"Jeremy Robinson is a fresh new face in adventure writing and will make a mark in suspense for years to come."
— David Lynn Golemon, NY Times bestselling author of CARPATHIAN

PULSE

"Rocket-boosted action, brilliant speculation, and the recreation of a horror out of the mythologic past, all seamlessly blend into a rollercoaster ride of suspense and adventure."
— James Rollins, NY Times bestselling author of THE EYE OF GOD

"Jeremy Robinson has one wild imagination, slicing and stitching his tale together with the deft hand of a surgeon. Robinson's impressive talent is on full display in this one."
— Steve Berry, NY Times bestselling author of THE KING'S DECEPTION

"There's nothing timid about Robinson as he drops his readers off the cliff without a parachute and somehow manages to catch us an inch or two from doom."
—Jeff Long, New York Times bestselling author of DEEPER

"An elite task force must stop a genetic force of nature in the form of the legendary Hydra in this latest Jeremy Robinson thriller. Yet another page-turner!"
— Steve Alten, NY Times bestselling author of PHOBOS: MAYAN FEAR

"Robinson's latest reads like a video game with tons of action and lots of carnage. The combination of mythology, technology, and high-octane action proves irresistible."
— Booklist

D0249534

ALSO BY JEREMY ROBINSON

The Jack Sigler Novels

Prime
Pulse
Instinct
Threshold
Omega

**The Chess Team Novellas
(Chesspocalypse Series)**

Callsign: King – Book 1
Callsign: Queen – Book 1
Callsign: Rook – Book 1
Callsign: King – Book 2
Callsign: Bishop – Book 1
Callsign: Knight – Book 1
Callsign: Deep Blue – Book 1
Callsign: King – Book 3

**The Origins Editions
(First five novels)**

The Didymus Contingency
Raising The Past
Beneath

Antarktos Rising
Kronos

Standalone Novels

SecondWorld
Project Nemesis
Island 731
I Am Cowboy

**The Last Hunter
(Antarktos Saga Series)**

The Last Hunter – Descent
The Last Hunter – Pursuit
The Last Hunter – Ascent
The Last Hunter – Lament
The Last Hunter – Onslaught

Writing as Jeremy Bishop

Torment
The Sentinel
The Raven

ALSO BY SEAN ELLIS

The Nick Kismet Adventures

The Shroud of Heaven
Into the Black
The Devil You Know
Fortune Favors

Standalone Novels

Dark Trinity: Ascendant
Magic Mirror
Wargod

The Adventures of Dodge Dalton

In the Shadow of Falcon's Wings
At the Outpost of Fate
On the High Road to Oblivion

Jeremy Robinson's Jack Sigler Novels

Callsign: King – Brainstorm Trilogy
Prime

PRIME

A Jack Sigler Thriller

JEREMY ROBINSON
WITH SEAN ELLIS

BREAKNECK MEDIA

For all my real U.S. military readers, putting their lives on the line to keep the rest of us safe.

PRIME

PROLOGUE: ZERO
Baghdad, 656 A.H. (1258 A.D.)

THE MOST BEAUTIFUL city in the world was dying.

Nasir al-Tusi sat astride his horse at the edge of the River Tigris and wept.

As an advisor to the Great Hulagu Khan, he should have rejoiced at this victory, but he felt only bitter sadness in his heart.

He couldn't believe what he was seeing—not just the horror of the city's destruction, the smoke and the blood, and the absolute ruin everywhere he looked, but what defied belief was that this had been allowed to happen in the first place. The Khan's quarrel was with the rogue Nizari Muslims, not the Abbasid Caliphate. Yet, seemingly against all reason, Caliph Al-Musta'sim had refused to pay tribute, in the form of military support, to the Mongol ruler. As a result, he had also become the Khan's enemy.

The Caliph had bragged that if the Khan tried to attack Baghdad, the women of his city would drive the Khan off. Indeed, when the Mongol army arrived at Baghdad, they found a city barely ready to repel an invasion. No army had been summoned. The walls had not been fortified to withstand the Mongol artillery. Even when Hulagu deployed his forces on both banks of the Tigris River and began preparations for the siege, the Caliph barely took note.

Too late to accomplish anything, the Abbasid ruler eventually sent out 20,000 horsemen to engage the enemy. Hulagu's forces, led by the cunning Chinese general Guo Kan, had destroyed several dikes, flooding the plain and drowning the cavalrymen, obliterating the Caliph's forces in a matter of hours. Instead of sending a fraction of his military force and paying a token tribute to the Khan, the Caliph had chosen instead to sacrifice his entire army in a futile display of arrogance.

The siege had been brutal and brief. The Mongols encircled the city with a palisade and commenced an artillery assault that shattered the city walls. Thirteen days after the Mongol army assembled on the banks of the Tigris, the Caliph signaled his surrender.

Hulagu was in no mood to negotiate. "Now that I have beaten him, the fool wishes to make peace? His treasury overflows with gold, yet he did not spend even a *dinar* to defend it. I will shut the fool up in his treasury. If he prizes his gold so highly, let him eat it."

As a scholar, al-Tusi cared nothing for the fate of the Caliph or his wealth, but there was something of inestimable value inside the walls of the defeated city that did interest him. Baghdad's greatest treasure was not its gold, but rather its scholars and its libraries, foremost of which was the House of Wisdom.

"You rule all the Earth now, Great Khan," al-Tusi had told Hulagu as the siege began. "With the knowledge in the House of Wisdom, you and your sons will rule Heaven and Earth for a thousand years...no, a thousand times a thousand years. You must preserve it."

Hulagu however had been unmoved. "Knowledge is like anything else that may be lost and found again. The Caliph's arrogance cannot be excused, and if it means the destruction of every book in the city, then so it will be."

Al-Tusi knew better than to argue with the Khan, though he knew of one book kept in the House of Wisdom that could never be replaced.

"However," Hulagu had continued, "there is truth in what you say. I appoint you, Nasir al-Tusi, as the protector of this great trove of learning. When the city falls, you will gather whatever remains, and then use it to establish a new House of Wisdom."

Despite the concession, al-Tusi had not expected the siege to end so quickly or so dramatically. Already, Guo Kan had led his forces into the city to 'prepare' for the Khan's arrival.

Al-Tusi wiped the tears from his eyes and urged his mount to continue toward the ravaged shell of Baghdad. The Tigris was running red with spilled blood, but there were pools of a black, oily substance on its surface, which al-Tusi recognized immediately. It was ink, the ink of thousands of scrolls and books that had been thrown into the river by the marauding invaders.

The destruction of the House of Wisdom had already begun.

I'm too late, he thought, and the tears began flowing again. *But perhaps they haven't found the Book yet.*

In his despair, he thought he could hear his father's voice, echoing from out of Paradise. *Inshallah, my son. If Allah wills it, you will save the Book. If it has been destroyed, then it is because Allah does not will you to possess it again.*

The sentiment brought him no comfort.

As he reached the city gate, the vast destruction became almost too much to bear. He wrapped his turban tightly around his nose and ears, a futile attempt to keep out the stench of death and muffle the screams of the dying. The streets were slick with blood, and the marketplaces that lined them were filled with what looked like heaping mounds of meat, swarming with black flies. In the distance, bands of infantrymen were methodically searching houses, a process which seemed to involve tearing them down to their foundations.

Al-Tusi felt a growing apprehension. The Khan had assigned an *arav*—ten horsemen—to serve as his escort, but in the mayhem and in the grip of bloodlust, it might be difficult for the marauders to distinguish friend from foe. After more than an hour of negotiating the ruins and circumventing the larger concentrations of victorious invaders, al-Tusi reached his destination.

Even from a distance, he could see that the House had not escaped harm. Pillars of smoke ascended from its courtyards. Soldiers stood on its open terraces, pitching manuscripts into the river, competing with each other to see who could throw them the furthest. Fighting an urge to shout at them, al-Tusi rode right up to the main entrance, where he was confronted by a group of Turkish soldiers.

"Let me pass," he ordered. His voice was weak, barely audible through the cloth he'd bound over his face. "The Khan commands that this place be spared."

"We don't take orders from you, Persian," the leader of the group sneered at him. Then the man cocked his head sideways as if contemplating something humorous. "But General Guo is waiting for you inside."

Guo Kan is waiting for me?

The Chinese general was aware that Hulagu had ordered al-Tusi to preserve the House of Wisdom, so why was he there, in the House, personally overseeing its destruction?

The Turk led him inside, following a route that seemed purposefully designed to make al-Tusi bear witness to the cruelty of the victorious army. Everywhere he looked, there was blood and ruin. Scores of scholars and scientists, the most learned men in the Islamic world, had been pinned with lances to the walls of the enormous reading rooms. The tables, where these men had read, translated and copied the scrolls in the House's collection, had been hacked apart to make a path for mounted archers, who were taking turns riding up and down the halls using the impaled men, some of whom were still alive, for target practice.

At last, he was brought to the highest tower of the House. He recognized this place, one of the many observatories where astronomers studied the heavens and mapped the stars. Although the din of the city's destruction was still audible, the observatory was, for the moment at least, still untouched. Shelves of scrolls and books lined the walls, all arranged according to the orderly filing system employed by the House's librarians. Tables, with every manner of machine and scientific apparatus, had been arranged in a ring around the center of the circular room. Guo Kan waited there, casually inspecting the devices as if they were wares in the marketplace.

"Ah, Persian. Come to pick the bones of the dead?"

Al-Tusi bit back a retort. He could ill afford to offend Guo Kan. The Chinese general was highly regarded by the Khan, and if Guo Kan decided to simply execute al-Tusi on the spot, Hulagu would probably not even take notice. Instead, al-Tusi simply inclined his head in a gesture of deference. "The Khan has ordered me to preserve as much of the library as is possible."

"The Khan is very wise." Guo offered a cryptic smile and gestured to the tables. "The treasures in this place are greater than anything in the Caliph's vaults."

Al-Tusi chose his reply carefully. "Unfortunately, ink and parchment is not so durable as gold. I fear much has already been lost."

The general seemed not to have heard. "With enough gold, one man can buy an army of ten thousand, but with knowledge...ah, with knowledge, one man can destroy an army. You are a man of learning, Persian. Tell me, what do you see here?"

"These are scientific instruments for taking the measure of the heavens." Though his answer had been immediate, reflexive, al-Tusi now scrutinized the machines and devices arrayed on the tables. Some were quite familiar—astrolabes, clocks and planetary models—but many of the others had nothing at all to do with astronomy.

"Are they indeed?" Guo watched him carefully for some hint of duplicity. "There is a scroll here that purports to hold the secret of Greek Fire. Over there—"

He gestured across to a table, upon which lay several enormous dome-shaped objects that looked like the lids of cooking pots. "Polished mirrors that can focus the rays of the sun and start fires, even at a great distance. I think these *scientists*—" Guo spat the word like a curse, "were trying to give the Caliph the victory of which he boasted."

Then he smiled again. "But, I am no scholar. I might be mistaken. Some of these machines do, indeed, appear harmless. Take this one, for example."

Al-Tusi's breath caught in his throat as he saw the apparatus Guo was inspecting. It looked at first glance, like a large basket or a pot—al-Tusi reckoned he could not have encircled its circumference with his arms. Instead of clay or woven straw, it was constructed of lacquered wood, a flawless joining of curved panels that resembled the shape of a gourd, resting on a rectangular base from which sprouted a number of metal levers, each engraved with a distinctive symbol—symbols al-Tusi himself had created, and which only a handful of other men had ever seen.

By all that is holy, they actually built it.

Now he understood why the Caliph had been so defiant.

Six years earlier, al-Tusi had been part of an unparalleled scholarly experiment. A group of intellectuals, scientists and visionaries from every part of the civilized world had set out on a quest to discover the source of life. They had originally thought to name the object of their search after the paradise described in the holy writings of the Jews and Christians, but their goal did not lie in Mesopotamia, where Eden was thought to have existed. Besides, even if the sacred writings were to be taken literally—something that none of the scholars truly believed—scripture explicitly stated that God planted his garden after the Creation was complete. Life could have begun anywhere. Instead, they named the thing they sought *prima materia*, the name Aristotle had used in antiquity, and the place where they eventually found it, they had called 'the Prime.'

For more than two years, they studied the Prime, unlocking its secrets and recording their discoveries in a book—*The Book*—written in a language of al-Tusi's devising. They knew the world was not ready for what they had learned. The Christian kingdoms lived in perpetual fear of scientific learning; the possession of knowledge was a dangerous thing, an affront to God, and anyone possessing such a book would be labeled a heretic and summarily executed. Even in the enlightened Islamic world, possession of such information was dangerous, but the men had agreed that the House of Wisdom, which had endured for nearly five hundred years, would be the best place to safeguard the Book. Al-Tusi himself had borne the manuscript, along with a second document, a parchment roll that contained instructions on how to unlock the secrets of the Book, to Baghdad, en route to his home in Persia. When he had entrusted it to the keeper of the House, he had given the man explicit instructions to keep the Book secret until the world was ready for such profound knowledge.

The fools, al-Tusi thought. *These discoveries were never meant to be used as a weapon; they cannot be used that way. It is an impossibility.*

He felt the general's eyes upon him, and he knew that he'd already given too much away by his reaction. He did his best to affect an expression of indifference, as he pretended to study the device. "It is an *urghan*. A musical instrument."

Guo pressed one of the levers experimentally, and a low note resonated from the wooden body of the *urghan*. The sound continued to echo in the room for a moment after he released the lever. "How does it work?"

Al-Tusi laid a hand on the wooden body of the instrument. He saw that several bowls also occupied the tabletop, each of them containing lumps of powder—ash, sulfur, salt and other substances that he did not immediately recognize. All of them were arranged in a circle around the *urghan*, just as he and his fellow scientists had done years before, along with leaves of vellum and paper, the latter inscribed with diagrams and notations in Arabic. Then he saw something else on the table. It was the parchment he himself had written, which explained, among other things, how to construct and use the machine. It lay unrolled and open for all to see.

But where is the Book? Surely they would be together.

Through a supreme effort of will, he maintained his neutral demeanor. "There is a bladder of air inside. It is filled with a bellows." He indicated another lever, which he began pumping with the heel of his hand. "There is a *ney* inside—a hollow reed with many different holes—and when you press one of these levers, it releases the air and covers one of the holes."

He demonstrated its operation with a few random notes, finishing with a discordant combination that, he noted with some satisfaction, caused the general to wince. "Not very useful as a weapon," al-Tusi continued. "I suppose with several of these you could make the enemy drop their swords and cover their ears."

"A musical instrument? It is nothing more than that?" Guo continued to watch him, as if he could read in al-Tusi's eyes the truth about the device. "I shall take it with me then. Perhaps I will learn its mysteries."

Al-Tusi shrugged, but this time he wasn't trying to hide anxiety. Guo had overestimated the *urghan's* importance.

Now if he will just get out of the way, I can find the real prize.

"Yes," the general went on. "Perhaps you will teach me how to play it."

"I am no musician," al-Tusi replied, staring at the *urghan*, surreptitiously searching the surrounding tabletop for the Book. "And I have the Khan's business to attend to here. I must try to preserve what little of the library you have not already destroyed."

With what he hoped was an air of casual disdain, al-Tusi turned away and started gathering scrolls and codices from the tables. He purposely ignored the parchment on the table with the *urghan*, hoping that Guo would lose interest, or more accurately, that he would be deceived by al-Tusi's apparent disinterest.

"I leave you to your task," Guo said, after a long silence. He strode toward the exit, pausing at the threshold. "I think I would like that instrument, though. I'll send some men to collect it. Please make sure nothing...untoward...happens to it."

As soon as the general was gone, al-Tusi let out the breath he had been holding, and he hastened back to the table. With barely restrained urgency, he began sorting through the papers arranged around the *urghan*.

Where is it? It has to be here.

His fingers lit upon the parchment. He was surprised at the memories a simple touch evoked, but he tucked the nostalgia away, along with the roll, which disappeared into the folds of his robes.

Let Guo have the urghan; *without this, he will never begin to grasp its true importance.*

But securing the parchment brought him scant comfort. The Book was nowhere to be found.

HE SEARCHED EVERY document in the room, and when he was done, he searched the other observatories and reading rooms. Over the days that followed, he would inspect every scrap of paper or parchment that Guo's soldiers had not destroyed—setting aside more than four hundred thousand unique documents—but the one book he sought most continued to elude to him.

There was a simple explanation, of course. The Book, that singular, irreplaceable chronicle of the experiments conducted at the Prime...the tome that, quite literally, contained within its pages, the secrets of life itself...was gone.

Destroyed.

Pitched into the Tigris like so much waste.

At first, al-Tusi was inconsolable, but as the days and weeks passed, he realized that perhaps his father had been right about such things. Allah had seen fit to remove the knowledge from the world.

The Caliph had tried to use the discovery as a weapon of war. No doubt, men like Hulagu and Guo would have attempted to do the same, and if they had somehow succeeded...

Al-Tusi didn't want to contemplate what that might mean.

Perhaps it was best that the Book was gone.

Inshallah

Yunnan Province, China, 2005

KATHERINE GELLER STARED at the endless emerald-green tea plants covering the distant hills, with a mixture of nostalgia and contempt. She was a coffee drinker and had been since her late teens, imbibing mug after mug of the beverage, sweet but without milk, as she studied and crammed to get through her university courses, and subsequently her PhD in Biology, along with Masters degrees in molecular biology, organic chemistry and epidemiology, respectively. Coffee was a drink she associated with ambition and the drive to succeed; tea just made her think of Richard.

They'd been good for each other, even if they hadn't been terribly successful as a couple. Richard had also been driven to succeed, and with the nearly limitless resources of his inheritance, his only limiting factor was the scope of his vision. She had helped him articulate his grandiose schemes, and he in turn had opened doors for her that she hadn't even known existed. They had pushed each other to new heights, competed with and dared each other, and in the end, extended their reach well beyond what either of them had thought possible to grasp. Perhaps because their personalities were so much alike, the intimate relationship that had started it all—which they both recognized from the outset as nothing more than a diversion—had withered on the vine. Not surprisingly, they were both better for it. He had gone on to pursue his ambitions, and she had returned to her true passion: research.

They were still close. His company was discreetly funding her current endeavor. She called every day on the Qualcomm satellite phone he had insisted she take along, but their conversations rarely evoked any kind of emotional response. The sight of the hills covered in tea however, reminded her of the god-awful fresh-cut peppermint tea that he was always trying to get her to drink, and that took her to more intimate places in her mind.

"Dr. Geller!"

Katherine shook her head to clear away the memories of her former lover. She turned toward the person shouting her name. Bradley Stafford, one of her graduate students and her chief research assistant, was hastening in her direction, waving a sheet of paper she knew would contain the raw data from the latest batch of samples. If Stafford's enthusiasm was any indication, the news was good. She took the report with a patient smile, and gave it a cursory once-over.

Good news indeed—excellent in fact.

"We found him, didn't we?" asked Stafford. "Patient Zero."

Katherine cast him a reproving glance. "We're just collecting samples, Brad. We've got half a dozen more sites to visit before we can even begin parsing the data."

Although her statement was accurate, she had a more compelling reason to be hesitant about declaring victory. In a lower voice, she added: "The last thing we need right now is for Han to get all excited and shut us down."

Dr. Han Li was their official liaison with the Chinese Ministry of Health, or to be more precise, their government-appointed babysitter. Although Katherine's team nominally had the full support and coop-eration of the Ministry, implicit in that agreement was the expectation that they would find nothing to upset the status quo, and certainly nothing that might reinforce the idea that the People's Republic of China was the birthplace of catastrophic infectious diseases. The Ministry had granted them access to archaeological sites in Yunnan Province only in hopes they might find clues that would lead them elsewhere, perhaps to India or one of the other hypothesized origination sites for the pandemic.

Katherine didn't want Han to know all the evidence pointed to the unarguable conclusion that the most devastating outbreak in the history of the world had begun right here in Western China.

Bradley wasn't wrong; they were closing in on Patient Zero—the source of the Black Death.

The Black Death.

The name wasn't just dramatic hyperbole. The outward symptoms of the plague that had swept across the known world during the fourteenth century were black pustules on the skin and a darkening of the fingernails as the tissue underneath began to necrotize. There was debate about how many had died from the plague, which reached its peak between 1348 and 1350, but it was generally believed that the pandemic had killed half the world's population. Estimates of the death toll ranged from 75 million to 200 million, making it even deadlier than the Spanish Influenza pandemic of 1918. Katherine imagined that the survivors must have felt like they were living through the tribulation prophesied in the Bible: "Then two shall be in the field; the one shall be taken, and the other left."

In the big picture of infectious disease, the Black Death was a statistical anomaly—a flash fire that had done a lot of damage in the short term, and then more or less burned itself out.

The strangest thing about the Black Death was that no one was really sure what it was. Common wisdom held that the plague organism was *Yersinia pestis*—the bacteria responsible for bubonic and pneumonic plague—which had jumped from rodent populations to humans through flea bites. Forensic evidence tied the bacterium to the Black Death, but some historians believed the evidence had been misread. Many of those who contracted the plague lived in climates where transmission by flea bites would have been extremely unlikely. Some scientists—and Katherine was among their number—believed that bubonic plague was coincidental with the actual cause of death, or that the agent responsible was either a unique strain of *Yersinia* or something that worked in tandem with the plague bacterium to enhance its lethality.

Katherine's team was trying to identify the original source of the pandemic, to find its earliest victims and hopefully to gather samples of DNA from the plague organism that would provide a definitive answer. But unlike viruses, which were really nothing more than chains of protein that could remain dormant for years or even centuries, bacteria were living cells that needed sustenance. When an infected person died, the bacteria in their body died soon after and began to degrade. Sometimes though, traces of bacterial DNA remained in the bones and teeth of victims long dead—traces that could be extracted in the mobile laboratory and sent off for analysis using a satellite Internet connection.

Archaeologists had identified several sites in Asia where the plague had ravaged the population. Entire villages had died and been reclaimed by the earth. It was in these places that Katherine hoped to find Patient Zero—figuratively at least—and to answer two questions: what really was the cause of the Black Death, and why had it appeared, seemingly from nowhere, to nearly wipe out humanity?

She tucked the report under her arm, and with Stafford in tow, she headed for the dig. This particular site, a village that had completely vanished from history during the early fourteenth century, had been a godsend. They had found dozens of remains in small clusters, families that had died in their homes with no one left to bury them. Over the years that followed, seasonal rains had caused the earth to swallow them up where they lay.

Satellite imagery and ground-penetrating radar had given them a rough map of the village, and now strips of engineer's tape showed where houses had once stood. Several of these had already been excavated, the remains catalogued and removed, but there were a few more at the north end of the village that were still being probed. Katherine walked between these, monitoring the progress of her graduate students and the archaeologists that were working with them, curious to see what new discoveries would be made, but any excitement she might have felt was tempered by the fact that Han Li was hovering nearby.

The Chinese doctor glanced up as she approached. "Dr. Geller, good morning."

His English was perfect, his manner as quiet and dutiful as always, but Katherine thought she detected a hint of agitation. She wondered if the data in the report had already reached him, but a moment later she realized that his anxiety arose from another source. Several of the team members were working in a new area, outside the map of the village. A new grid of tape was being laid out just beyond the eastern perimeter, and several of the team members were eagerly watching the proceedings.

"What's going on over there?"

"A discovery has been made," Han explained.

Katherine pushed past him and approached Bill Smythe, the ground-radar technician who was overseeing the new operation. "Bill, why are you setting up here?"

Smythe made no effort to hide his excitement. "We found something. There's a large void here, less than two meters down."

It took a moment for her to process. The void could be a root cellar, not the likeliest of places to find the bodies of plague victims, but if there were remains inside, they would have been shielded from the elements—possibly even mummified. Katherine made an effort to quell her rising enthusiasm. It was better to be surprised with success than with disappointment. "Find a way in. The rest of you have work to do."

Fifteen minutes later, Smythe reported back that he had found what appeared to be the original entrance to the cellar, a staircase that descended into the void. Laborers used picks and shovels to loosen the earth, and in short order, they created a hole large enough to accommodate a person.

Before descending into the dark space, Katherine donned a HEPA respirator mask and latex gloves—the same bio-safety level-two equipment worn by the team as they dug up the village. It was a precautionary measure, and not just because of the very remote chance of exposure to

Yersinia; there were other pathogens—bacteria, viruses, fungal spores—that might be lurking in the sealed environs of the cellar. Thus equipped, she lowered herself into the opening, with Han and Stafford right behind her, the latter recording everything with a handheld video camera equipped with a brilliant LED spotlight.

The descending staircase was uneven, littered with fallen dirt and rock from the excavation, but the space beyond was untouched by time. Katherine directed the beam of her flashlight into the dark depths of the enclosure, and realized immediately that this was no root cellar.

It was a tomb.

The chamber was filled with statuary—dogs, dragons, traditional representations of the Buddha—but there were also elements that, to Katherine's uneducated eye at least, did not appear to be Chinese in origin. Weapons of war—swords, lances, bows and quivers full of arrows—were prominently displayed, along with life-sized ponies, saddled but riderless. The pieces appeared to have been arranged with *feng shui*—Chinese geomancy—in mind; the statues formed a maze designed to confound evil spirits who preferred to travel in straight lines.

Han placed a restraining hand on Katherine's shoulder. "Dr. Geller, I must insist that we withdraw until I can advise the Ministry. This is a significant archaeological find, and has nothing to with your research."

Katherine gazed back at him. He was right; this tomb had probably been laid long before the outbreak of the plague, and it was unlikely that it would yield any clues relating to their search.

Nevertheless, her curiosity was burning. This was a once in a lifetime opportunity. "We should collect environmental samples as a baseline. And while we're at it, we can make sure it's safe for the archaeological team." She patted his arm in what she hoped was a comforting gesture. "Don't worry; I won't touch anything."

Katherine felt his hand slip away, and realized that he was as eager to plumb the tomb's depths as she.

They moved through the maze, leaving a trail of footprints in the layer of dust on the earthen floor but otherwise disturbing nothing. The path wound around the outer edge of the enclosure, then spiraled in toward the center where they found a bier, upon which lay an ornate sarcophagus with a terra cotta effigy, presumably the occupant of the funerary container. Han played his light across the familiar looking ideograms inscribed on the sarcophagus, but shook his head signaling incomprehension. Then he turned his beam to an object that had been conspicuously placed alongside the bier.

"This doesn't belong here." He reached out and placed a gloved hand on it, as if to confirm its solidity.

Katherine directed her light onto it as well. It didn't look like a Chinese artifact; the symbols on its exterior were vaguely familiar, but definitely not in the style of the ideograms on the sarcophagus. It showed considerable decay and looked like it might have been damaged prior to its placement, so a positive determination of its purpose was impossible. Like the identity of the tomb's occupant, the object would be something for the experts to figure out, but it was a mystery that had no bearing on her own research.

She was about to turn away when her light fell on Han's fingers. She gasped behind her mask.

A black film clung to the latex membrane of his glove. He saw it as well, and his face twisted into a perturbed frown.

It was probably nothing, just centuries old dust. Nevertheless, Katherine felt her pulse quicken. "Let's get out of here."

They negotiated the maze back to the entrance where the rest of the team had gathered, eagerly awaiting a report on their discoveries, but Katherine gestured for them to stay back and called for a specimen kit.

Both of Han's gloves were now almost completely covered in the black film. Using forceps, she peeled them off his hands and dropped them into a plastic bag, only then allowing herself a small sigh of relief. Whatever the substance was, it was now safely sealed away.

"Dr. Geller!" It was Stafford. The graduate student had been recording her activity with his video camera, but now he seemed to have forgotten all about this task. He had one hand extended toward her, and she saw the same black film on his gloves. But he wasn't showing her—he was pointing at her. "Your face."

She reached up reflexively but caught herself before making contact. Not that it would have mattered; she knew what she would find. *Damn it. This isn't happening.*

But it was. They'd been exposed to something in the tomb.

"Isolation protocols," she said, the words barely getting past the lump in her throat. "Everyone stay back."

There was an emergency wash station in the lab tent; all three of them would need to be disinfected, their clothes and shoes destroyed...

Suddenly, Han let out a choked gasp and collapsed to the ground.

Katherine stared in disbelief at his motionless form. Han's cheeks bore several dark smudges and the rims of his eyelids were encrusted with the black substance, but this wasn't the cause of his distress. The doctor's skin was cyanotic; he was suffocating.

It wasn't possible. *He couldn't have inhaled it,* she thought. *He's still wearing his mask, for God's sake.*

His mask!

The filter cartridges on Han's respirator were weeping beads of a fluid that looked like crude oil. The substance had clogged the filters; that was why he'd passed out.

She frantically ripped the mask away, revealing the doctor's blue-tinged lips but also a scattering of black blemishes around his mouth and nose.

Han still wasn't breathing.

Katherine discovered that she was also having difficulty drawing breath, and against her better judgment, she removed her own respirator. She was trying to figure out what to do next when a cry sounded from the gaggle of onlookers.

Like some biblical miracle, the crowd parted, the team members retreating in a panic from one of their own. A female archaeologist—Katherine couldn't remember her name—was gazing in stunned disbelief at her hands, and even from a distance, Katherine could see that the woman's fingernails had turned completely black.

Then another shriek went up, and pandemonium erupted.

My God! What have we unleashed?

Stafford abruptly fell to his knees and pitched forward, face down and unmoving, but Katherine made no effort to loosen his mask.

She felt a rattle in her lungs with her next breath, like the beginnings of a chest cold.

Whatever it is, it's fast.

Something about that realization soothed her. Her fear receded, replaced by a calm that was clinical but at the same time, almost reverential.

She had discovered something new, something unique, and that was what she had lived for. So what if it killed her?

She unclipped the satellite telephone from her belt and hit the redial button.

The call connected almost right away, but there was a momentary delay as the signal traveled into space and then back down to its destination. "Katherine? I wasn't expecting you to call so early."

She tried to answer, but there was no breath in her lungs to form the words. Her only reply was a mewling sound that turned into a coughing fit. Black phlegm sprayed across the backlit display of the phone handset.

There was another maddening pause, and then the tiny speaker erupted with a strident: "Katherine!"

Dark clouds gathered at the edge of her vision, but the coughing spasm had cleared some of the fluid from her lungs. She managed to draw a shallow breath and willed herself to speak one last time.

"Richard. I've found something."

CIPHER

ONE
Iraq, 2006

THEY SEEMED TO materialize out of thin air, like ghosts, or perhaps more in keeping with the superstitions of the region, like *jinn*—spirits of smokeless fire that inhabit the space between earth and heaven.

Not that there was anyone around to notice.

Even if the inhabitants of Ramadi had been inclined to venture out after dark, a curfew was in effect and the streets were patrolled by a combined force of United States military personnel and soldiers of the newly reinvented Iraqi Army. At two a.m., anyone wandering the streets was likely to be shot on sight.

The eight men who moved swiftly and soundlessly through the night weren't worried about being discovered. They had timed their advance perfectly to avoid detection by the patrols, and it was unlikely that anyone glancing out a window into the darkness would have been able to distinguish them in their camouflaged uniforms with matching body armor and helmets. Peering through the monochrome display of their PVS-14 night-vision devices, they advanced to the front of the target house and assembled in groups of four on either side of the door, bunched together like coiled serpents preparing to strike, which was more or less exactly what they were.

The second man in formation to the right of the door whispered into the lip microphone of his radio headset. "This is Cipher Six. By the numbers. Last chance. Go or no-go? Over."

The replies crackled in the earpieces of the headsets worn by all six men.

"Eagle-Eye One. Go. Over."

"Eagle-Eye Two. Go. Over."

"Eagle-Eye Three. Do it. Over."

"Cipher Seven, good to go. Over."

Cipher Six, a man named Kevin Rainer—formally Lieutenant Colonel Kevin Rainer, though no one had called him that since he earned his *green beanie*—nodded, a gesture that went unnoticed by the other seven men arrayed around the door. The gesture *was* seen by the three sniper teams—Eagle-Eye One, Two and Three—who watched over them all from a distance.

The Eagle-Eye snipers were literally able to see through the walls of the house with their thermal scopes, verifying that only two occupants were within, but heat signatures could reveal only so much. Were the men wide awake but lying still on their beds? Would they be instantly alerted to the presence of intruders and snatch up a handy AK-47 or activate the detonator on an IED? Were they even the right men?

"Danno, go."

The third operator in the stacked group on the left side darted forward and knelt in front of the door. One gloved hand came up to test the knob. It didn't move, but Daniel Parker had been expecting that; he would have been surprised if the door had opened on the first try. On any other night, he might have blasted the door off its hinges with a shotgun, used a shaped charge to blow out the latch plate or simply kicked the damn thing down, but not tonight. This mission demanded a more subtle approach.

Parker took a lock-picking gun from a pouch on his tactical vest and slid the metal pick into the keyhole. There was a faint clicking noise as he worked the trigger lever, but a moment later the cylinder rotated, allowing him to ease the door open a crack. He slid a hand inside the gap, probing for trip wires or some other booby trap. Finding nothing, he gave the door a push and then spun out of the way, as Rainer's team moved fluidly inside.

There was the briefest pause and then Rainer's voice whispered across the radio net. "Room clear. Move in, Jack."

Parker fell into line behind his team leader, Jack Sigler, as the second group filed into the house. All but one of the members of the first group were spread out throughout the front room in tactical positions. The remaining operator stood guard over a figure that lay face down and motionless on a mattress in the corner, his hands secured behind his back with flexi-cuffs.

Just as they had rehearsed dozens of times...hundreds of times...Sigler's team lined up on the corner of the hallway, and at a gesture from their leader, each advanced into the unknown space beyond. Sigler was the second man into the room, as was their protocol, and he broke to the right. Parker, in the number three position, peeled left behind the point man, Mark Adams. Another mattress was positioned along the far wall right in front of Parker, and a bearded man lay sprawled out atop it, snoring loudly.

Sigler and the fourth man in their stack, Casey Bellows, visually scanned the rest of the room, while Adams moved directly toward the sleeping man, with Parker close behind him. A narrow beam of green-tinged light—invisible to the unaided eye—lanced from the AN/PAQ4 targeting laser mounted on the upper receiver of Adams's suppressed Heckler & Koch HK416 assault rifle. As seen through the night-vision devices each member of the team wore, it appeared as a bright, wavering point on the supine man's forehead.

The sleeper stirred and opened his eyes.

Adams froze in mid-step. Below the brilliant spot of the laser, a pair of white dots appeared—the man's pupils, fully dilated and reflecting only the infrared spectrum of light—staring right back at Parker.

Then the man rolled over onto his side, facing the wall.

Parker didn't exhale the breath he was holding. Maybe the man was still asleep, maybe he was just playing possum; either way, in another three seconds he would either be bound and gagged, or bagged and tagged. Parker activated his own PAQ4, aiming at the back of the man's head, as Adams moved in for the capture. Before the man could even begin to wake up, he was flipped onto his stomach. The flexi-cuffs were pulled tight around his wrists and a strip of olive drab '100 mile an hour' tape was slapped over his mouth, to preemptively silence his uncomprehending protests and cries of alarm.

Adams gave a thumbs-up signal, indicating that the captive was under control, after which Sigler's voice whispered across the net: "Room secure."

"Roger," Rainer answered. "Cipher Seven, we are ready for pick-up. Over."

Cipher Seven, Doug Pettit, who presently sat behind the wheel of an up-armored M1151 HMMWV—a Humvee to the rest of the world—idling quietly with no lights showing, half a mile away, replied immediately. "Roger, Six. We're on our way."

"All right, boys," Rainer said. "Clean up time."

A falsetto voice cooed in Parker's earpiece: "Knock, knock. Housekeeping."

It was probably Jesse Strickland, who styled himself the team's court jester. Someone groaned in response, but that was the end of it. The team went to work. Parker lowered his assault rifle, leaving Adams to look after the prisoner. He took a large green nylon pouch—a standard military-use body bag—from a pocket. He held it open so that Sigler could begin dropping stuff in. Everything but the furniture went into the bag: loose papers, books, articles of clothing and even a collection of empty soda bottles. There was no telling what might be worthwhile, and this was not the time or place to make such judgments. There would be plenty of time to sort through it all later, when they were back safely behind the wire.

Thirty seconds later, the eight men, along with two captives and three bags full of what might or might not be important evidence, hustled from the door of the house to a row of waiting Humvees. Parker heaved his burden through the rear door of the fourth vehicle in line and then climbed inside, slamming the heavy door shut and engaging the combat locks. Sigler settled into the front passenger seat and secured his door.

There was another round of radio check-ins, with each driver reporting their readiness, and then the convoy pulled away. Despite being in armored vehicles, the team remained vigilant. The mission had gone flawlessly to this point, but the last thing any of them wanted to do was jinx things with a premature round of self-congratulation. It took only a single roadside IED to ruin an otherwise perfect outing. They avoided the known patrol routes, where insurgents most often targeted occupation forces, and instead risked a course that led them through neighborhoods that were known to be sympathetic to the opposition, reasoning—or rather hoping—that *Hajji* would be less likely to blow things up on his own doorstep. Nevertheless, every man in the team knew that no amount of preparation and planning could guarantee success; luck always played a part.

This time, their luck held. Twenty minutes later, they rolled under the arch that guarded the entrance to Camp Blue Diamond. The mission had gone flawlessly. They had captured both of the al-Awda couriers and gathered a ton of evidence, without firing a single shot...or being fired at.

It was a great way to end their four-month deployment to Iraq.

TWO

THE ARRIVAL OF a helicopter at Camp Blue Diamond—formerly the An-Ramadi Northern Palace, where Saddam Hussein's half-brother had once lived, and presently headquarters of US Marine Corps 1st Division—was a common enough occurrence that Jack Sigler rarely took note. Something about this one was different, though. The deep bass thump of the rotors beating the air above the Euphrates River, as the bird made its final approach, resonated through his body like an alarm and fanned an ember of anxiety in the pit of his stomach. He poked at the food heaped on his tray—two hamburgers, a mini-pizza and an unopened bag of Cool Ranch Doritos—but his appetite had disappeared.

Daniel Parker, seated across the table from him, instantly picked up on Sigler's discomfort. The team's only African-American operator, Parker had a round, youthful face that was incapable of concealing his emotional state. "Someone just walk across your grave, Jack?"

"I just remembered something I need to take care of." He stood, and in a single deft motion, scooped up the tray, dumped its contents into a nearby trash can and flung it like a Frisbee onto the tray rack. "I'll catch up with you later."

Parker stood as well. "Well that's a coincidence. I just remembered that I need to take care of something, too."

"Yeah? What's that?"

"You tell me."

Sigler regarded his teammate and friend with a wan smile, an expression that seemed completely alien on his rough, unshaven face. With his shaggy hair and hard expression, Sigler had been often told he resembled Hugh Jackman, or more precisely, that actor's film portrayal of the comic book superhero Wolverine; Wolverine didn't smile.

Before Sigler could answer, the Motorola Talkabout radio clipped to his belt crackled to life. "Jack, it's Kevin. I need you at the TOC."

Parker's eyebrows went up. "Damn, Jack. Spidey-sense, much?"

"I'm wondering that myself," Sigler muttered. The ominous feeling that had started with the approach of the helicopter was blossoming into something like paranoia. He keyed the transmit button on the radio. "Be there in five."

It took him only three minutes to walk briskly from the dining facility in the main palace building, to FOB McCoy, the smaller, walled-off compound where Cipher element had set up shop. Above the always-locked metal door was a crudely painted sign that read 'Animal House,' presumably a reference to the college fraternity in the classic John Belushi movie of the same name: Delta Tau Chi—Delta House. The sign had appeared one night, a few weeks after they'd arrived in country—most likely some jarhead acting on a dare—but Kevin Rainer, Cipher element's commander, had left it there. Although their unit designation was supposed to be classified, why bother denying what everyone at Camp Blue Diamond already knew; Cipher element was part of the 1st Special Forces Operational Detachment-D, the US Army's elite counter-terrorism interdiction unit, better known simply as *Delta*.

Sigler went directly to the tactical operations center (TOC)—known informally as *The Lair*—which served a dual purpose as both communications hub and conference room. Rainer was seated at the end of the long rectangular table, along with Doug Pettit and two other people—an athletically built, brown-haired man, and a woman—in civilian clothes. The man was Scott Klein, a CIA officer who had been working closely with Cipher element to disrupt communications between the different local insurgent groups, but it took Sigler a moment to recognize him; he was having trouble tearing his gaze away from the woman.

She was, in a word, stunning.

She was seated, but Sigler guessed that she was about the same height as Klein; the Company man was about 5' 10". Her blousy top mostly concealed her figure, but her arms, where they emerged from her rolled up sleeves, were slender and toned. It was her face however, framed in a cascade of long and straight black hair that arrested Sigler's attention. Her almond-shaped eyes, the irises brown with flecks of gold, hinted at some recent Asian ancestry, as did her high cheekbones, but her face was longer, with a prominent forehead and a strong jaw.

"Hel-lo," murmured Parker, slipping into the Lair behind Sigler.

Command Sergeant Major Pettit, Cipher element's senior non-commissioned officer, directed a scathing look at the young operator, but no one else at the table seemed to notice, least of all the woman, whose attention was fixed on the screen of her laptop computer.

Klein rose and extended a hand to Sigler. "Jack, good to see you."

Sigler accepted the firm handclasp, but his reply was guarded. "Scott. Why do I have the feeling that you're about to ruin my day?"

Klein's grin confirmed Sigler's suspicions, but the CIA officer withheld further explanation until Sigler and Parker were settled in at the table. "First, congratulations are in order. The guys you nabbed last night turned out to be a lot more important that we expected."

Sigler felt his apprehension growing; he could tell where this was headed. The couriers had given up something actionable—maybe a location for a high value target—and now Cipher element was going to have to postpone their rotation back to the States to take on one more mission.

Ordinarily, that wouldn't have bothered Sigler. It wasn't as if he had anyone waiting for him back home.

He wasn't really sure what 'home' was anymore. For the last eleven years of his life, home had been wherever the Army sent him, and somehow that seemed more real to him than his childhood home in Richmond, Virginia. His mother still lived there, but he didn't visit often. There were too many bad memories at the house on Oak Lane: memories of his sister Julie who had always been there for him, and of his father who never had.

He'd been adrift back then, a punk, more interested in skating and hanging out with the other losers in the neighborhood, than in trying to be a good son. He didn't care what his mother or his mostly-absent father thought of him, which seemed to suit them just fine. Julie, however, had refused to give up on him. In her own gentle but insistent way, she had equipped him to make his own path in life, encouraging him to find a dream and follow it, just as she had ultimately done.

When he was fourteen, Julie had joined the Air Force, intent on becoming one of the nation's first female fighter pilots. Two years later, against all odds, she had succeeded. Then, just a few weeks before she was to wed her high school sweetheart, while on a cross-training flight in a Navy F-14, she crashed. Julie's death had been the final straw for an already strained domestic situation. Three months later, Sigler's father left abruptly and didn't come back. Shortly thereafter, Jack Sigler left as well, to join the Army.

Unlike his father, Sigler wasn't running away. At first, he'd thought that it was Julie's death that had motivated him to enlist, but later he realized that it was really his memory of her life that was driving him. Military service had given her focus, a challenge she knew she was capable of meeting and beating, and that was what he felt he needed. His mother, though heartbroken, had agreed to sign the waiver that would allow him to enlist at seventeen.

The rigors of basic training had shown him what he was capable of accomplishing. His natural athleticism and agility made him a perfect candidate for specialized training—Airborne school, the Rangers—but he wasn't content to simply test his physical prowess. While serving in the 101st Airborne, he managed to earn a college degree, and then he attended Officer Candidate School. Not long after receiving his commission, he set his sights on a new goal: Special Forces selection.

The challenges...the successes...had transformed him.

He'd joined the Army because he wanted to make a difference, to do something that would have made Julie proud, and now here he was, leading a team of the most elite counterterrorist shooters in the world, saving lives by taking out the bad guys before they could kill innocents.

Making a difference.

The uniform was home. He preferred being on alert status, whether forward positioned as they had been for the last four months, or standing by in the on-deck circle at Fort Bragg, waiting for the shit to hit the fan somewhere.

Yet somehow, this time he'd actually been looking forward to going back to the States, and he wasn't the only one.

Casey Bellows had seen his newborn son only via webcam. Mark Adams, the old man of the team at thirty-eight, was just two years shy of his twenty, and he had already received approval for transfer to a non-deployable headquarters unit. Even the Boss, Rainer, had made no secret of his plan to leave active duty and start up his own private security firm.

They'd had a good run, but maybe it was time to cash out and enjoy their success, not risk it all on one more throw of the dice.

Stow it, Sigler, he admonished himself. *This is what you signed up for.*

Sigler focused on Klein.

"Sasha can explain it better," Klein continued, with a gesture to the woman. Then he hastily added, "Sorry, I skipped the intros. Jack, Danno, this is Sasha Therion. We brought her in to consult on this..."

He paused, as if expecting the woman to engage with the conversation, but she continued to gaze at her computer screen, seemingly hypnotized.

Sigler felt compelled to speak, if only to end the awkward silence. "Brought her in? I thought your new boss put the kibosh on outsourcing."

It was no secret that Domenick Boucher, the new director of the CIA, under orders from the President, had put an end to the former administration's practice of outsourcing the detainment, rendition and interrogation of suspected terrorists. It was partly as a way to restore accountability to the relevant agencies and partly to stop the hemorrhage of taxpayer dollars into what some journalists had taken to calling the 'terror-industrialist complex.' The President had made other changes too, some public and some under the radar, to stream-line the nation's intelligence-gathering apparatus and repair the lingering damage to America's public image following too many inci-dents of abuse, brutality and torture—oft times with official sanction.

The President, a former Army Ranger, was by no means soft on national security issues, but he did have what one primary opponent had disparagingly called 'an obsolete sense of integrity.' Old-fashioned maybe, but not obsolete. Evidently the American people had liked the idea of a leader with integrity.

Klein shook his head. "This is different. But, I should let Sasha explain."

When she failed to pick up the cue a second time, the CIA man laid a hand gently on her forearm, and as if speaking to a young child, he said: "Sasha, why don't you tell the men about your work?"

The woman looked up suddenly, the spell broken. She glanced around the table as if just realizing that she wasn't alone. "Uh, I do the math."

Sigler stifled a laugh, but he noticed that Parker was now sitting up a little straighter. Daniel Parker, a self-confessed science geek, was the antithesis of most African-American stereotypes: a man who would count it a greater honor debating astrophysics with Neil deGrasse Tyson than playing one-on-one with Allen Iverson...though if push came to shove, he would probably acquit himself equally well in either situation.

"Sasha is, among other things, a cryptanalyst," explained Klein. "We might have stopped outsourcing the dirty work, but we can't afford to keep people with her talents on the payroll."

Sigler connected the dots. "So we found some kind of coded message."

Klein pursed his lips. "Not exactly."

"This is what you found," Sasha declared, as if abruptly deciding to take an interest in the conversation. She turned the laptop around and showed them the screen, and the image on it that had so captivated her.

The display showed what Sigler could only assume was a digital copy of one of the documents they had recovered during the previous night's raid. It didn't look familiar, but then he hadn't really been looking when they'd done the collecting. He recognized the delicate curves of Arabic script, but there was a block of writing in the middle that looked like nothing he'd ever seen before. The letters might have been Greek or perhaps Cyrillic, but interspersed among the not-quite-familiar letters were other shapes that looked almost like Chinese characters:

"What does it say?"

"I don't know," Sasha replied, looking genuinely bothered by the admission.

The CIA man broke in impatiently. "It's evident from the accompanying message that the enemy *does* know what it says, and that it's critical to the development of a biological weapon."

Sigler had been in the Unit long enough that such a declaration no longer surprised him. The stakes were always high. America's enemies were bent on acquiring bio-weapons or loose nukes. It was the Unit's job—*his* job—to nip those deadly aspirations in the bud.

"The intel you collected," Klein continued, "doesn't tell us what exactly, but it does tell us where: an old Republican Guard depot about thirty klicks northeast of Samarra."

Sigler reviewed his mental map of the region, but the area didn't ring any bells. Samarra lay between Baghdad and Tikrit, along the eastern leg of the Sunni Triangle, where nearly all of the insurgent activity had been focused lately. East of the triangle, there was a whole lot of nothing, all the way to the Iranian border.

"We had no idea this place even existed; it doesn't show up on any of our satellite imagery, going back all the way to the First Gulf War, so we have to assume that it was decommissioned sometime following the end of the war with Iran. We should have a UAV over the site within the hour, but we're thinking most of it's underground. Saddam probably buried it to hide it from UN weapons inspectors. That's probably why we didn't find it sooner." Klein shifted forward in his chair.

Here it comes, thought Sigler.

"The window of opportunity on this one is narrow. Once they figure out their couriers got nabbed, if they haven't already, they'll pick up and move. We need to hit this place ASAP." Another pause.

"Tonight."

Sigler didn't question the assessment. Klein wasn't asking for his opinion or advice; the CIA man was telling him to get ready. "I'll tell the boys."

"Slow down. There's more." He glanced at Sasha. "You're going to have a ride-along."

This time, Sigler wasn't able to hide his dismay. "You're shitting me, right?" He glanced over at Rainer, but the Boss was stone-faced. "You mean you'll bring her in once we secure the site?"

Klein shook his head. "Miss Therion needs to be there with you."

For the first time since her introduction, Sasha seemed to be aware of the discomfort her presence was creating. "The Iraqis know how to crack this code," she said, tapping the computer screen emphatically. "And we don't. We don't even know where to begin. I have to be there. I have to be the first one inside."

Rainer cleared his throat. "The decision is made, Jack."

"With all due respect, sir, I would like to say for the record that this is a piss-poor idea." Sigler hoped that his use of the military honorific—something that was almost never done in the Unit—would convey that this wasn't just run-of-the-mill bitching and moaning.

Rainer's reply was succinct. "Deal with it."

Sigler glanced at Klein, who now seemed to be making a studied effort to avoid meeting his gaze, and then at Sasha. "I don't suppose you've been trained for field work. Can you shoot?"

Before she could answer, Klein spoke up. "Don't worry about that, Jack. I'll take care of her. You guys just need to get us through the front door."

A dozen different retorts flew through Sigler's mind, but this time he checked himself. He stood up. "I'm going to need that imagery from the drone as soon as you can get it to me. The more I know about the site..." He let the thought trail off; there was nothing to be gained by stating the obvious. He motioned for Parker to follow, but to his surprise, his friend waved him off.

"Actually Jack, I'd like to have a word with Miss Therion."

For a moment, Sigler wasn't sure he'd heard correctly, but before he could inquire, Pettit snapped: "Parker!"

Usually, a stern look from Cipher element's top NCO would be enough to put any member of the team in their place—even Sigler, who, as the platoon leader, outranked him. Pettit rarely had to chastise with words, but when he did, everyone sought cover.

Parker, however, didn't even blink. He pointed at the computer screen and kept his gaze on Sasha. "I know what that is. So, either you can talk to me, one-on-one, and tell me what's really going on here, or I can walk out that door and tell the rest of the team that we're about to go put it on the line over an undecipherable medieval manuscript that's probably a hoax."

Sigler gaped at him. So did nearly everyone else. Klein swore softly under his breath.

Sasha shook her head. "It's not a hoax. That much, I'm sure of. And this could be the closest anyone has come to cracking the code in over four hundred years."

"What the fuck?" growled Pettit, turning to Rainer in disbelief. "Medieval manuscript? Is this shit for real?"

Rainer didn't respond to his sergeant major. Instead, he stood abruptly and motioned toward the door. "Gentleman, let's give Danno and Miss Therion a chance to get acquainted."

THREE

RAINER'S ABRUPT DECLARATION caught even Parker by surprise, and he didn't hide his elation very well; he grinned so hard, his jaws started to hurt. As the others filed out of the TOC, Sasha just stared at him in what he guessed was complete disbelief.

Yeah, that's right, he thought, nodding his head ever so slightly. *The black man was the smartest guy in the room. Bet you didn't see that coming, princess.*

"So," she said, when they were alone. "You know about the manuscript?"

He shrugged, but his irrepressible grin foiled his attempt to appear nonchalant. "Maybe. Or maybe I was just trying to find an excuse to be alone with you."

She blinked, uncomprehendingly. "Why would you do that?"

That dulled Parker's smile just a little. This girl wasn't pretending to be aloof as a way of fending off unwanted advances; this was who she really was. "I've dabbled a little in number theory and mathematical codes. I like to do brain teasers. Lateral thinking puzzles, cryptograms...stuff like that. I must have come across an article about it somewhere and it stuck in my head.

"Probably when I was at Yale," he added with a wink.

That seemed to penetrate her shield of inscrutability. "You went to Yale?"

His only answer was an airy wave. He hadn't attended Yale as a student, but he had grown up in New Haven, where his father still worked at the University as a janitor. He'd spent a lot of time on the campus while growing up, and he had, for a short while, dared to dream of attending the Ivy League institution. It was a dream that could not withstand the harsh realities of socio-economics and race politics.

His higher education—still a work in progress—had come through distance learning programs, but Sasha didn't need to know that.

"The article called it 'the most mysterious manuscript in the world.' An entire book written in a language that no one has ever seen before, and which no one is able to translate. Not even the NSA. That's pretty crazy shi...ah, stuff."

Sasha nodded. "It's one of the greatest puzzles in cryptology."

It was officially designated MS 408 of Yale University's Beinecke Rare Book and Manuscript Library, but it was more commonly known as the Voynich manuscript, so named for the early 20th century antique book dealer who brought it into public awareness.

The book's vellum pages, over two hundred and forty altogether, were decorated with elaborate full-color illustrations, mostly of plants, rendered with extraordinary detail—almost like a biology textbook— which had led many to believe that it was a book of herbal remedies from the Middle Ages. The pages also depicted star charts, along with more symbolic pictures—several of the paintings featured crudely drawn, almost cartoonish images of naked pregnant women, cavorting about in green pools, dancing along the edge of spiral star clusters, or emerging from plant root systems that looked suspiciously like the veins and arteries of a human body. What made the Voynich manuscript remarkable though was its text. The entire book had been written using a completely unknown alphabet system that had confounded all attempts at decipherment.

Theories about its origin were diverse. Some believed it to be the work of an herbalist or apothecary, who had developed the unique code to protect his recipes from competitors. Others believed it to be a hoax—created by a confidence artist during the reign of Queen Elizabeth or perhaps even by Voynich himself in the early 1900s—and opined that the reason the book's code couldn't be cracked was that the text had been generated randomly, to make it seem that the book contained some great mystery. Hoax or not, since its appearance in 1912, more than a few people had wasted years of their lives in a vain attempt to solve its riddle.

The mystery of the Voynich manuscript was exactly the sort of puzzle that captivated Parker. He had read numerous articles about the book, staying current on the latest research and theories about its origin, so he had immediately recognized the text excerpt on Sasha's computer screen. On a personal level, he was intrigued by the admittedly bizarre notion that Iraqi insurgents might be on the verge of cracking the Voynich code. The fact that this beautiful, if somewhat socially awkward cryptanalyst not only shared his interest but was obsessed with finding the solution, made it even more appealing.

But it sure as hell wasn't a good reason for Cipher element to risk their lives.

He shook his head. "The Voynich manuscript is almost certainly a hoax. The best theory I've heard is that it was produced by an English charlatan who claimed, among other things, to be able to turn lead into gold. The reason no one can read it is that there's nothing there to read; it's just a jumble of random symbols that don't mean anything."

"You are talking about the Edward Kelley hypothesis?" Sasha shook her head. "That has been categorically disproven."

"Categorically disproven? I wasn't aware of that."

"At my request, the agency secretly tested pieces of the manuscript. Carbon-14 dating confirms that the parchment dates to between the 13th and 15th centuries, at least two hundred years before Kelley lived."

"So it's old. That proves nothing. Different crook, same scam."

She pursed her lips. "You could be right. But the documents your team recovered indicate that al-Awda is in the process of decoding it. They believe it will help them create a new bio-weapon."

Despite his desire to impress her, Parker couldn't hide his incredulity. "Really? A medieval cookbook is going to tell them that?"

"You must be unfamiliar with the science of ethnopharmacology." Sasha's tone was flat, matter of fact, but the statement was a disparaging slap in the face to Parker. "It's the study of traditional medicines used by different ethnic groups, to discover new drugs and medicines. Traditional knowledge is the basis of modern pharmacology; there's every reason to believe that the Voynich manuscript might contain important new insights into healing medicines. However, if the information you recovered is accurate, the book might also contain important historical information about the plague."

That got Parker's attention.

If the Voynich manuscript did date back to the 1400s, then it wasn't too much of stretch to believe that it might contain knowledge about the Black Death, which had ravaged Europe less than a century earlier. The plague bacteria had already been used as a bio-weapon; it was widely believed that the first outbreak of the disease in Europe had occurred after an invading Mongol army catapulted infected bodies into the besieged city of Caffa. Seven hundred years later, the organism that had caused the plague—*Yersinia pestis*—remained a pathogen with deadly potential for exploitation as a germ warfare agent.

Ultimately, it didn't matter whether the Voynich manuscript really contained information about the plague, or even if it could be decoded at all. Somebody was trying to cook up a nasty new weapon, and it was his job—his team's job—to identify them and put them in the ground.

"That's good enough for me," he said, rising to his feet.

Sasha's face creased in confusion. "You...believe me? Just like that?"

"It doesn't matter what I believe." His grin was back, but this time it was a cold smile of anticipation. "I've got a job to do. It's going to be a busy night."

FOUR
Washington, D.C.

DOMENICK BOUCHER WAITED patiently for the President's daily national security briefing to conclude. As Director of the Central Intelligence Agency, he'd been the first to speak, providing the Commander-in-Chief with a succinct snapshot of how the world had changed during the previous twenty-four hours. He had then listened attentively as other members of the National Security Council had done the same, but all the while his thoughts never strayed far from the one piece of information he had withheld; he clenched it in his mind, like a hand grenade with the safety pin removed. It was an apt simile. He was about to drop this particular grenade on Tom Duncan's desk, and the odds were good that neither of them would be able to escape the shitstorm of political shrapnel that would follow.

When the President finally dismissed the meeting, Boucher stood with the rest of the attendees but didn't join the exit queue. President Duncan settled into the executive chair behind the Resolute Desk and leaned back, crossing his arms over his chest. "Something on your mind, Dom?"

Boucher pursed his lips. "Mr. President..."

"It's just us, Dom. Spit it out."

Easier said than done. Boucher wasn't just the DCIA; he was also Tom Duncan's friend, and that made this so much harder. He took a single sheet of paper from his leather portfolio and placed it in on the desktop. Duncan ignored it, maintaining eye contact with Boucher, compelling him to speak.

"Last night, a Delta team running CT operations in Ramadi captured two couriers working with the al-Awda resistance—"

"Refresh my memory."

"Al-Awda is Arabic for 'The Return,' as in the return of Saddam Hussein. It's a small group, made up of Ba'ath party members and Saddam loyalists. They've mostly been marginalized since Operation Red Dawn, but information recovered last night suggests that they are still active. We think they might have set up shop at a remote site east of

Samarra..." Boucher paused a beat then dropped the grenade. "It looks like the place is an undocumented Iraqi bio-weapons laboratory."

Duncan processed this for a moment then leaned forward, his palms flat on the desk to either side of the unread brief. "Undocumented? Christ, Dom, are you telling me that we've finally found the smoking gun?"

"I'm afraid it looks that way."

In October 2002, after several months of evident non-compliance on the part of Saddam Hussein's government with UN weapons inspectors, the United States Congress voted to authorize military action against Iraq. Four months later, the US Secretary of State, speaking before the United Nations Security Council, presented evidence of an ongoing Iraqi effort to develop weapons of mass destruction (WMDs), with the intent of using them against Western nations. Shortly thereafter, the war began. Almost two hundred thousand soldiers from the United States and three other countries, swept across the border, and in just twenty-one days of fighting, toppled the Ba'athist regime of Saddam Hussein.

But no WMDs were found.

As the triumphant victory turned into a prolonged occupation and a brutal campaign against insurgent guerillas—news pundits began calling it a 'quagmire'—the rationale for the war came under intense scrutiny. What had, in the days leading up to the invasion, seemed like a 'slamdunk'—damning evidence of an impending strike against American interests utilizing a deadly combination of biological, chemical and nuclear weapons—now seemed like a fallacious pretext for a war of imperialism.

It would later be revealed that much of the so-called evidence had been fraudulent, supplied by Saddam Hussein's political rivals, who had—successfully it seemed—tricked the nations of the West into toppling the hated dictator from power. While many would subsequently argue that Saddam's overthrow was justified, even absent the threat of illegal weapons programs, the perception that America had been deceived into starting the war haunted the former President to the end of his first and only term in office, and his decision not to run for a second term paved the way for the election of dark horse candidate Thomas Duncan.

Duncan, a former combat veteran, was intimately familiar with the very real cost of war, in both treasure and blood. His policy from day one in office was that there would be no hand wringing or recriminations over the miscalculations of the former administration, but he did intend to give the American people exactly what he had promised in the campaign—a government that was accountable for every dollar and every drop of American blood spent in the war effort.

Although there was no easy solution to the Iraq problem, Duncan was aggressively pushing his advisors for an exit strategy that would ensure long-term security and stability in the region. It was a politically popular position, and the war hawks in Congress, still stinging from the WMD fiasco, were keeping their heads down.

The discovery of a 'smoking gun'—a secret bio-weapon production facility leftover from Saddam Hussein's regime—would change all of that. A single shred of evidence, even circumstantial evidence, might be used to justify the war in the court of public opinion. Although doubts would linger, the uncertainty would undermine the President's position. The hawks would demand a more aggressive approach to foreign policy, with pre-emptive military action as a tool of statecraft, and more American soldiers would pay the price with their lives.

Duncan shook his head. "It is what it is, Dom. I won't lie to the American people. Sunlight is the best disinfectant, and the sooner we get this out in the open, the better."

"In point of fact, we don't actually know what *it* is. That's what the D-boys are going to find out tonight."

The President sighed, then lowered his eyes and scanned the brief. "What's this about a cryptanalyst?"

Boucher stifled a laugh. "The code the insurgents are using triggered an internal protocol that's been around since the days of the OSS. Sci-Tech says it's a code that's never been cracked, the holy grail of crypto. They begged and pleaded for me to deploy their expert with the team, and I saw no good reason to refuse. Her presence won't put the mission at risk."

The President did not pursue the issue. "I want to watch the game. Transfer control of this to the Situation Room. I want General Collins there, too. Those are his boys on the ground."

Boucher frowned. Some in the media had opined that, if the President had a failing, it was that he didn't like to relinquish control to his subordinates. The DCIA knew better; Duncan wasn't a control freak, and he didn't hire anyone without absolutely trusting them to get the job done.

He just misses the action.

"I'll order the pizzas."

FIVE
Iraq

THE THREE MH-60L Black Hawk helicopters from the 160th Special Operations Aviation Regiment, arrayed in an echelon-right formation, cruised through the darkened sky high above the Mesopotamian flood plain, performing the very task that had earned them the unit designation of the 'Night Stalkers.' Huddled together with Parker and the rest of his squad in the middle aircraft, Jack Sigler peered through his night vision scope, looking over the shoulder of a Black Hawk crew chief seated behind an M240H machine gun. He could make out a distant glow—the lights of Baghdad—far to the south, but below them, there was only the flat featureless desert landscape.

Featureless, but not quite empty.

The reconnaissance drone had uncovered the desert's secret: a low, cinderblock structure, half buried by windblown dust, just to the east of what the map called Buhayrat Shari Lake. The lake was now just a dry salt flat, two miles across and almost twenty miles long. The drone had showed them the target building, but revealed no sign of activity—no cooking fires burning, no vehicles, not even tire tracks. The facility looked abandoned, but looks could be deceiving.

After completing the initial sweep, the drone returned for refueling, but it was back in the air now, feeding real time infrared imagery to the PDA Rainer carried with him in the trailing helo. Sigler kept expecting the Cipher element leader to keep them updated, but Rainer had been uncharacteristically quiet. With the exception of Strickland's *sotto voce* whispered: "Mommy, are we there yet?" comment, everyone else had remained quiet as well.

Maybe no news is good news, Sigler thought. *Guess we'll find out in about five minutes.*

Four minutes and fifty seconds later, the crew chief at the gun twisted around and tapped him on the arm. The Night Stalkers crew members wore headsets that gave them access to their own radio net and internal comms, but as a matter of operational security, they didn't have Cipher element's frequency. The Delta team's radios did include a separate channel so they could communicate with the Night Stalkers—who were using the unit callsign 'Beehive'—but this close to the objective, the last thing Sigler wanted to do was mess with the radio settings. At this point in the mission, gestures and hand signals were the preferred form of communication.

Sigler passed the tap on to the rest of the squad, and almost in unison, they gave their equipment a final pre-combat inspection.

Rainer's voice squelched in his earpiece. "Eagle-Eye, this Cipher Six. Let me know when you're in position. Over."

A few hundred yards ahead, the lead Black Hawk executed a tricky near-vertical descent, flaring into a hover just a few feet above the arid terrain. Though he couldn't see them, Sigler knew that the six Eagle-Eye snipers were piling out of their ride and establishing a defensive over-watch position a kilometer away from the target.

The helicopters were quiet, but the desert was a big empty place and sound carried. Even at this distance, the insurgents in the building were probably sitting up and taking note. The Black Hawks were always at their most vulnerable during touchdown, when they were close to potential hostiles and unable to execute any kind of evasive maneuvers. It would be the job of the snipers to deal with any opposition during the interminably long half-minute or so required for other two Night Stalker birds to debark their passengers.

The snipers gave the 'all-clear' a moment later. Immediately, Sigler heard a change in the pitch of the turbines, and then he felt his stomach lurch and rise into his throat as the helicopter dropped like a runaway elevator. The downward motion stopped abruptly, and Sigler saw the crew chief waving, giving his all-clear.

The ground looked tantalizingly close, but Sigler knew from experience that night-vision devices screwed with depth perception, and with forty-odd pounds of gear strapped to his body, it paid to err on the side of caution. With his knees bent slightly to absorb the impact, he jumped from the hovering helo. As soon as his feet made contact, he dropped into a low shooter's stance and began moving forward, sweeping the foreground with the barrel of his HK416 assault rifle.

The squared-off outline of the building was visible about fifty meters away, but it looked as desolate as the rest of the bleak landscape.

"Last man out!" someone behind him shouted into the radio, and then the Black Hawk's turbines roared and the downdraft of the helicopter's ascent nearly blew Sigler over. When the maelstrom began to subside about ten seconds later, he keyed his mic. "Cipher Six, this is Cipher One-Six. We're in position. No sign of rain. Over."

"Roger, One-Six. You know what to do."

Sigler gestured for his team to line up behind him, and he began advancing toward the building. He stayed in his hunched over stance, his gaze flitting between the front of the building and the ground directly in front of him.

"Cipher element, this is Eagle-Eye two. Nothing on thermals."

Sigler frowned in dismay but kept moving. The cinderblock structure, unlike the shoddy house they had raided the previous evening in Ramadi, was an effective enough insulator to mask heat signatures from the thermal scopes.

The six men reached the front of the building. Sigler lined up beside the entryway—there was no door. Three operators were behind him, while the remaining two men posted at the corners to watch the sides and the rear of the building.

Unit SOP called for a dynamic entry, moving in fast, identifying and eliminating hostiles in the blink of an eye, but Sigler hesitated. The open doorway, a dark hole in the green-gray of the building, beckoned him. Without a door to kick down, it would be the smoothest entry ever. What could be easier?

Too easy.

Instead of giving the signal that would start the countdown, Sigler eased forward and peeked around the doorpost.

Someone behind him hissed a warning. Almost from day one in basic training, soldiers were taught to never present a silhouette target to an enemy. If the insurgents were inside, waiting to meet the attack that they must surely suspect was coming, then he was a dead man.

No shot came.

The green display of his night vision showed what looked like sleeping forms, wrapped in blankets. There was no sign of movement within.

Sigler eased back. Nothing about this felt right.

It was decision time; he had to either go now or abort. His instincts were screaming for him to do the latter, but he didn't have a shred of evidence to back up that call.

Rainer's voice scratched in his ear. "Jack, why are you still on the wrong side of that wall?"

Sigler ignored the question. He activated his PAQ4 and directed the laser beam into the room, easing out once more into the danger zone. The green light stabbed into the dark interior, illuminating the space but revealing nothing more...

Something glinted in the laser light, right in front of him. A thin strand of monofilament was stretched across the door frame just above ankle level.

He keyed his mic. "All Cipher elements, this is One-Six, I'm calling the game. Fall back to rally one."

"Jack?" Rainer didn't bother with brevity codes.

"This is a set up, Boss."

Sigler wasn't sure what Rainer's reaction would be. Another SOP was that anyone could pull the plug on a mission for any reason—he might catch hell in the after-action review if it turned out to be nothing but a case of jitters—but this close to the objective...

"It's your call, Jack."

Sigler led his squad back out, taking care to step only in the boot prints that marked their initial approach. Rainer was waiting at the designated rally point, two hundred meters from the building, along with Pettit, Klein and Sasha.

Sigler got right to the point. "It's wired. We were expected."

Sasha spoke up. "You don't understand. I need to get inside."

"No ma'am," Rainer said. "You don't understand. There's nothing in there. This was a trap."

"Shit," growled Klein. "Can we at least sweep the place for NBC residue?"

If the facility had been used as a bio-weapons laboratory, it was conceivable, however unlikely, that trace evidence might be found.

"Negative. We're done here. I'm calling the birds," Rainer said.

Best news I've heard all day, Sigler thought.

SIX

SASHA THERION STUMBLED along behind Klein, trying to make sense of what was happening...trying and failing.

She'd come here to learn about the Voynich manuscript. It wasn't just a book of herbal remedies. It contained something so much more fantastic than that... It had to. That was why its author had gone to such extraordinary lengths to encipher the text. The insurgents knew it, too. They had cracked its code, or were close to doing so, and planned to use its centuries' old secret to make a weapon that could destroy life.

So why were the soldiers leaving?

Sasha didn't like it when people changed the plan at the last minute. Plans were good; they were the only way to ensure orderliness. Changing plans meant introducing uncertainty into the equation, and uncertainty was a sure path to chaos. And chaos was relentless...insidious.

If they would just let me do what I came here for...

The helicopter swooped down, beating the earth all around her with its rotor wash. She felt Klein's hand on her shoulder, urging her to duck low. She didn't like it when people touched her, but she complied. A few seconds later, she was bundled inside and guided onto one of the bench seats. Klein sank down next to her, and a moment later, the Black Hawk climbed back into the sky.

She peered through the eyepiece of the night vision monocular the Delta operators had supplied her with, looking first at the Agency man and then at Rainer. She had to explain it to them, make them understand how important it was that they accomplish their goal.

One of the helicopter's crew leaned back and craned his head toward Rainer. He was shouting, but his voice was barely audible over the strident whine of the turbine engines. "What happened?"

"A complication," Rainer answered. "The plan is the same."

Sasha didn't understand. How could the plan be the same if they were leaving?

The crewman just nodded.

"Do it!" Rainer shouted.

Sasha was still trying to make sense of this when the Delta team leader brought his carbine up and fired two shots.

Klein jerked in the seat beside her. Sasha flinched, as a hot blast of sulfurous exhaust sprayed her face. Then she felt something else, something warm and wet on her shoulder. Klein had slumped against her with blood trickling from a pair of tiny holes in his forehead, and gushing from the enormous opening in the back of his skull.

The crewman Rainer had spoken with stretched out his arm, pointing across the cabin in the direction of his counterpart on the opposite side. As the other crewman started to turn, a tongue of flame leapt from the pistol in the first man's hand. The second man slumped forward over his machine gun. At almost the same instant, there was another report from the cockpit.

"What the—" the man Sasha knew as Pettit stiffened on his seat, trying to get his own weapon up, but Rainer was already swinging his gun around. Two more shots erupted from Rainer's carbine and punched into Pettit's face.

Sasha didn't know what was happening...except in a strange way, she did. It was exactly what she'd been afraid of; they had changed the plan, and now chaos was descending.

They're going to kill me next, she thought, and maybe that was okay. Everyone died, no matter how they fought against that inevitable outcome. Life, with all its endless unpredictable possibilities, always reduced to zero in the end, the final victory of order over chaos.

But the Delta team leader didn't shoot her; he didn't even point his gun at her.

"Sorry you had to see that," he shouted. "But if you'll just sit tight, everything will make sense in a little while."

Sasha very much doubted that.

SEVEN

SIGLER WAS THE last to climb aboard the second Black Hawk. As he got in, he flashed a thumb's up to the crew chief and shouted: "Last man!"

Then the crew chief did something unexpected. He held up his hand with forefinger and middle finger extended, just like the peace sign, or V for Victory...or, Sigler realized, the number two. The crew chief was telling him to switch to channel two on his radio, which was preset with the Night Stalkers' frequency.

"This is Cipher One-Six," Sigler said when the he'd made the switch. "Do you have traffic for me?"

"Cipher, this is Beehive Six-Four. I've lost contact with Beehive Six-Six, and they are presently heading away from our position on a bearing of three-three-zero. Do you know what's up? Over."

Beehive Six-Six was the Black Hawk with Rainer's group, and the compass heading meant they were flying north-northwest. Ramadi lay to the south.

"Standby." He switched to the Delta channel. "Cipher Six, this is Cipher One-Six. Come in, over."

No answer. He tried two more times, unsuccessfully. He was about to switch back to update the pilot, when a voice sounded in his earpiece. "Cipher One-Six, this is Eagle-Eye Three. What the hell's going on?"

Even without the callsign, Sigler recognized the voice of Lewis Aleman. The tall, athletic sniper shared Parker's interest in science and technology, and the two men often hung out together, salivating over the Sharper Image catalog like it was the Sport Illustrated swimsuit issue.

"Wondering that myself, Eagle-Eye. Are you guys on the bird?" Sigler saw the crew chief motioning for his attention again, but waited for Aleman to answer in the affirmative. "Roger, Eagle-Eye. Standby."

He switched to the Night Stalkers' frequency. "Go for Cipher element."

"Cipher, this is Beehive Six-Four. Beehive Six-Six is...they're bugging out, and they ain't taking our calls. This is your show, Cipher. What do I do?"

Sigler's brow furrowed in disbelief; there was no protocol for a situation like this. He leaned over the crew chief's shoulder and stared out the door, hoping to catch a glimpse of the departing Black Hawk, as if visually confirming what he'd been told would give him some insight about what to do next.

He didn't see the helicopter. Instead, he saw a flash on the ground, perhaps a mile to the west, then another.

Abruptly, the display in his night vision device flared bright white, like a high intensity spotlight beaming directly into his retina. He reflexively tore the monocular away, but the damage was done; a greenish blue spot filled his right eye.

His left eye however, fixed on the source of the light: two parachute flares, fired from mortar tubes, were blazing like tiny suns in the night sky.

"Shit! Get us out of here, Beehive!"

His warning was unnecessary; the pilots had seen the flares as well and were already taking evasive action.

Two deep booming sounds reverberated through the airframe, the reports of the mortar launch finally reaching them, and then

Sigler's good eye detected more flashes on the ground, and pinpoints of light streaking into the sky. Sigler recognized them instantly; RPGs...rocket propelled grenades.

The effective range of the RPG was only about a hundred meters. Beyond that, there was less than a fifty percent chance of hitting a stationary target. At a thousand meters, the grenade would self-destruct. Sigler's helicopter was well outside that radius, but Beehive Six-Five was a lot closer to the source. The air around the helicopter carrying the snipers suddenly came alive with flashes, as the grenades began exploding. Sigler thought the helicopter had weathered the barrage, but a moment later he heard a voice over the radio: "Shit! We're going in."

Beehive Six-Five wobbled in the air and began corkscrewing downward.

There was a thunderous eruption right in front of Sigler; the crew chief had opened up with his M240. Red arcs—tracers—described the path of the 7.62 millimeter rounds as they lanced toward the source of the RPGs, but it was impossible to distinguish a target or judge the effectiveness of the fire.

A puff of dust below marked the spot where Beehive Six-Five finished its fateful plunge. Sigler knew exactly what he had to do next. "Six-Four, get us as close as you can. We'll do the rest."

"Roger, Cipher." The pilot's voice was steady and professional, without a trace of hesitation. "I'll try to make it a short walk."

Sigler switched channels. "Eagle-Eye, do you copy?"

There was an interminably long silence, but then someone broke squelch. Sigler heard several seconds of gunfire, then a cough. "Cipher. Could use a little help here."

It was Aleman.

"On our way, Eagle-Eye. What's the count?"

"Two and two." Two dead, two injured badly enough to be out of the fight. After a beat, Aleman amended: "I think. Having trouble telling which way is up right now."

"Sit tight, Eagle-Eye. Help is on the way."

The Black Hawk set down about fifty yards east of the crash site, well out of RPG range, but in between bursts from the M240, Sigler could hear the distinctive crack of bullets ricocheting off the armored exterior of the helicopter. As soon as the crew chief threw open the door on the sheltered side, Sigler's team poured out onto the desert floor.

When the last man was out, Beehive Six-Four rose again into the sky, and the door gunner continued to hurl bullets in the direction of the muzzle flashes. Sigler's men broke into pairs and began moving toward the crash using the tried and true individual movement techniques taught to every soldier: three to five second rushes, measured out to the rhythm of the mantra *I'm up, he sees me, I'm down...* Then drop to the prone, roll left or right, it didn't matter which as long as you didn't get into a pattern, and give your buddy some cover fire so that he could make his move.

There was another pair of booms and two more flares appeared in the sky overhead. The enemy probably thought that lighting up the sky would level the playing field, removing the technological advantage of the Delta team's night vision. And maybe it would do that, but stealth and darkness weren't the only tools in the Delta toolbox. One Delta operator was easily worth ten...twenty...or even fifty insurgents.

Sigler tried to do the math as he dropped to the prone once more, rolled left, and then squeezed a pair of shots in the direction of a distant muzzle flash. His eyesight was almost back to normal, and he could easily distinguish at least twenty separate jets of flame. Maybe fifty to one was pushing it a bit. He didn't know how many hostiles they were facing, but it was evident that someone had put a lot of thought into this trap, which meant these weren't run of the mill durka-durkas sprayin' and prayin'.

Inside job.

He bounded up and made another rush. He was close enough to the crash site to see men huddled behind the wreck, popping up every few seconds to provide covering fire. Two more rushes would get him there, maybe one if he didn't stop...he was close enough now that the wreck would cover his approach.

Someone in Beehive Six-Six was working with the enemy. Klein. It had to be Klein. The Company man had sold them out, sacrificed them...but why?

He reached the downed helicopter and went immediately to the nearest man. It was Lewis Aleman. The Delta sniper had his H&K PSG 1 sniper rifle beside him, but his left hand was clutching a Beretta M-9 handgun. It took Sigler only a moment to realize why Aleman had opted to use the pistol; his right hand, cradled protectively against his abdomen, looked like a mass of raw meat.

Sigler took a mental step back and assessed the situation. The Black Hawk sat upright on the desert floor, but the crash had crumpled its frame like a beer can. The doors had sprung open, leaving an open space through the middle, and two men—one wore an olive drab flight suit, marking him as a surviving crewmember, and the other was a Delta sniper—were working the fixed machine gun on the far side. Sigler also saw a body inside, a crewman impaled on a piece of metal.

There were two other motionless forms on the ground outside the Black Hawk. Both wore desert camouflage, torn and dark with spilled blood. Sigler couldn't tell if they were alive or not. He turned back to Aleman. "Sit rep?"

The sniper grimaced. "Pilot's alive...at least he was...trapped in the cockpit. Co-pilot has a broken leg...maybe some ribs."

"Our guys?"

Aleman motioned to the still forms on the ground. "Bell's hurt bad. Broken back, I think. Martinez is done."

"Did you get a look at the other side?"

"Yeah. There's a whole fucking lot of them."

The rest of Sigler's team reached the wreck and fanned out to join the Black Hawk's defenders. Sigler took charge. "Danno, Jess...get that second 240 back in action. Jon, I need an LZ. Casey, Mike, get the wounded ready for transport."

As the men quickly went to their assigned tasks, Sigler called up to the remaining Black Hawk, which continued to circle high above them. "Beehive Six-Four, this is Cipher. We're establishing a casualty collection point fifty meters from my location. Will pop white smoke when ready for pick-up. How copy?"

"Good copy, Cipher. Stay on this channel. Have requested CAS, but no word on ETA."

CAS—close air support—was exactly what they needed right now, but Sigler wasn't going to hold his breath and hope for someone to come pull their asses out of the fire. He turned back to the wreck, where Parker and Strickland had succeeded in liberating the M240H from its pintle mount. Strickland cradled the machine gun in both arms, while Parker gathered up full cans of ammunition—two in each hand. Sigler gestured for them to set it up at the nose end of the helicopter, and then he moved forward to the cockpit door.

The pilot sat unmoving in his chair, the control panel closed over his legs like the jaws of a devouring monster. His head lolled to the side and blood dripped from the bottom edge of his helmet. Sigler turned away.

He joined Parker and Strickland just as the latter opened up with the M240. Parker was right next to his teammate, ready to slap in a fresh belt of ammo as soon as it was needed. Sigler dropped down next to him.

"How many?"

Parker craned his head to answer. "I make out three different groups...at our ten, twelve and two."

The mortars boomed again, throwing another pair of flares into the sky, and this time Sigler was able to mark their location, positioned behind the line of riflemen.

"I don't like this, Danno. Pretty soon, they're gonna figure out they can do more with those cannons than just pop flares."

"So we can't stay here. What's the play?"

Sigler did a rough head count. There had been ten men aboard the Black Hawk. Even if they left the dead behind, a thought that galled him, he didn't think the remaining bird could get them all out. "We evac the casualties, then fall back to the original objective. Buy some time until another bird gets here."

Parker nodded, but before he could say anything, the ground in front of them erupted in a spray of dust. Sigler instinctively dropped, but just as quickly, he rolled into a prone shooting position and triggered a few shots of suppressive fire. He expected to hear Strickland jump in with the 240, and when that didn't happen, he called out: "Danno, Jess, still with me?"

"Jack," Parker called. "Jess is hit."

Sigler muttered a curse and spider-crawled back to the impromptu machine-gun emplacement where he found Parker with both hands pressed to the Strickland's neck in what seemed like a futile effort to stanch the rhythmic spurts of blood.

"Keep pressure on the wound," Sigler instructed. "I'll pull him behind cover."

At a nod from Parker, he grabbed the stricken soldier's legs and began hauling him back behind the shadow of the helicopter. Parker kept one hand on the wound and dug a field dressing from his tactical vest with the other. It was probably a wasted effort, but Sigler didn't tell Parker that; Delta operators never gave up, especially when it came to saving one of their teammates. Braving the kill zone once more, Sigler crawled out to retrieve the 240.

"Jon! Where's my LZ?"

From about fifty meters away, Jon Foley on one end of a litter carrying an immobilized Delta sniper, shouted: "Open for business!"

Sigler helped Parker carry Strickland to the casualty collection point, and then he keyed his mic. "Beehive, this is Cipher. Watch for smoke."

The Black Hawk set down, practically on top of the hissing smoke grenade, once more shielding the Delta team while they loaded their wounded men and dead. Sigler kept a mental tally; the score now stood at three dead, including the pilot whom they'd been unable to free from the wreckage, and three seriously wounded. He realized someone was missing. "Where's Aleman?"

He spied the lanky sniper, still in position at the wrecked bird, and somehow firing an assault rifle one-handed. Sigler switched to the Delta team channel. "Aleman, get your ass on this bird!"

Aleman's voice came back, crystal clear. "Sorry, did not receive your last."

Sigler considered repeating himself, but then thought better of it. There was no telling how long it would be before help arrived; as long as Aleman was willing and able to pull a trigger, there was no reason not to keep him in the game.

As the last of the litters was loaded onto the Black Hawk, the crew chief leaned in. "If we dump some weight and get real cozy, we might be able to get everyone on."

"Dump some weight? You mean like the guns and all the ammo?"

The crew chief shrugged. "I didn't say it would be pretty."

The Black Hawk was rated to carry a maximum of eleven troops along with its crew of four. Dropping the armaments and other extraneous equipment might allow them to stretch that limit a bit, as would leaving the bodies of the dead behind, but Sigler didn't like the math. "Just hurry back."

The crew chief nodded solemnly and then climbed aboard and slid the door closed. Sigler crouched low and hastened out from under the rotor wash as the idling turbines began whining louder.

He was halfway to the wreck when he saw a flash in the corner of his eye.

A small group of insurgents—or maybe it was just a lone fearless soul, hell-bent on earning his virgins in Paradise—had flanked them, circling around to the south of the crash site.

In the time it took him to turn his head, the RPG crossed the distance to its target.

The warhead—a PG-7VR tandem charge grenade—had been designed to destroy tanks with modern reactive armor. It did this by first exploding a small shaped charge that released a high-velocity jet of metal in a superelastic state, which can cut through solid steel. The second, larger high-explosive charge would then penetrate deep into the wound and detonate inside the target.

The rocket snaked in under the rising helicopter's rotors and struck below the exhaust vent on the port side. The shaped-charge blast cut through the Black Hawk's exterior like it was made of tissue paper. A millisecond later, the three pounds of high-explosives in the main charge detonated, and Beehive Six-Four blew apart at the seams.

EIGHT
Washington, D.C.

THE PRESIDENT'S PALM came down on the tabletop with a resounding smack that echoed like a pistol-shot in the crypt-quiet Situation Room.

The operational command center in the White House basement was all but deserted. The President had only intended to observe the Delta team operation, and so he had eschewed the normal cadre of advisors, aides and support staff. The were only two other men in the room besides Boucher. Lieutenant General Roger Collins, commander of the Joint Special Operations Command, was a thick, beefy man with puffy, red features and a poorly-kept secret love affair with the bottle. Collins's aide was a compactly built man with a silver-gray buzzcut, colonel's eagles on his epaulets and a black name plate that read 'Keasling.'

Collins shook his head. "Well...shit."

Boucher winced as the President's eyes sent daggers through the air at the three-star general. "Shit? That's all you've got? Shit?"

Domenick Boucher swallowed nervously and returned his gaze to the television screen, where the crisis was playing out in real-time. The feed was from an infrared camera mounted on a circling Predator UAV, and the images were rendered in an eerie inverted black and white, with the grayscale hues serving as an indication of temperature. The expanding cloud of white smoke that now occupied the space where one of the Army helicopters had been a moment before, could only mean one thing: the Black Hawk had become an inferno.

Until the President's outburst, Boucher had felt as paralyzed as Collins. He'd watched in mute disbelief as the operation had fallen apart before his eyes, turning from a simple raid into a full blown battle. But Duncan's anger galvanized him.

Focus, he thought. *What are the priorities?*

He'd never faced a crisis like this as the Director of the Central Intelligence Agency. There was rarely a need for the DCIA to be hands-on, but Boucher had come up through the ranks and witnessed some of the nation's worst moments from the other side of director's desk.

I've got people in the field... He shook his head; Klein and the crypto consultant were on the helicopter that had taken off without warning. There was nothing he could do to help them; no way to reach them. *Why? Why did that Black Hawk go rogue? Who was giving the orders?*

He dug his cell phone from a pocket, then just as quickly put it away. The Situation Room was shielded; no radio signals could get in or out. He would have to make do with one of the hard-wired telephones, which like all the other technology in the Situation Room, was painfully obsolete and actually less secure than Boucher's encrypted digital phone.

Collins was still fumbling for an answer. "Sir, there's not a hell of a lot I can do."

"You can get those men out of there." The President's voice was low and flat, a steel blade hissing from between clenched teeth.

The general, perhaps without thinking it through first, shook his head. "Mr. President, it's not that simple. We're not coordinating with Defense on this, and if we make that call, we'll have to disclose the whole operation. We won't be able to keep the mission a secret."

"Do you think those men out there give a damn about that?"

"That's what we pay them for, sir."

Boucher wasn't the only man in the room shocked into action. The general's aide likewise leaped for a phone. The President's eyes followed him, but he made no move to interfere or ask for an explanation; the man was doing *something*, and Boucher knew that counted for a lot in Duncan's book.

Collins finally seemed to grasp the concept as well. He swiveled his chair toward Keasling. "Mike, get some CAS out there."

Keasling looked up but didn't pull the receiver away from his mouth. "Calling the Air Force now, sir."

"Doesn't the 160th have attack choppers?" intoned the President, somewhat mollified. "Little Birds?"

Boucher recalled that Duncan had seen the Army's special operations helicopters in action when he'd served in Mogadishu, nearly two decades earlier.

Keasling didn't seem the least bit nonplussed. "With respect, Mr. President, I think the Night Stalkers need to be grounded."

Collins was indignant. "Mike, what the hell?"

Keasling pointed to one of the screens that showed an air traffic control radar map of Central Iraq. "Beehive Six-Six has gone AWOL. I don't know who's in command of that aircraft or what they're doing, but I'd say there's a better than even chance that at least one of the crew is involved in this action."

The announcement stunned Boucher. That was the piece of this puzzle that refused to fit. Someone had set a trap for the Delta team, that much was obvious, but the ambush at the site was only part of the equation; someone had been working from within their ranks to make sure that Cipher element was in the wrong place at the wrong time.

He heard a voice in his ear and realized his telephone call to the Director of Operations had finally gone through. "This is Boucher," he said in a low whisper. "We have a situation involving operations with Cipher element. I need all hands on deck."

There was a moment of silence at the other end, and Boucher could imagine the DO biting back a river of questions. "Understood. I'll sound the alarm. Will you be joining us?"

"Not sure. I'm with the President now. I'll either meet you there or set up a conference call."

The President quickly grasped the import of Keasling's statement. "You think there are others involved?"

Keasling nodded. "Or the rogue agent might have sabotaged the support aircraft. Either way, we need to keep the Night Stalkers on the bench for now."

"So what else can we do to help those men?"

"I'm trying to divert immediate close air support, sir. And I've put the word out to all our operators in the region. 1st Ranger is attached to 7th Group at COB Speicher—al Sahra airfield, near Tikrit. They can be there in a couple hours."

"A couple hours? Our boys could be dead by then."

A strange gleam lit in Keasling's eyes. "Sir, with all due respect, I wouldn't bet on it."

NINE
Aden, Yemen

A MAN IN a white waiter's uniform pushed a food service cart out of the elevator and down the hallway. It was an hour after midnight, and the corridor was still and silent. Upon reaching his destination, one of more than a dozen nearly identical doors on either side of the hall, the waiter stopped and consulted a slip of paper on the cart, as if to verify that he was in the correct place. He stood motionless for a moment and could just make out a murmur of voices—probably from a television set inside—then he rapped his knuckles loudly on the door.

Several seconds passed. He was about to knock again when a voice issued from behind the panel. The terse inquiry was in Arabic, a language the waiter did not speak fluently, but the meaning was clear enough.

"I have food," he called out. He spoke in English, but with an accent that might reasonably have been mistaken for German. "You order room service, *ja?*"

The door opened a crack, and through that narrow space, the waiter saw an unsmiling bearded Arab man, not quite as tall as his own six feet. The Arab appraised the waiter with a laser-like stare, taking in his dirty blond hair and long goatee—features that looked decidedly out of place in the region. Then he opened the door wider and took a half-step into the hall. Despite the late hour, the man was fully dressed, though he had chosen western attire—a brown sport coat over a white cotton dress shirt and khaki chinos—instead of the garb preferred by his kinsman. He glanced left and right, then returned his attention to the waiter.

"No room service."

The waiter picked up the slip of paper and held it out for inspection. "You order food, *ja?* See right here?"

The Arab ignored the paper. "No."

The waiter took another look at the slip. "Did someone else in the room order? You have others in the room with you?"

A perturbed look crossed the man's face, then he stepped back inside and rattled off an inquiry in Arabic. The waiter seized the opportunity to advance his cart into the room, but the Arab blocked his entry, stopping the cart with such suddenness that the waiter had to steady himself by grasping the door frame. There was an angry look in the Arab's eyes as he pushed the cart back into the hall.

"No order," he said forcefully. To make his point even more explicit, he drew back the lapel of his jacket, revealing something metallic—the brushed chrome slide action of an enormous pistol in a shoulder holster. "You go now."

This time, the waiter offered no protest, but almost scurried back, with one hand raised in a gesture of surrender. The Arab watched the blond man retreat all the way to the elevator, before turning back inside and slamming the door.

Instantly, the waiter reversed course and hurried back to the same room's door. As he moved, he tucked his chin against his right shoulder, and when he spoke into the radio microphone clipped inside his white uniform jacket, all trace of the quasi-German accent was gone. "This is Juggernaut. Package delivered."

A man's voice—a laconic Texas drawl—sounded in the flesh colored ear bud connected to the radio. "Roger, Jugs. Receiving, Lima Charlie."

Lima Charlie, the NATO phonetic alphabet equivalent of the letters L and C, meant the signal from the tiny transmitter that had been surreptitiously placed in the hotel room was being received "loud and clear."

A murderous gleam appeared in the waiter's bright blue eyes. "Damn it, Houston. I fucking hate it when you call me 'Jugs.'"

The man at the other end of the transmission—Sonny Vaughn, the team leader who went by the callsign 'Houston'—didn't take the bait. "You've got 'em riled up. They aren't buying your bogus waiter schtick."

"It was your stupid idea," groused the ersatz waiter—Stanley Tremblay, callsign 'Juggernaut.' "A German waiter in a fucking Arab country? Really?"

"I explained all this, Jugs. A lot of European tourists come here. And half the workers in Arab countries are foreigners. Besides, the whole point was to stir things up...whoa, standby." There was a long silence. "Bingo. These are our guys all right. Two men... They know they've been made."

"Is the kid here?"

"Negative." Pause. "Someone's making a call."

"Shit."

Tremblay swept the stack of neatly folded dinner napkins off the cart. He reached down and plucked up the Beretta 9 mm semi-automatic pistol equipped with a suppressor that nearly doubled its barrel length, concealed beneath. He gave the hotel room door a gentle push—the strip of tape he'd surreptitiously slapped over the strike plate during his first attempt to enter, had prevented the latch from engaging—and moved inside like the Grim Reaper in stealth mode.

In the space of two seconds, he fired four shots—two pairs of bullets for each of the two men standing in the front room. The big Arab that had met him at the door had only enough time to whirl around in surprise before the Beretta gave him the kiss of death. The other man, also of Arab ancestry, but smaller in stature, didn't even have time to look up from the cell phone he was dialing.

With the gun still held at the ready, Tremblay quickly moved to the second body and scooped up the phone in his left hand. He could hear a tinny voice issuing from the speaker, but he ignored it and thumbed the 'end' button.

"Got a number, Houston. Find a name to go with it." He started to read the digits from the phone's display, but before he could finish, it started vibrating in his hands. "Shit. He's calling back. How do you say 'butt-dial' in Arabic?"

"Never mind that, Jugs. Hold the phone next to the radio. I'll try to bluff 'em."

The phone squirmed like a living thing in his hands. Tremblay hastily unplugged the mic and earbud wires from the radio unit clipped to his belt, then held the cellular phone next to it and hit the button to accept the call.

The conversation that followed was brief and incomprehensible. Despite his southern roots, Vaughn did a passable job of mimicking the voice of the phone's former owner—an imitation based on the snippets of conversation he'd overheard from the listening device—but when the call ended, there was a note of urgency in his next transmission.

"They're spooked, pardner. I got an exact GPS location from the call: Mualla, the port district."

"The kid is there?"

"Hope so. But we can't wait for you."

Tremblay scowled. "Story of my life. I do all the work, but you guys get to have all the fun. Come pick me up when you're done."

"Roger, out."

Tremblay tossed the phone aside and turned for the door. His disappointment at being left behind by his teammates was sincere, but the clock was ticking, and the two minutes it might take him to exit the hotel could mean the difference between rescuing the kid or recovering his headless body.

The 'kid' was the adult son of the US Ambassador to Saudi Arabia. He'd been abducted while vacationing in the area—sailing or some other damn fool diversion of the idle rich. Tremblay and his three teammates from Delta's elite Alpha team had managed to identify the kidnappers. They were al-Something-or-other...there were so many damn terrorist groups in the Arab world that he'd given up trying to keep them straight. Alpha had tracked them here to Aden's Gold Mohur Resort, but evidently the bad guys had split up. Two of them had been living it up here at the hotel, while an unknown number were babysitting the hostage on the other side of the city.

The attack came before he took a single step.

Something tipped him off. The creak of the floor as the man attempted to sneak up behind him, a shadow moving on the wall, the rush of wind as the man drew back to hit him... Whatever it was, the premonition saved his life. He half-turned and threw up a hand to block the chair that his assailant was about to smash down on his head.

There was a splintering sound as the chair came apart on impact. Pain throbbed in Tremblay's forearm and the pistol flew from his nerveless fingers, even as he staggered under the blow. Then, like a player in a slapstick movie, he tripped over one of the bodies on the floor and fell squarely on his backside.

The attacker pounced on the gun.

There wasn't time to seek cover, so Tremblay did the only thing he could think of: he grabbed the body he'd tripped over—the corpse of the big man that had met him at the door—and hauled it front of him like a human shield.

Something heavy fell out from beneath the man's jacket and slammed like a sledgehammer into Tremblay's crotch. Even as he grimaced against this fresh wave of pain, he heard a faint coughing sound and the rasp of the Beretta's bolt sliding back and ratcheting another round into the firing chamber. There was a faint tremor as the bullet punched into the dead man, but Tremblay barely noticed. His attention was fixed on the thing that had just punched him in the nuts.

It was a Desert Eagle Mark XIX. The weapon was a monster. Its ten inch barrel was almost as long as the Beretta with its attached suppressor, and at about five pounds, it weighed more than twice as much as the standard issue military sidearm. A cursory glance at the half-inch diameter of the barrel confirmed what Tremblay already suspected: the Desert Eagle was outfitted for the .50 caliber Action Express round.

He grabbed the pistol in his left hand, awkwardly reinforcing his grip with his still half-numb right hand, and shoved the enormous pistol against the back of his very dead human shield, pointing it in the direction of his assailant. His thumb swept the safety off and his finger pulled the trigger.

The report sounded like cannon-fire. It felt like it too...or maybe like holding a stick of dynamite. Because he'd been in a sitting position, there had been no way to brace his body against the recoil. Newton's Third Law of Motion ruled against him and he toppled backward, barely keeping the gun in his clenched fist. He still fared better than his attacker though. The bullet had punched through the dead man's soft abdomen, and continued forward undeterred, striking the man halfway across the room, spattering both men's blood onto the walls and even the ceiling.

Tremblay quickly shook off the effects of both the unexpected attack and his stunning rejoinder, and scrambled to his feet. The report from the Desert Eagle had been loud enough to wake the dead, to say nothing of the other guests at the resort, and that was going to make getting out a bit trickier than he'd planned. He hastened to the room entrance, which was still open after his violent intrusion. In the hallway beyond, doors were opening and a growing tumult of voices was audible, but he didn't step out to investigate. Instead, he stripped away the piece of tape he'd used to confound the latch bolt, and firmly closed the door. That would buy him a few minutes to figure out what to do next.

Remembering that he'd been caught off guard once already, he spun around with the Desert Eagle at the ready and quickly checked the suite to make sure there were no other occupants waiting in ambush. There were no more surprises of that sort, but he did find an open door leading to an exterior balcony where he suspected the third man had been lurking. The balcony also gave him an idea on how to make his exit.

He returned to the front room to retrieve his Beretta, a much more efficient weapon for field work than the overly powerful Desert Eagle, but as he was about to discard the latter, he hesitated.

Stan Tremblay had a deep appreciation for a well-engineered piece of killing technology. True, the Desert Eagle was about as useful to a stealthy Delta operator as a Lamborghini Diablo was to a soccer mom, but that didn't make it any less a thing of beauty. Besides, the Fates had literally dropped it right in his lap, and not a moment too soon...obviously, the universe wanted him to have it.

Despite the urgency of his situation, he flashed an approving grin at his unassailably logical conclusion, and searched the body of the big Arab for spare magazines. To his utter delight, he found that the dead man's shoulder holster rig contained not only four more seven-round magazines, but another identical pistol on the opposite side.

Tremblay let out a low whistle. "Holy shit, pal. Trying to over-compensate for something?"

Since breaking up a matched set seemed like bad luck, and it was probably dangerous to just leave them lying around, he appropriated the holster for himself and once he'd looped it around his own shoulders, he returned the first pistol to its place. He shifted the rig experimentally; the added weight felt strangely comfortable.

He lingered in the suite a moment longer, searching the closets until he found a baggy windbreaker jacket that would both conceal his new acquisitions and be a little less conspicuous than the white waiter's outfit. Then he headed back to the balcony and swung over the rail.

Despite his size, or maybe because of it, he moved down the exterior of the hotel like King Kong on the Empire State Building. He'd grown up with the woods of New Hampshire as his playground; climbing was second nature to him. He swung between balconies, made dynamic leaps between the patios when necessary and finally dropped the last ten feet to the concrete deck that surrounded the entire building, whereupon he immediately melted into the shadows.

He considered trying to steal a car from the parking lot, but rejected the idea. Someone was bound to contact the authorities in response to the shooting; the last thing he needed was to roll up to a police checkpoint with a hot ride, a small arsenal and a bogus Canadian passport. Instead, he employed the method of travel that had served soldiers like himself well for untold millennia. He started walking.

The airport was only about six miles away, a distance he could have traversed in about an hour without even breaking a sweat, but when he emerged from the hills that separated the Gold Mohur coastal area from the residential areas of Aden, he was able to hail a taxi cab and shorten the journey. Forty minutes after leaving the hotel, he was on the tarmac at Aden International Airport where a USAF C-17 waited. As he hiked up to the open rear ramp of the enormous cargo jet, Vaughn stepped out to meet him.

Vaughn was a little shorter than Tremblay, but solidly built. He had wavy brown hair and a neatly trimmed beard that was—like Tremblay's goatee—against Army regs, but Delta wasn't like the regular army. Unit operators needed to be able to blend in with the general population as much as possible, and that meant some rules had to be bent a little. The Texan's expression was uncharacteristically grim.

Tremblay nodded to him. "Houston, we have a problem?"

"Shake a leg, Juggernaut. There's a fire."

Tremblay's brows creased but he withheld his questions until he was on the ramp. "What the fuck, over? Didn't you get the kid?"

"We got the kid; zero complications. Handed him off to State fifteen minutes ago. This is something else." Vaughn waved to one of the flight crew, then ushered Tremblay forward to where the rest of the team was waiting. When Tremblay was seated, Vaughn spoke again. "You know about Cipher element, right?"

"The CT unit working with the Agency." Cipher element wasn't a unit, per se, but rather an assignment, and the plan was for every Delta squad to get their turn. Most of the current Cipher roster were from Bravo team, but Tremblay knew a few of them.

"That's right. Well, we just got word that they are in the shit. Right now, as we speak."

Tremblay frowned, trying to recall the names of the men he knew who were currently deployed with Cipher. "What went wrong?"

"What didn't? All I know for sure is that they are stranded in the desert and they could use a few more shooters."

He let it hang right there, and Tremblay couldn't tell if Vaughn was ordering them into the fight or asking for volunteers.

It didn't matter really. Either way, he was going.

TEN
Iraq

AFTER THEIR INITIAL success, the tide of the battle had shifted against the insurgents. They still had superior numbers on their side; the original force of one hundred and eighty-five *mujahideen* had been whittled down to about a hundred and thirty, while by their best estimates, the surviving Americans numbered less than a dozen. Their greatest asset however, the element of surprise, had been thoroughly expended. The Americans had suffered heavy losses in those first few minutes of combat, but once the initial sting had worn off, the Americans' superior training and technology had swung the pendulum in the other direction.

Two groups of American soldiers, working in concert with some hidden observer, had flanked their position and destroyed the mortar emplacements before they could be used to deadly effect. One of the fire teams had been cut off and annihilated, but the damage was done. With the mortars gone, the insurgents had lost their ability to light the battlefield, to say nothing of having the capacity to rain down destruction from a safe standoff distance.

The battle had begun with a cacophony of shots and explosions, but now, as the various pieces on the chessboard moved to gain strategic advantage, silence dominated the night, with only occasional scattered gunfire—spooked insurgents, shooting at phantoms. The American rifles and machine guns had not been heard for nearly half an hour.

The insurgents, motivated more by impatience than courage, advanced to the site where the helicopters had gone down. Smoke still seeped from the burned-out remains of the Black Hawk helicopters, which had both been completely destroyed with incendiary charges. Using hooded flashlights, they scanned the area and quickly discovered the trail left by the retreating soldiers—a trail of blood from bodies dragged across the dry floodplain. The Americans were fleeing to the old lake monitoring station—the bait that had been used to lure them out into the desert in the first place. The *mujahideen* set out at dead run, confident that victory was nigh.

There was no sign of activity at the concrete building, but a faint glow was visible inside. The bulk of the fighters spread out, taking up over-watch positions, while a small knot crept forward, their weapons trained on the door. The leader of the group noted the deactivated tripwire, lying on the sand of the entryway. He dug a Russian-made F1 fragmentation grenade from his satchel, pulled the safety pin and lobbed it through the open doorway.

The grenade detonated with a dull thump. The concrete walls withstood the blast, but the explosion blew the metal shutters off the windows, sending them spinning like shrapnel into the night. A column of dust and smoke vomited from the door.

No one inside could have survived, but the insurgents needed to be certain. After waiting a few seconds for the smoke to clear, they rushed inside. A few moments later, one of them emerged and called out with his report.

No bodies. The building was empty.

More of the fighters came forward, as if to confirm for themselves.

THAT WAS THE moment for which Jack Sigler had been waiting.

He pumped the M57 firing device three times, but once was enough to send a small electrical charge through a fifty-meter long strand of insulated wire and detonate the blasting cap in the M18 Claymore anti-personnel mine.

A storm of steel pellets obliterated the advancing group. At the same instant, the surviving Eagle-Eye snipers reached out with their rifles and started picking off targets of opportunity. The men searching the building rushed out, only to be met by a hail of bullets from the Delta operators concealed in low fighting positions less than a hundred meters away.

Primal fear momentarily overcame fundamentalist zeal; the insurgents abandoned their defensive positions and fled.

Sigler keyed his mic. "Cease fire, I say again, cease fire and move to zero."

He didn't wait for confirmation. Everyone knew the plan.

After Beehive Six-Four had gone down, the priorities had changed. Up to that moment, the plan had been to simply stay alive long enough to get everyone out. Survival and victory were the same thing now; staying alive meant defeating this enemy, destroying them completely.

Sigler possessed the ability to think analytically—strategically— even under the worst conditions. His instructors at OCS had quickly recognized his innate talent, and they had sharpened it by running him through increasingly difficult scenarios and simulations. He'd learned how to outwit his opponents, overcome seemingly impossible odds and perhaps the hardest lesson of all, when to gamble with the lives of his men.

Half a world away, observers at Joint Special Operations Command painted a picture of the battlefield from real-time imagery, supplied by the UAV circling overhead. Sigler had divided the survivors into four groups. One group, comprising most of the remaining snipers and the lone surviving crew chief from the downed Black Hawk would fall back to the original objective to disarm the booby-trap and set up an ambush of their own. The rest of them—six men, including Sigler and Aleman acting as spotters—would flank the insurgents and take out the mortar emplacements.

They'd succeeded in accomplishing that task, but one of the forward teams—Jon Foley and Mike Adams—had been cut off during their retreat. The disembodied voice from JSOC had confirmed their deaths.

There were just eight of them left now—four snipers, including Lewis Aleman, whose right hand was broken and useless; one warrant officer from the Night Stalkers; and the three surviving members of Cipher element—Daniel Parker, Casey Bellows and Sigler. They were desperately low on ammunition, and every shot had to count. That was the bad news. The good news was that help was on the way...or so HQ kept telling him.

Sigler sprang to his feet and hurried to the corner of the building to provide covering fire for the rest. Parker appeared beside him, still hauling the M240. A loop of ammunition, about twenty inches long, hung from the feed tray; fifty rounds, maybe less...after that, they might be able to beat someone to death with it.

The snipers had the farthest to run, and before they could reach the relative shelter of the structure, the insurgents seemed to collectively recover their nerve. Sigler heard the low crack of Kalashnikov rifles firing, and then realized that rounds were ricocheting off the cinder block walls behind him. The snipers were zigzagging, trying to stay one step ahead of the incoming fire.

"Move your ass!" Sigler shouted, more out of frustration than anything else, and then he fired in the direction of the muzzle flashes
closest to the running men. Beside him, Parker ran out the last of the
ammo belt, and then immediately switched to his carbine.

With a howl of divinely inspired ardor, a dozen insurgents broke
from cover and started running toward the building, sweeping their
AK-47s ahead of them as they ran, firing at random intervals. A round
caught one of the snipers in the leg, and he went down in the open.
The other man skidded to a halt, trying to reach his fallen comrade,
but was driven back by a storm of lead.

Sigler held his ground. Two shots, new target...two shots, new
target. Enemy fighters went down, one after another, but not all of
them stayed down. Two shots, new target...two shots, new target...

Click.

It wasn't a surprise. He habitually counted his shots so that he
could be ready for a fast reload. The problem was he didn't have any
more magazines.

"I'm out!"

"Well you ain't getting any of mine," Parker shouted back, firing
with the same rhythm.

Then his weapon fell silent, too.

Six of the original twelve *mujahideen* were still on their feet, still
advancing.

Sigler drew his KA-BAR knife from its sheath. "Danno, let's teach
these assholes that you don't bring a gun to a knife fight."

"Foxtrot Alpha," Parker replied, drawing his own blade—a standard
issue M7 bayonet—and standing beside Sigler to meet the charge.

Something popped in the air high above them. For a moment,
Sigler thought it must be another flare, but the sound repeated twice
more in the space of a second, without any other accompanying
fireworks. Just as Sigler started to look up, something big slammed
into the ground fifty meters north of their position.

Suddenly, the head of the nearest insurgent exploded like a
watermelon at a Gallagher show. A loud report echoed from above
like thunder, and then there was another, and another, and one by

one the charging fighters went down, their bodies erupting in geysers of blood.

A dark figure dropped out of the sky, landing less than twenty meters from the corner where Sigler and Parker were preparing to make their stand. He wore a black jumpsuit and helmet, but Sigler could distinctly make out a wisp of blond hair sprouting from the man's chin. The paratrooper wielded a pair of enormous pistols, one in each hand, and as he fired them out, the last of the charging insurgents went down.

The newcomer shrugged out of his parachute harness before the canopy could settle around him, then hastened to join Sigler. He kept his pistols aimed in the direction from which the attack had come, but the balance of the enemy forces were well beyond pistol range, even a pistol as massive as the Desert Eagle. When he reached Sigler's side, they all hastened into the relative safety of the concrete building.

"Heard you guys were throwing a party," the blond man said, grinning. "Hope you don't mind us crashing."

Sigler was almost too stunned to reply. "The more the merrier, but I hope you brought some beer. We're out."

One of the other paratroopers stepped forward. "No beer, but we have these." He passed over a clutch of magazines. "Sonny Vaughn, call me 'Houston.' Smiling boy over there is Stan Tremblay—Juggernaut." He jerked a thumb toward the third paratrooper. "That's Silent Bob. We're Alpha team."

In a rush of understanding, Sigler realized that these men had performed a HALO—a high altitude, low opening—parachute jump. The dangerous technique, which involved jumping out of a jet aircraft from an altitude of 35,000 feet, freefalling for two minutes, and then popping a chute just three hundred feet above the ground, was usually reserved for stealthy insertions into enemy territory, but it was an effective way to get a shooter onto the battlefield in a big hurry.

Alpha team...HALO jump... These guys are Delta.

For the first time since the battle had begun, Sigler felt a ray of hope. He took one of the magazines and reloaded his carbine. "Any more of you guys on the way?"

"Cherry should be around here..." Tremblay started to say, but Vaughn cut him off.

"Cherry burned in. What you see is what you've got."

Sigler remembered the loud impact that had preceded the paratroopers' arrival. There were no second chances with a HALO jump. You could get hypoxic during the long free-fall, or giddy with nitrogen narcosis... Your hands could freeze... Your chute could malfunction...and that was it. Game over, permanently.

"Aww shit, really?" Tremblay shook his head.

Three men. Sigler's candle of hope flickered a little. Still, they were Delta operators, and that was nothing to sneeze at.

Parker clapped Tremblay on the shoulder. "You saved our asses with those hand cannons of yours. Is that Alpha standard issue? Jack, you gonna get us some of those?"

Tremblay sucked in a breath and then stoked his grin back to life. "I found these babies just lying around. They were too shiny to pass up."

"Hang on to them. You'll probably get another chance to use them."

Sigler cleared his throat. "If you girls are done fixing your makeup, there's work to do."

"Roger that, boss. What's the plan?"

Sigler had been pondering that very question. The enemy knew where they were, and the odds were good that they were already planning another mass attack. He hastily outlined his defensive plan: two sniper teams on the roof, shooters at every window.

Each of the Alpha team shooters had brought along eight thirty-round magazines, and they divided these so that everyone had at least two full mags. The newcomers had also brought along another five hundred rounds of loose ammunition. Everyone immediately set about reloading empty magazines, but it was a tedious chore, and Sigler doubted very much that enemy would give them time to complete it.

They got about four minutes.

The insurgents had used the brief lull to send a flanking element around to approach from the south. When one of the snipers on the roof spied their approach and started picking off targets, it was like opening the floodgates. The enemy fighters charged like a swarm of warrior ants.

The small concrete building seemed to vibrate with the rising crescendo of gunfire. The Delta shooters were the best in the world at their job, but for every insurgent that went down, five more advanced another ten meters, pouring lead at the defenders. The air was thick with sulfurous smoke and dust; the relentless assault pulverized the concrete walls.

Then a different sound cut through the tumult. There were long eruptions of noise that overpowered the random staccato pops of the AKs and HK 416s. It was the distinctive report of a Browning M-2 .50 caliber machine gun—affectionately nicknamed "Ma Deuce."

And Ma Deuce never traveled alone.

Someone let out a whoop. "Hot damn. Now it's a party."

For a second, Sigler thought it was Jess Strickland, but then he remembered that Strickland had died when the helo blew up.

Must be the blond guy, Tremblay.

He didn't dare look back. Twenty fighters...maybe more...were attempting to cross the last thirty meters to reach the building. There wasn't even time to aim; he just kept pulling the trigger.

Out of nowhere, a blocky shape blasted through midst of the charge.

It was a Humvee.

Bodies went flying, and some were crunched under the heavy tires as the armored vehicle rolled to a stop between the besieged structure and the advancing horde. The Humvee's gunner swept left and right with the .50 cal, but right below him, the rear door flew open and a soldier emerged, waving frantically to the men in the building.

Sigler got the message. "Our ride's here! Move out."

The Humvee was the first in a line of five similar vehicles, which had deployed in a semi-circle between the building and the two advancing fronts of enemy fighters. While the turret gunners laid down suppressive fire from their M240B and M2 machine guns, the rear doors on the sheltered side were thrown open to admit the beleaguered defenders. Sigler directed the wounded to the nearest trucks, and then with Parker right beside him, he headed for the front vehicle.

A familiar percussive boom thundered across the desert—an RPG launch. He didn't see the rocket, but a moment later, the grenade impacted the front end of the lead truck. The high-velocity jet cut into the engine block like a Jedi lightsaber, and the subsequent detonation flipped the Humvee onto its side.

Parker was halfway in the truck when the grenade hit. The force of the explosion spilled him out, and he fell next to Sigler, who had thrown himself flat. The armored vehicle rose above them like a looming wave, and they scrambled to avoid being crushed beneath it. The soldier manning the machine gun was catapulted from the turret and hurled against the side of the building.

Then something extraordinary happened. The soldier sat up, shook his head like a football player trying to shake off a hit and then slowly climbed to his feet and stalked toward the wreckage of his vehicle. He was big, at least as tall as Sigler but broader, and in his full body armor he looked like a walking mountain. He strode past the two Delta operators, glancing their direction as if to verify that they weren't seriously hurt. Then he went right back to his weapon.

Sigler wasn't sure what the big soldier expected to accomplish. With the Humvee on its side, the M2 was useless. The heavy machine gun was hanging from its mount like a broken wing, its long barrel jammed into the ground, but the soldier approached it like this wasn't even a minor inconvenience and pulled the quick release pin on the swivel mount, wrestling the gun into his arms.

Parker whispered something, a name perhaps, and Sigler saw the look of recognition on his friend's face, but there wasn't time to ask for clarification. He didn't know what the walking mountain planned to do with the Ma Deuce—it wasn't the kind of weapon you could shoot from the hip—but figuring that out wasn't his problem. He got to his feet and raced to the turret hole in the Humvee's roof and stuck his head inside to check for survivors.

The vehicle's only occupant was the driver, who was dazed but alive and apparently unhurt. Sigler could hear rounds plinking off the armored underside of the Humvee, but as long as the insurgents didn't hit it with another RPG, they were safe for the moment. As he helped the driver extricate himself, he heard the M2 booming again.

The big soldier had somehow braced the gun against the Humvee's tire, and Parker was right next to him with a spare can of ammunition.

"Leave it!" Sigler shouted. "Time to go."

Sigler wasn't sure the walking mountain had heard the order, much less that he would follow it. The guy looked completely zoned in. Sigler had seen soldiers get all jacked-up on adrenaline, screaming obscenities and lost in the fog of war, but this was different. The big soldier reminded him of Schwarzenegger in the Terminator movies—intense but dispassionate, methodical, efficient...unstoppable.

But it was time to go.

There was an incendiary grenade mounted on the Humvee's center column—a self-destruct measure in case the vehicle had to be abandoned, which was exactly what they were going to have to do. Sigler didn't bother to remove it from the mount; he just pulled the pin and let it burn.

"Fire in the hole!" he shouted as he ran past Parker.

A tiny supernova erupted inside the vehicle, spilling blinding radiance and intense heat through the opening as the thermate grenade, burning at over 3000 degrees Fahrenheit, vaporized synthetic fabrics and plastic, and set the very metal itself on fire.

The big man just nodded, and then with the same degree of effort that someone might use to drop a hamburger wrapper in a trash can, he stuffed the M2 into the turret and ran after Sigler.

The big guy and the driver piled into the next truck in line, while Sigler and Parker ran for the one behind that. The turret gunners were firing at a cyclic rate, burning through ammo to keep the enemy from shooting any more RPGs, but with everyone aboard, the drivers took off.

The sound of bullets smacking into the armor plate was strangely comforting—like rain on a tin roof, but in a few seconds, they were well out of range of the insurgents' rifles.

The quiet was even better.

ELEVEN

THE MOOD IN the Special Forces compound at Contingency Operating Base Speicher was somber. The Delta shooters busied themselves with maintenance tasks—cleaning their weapons, inspecting their equipment to ensure that all was ready for the next mission and even grabbing some food and shut-eye—but hardly anyone spoke. The brief sense of elation that accompanied their salvation was tempered by the knowledge that, for several of their friends, the help had arrived too late.

Every career Spec Ops shooter had experienced the emotional conflict that occurs when not everyone makes it back from a mission, but this instance was on a different order of magnitude. Only three members of Cipher element remained. Four of the snipers had survived, though two were wounded—including Lewis Aleman, whose crushed hand would almost certainly spell the end of his career as a Delta operator. Of the eight men comprising the flight crews of two Night Stalker Black Hawk helicopters, only one had made it back. Everyone on Beehive Six-Six was MIA. Perhaps even worse, the survivors knew that their lives had been bought with the blood of those who had come to save them, including Sonny "Houston" Vaughn, the Alpha team leader, who had caught a bullet on his way to the Humvee and died in Stan Tremblay's arms on the ride back.

Sigler's black mood wasn't just due to survivor's guilt, though. He was angry. The deaths of his teammates weren't just the fortunes of war; someone had set them up and sent them into a trap.

He was going to find out who that someone was. Then, he was going to kill them.

They'd returned to the regional base just as dawn was breaking in the east. The 7th Special Forces team—the guys that had come riding to the rescue—had given the survivors a hut to recover in, but Sigler had been kept busy with administrative tasks, seeing to the needs of the wounded and of course, reporting the details of the disaster to headquarters. Thus far, JSOC had not responded to his requests for information that might help identify the persons responsible for the attack.

As he sat with the tattered remnants of Cipher element, Eagle-Eye and Alpha team, meticulously disassembling and cleaning his weapon—an activity that was, for a soldier, something akin to meditation—he searched his memory to see if the answer lay somewhere in the events of the previous night. He was physically exhausted, but his mind would not let go of the mystery.

Someone had set a trap for them...why? He rejected the obvious answer—to kill them. There were plenty of ways to accomplish that.

But if killing Cipher element wasn't the primary objective, then what was?

He was working through the possibilities when two men he didn't recognize strode into the room. One of them was wearing civilian clothes—khakis and a long-sleeve, pale-blue dress shirt—the other was wearing ACU fatigues. The name-tape over his breast pocket said 'Keasling,' but it was the rank badge in the middle of the man's chest that got Sigler's attention: a single black star.

He jumped to his feet and was about to call the room to attention, but the general waved him off.

"Stand easy, men." Keasling regarded each man in turn, and finally brought his attention back to Sigler. "I won't bullshit you. We are at condition FUBAR. Sixteen hours ago, the President did two things: He asked General Collins for his resignation, and he hired me to run the Joint Special Operations Command. I'm your new boss."

Glances were exchanged but no one spoke. Keasling gestured to the civilian. "This is Domenick Boucher, the Director of the CIA. Gentlemen, we are here to fix this train wreck."

Stan Tremblay folded his arms over his chest and leaned back in his chair. "You're the new JSOC? That's a three-star billet. That must have taken some grade-A ass kissing."

Keasling's right eye twitched, and for a moment, Sigler thought the general was going to blow a gasket, but then the twitch went away. "I guess the President liked my smile. Now, if you're done busting my chops, *sergeant*, there's work to do. We're in the dark, men."

Sigler pointed a finger at Boucher. "Why don't you start by talking to him? It was his people that sent us out there in the first place. Last I heard, they were both aboard the Black Hawk that went missing."

Boucher glanced at Keasling, as if silently asking for permission to answer, and then cleared his throat. "Then let me update you. After leaving you, the helicopter designated Beehive Six-Six crossed the border with Syria and continued on to Damascus. The pilot flew nap-of-the-earth to avoid ground radar, but we were able to track him from an AWACS plane.

"Our assets in Syria searched the abandoned helicopter and found the remains..." He swallowed, as if this was the first time he'd put it in words. "They positively identified the remains of Officer Scott Klein, along with two members of the flight crew, and one of your men."

One? The implications of that punched Sigler in the gut. "Who?"

"Sergeant Major Pettit," said Keasling. "He was executed; they all were. Point blank range; no sign of a struggle. We have to assume that everyone who was not found dead on that helo is on the side of the enemy."

Sigler felt his blood go cold. The enemy now had a face and a name: Kevin Rainer, his commanding officer. Rainer had led them into the trap and left them there to die.

Boucher continued. "Three Caucasian men and a Eurasian woman were spotted at Damascus International Airport, boarding a flight to Doha, Qatar. From Qatar, they caught a connecting flight to Yangon—"

Tremblay scratched his goatee. "Yangon? That's somewhere in East Butt-Fuck, right?"

"Close," Sigler said. He wasn't sure about Tremblay's impulsive need to turn everything into a joke. Sometimes, it was good to have someone around to help lighten the mood, but there was such a thing as too much. "Most people still call it Rangoon. It's in Myanmar...which most people still call Burma."

"Goddamn," Tremblay muttered sourly. "Can't these people just pick a name and stick with it?"

"They're in the air right now," Keasling said, steering the discussion back on point. "We don't know if that's their final destination, but our assets in Yangon will pick up their trail." He looked around the room again, once more making eye contact with each man in turn. "I'm acting under the assumption that some of you here might be interested in payback."

Sigler could tell that Keasling had been hoping for a cheer or a rousing "Fuck, yeah!" but the subdued mood persisted. After a few seconds, Parker broke the awkward silence.

"Mister...Boucher, is it? Why don't you tell us what's really going on?"

Keasling frowned and looked as if he was about to tell Parker to shut up, but Sigler quickly backed his friend up. "I think we all deserve some answers, sir."

Boucher sighed. "Honestly, I wish I knew. I had the same intel as you going into this. I've got a team conducting forensic analysis of the documents you recovered in Ramadi. Our working theory is that the message that sent you out there—the message about a bio-weapons factory—was probably planted."

By Kevin Rainer, Sigler thought. *The promise of a WMD was irresistible bait for the trap. But why?*

Why had the Delta commander sold out his men?

"You're all missing the most important thing," Parker interjected. His expression was taut, like he was about to explode. "The message wasn't just about bio-weapons."

Keasling looked to Boucher for confirmation. The Director of the CIA nodded. "The message contained a specific reference that led to one of our cryptanalysts being sent along."

"Sasha Therion," Parker supplied.

"That's right. We're considering the possibility that she might have been involved."

"Bullshit."

Sigler coughed to get his friend's attention and flashed a warning glance. *Take it down a notch, Danno.*

In a more subdued voice, Parker continued: "That reference to the Voynich manuscript... There was a reason for that. They...whoever they are...needed your expert on the manuscript."

The Delta operators in the room stared at Parker in disbelief; it was as if he'd suddenly grown horns or begun speaking in tongues. But Boucher just nodded. "That's a scenario we're considering."

"Considering? Well consider this. Someone turned at least three operators to make this happen. Whoever is behind it has money and influence, and for some reason they think that a medieval manuscript that no one can read is worth all this trouble. So what you should be considering is: what do they know that we don't?"

Parker's comments had aroused Sigler's curiosity; he wasn't sure if his friend was really on to something or if his concern arose from a schoolboy crush on the enigmatic Sasha Therion, but he made a mental note to ask his friend for further clarification.

Keasling shook his head. "That doesn't matter. All that matters is stopping them. That's your new mission."

Keasling's final statement went through Sigler like an electric shock.

Your new mission.

My new mission.

As if reading the unasked questions in the faces of the men in the room, Keasling continued. "Sigler, you're Cipher Six now. Organizational structure is at your discretion. Tremblay and Roberts, you're TAD to Cipher element for the duration of this mission..." He glanced at Sigler. "Unless you have an objection to that?"

Sigler glanced at Tremblay and the man he knew only as "Silent Bob," but their faces were unreadable. Even though Delta operators were consummate professionals, every team relied upon the unique chemistry of its individual members. It was impossible to predict whether the remnants of Cipher element and the survivors from Alpha team would mesh seamlessly, or burn up in a fireball of friction. "No objection from me."

"If you need additional personnel, you can draw from 7th Group. I'll travel with you to Myanmar and liaise with our assets on the ground." The general checked his watch. "It is now 1630. I want to be in the air no later than 1800. Now, if there's nothing else..."

Sigler recognized that was Keasling's way of signaling that the discussion was at an end, but he knew this might be his only opportunity to show everyone in the room that he was ready to be their leader. "Actually, sir, there is one thing."

Keasling frowned. "Go on."

"I'd like to change the mission designation. We're not really Cipher element anymore, so it doesn't make sense to keep using Cipher callsigns."

"Bad juju, is that it?"

Sigler shrugged. "If you like."

Keasling waved his hand as if the matter were of no consequence. "Fine. Use your Delta handles. Make sure to submit an updated roster. Just out of curiosity, Sigler, what's your callsign?"

"Elvis, sir."

Keasling made a face. "How on God's green Earth did you get tagged with that?"

Tremblay gave a theatrical gasp. "Sir, are you disrespecting the King of Rock and Roll?"

Sigler couldn't help but grin. "I've always kind of been an Elvis Presley fan. TCB—'Taking care of business'—is sort of my unofficial motto."

"I loathe Elvis Presley. My ex-wife ran off with an Elvis impersonator," Keasling groused. He squinted at Sigler. "But in the interest of getting this show on the road, let's say we compromise. Your new operational callsign is—"

"Pelvis!" Tremblay chortled.

Keasling ignored him and spoke just one more word: "King."

FACTOR

TWELVE
Mandalay, Myanmar

EVERYONE NOTICED THE blonde woman.

She wore a tight beige T-shirt that clung to the firm contours of her breasts, exposing just enough of her décolletage to be enticing without being obvious, and a pair of dark green cargo shorts that had been rolled up a couple of times to reveal even more of her toned and tanned legs. Her long hair was pulled back—though hardly restrained—in a pony tail that conveyed that elusive girl-next-door allure; a seemingly effortless beauty, all the more desirable in its apparent innocence.

She seemed oblivious to the attention, yet there was something intentional about the way she leaned, almost seductively, over the perfume counter at the duty free shop. Every few minutes, she would ask the man behind the counter questions about price or request a tester bottle, spritzing a small amount of aerosolized *eau de toilette* into the air. Occasionally, her eyes would dart to the concourse outside the shop, often encountering a lascivious stare from a male passerby, or less frequently, a jealous sneer from less appreciative females. She would then, regardless of the expressions or gender of any onlookers, arch her back like a cat stretching after a nap—an action that drew even more attention to her breasts—and then return to perusing the perfume selection.

Wherever she went, everyone noticed the blonde woman, and a few of those who noticed took the added step of inquiring about her.

Those who did would be informed that the woman was a Canadian humanitarian worker with the Red Cross...or maybe it was UNICEF... Her specific affiliation remained the subject of some debate. She had been in country for several months now, visiting clinics, dispensing vaccines and medical supplies...generally getting noticed, but somehow never staying in one place long enough to allow idle curiosity, or even a flush of arousal, to escalate into something more overt.

Everyone noticed her, and that was exactly what she wanted, not because she craved attention, but because while they were busy looking at her, they hardly noticed that she was looking back.

The three Caucasian men who got off the plane that had just arrived from Yangon certainly noticed her, even the one who had his arm draped possessively over the shoulders of his female traveling companion—a Eurasian woman who, for a change, paid the blonde woman no heed.

The blonde happened to look up at just that moment and met the man's stare. She smiled, stretched, and then turned back to the counter. "This one," she said, pointing to the fragrance she had most recently sampled. She laid a 100 *kyat* note—worth about fifteen US dollars—on the counter and took her purchase. "Keep the change," she said, flashing the man the same smile she'd shown the three Westerners. She exited the store, joining the flow of disembarking passengers.

She moved casually, making no effort to hurry and no effort to avoid being noticed, but always keeping the three men in sight. It wasn't difficult; like her, they stood out in the crowd of Asian faces. She moved with the crowd to the exit and got in the taxi line, while the Westerners climbed into a waiting sport utility vehicle. As their ride pulled away from the terminal building, she took out her cell phone.

"Red Toyota Fortuner," she said, getting right to the point. "Brand new. Can't miss it."

"New?" came the response. New vehicles were a rare thing in Mandalay. The military rulers of the country imposed strict limits on the number of cars that could be imported. Only the very wealthy could afford to buy them, and in Myanmar, most of the wealth came from illegal activities—primarily from the drug trade. "Do you think our friends are involved?"

"As Lieutenant Ball would say: 'Signs point to yes.'"

The man on the other end gave an easy laugh. "Any idea which flavor?"

"'Reply hazy, try again.'"

"Well, at least this won't be too much of a distraction. Might even be the break we've been waiting for."

"'Cannot predict now.' Just keep your distance. The sooner we can hand this off to those Delta testosteroids, the sooner we can get back to our own mission."

There was a momentary pause on the line, and then the man spoke again. "I've got them."

"Then hang up and drive, pretty boy."

"'You may rely on it.'"

THIRTEEN

SHIN DAE-JUNG KEPT a healthy interval between the red Toyota and his own Honda Rebel 250, though once his quarry left the urban environs of Mandalay, it was more a matter of trying to keep up with the Toyota rather than holding back. The other driver, evincing the kind of confidence that can only come with familiarity, maintained an average speed of about seventy miles per hour. Shin had to keep the speedometer on the motorcycle pegged to keep a visual fix on the red vehicle, which barely slowed through the series of hairpin turns that wound between the hills between Ongyaw and Thon-daung-ywa-wa.

It had come as no little surprise when the target vehicle had left Mandalay behind. Now, nearly sixty miles out and nearing the border of the rural and mostly uninhabited Shan state, he wondered if he had not been given a fool's errand. He briefly lost sight of the red Toyota when the road straightened as it approached Pyin Oo Lwin, gateway to one of Myanmar's very few—and thus far unsuccessful—tourist attractions, the Kandawgyl Botanical Gardens. His assignment in the country that many still called Burma had taken him to all of its major cities, but he rarely traveled those long distances by road, and so he was unfamiliar with the highways. He did know that the further out the target vehicle went, the less likely he would be able to successfully track them to their destination.

It was a white-knuckle ride, even for someone like himself, who routinely indulged in dangerous activities: combat in Iraq and Afghanistan; covert insertions into Pakistan to kill or capture terrorist leaders and North Korea, where he could pass as a native, to reconnoiter suspected nuclear weapons facilities; recreational SCUBA diving, particularly the exploration of sunken wrecks; and perhaps riskiest of all, maintaining his hard-earned reputation as a Korean Casanova.

He had actually been looking forward to just such an amorous encounter tonight at the Sunrise Hotel Mandalay, where he was supposed to meet with Giselle, a beautiful but slightly homesick Swiss Doctors-Without-Borders doctor. When he'd gotten word of this little errand for the Delta boys, he had expected that he would have to ask for a rain check, but then again, if the red Toyota slipped away, he might make it back in time for cocktail hour.

He spied the Fortuner, a red smudge that appeared for just an instant on the black ribbon of highway heading out of Pyin, and then it vanished over the horizon. With the throttle wide open, he blasted through the town. He continued along the highway, scanning the road ahead for another glimpse, but the Toyota was gone.

Damn it, where did they go?

He felt a growing sense of apprehension. He was a realist—sometimes, shit happened, and that was just the way it was—but he was also a soldier, taught to live by the simple, if simplistic slogan: "failure is not an option."

His failure was not in his inability to match pace with the Toyota, but rather in choosing the motorcycle for the pursuit. In the urban environs of Mandalay, it was perfect for shadowing someone. How could he have known that the target would go for a drive in the country?

He was scanning the highway ahead so intently that he completely missed the narrow dirt road that veered off to the south. He did notice a cloud of dust settling, but he was half a mile down the road before it clicked.

Dust cloud.

They turned off.

He geared down, resisting the urge to squeeze the brakes. At seventy miles per hour, that was a good way to lose control, and he had no desire to end up smeared across a stretch of Burmese blacktop. Instead, he waited until he was only doing about forty, and then leaned forward and squeezed the front brake.

The front tire left a streak of rubber, but the back end of the Rebel lifted off the ground, the drive wheel spinning free. With a little wiggle of his hips, Shin swung the bike halfway around, pivoting on the front wheel, and as the rear tire touched down, he twisted the handlebars the opposite way and goosed the throttle again, accelerating out of the turnaround.

He felt a surge of excitement that was partly due to the realization that he hadn't lost the Toyota after all, but mostly because of having pulled off a near perfect "stoppie."

Too bad there'd been no one around to see it.

He raced back down the highway, and this time he had no difficulty spotting the dirt track. He also saw that the road was blocked by a metal gate. An old Bamar man wearing what looked like military fatigues, stood at the gate and watched Shin approach with unveiled distrust.

Shin weighed his options as he turned toward the gated road and brought the motorcycle to a stop a few feet away from the old man. He was a park ranger, Shin decided, or at least he was meant to look like one.

Putting on his most sincere smile, he addressed the man in Mandarin Chinese. "Is this the entrance to the botanical gardens?"

The old man blinked at him and then tried his best to reply in the same language. "No Chinese speak. Go away."

Though conversationally fluent in the Burmese language, Shin was trying to pass himself off as a misguided traveler. Chinese visitors were about the only tourists who came to Burma, and some parts of the country had as many Chinese inhabitants as Burmese. Shin was Korean, but he doubted the Bamar man would be able to make the distinction.

"English?" Burma had been a British colony until 1947; the old guy might even remember the Colonial era.

The man nodded, but remained wary.

"I looking for gardens," Shin continued in his best attempt at broken English.

The man pointed back down the highway. His own command of English was passably good. "The gardens are that way, five kilometers."

Shin knew he was reaching his limit of questions, but he thought he could get away with one more. "What this place?"

"It is a wildlife refuge. No one is allowed inside."

"Wildlife? What kind? Good for pictures?"

"*Buru*," the man answered.

"*Buru*?"

The man nodded as if the question somehow signified Shin's comprehension. "*Nagas*. Very dangerous. No pictures."

Well that clears it right up. First buru *and now* nagas?

Shin knew of an ethnic group called the Naga that lived in the northwestern region of the country, but he didn't think the old man was talking about them. Naga was also the name of a serpentine demon in Hindu and Buddhist mythology. The term was also sometimes translated as 'dragon,' which didn't make much sense either. Maybe it was a spooky story concocted by the government or someone else with a desire to keep people off this road. Regardless, it was time to be moving on.

He thanked the old man and pulled back onto the highway. This time, he kept his speed to a nice safe forty mph, and as soon as he was out of the gatekeeper's line of sight, he let go of the throttle altogether. He coasted the bike off the road and parked it in a stand of trees.

He shrugged out of his backpack and dug inside to retrieve his Garmin GPS unit and a paper map of the country. Neither showed the dirt road, much less indicated a wildlife refuge, but the map did show both the curves of the highway and the course of several rivers and streams that meandered through the valleys between the plateaus. He quickly plotted a course into the GPS that would eventually cross the dirt road—well away from the old man standing guard at the gate—and entered the waypoints into the device.

In addition to the navigations aids, his backpack contained what he had come to think of as essential equipment for any mission. There was enough gear to set up a hooch—a rainproof poncho and a quilted poncho liner, and some elastic bungee cords. There was food—a couple of granola bars, two MREs, a liter bottle of water and some iodine tablets for field-expedient purification if the need should arise, and it was looking like it might. What he didn't have was a weapon, at least not in the backpack.

After checking to make sure no one was around to observe him, he wiggled the motorcycle's seat cushion until it came free, revealing a hollow space underneath, which contained a few items of gear that he preferred not to have to explain at a police checkpoint: a SIG-Sauer 9 mm pistol, two fifteen-round magazines, a small set of binoculars and a PVS-14 night vision monocular. He loaded a magazine into the pistol and slipped it into his waistband, at the small of his back. The spare magazines went into a pocket and the PVS-14 went into the backpack.

The idea of the cross-country trek didn't bother him in the least. Though he didn't know exactly how far he would have to travel, he had a feeling he would catch up to the Toyota—and discover its occupants' final destination—before nightfall. Dirt roads were difficult to travel, especially in this region, which was plagued by seasonal monsoon rains. It might take hours to negotiate the crevices and craters created by erosion. The vehicle might not be able to travel much faster than he could run.

But before he set forth, there was one last thing he needed to do.

He took out his phone and dialed a number. It rang once, and then he heard a familiar voice—her voice. "Hello?"

"Giselle, *mon cheri*. I am so sorry..."

FOURTEEN

4163...

Sasha ran through the factors in her head. She discounted three out of hand; the individual digits did not add up to any multiple of three. *Seven? No. Eleven?*

She ran through the division. *Forty-one minus thirty-three leaves eight...eighty-six minus seventy-seven is nine...ninety-three... No.*

Seventeen? Nineteen? Twenty-three?

Yes... Twenty-three from forty-one leaves eighteen, for one hundred-eighty-six. Eight times twenty-three is one-eighty-four...which leaves two...twenty-three!

4167...

The digits added up to eighteen. Three was a factor. *Next.*

4169...

Sasha already knew that the number was not a prime—she had memorized the first two thousand prime numbers—but when she was faced with a problem for which the solution was not readily apparent, she would work her way down the number line, testing every number to see if it was prime, a number that was divisible by only itself and one. The activity helped sharpen her mental subroutines and gave her brain a chance to process the problem in the background. Once in a while, the problem might relate to her work—a particularly tricky code that would not yield to a brute force attack—but more often than not, the problems that confounded her the most had nothing to do with codes or numbers or anything that could be expressed in the precise language of mathematics. Instead, her consternation arose from the chaos of human interactions. She would use the technique to stave off boredom, such as when forced to sit in a doctor's waiting room. She was always punctual, and could never understand why medical professionals could not afford their patients the same courtesy. Other people would read magazines or play games on their cell phones... Sasha worked out the primes.

This situation was a lot like waiting at the doctor's office, except it had gone on now for...how long? *Long enough to get to over four thousand.*

She knew she should probably be afraid. Rainer had killed Scott Klein, for no reason she could fathom, and it seemed likely enough that he would kill her too, but that prospect did not frighten her nearly as much as the ongoing uncertainty. More than anything else, she hated not understanding what was going on around her.

After leaving the helicopter in Syria, he and the other men had been polite, if a bit abrupt at times. She had not been mistreated at all, aside from the simple fact that she was their prisoner. Rainer had promised that he would explain everything once they arrived at their destination, so with every stop along the way, she had asked him again.

"Not yet," he had told her as they deplaned in Yangon, and then they had moved through the airport to another concourse to wait for yet another flight. "Soon, everything will make sense. Trust me."

Rainer seemed to understand that threats of violence were not the way to gain her compliance. He did not seem put out by her repeated inquiries; if anything, he regarded her almost playfully, as if he was in possession of a secret that he was dying to share with her.

Now, as she bounced between the other two men in the back seat of the Toyota, with Rainer in the front passenger seat along with the Chinese man who had met them outside the airport, she sensed the long-awaited answer would come very soon. Speculation about what it might be was almost as frustrating as the waiting.

She was contracted to work for the US government, and as such was privy to matters that were classified as Top Secret, but the men who now held her captive had access to the same materials.

Did they need her to break a code?

That seemed likely enough, and yet why the elaborate deception? Why lure her to Iraq and then subsequently spirit her off to Myanmar, when they could have just abducted her off the streets of Georgetown?

It was a human problem; imprecise and unpredictable. Human variables were too chaotic.

4171…

She was still sifting through the factors when the Toyota crested a hill, revealing a fenced compound with four buildings nestled in a valley between two lushly forested hills. As the Toyota drew near, two men rushed out to open the gate ahead of their arrival. They were wearing civilian clothes, but carried guns—maybe they were AK-47s, she really didn't know for sure. She thought it might be some kind of paramilitary base, but it looked almost like a school yard; there was even a rickety looking playground in one corner of the compound.

They got out in front of one of the buildings and Rainer escorted her inside. This, at last, had to be their ultimate destination, and now he would tell her the reason for his actions. But Rainer offered no explanation. Instead, he motioned to a row of cheap, molded plastic chairs that lined the wall near the entrance, and then disappeared down a hallway, leaving her alone.

For a fleeting moment, she thought about simply getting up and leaving; it wasn't like she was handcuffed to the chair. She could hide somewhere, bide her time and wait for an opportunity to sneak out of the compound...stowaway in one of the cars in the parking lot perhaps.

No. Too many unknowns, too much uncertainty.

Rainer returned a moment later, accompanied by a tall, handsome man. Although she seldom paid attention to the latest fashion, Sasha thought his clothes looked expensive. He smelled amazing too.

The man greeted her with a smile. "Ms. Therion, is it? A pleasure to meet you at last."

Sasha didn't know exactly how to respond. She couldn't read facial expressions very well; smiles were just another unpredictable human variable. "Who are you?"

The man glanced sidelong at Rainer. "She doesn't know?"

The turncoat Delta operator shook his head. "I didn't tell her anything."

"Well, it's not that important." The man flashed his smile again. "You're not here to see me, after all."

"I don't know why I'm here."

"You are here because I have a problem. You see, I'm used to getting what I want. It's one of the perquisites of having more money than God. When I am confronted with a problem that I can't solve, I bring in the very best people to solve it for me. That is why you are here."

"Are you...offering me a job?"

He threw back his head and laughed. "That's exactly what I'm doing."

She was dumbfounded.

"This would be easier if I just showed you. Please come with me." He beckoned to her, and even though she had decided that she wasn't going to trust him, there seemed no alternative but to go along with him.

He guided her to a bleak-looking conference room. The chairs were the same as those in the lobby, and the table looked like something from a school cafeteria. He seemed to sense her train of thought. "I hope you'll forgive the rather austere appointments. I usually spare no expense when it comes to decorating, but the secretive nature of our work here meant that I had to make do with what was available. But here, this is what I want you to see."

He held up a small plastic rod, which she immediately recognized as a thumb drive. As if on cue, one of Rainer's cohorts stepped into the room and set a laptop computer down on the table—her laptop computer, which she had not seen since setting out on the ill-fated raid more than twenty four hours previously. The man opened the hinged screen and tapped the power button.

After the device booted up, her host plugged the thumb drive into the USB port. Understanding what was expected of her, Sasha entered her password to unlock the computer and then opened the directory for the portable memory stick. The folder contained several image files.

"Try the 'slide show' option," her host suggested.

She did, and after a few seconds the screen went black as the first image loaded. It was a photo, but of what exactly, she couldn't tell. Misshapen and irregular, blackened and corroded, it looked like something recovered from a fire. The image changed, showing it from a different angle, but the mystery of what it was remained unresolved.

Except she did recognize something.

She moved her face closer to the screen, peering intently at something that protruded from the object. She couldn't guess what its function was, but there was a symbol on it, a single character that she instantly recognized. Before she could process the information, the image changed again, and as if anticipating her desires, the next image was a close-up of the symbol:

"That's the script from the Voynich manuscript!"

Her host smiled. "Yes, it is."

She felt closer to an understanding of what was going on, but there were still too many unknowns. "Did the Iraqis find something that can decode the manuscript?"

"Oh, good heavens, no. And if they did, they wouldn't know what to make of it. I'm afraid the ruse in Iraq was necessary to draw you out into the open. You see, I knew the CIA would be very interested in any discovery relating to the world's most famous unsolved code...interested enough to send their best person out to investigate, though I had no idea who that person would be. There are many so-called 'experts' with pet theories about the Voynich code, but I needed the very best."

There was an infallible logic to the answer, and that appealed to Sasha, but it hardly justified what had been done to her. "You had all those people killed, just so you could get me here?"

Her host glanced nervously at Rainer, but then his expression hardened. "Maybe I haven't made myself clear to you, Ms. Therion. I get what I want, no matter the cost."

She swallowed. "I understand."

"Good." He put his hands on his hips and looked around the room as if to collect his thoughts.

"So what do you want? From me, I mean."

The man gestured again at the computer. "The object in those photographs was discovered last year in a crypt in the Yunnan

Province of China—just a few hundred miles from here, actually. As you can see, the artifact has markings on it that are identical to those found in the Voynich manuscript. It's badly damaged of course, but there are eight definite matches, and another fourteen probable matches, to Voynich script. I'm sure you, of all people, understand how significant that is."

She stared at the computer screen as it continued to cycle through the images of the strange object. "What exactly is it?"

"That is one of the questions I am hoping that you will be able to answer. Our best theory is that it is an antique code machine."

Sasha pondered that. The existence of a machine designed to facilitate enciphering or deciphering was not beyond the realm of possibility, but it seemed unlikely in this instance for the simple reason that the Voynich script remained so unique. If it had been produced using a machine, then surely other documents would have been found utilizing the elaborate—and still impossible to decrypt—substitution alphabet.

More unknowns.

Then she realized that the function of the device didn't matter nearly as much as the simple fact of its existence. It was tangible proof that the Voynich manuscript could be deciphered...it was meant to be deciphered.

By her.

Sasha felt as if someone had wiped her mental chalkboard clean. All the uncertainty surrounding her abduction, the actions and motives of her captors, even her ultimate fate when all of this was done...all of those variables had been erased.

"I need to see this machine. The real thing, not just pictures. Can you arrange that?"

The man regarded her with a taut expression, as if it was he that now harbored uncertainties about the situation. "Ms. Therion, because I want you to be able to solve this problem for me, I'm going to be straightforward with you.

"The sealed crypt in which this object was found, was infected with a particularly nasty strain of proto-bacteria—an organism very similar to the bacteria responsible for bubonic plague. The first people to enter were exposed and died in a matter of minutes."

"There's a connection between the manuscript and the plague?" Sasha recalled her earlier conversation with Daniel Parker. The document that had prompted the Agency to send her to Iraq in the first place, had suggested just such a link, but following Rainer's act of treachery, she had assumed it to be just so much window dressing to sell the deception.

"There is...let's call it a circumstantial connection. Archaeological sites contain all kinds of strange things—bacteria, fungi, viruses, even prions, which have been hidden away for thousands of years. Investigating those ancient mysteries is my specialty, though in this case, my motives are..." He trailed off as if realizing he'd said more than he intended. "I tell you this only because you need to understand that you can't interact directly with the artifact. It's here, in the facility, but it is still hot. Any attempt to decontaminate it would probably destroy it completely. Bio-safety level-four protocols are in effect. The closest you will be able to get to it is in a full environment suit."

Sasha nodded in agreement without even considering the precondition. She didn't care about the safety considerations; she was here for just one thing. The Voynich manuscript was a mystery that seemed unsolvable, a variable that kept the equation from balancing.

But she would solve it, and when she did, it would transform chaos into order.

FIFTEEN
Washington, D.C.

DOMENICK BOUCHER SANK wearily into the chair at the conference table in the White House Situation Room, and gestured for his traveling companion, Staff Sergeant Lewis Aleman, to do the same. Despite the fact that Aleman's right arm was heavily bandaged and nestled in a protective sling across his chest, he looked alert and ready for action, which was more than Boucher could say for himself. He'd caught a few hours of sleep on the flight back from Iraq, but anxiety over the unfolding crisis had robbed him of anything vaguely resembling rest.

Despite his injuries and over the protestations of the doctors at the base in Tikrit, Aleman had insisted on accompanying Boucher back to the states. "I need to be a part of this," the Delta sniper had argued. "If I can't be in the fight, then at least let me coordinate the mission from the TOC."

There was a lot to recommend granting the request. Aleman was familiar with the team and their protocols, but more importantly, he was already read in. With the full extent of the conspiracy still un-known, Aleman was one of a very few people that were above suspicion. Until more was known about the enemy, secrecy was paramount. That was why the President had directed the operation be run from the Situation Room.

Boucher was in the process of establishing a secure satellite link with General Keasling when the President entered the room. Aleman immediately snapped to attention and somehow managed to extricate his hand from the sling to offer a salute. Boucher also started to rise but Duncan waved him off.

"I've only got a few minutes, so let's dispense with all the formali-ties." Duncan nevertheless returned Aleman's salute. "Sergeant, as one shooter to another...helluva job. I promise you that your sacrifices will not be forgotten, and I will see that the deaths of your teammates are avenged."

"Yes, sir."

Duncan turned to Boucher. "Do we have the General on the line?"

Keasling's voice issued from the speakers. "I'm here, Mr. President."

"Good. Let's have the sitrep, gentlemen."

Boucher went first. "We've conducted preliminary forensic test-ing on the intel recovered from Ramadi, but there's nothing conclusive. The paper and ink are of the same type available for civilian use in Iraq. The only trace DNA evidence was from the people that we know handled it: the Delta team and our own analysts."

"Wouldn't that support the idea that it was a forgery?"

Boucher nodded. "The most likely conclusion is that Lt. Col. Rainer created the document and planted it during the course of the raid. But it's also possible that the insurgents were working with him—sacrificial lambs, so to speak—to further reinforce the illusion."

Duncan frowned. "Let's cut to the chase. Is there a WMD lab out there somewhere?"

Boucher knew the President well enough to recognize that the man wanted a truthful answer, but he hated having to admit to his own uncertainty. "I wish I could say unequivocally that there is not, but..."

"I read you, Dom. Keep digging." Duncan turned away, directing his voice toward the speaker box. "Mike, what's your situation?"

"Sir, we've tracked Rainer and the others to Mandalay. Our people on the ground have placed them at a remote facility east of the city. We're in the air now. Once we arrive and get the lay of the land, I will have a better sense of what our options are, and I'll develop contingency plans."

Boucher had no difficulty reading between the lines. Keasling was anticipating a covert assault on the Burmese facility, an action that was technically illegal and which carried enormous diplomatic risk, to say nothing of the danger to the Delta operators. Of course, that was the very reason why Delta had been created; sometimes, the strict letter of the law had to be broken in the interest of the greater good. Delta's job was to take those risks in a strictly unofficial capacity, giving the President full deniability, and if things went south in the field, they were on their own.

"Contingency plans," Duncan muttered, and then he shook his head. "We are in this mess because the system we've inherited—the way things have always been done—is completely ass-backwards. We've got too many agencies working at cross-purposes. Hell, sometimes actively working against each other. Too many 'yes men' who think it's their mission in life to either tell me exactly what they think I want to hear, even if it means cooking up the evidence to support it, or to protect me from knowing the truth."

It wasn't the first time Boucher had heard Duncan utter some variation of those words. He'd told the American people as much during the campaign. The bitter pill he'd been forced to swallow upon assuming the office of Chief Executive was that it truly was impossible for one man, no matter how dedicated and passionate, to overcome the inertia of bureaucracy. It had nothing to do with the limits of Constitutional authority; there were simply too many moving pieces. Too many human parts.

But there was something different about the way Duncan said it this time. Boucher saw a faint gleam in his old friend's eyes as he continued. "Enough. No more contingency plans. No more 'cover your ass.' As one of my predecessors famously said, the buck stops here."

He looked Boucher in the eye. "Dom, I trust you implicitly, and I know it's your job to keep me from going off the rails, but right now I need you to just shut up and listen."

Boucher felt an electric tingle in his extremities. *What the hell is he doing?*

"General Keasling, we don't know each other very well, but I think I'm a pretty good judge of character. I wouldn't have given you that star if I didn't think you were up for the job."

Boucher knew that Duncan had been prepared to frock Keasling as a Major General—the rank associated with his new position as the leader of JSOC. It had actually been Keasling himself who had insisted he not be advanced three full pay grades, a promotion that would have ignited a firestorm of jealousy in the Army high command.

The satellite connection couldn't completely mask Keasling's guarded reply. "Thank you, sir."

Duncan just smiled. "Oh, don't thank me until you've heard the rest."

SIXTEEN
Mandalay, Myanmar

JACK SIGLER—CALLSIGN: King, climbed out of the taxi and scanned the street ahead. He turned a slow arc, checking the area, high and low, from the ten o'clock position to the three. The other men who had been sandwiched together in the back of the vehicle did likewise upon emerging, each checking a different quadrant, overlapping their sectors of responsibility to identify potential threats.

They had all exchanged their combat fatigues for civilian clothes. King now wore blue jeans and a black T-shirt with a picture of Elvis Presley, which Stan 'Juggernaut' Tremblay had purchased for him at an airport gift shop. To further reduce their visibility, it had been decided to move from the airport to the Mandalay safe-house in two separate groups. King's group, which consisted of Tremblay, Silent Bob, and a sniper named Meyers, who went by the callsign 'Dark,' had taken the lead, traveling by taxi. General Keasling, 'Irish' Parker, 'Roadrunner' Bellows, 'Race' Banion—the other sniper from the Eagle-Eye team—and heavy weapons specialist Erik Somers, the last addition to their team, would follow in a pair of rented SUVs.

Somers had been brought on board just before leaving Tikrit. King knew him only as the big guy who had manhandled the M2 during the extraction the previous night, but he'd come with a personal recommendation from Parker. The two men had gone through Delta selection together. An intense but quiet figure, Somers was Iranian by birth, but had been adopted by an American family shortly before Ayatollah Khomeni's government closed off Iran from the rest of the world. He was a former marine who had switched services to become a Ranger, and he possessed seemingly superhuman strength, which should have made him an ideal candidate for Special Forces. According to Parker, Somers had aced the course but hadn't made the final cut. There could have been a number of reasons for that, not the least of which was team chemistry. That was something that weighed on King's mind as he contemplated both the mission ahead and the other special assignment General Keasling had given him.

The street was bustling with activity, all of it seemingly harmless, but the men remained vigilant as they followed King along a maze-like path between the freestanding buildings and eventually up a rickety wooden staircase that led to the second story balcony. He found the door with the yellow smiley face sticker he'd been told to look for; someone had used a pen to add fangs and sinister eyebrows to the iconic image.

Tremblay, with a mischievous grin, nodded at the decal. "I'm going to fit right in here."

King appraised him with a sidelong glance. It was still a little hard to reconcile this blond man with his punk-rocker goatee and an always ready one-liner, with the guy that had dropped out of the sky wielding .50 caliber death in both hands. He had no doubt of Tremblay's ability in combat—he'd already witnessed it first hand—but a successful team had to be able to work together every day of the week, not just on the day of the big game.

Two hours ago, it wouldn't have mattered. Two hours ago, his orders were simple: take the team you've got and go after the bad guys. But then, Keasling had taken him aside. "The President has ordered me to put together a new unit; fast, mobile, unlimited resources, non-existent radar signature, if you take my meaning. He and I both agree that you are the ideal candidate for field leader."

King had been in the Army long enough to be extremely wary of 'special assignments.' "Sir, that's already Delta's job description."

Keasling's expression at that moment had spoken volumes. The general hadn't seemed particularly happy about this development either, but he wasn't about to contradict the President. He clearly expected the same from King. "Think of this as the *Delta* of Delta. The difference is that you will get your orders directly from a handler in the National Security office. Administratively, you'll still be part of JSOC, but in all other respects, you will completely bypass the chain of command."

King had decided to keep the rest of his opinions to himself. "When does this go into effect?"

"It went into effect five minutes ago, when the President told me to make it happen. Obviously, we've got some growing pains ahead of us, but arrangements are already being made for a live uplink to your new handler."

Keasling hadn't asked if he wanted the job; maybe that wasn't even an option, but King figured the general had known all along that he wouldn't refuse.

Which meant he now had to think about trying to select a team of operators for this 'Delta of Delta,' while at the same time planning for the mission already underway. It was evident that Keasling expected him to build his new team from the current group, but King knew that no matter how outstanding the shooters were as individuals, what really mattered was whether they could work as a team.

He tried the door—unlocked, as he'd been told it would be—and went in. The space beyond was dimly lit by sunlight filtering through the curtained windows, and it took a moment for his eyes to adjust to the relative darkness. Cardboard boxes and blankets hanging from a web of clotheslines had been used to partition the area, but his attention was immediately drawn to the center of the large open, room where an impromptu assemblage of foam mats had been laid out in a square and bordered with ropes on all four sides. It was a boxing ring.

A strange repetitive noise emanated from the shadows—a slapping sound interspersed with grunts of exertion. He glimpsed a ratty-looking heavy punching bag hanging from a metal frame in a corner of the room. The bag quivered from persistent blows, and as he advanced toward it, he saw the person responsible for the assault on the other side.

Tremblay let out a low whistle. "I think I'm in love."

King's first impulse was to agree. The person pummeling the heavy bag was a woman—blonde and petite, wearing a tight-fitting T-shirt that clung tantalizingly to her curves and a pair of short shorts that covered just enough to set the imagination on fire. The perspiration running in rivulets from her face and dampening the fabric of her shirt did nothing to diminish the sheer sexiness of her appearance; in fact, it made her even more appealing.

The scene was surreal; the woman could have been a model, posing for a camera shoot, but there was nothing simulated about the punches she was throwing. She glanced up as they approached, but gave the bag several more hits in rapid succession before formally acknowledging their presence.

"You must be the Delta boys." She offered a coy grin, and rested her boxing-gloved hands on her hips. "Sorry, you caught me in the middle of my workout. I wasn't expecting you until later."

Tremblay matched her smile. "And we weren't expecting...*you*."

"Down boy," King muttered. He turned to the woman. "What's the word of the day?"

She raised an eyebrow. "So, right to business? That's okay. I like that in a man. The word of the day is 'timberline.'" She paused and locked stares with him. "I've shown you mine..."

"The counter-sign is 'grapefruit.' I'm King. Laughing boy here is Juggernaut, and the other stooges are Bob and Dark. Are you Baker?"

It had not been made clear if that was her real name or a mission callsign, but when she nodded, Tremblay gave a little gasp of comprehension. "I've heard about..." He turned to King. "Do you know who this is? The Legend of Zelda?"

King shook his head, mystified. He didn't think the other man was talking about the old Nintendo game.

Tremblay turned back to the woman. "That's who you are? Zelda Baker. The first woman to ever make it through Ranger school."

King's brow furrowed. The statement didn't make any sense. Females weren't eligible for Ranger school because of the military ban on women in combat occupation specialties.

"I thought it was just scuttlebutt," Tremblay continued. "G.I. Jane bull-shit. Some general had the nutty idea that Spec Ops needed to be co-ed, so he set up a special pilot program to start training women for the Unit."

King glanced at her. She was still smiling, but there was a dangerous gleam in her eyes. "I've never heard anything about this," he said.

"A buddy of mine was an R.I. They wanted to keep it all very hush-hush in case things went horribly wrong...which is exactly what happened. Only one of the candidates made it through, which just showed what a stupid idea it was to begin with—"

Zelda cleared her throat. "Standing right in front of you, Prince Charming."

The Delta shooter swallowed nervously. "Ah, sorry...but you know what I mean."

"Actually I don't. I'd love to see how you're going to get out of that hole by digging deeper, but we should probably cut to the chase."

King wanted to hear more about this woman—Zelda Baker, evidently the first and only female Army Ranger. Keasling had told him that their contacts in Myanmar were military intelligence; aside from that, he hadn't known what to expect...but as Tremblay had so eloquently put it, he hadn't been expecting her. But she was right; they were on the clock. "I was told that your people are maintaining surveillance on the subjects. Is that correct?"

"My people?" Her lips curled in something that might have been a wry smile or a sneer—he couldn't say for sure.

She gestured for them to follow her into one of the partitioned areas, which had been converted into a makeshift office. There was a wall map of Southeast Asia tacked to one wall and a pad of butcher paper on an easel in a corner. A folding card table served as a desk, but most of its surface was taken up by electronic equipment—a military radio, a computer terminal and a fax/copier/scanner. The only decorative item in evidence was a stuffed toy sitting on the table right next to the computer. It was a Ranger Bear, just like those sold in the Post Exchange—a teddy bear in camouflage BDUs complete with a black beret, but this one had been modified. The bear's head had been removed, and in its place was a Magic 8 Ball. King noticed that someone had pinned a silver rank bar to the beret.

Zelda saw him looking at the doll. "That's Lieutenant Ball. He usually makes better decisions than a real officer."

She stripped off her padded boxing gloves and tossed them down next to the disfigured bear, then sank into a chair. "Let me tell you about 'my people.' It's just the two of us—me and Shin—and I really don't have time for this bullshit.

"There's a quarter of a million troops in Iraq 'fightin' the evildoers.'" She emphasized her contempt with air quotes. "But do you know where the tangos get their guns? Or the money to build IEDs to blow your asses up? Right here. This is where the evil begins."

"Drugs." King understood immediately what she was talking about. Opium trafficking in the Golden Triangle was keeping Al Qaeda and other terrorist groups flush with cash. He also knew that the CIA and FBI were actively working to shut down the criminal agencies that were facilitating those activities, but evidently Zelda saw her mission as more than just orders to be followed; it had become personal.

She waved dismissively. "Drugs. Sex slaves. Child soldiers...anything that can turn a profit for the triads."

"Look, I get it. You're fighting the good fight here, and you don't appreciate being pulled off that to do favors for us. But we're on the same side."

She regarded him thoughtfully. "Are you sure about that? The guys we've been trying to take down—the 14K triad—they've got a particularly brutal revenue stream: they kidnap people off the streets and harvest their organs. Care to guess who buys them? Rich, connected people—people back in the states—who don't want to have to wait for a donor match. Do you think the people in power *really* want to shut them down?"

King realized that he had to take charge of the situation. "It's not our job to figure out what they really want. We follow the orders we're given."

"'Ours not to reason why,' is that it?"

"That's what you signed up for, soldier."

The faintest glimmer of a smile returned to her full lips, and then she did something completely unexpected. She arched her back and stretched lazily, like a cat rousing from a nap. "Well then, what are your orders, sir?"

"General Keasling will have those for you when he arrives. For now, I'd like all the intel you've got on the subjects. I understand your man—Shin—is currently conducting surveillance?"

"He checks in at the bottom of the hour, so it will be another forty-five minutes before I hear from him." She tapped a folder on the tabletop. "He calls me, I don't call him. That's the rule. His communications logs are all here, so feel free to look through them. That's all I've got for you really. If there's nothing else, I'd like to finish my workout." Zelda stood and picked up the boxing gloves, and then flashed her seductive grin again. "Actually, I could use a sparring partner. What do you say, King? Are you up for it?"

Tremblay made a low sound, like an exaggerated groan of pleasure. "My God, that's so hot."

King stared back at her in disbelief. To all appearances, she was coming on to him, but his instincts were shouting down his libido. He doubted very much that what she wanted was something as banal as sex. This woman was smart and tough—tough enough to survive one of the most difficult programs in the Army; she was someone who knew what she wanted and would blow through any obstacle in her way. It was a game to her...

No, he thought, *not a game*. This was animal behavior, the she-bear marking her territory.

I do not have time for this shit.

By making the first move, throwing down the gauntlet, she had already won. She had put him on a defensive footing, established the battlefield, dictated the terms of victory. If not for the fact that he had been unwittingly outmaneuvered, he might have applauded her decisiveness.

Worse, she had defined him: a soldier, following orders without thinking; an officer, inept and unworthy of respect; a man... Oh yes, that was it. That was the thing that bothered her the most.

He didn't think she was a lesbian; even if she was...*Don't Ask, Don't Tell*. That was the policy. Regardless, she definitely had issues when it came to men.

He realized that she wasn't the only one watching to see what he would do and how he would play the game. All eyes were on him. If he played along, did what she wanted, he'd look weak, unable to say no to a pretty girl...

Okay, 'pretty' might be understating it. She's Playmate-of-the-Month material.

Did he dare refuse? He had every right to, but his fellow Delta shooters were expecting him to stand and deliver. If he didn't... Well, like the old saying went, you never got a second chance to make a first impression.

There was another saying he liked even better: The best defense is a good offense.

A smile slowly curled the corners of his mouth. "You know, maybe I should ask your CO what he thinks about this."

A flicker of doubt dulled the mischievous gleam in her eyes. "My CO?"

He picked up the stuffed bear and rolled the black plastic sphere into his palm. "Lieutenant Ball. Should I play grab-ass with Baker?"

Zelda frowned.

He gave the ball a vigorous shake then turned it over and looked at the little window where the answer was displayed.

Reply hazy, try again.

"Well, I'll be damned," he said, returning the toy to its place. "Lieutenant Ball says to go for it. I guess it's on."

SEVENTEEN

SHIN DAE-JUNG CONSIDERED it a matter of personal pride that he never complained about anything. Whether it was a duty station, another soldier, a particular mission...even Army chow in all its legendary inedibility, he faced each bump in the road of life with the implacability of a Buddhist monk.

But just this one time, he was tempted to make an exception.

It wasn't that there was anything particularly miserable about the assignment. He had humped cross-country for a good ninety minutes, a distance of at least six miles over uneven terrain, but that was just a walk in the park for someone like him. At one point, his foot had broken through a thin crust of dirt concealing some kind of animal burrow, and he'd twisted his ankle, but that kind of thing was to be expected. The low valleys between the hills seemed to be riddled with similar pitfalls, and to avoid more stumbles, he'd kept to the high ground, which had added to the length of his journey, but that too was just something that had to be done. When he'd reached his destination, a low hill west of the fenced compound, he'd hunkered down on the hard earth under his camouflaged poncho, motionless, as various bugs, critters and creepy-crawlies meandered across his body—par for the course. His thermal poncho liner didn't quite keep him toasty warm through the long chilly night, but he'd been colder before.

No, what had ramped up the misery factor was the fact that he could have...he *should* have...spent the night nuzzled up next to a very satisfied lady doctor.

Someone was going to get an earful when he got back; not Zelda—this wasn't her crazy idea—but the Delta boys... Oh, yeah, they were going to hear about what he'd given up to run their errands. The thought made him smile; the Delta operators would probably be a lot more sympathetic to his sacrifice than the blonde Amazonian war-goddess.

Ah well, as Giselle might say: c'est la vie.

The arrival of the helicopter made him forget all his woes.

It had come just after his last check in. He'd been busy drawing a diagram of the compound, noting the position of each building, as well as the exact coordinates for everything: the buildings, the fenced perimeter and even what appeared to be an obstacle course in the northeast corner. With precise enough coordinates, the Delta boys would be able to draw a near perfect map of the compound from just his radioed description.

The sound of voices drifting up from the compound grabbed his attention. He scanned the compound with the binoculars until he found the source of the noise; a small crowd of people—twenty or more—milling around the area he had dubbed 'the course.'

Everyone in the group had black hair and dark complexions, marking them as native to the region. Most wore simple clothing: dingy t-shirts and what might have been canvas trousers. All appeared to be male, but that was something he couldn't confirm. What he could determine with more certainty, based on the differences in size, was that some of them were just children.

Shin immediately got the sense that they were all prisoners.

Two men however, were not wearing the "uniform" of the captives. They were also Asian, but they looked like they'd just stepped out of a hip-hop music video—baggy jeans, T-shirts with fashion-designer logos prominently displayed, caps with the visors turned sideways. The effect would have been comical if not for the Kalashnikov rifles they wielded.

Then something truly unbelievable happened. The milling group fell into a neat military-style rank in front of the two 'gangstas,' and then, two at a time, they headed into the obstacle course.

They moved with astonishing speed and alacrity, bounding over hurdles and scrambling up ropes like soldiers at boot camp.

Shin realized that was exactly what it was. He assumed the men were conscripts, taken against their will and brought here to be trained and indoctrinated as soldiers, but it was equally possible that they were volunteers.

So what was this place? Headquarters for a local warlord? A secret terrorist training camp?

He wasn't due to check in for another thirty minutes, but this news seemed to warrant an unscheduled call. But before he could dial Zelda's number on his satellite phone, the helicopter arrived.

Because he was peering intently through his binoculars, he heard the beat of the rotors and the strident roar of the turbines before he made visual contact, but after only a few seconds of searching the sky, he found it—a sleek black Bell 430, coming up from the south, right behind him.

He huddled under his blind as it passed overhead, then he trained the binoculars on the aircraft as it touched down on the roof of the structure he had designated 'Building Two.' As soon as its wheels touched down, the pilot killed the turbines and let the rotors spin themselves out, a process that took several minutes. Finally, when the long airfoil-shaped blades were completely still, the doors were thrown open and the passengers began disembarking.

They were all Caucasian, and although too far away for Shin to distinguish faces through the low-powered binoculars, there were enough clues for him to approximate what was happening. The focus of everyone's attention was an infirm figure with thinning gray hair— Shin assumed it was a man—who was assisted out of the helicopter and into a waiting wheelchair.

Shin and Zelda had been investigating reports of people—children particularly—disappearing off the streets. There were a number of possible explanations, and all of them represented humanity at its most evil—young girls sold to brothels throughout Asia and young boys turned into infantrymen for warlords and rebel armies. There were even rumors that a Chinese criminal organization, the 14K triad, was abducting people, harvesting their organs and selling them on the black market.

Not just rumors anymore, Shin thought. But the triad wasn't smuggling the organs out of the country, a time-consuming endeavor that could damage the tissue. Instead, they were bringing the recipients here, to receive their new organs fresh from the unwilling donor.

A paramilitary training camp and a secret organ transplant clinic. The triad had built a one-stop shop for the flesh trade.

He reached for the satellite phone, but before he could dial the number, it started to vibrate in his hand.

EIGHTEEN

AT FIRST, KING wasn't sure what would happen. That lasted about fifteen seconds.

Tremblay who had appointed himself referee and timekeeper, had leaned in close as a shirtless King clambered over the ropes. "So, what's your plan? I mean, you're not actually going to hit a girl, are you?"

King was still pondering the question as Tremblay gave a shrill whistle signaling the beginning of the first round.

Zelda was grinning as she darted to the center of the ring. The mouth guard clamped between her teeth made her lips seem unnaturally full, but there was an intensity in her unrelenting stare that was like nothing King had ever seen before, not even in the eyes of men who had tried to kill him. He approached the center cautiously, his gloves up and ready to fend off her attack.

She jabbed at his gloves, testing his defenses. He effortlessly batted her punch aside. She jabbed again, but it was a feint; as he tried to block, she side-stepped and then threw a left upper-cut that connected solidly on his chin.

For a second, all he saw was stars.

It wasn't the hardest hit he'd ever taken. He'd had his bell rung plenty of times before. The difference this time was that he had—foolishly—not been expecting her to hit quite that hard.

He staggered back, flailing his arms to ward off her attempt to follow through, and when he could, he threw a wild cross-body punch that somehow made glancing contact.

Somebody gasped... He couldn't say for sure who, but his vision cleared enough to see Zelda's hair, flashing gold, as she moved in for another attack. This time he didn't bother trying to block her. Instead, he went on the attack, and this time he didn't hold back.

Hit a girl? Ha!

There were a lot of words that could be used to describe Zelda Baker—and she had probably heard them all—but 'girl' he decided, was not one of them.

Time passed in a blur of disconnected perceptions. In his more lucid moments, it would occur to him to press the attack. Sometimes it worked, and he succeeded in driving her back against the ropes, but invariably she would find a way to turn the tide. What she lacked in size and strength, Zelda made up for with skill; it was plainly evident that she'd received formal training. She was fast on her feet, flitting about the ring like a moth. She knew how to use the clinch to recover her wits when King landed a blow that should have put her on the mat.

At one point, as he sat slumped in a folding chair during one of the breaks between rounds, Tremblay knelt beside him. "Boss man, I got nothing but respect for you, but how long are you going to keep this up?"

Before King could answer, he heard Zelda's voice, strained and breathless from the exertion, reach out from the opposite corner like another punch to the jaw. "Had enough?"

He met her gaze. "I was going to ask you the same."

She laughed. "I'm just getting warmed up."

King shrugged. "Couple more rounds then."

Tremblay shook his head and handed King a towel to mop the perspiration off his face and shoulders. "Just in case you've lost count, we're at six."

Six? He had lost track.

Tremblay took the towel and gave another shrill whistle to mark the start of the seventh round. King hauled himself to his feet and waded once more into the fray.

It had stopped being a fight—it had never been much of a sparring match—and turned into something more like a marathon, a test of the limits of human endurance. It was a test, not of skill in combat, but of will. In both respects however, it seemed they were equally matched.

They circled, threw punches, fell against each other, and then repeated the dance, spiraling ever closer to total collapse. Zelda's face was flushed and puffy, her lower lip looked like a piece of raw meat, and she didn't seem quite as light on her feet now, but the determination in her eyes remained undimmed. King's own arms felt like they were made of rubber, and the padded leather gloves felt as heavy as lead weights.

All his attention was focused on her. He watched her eyes, searching for that flicker of movement that would telegraph where and when the next blow would come. He watched the set of her body and where her feet went; it had taken him a while to realize that she would plant her feet in a variation of a shooter's stance just before striking.

The rest of the world had ceased to exist for him. His only connection with anything outside the rope circle was Tremblay's shrill signal that another round had come to an end. Perhaps that was why it took him a moment to process the voice that boomed like a thunderbolt in the dimly lit room.

"What the fuck?"

As the words finally penetrated the filter, King and Zelda, as if by mutual accord, relaxed their stances and turned their attention to the group of onlookers, which had more than doubled in size. The rest of the team had arrived, but it was General Keasling, glowering at the edge of the ring, who seemed to suck the oxygen out of the room.

Keasling's face was a mask of barely contained rage. "What in God's name do you think you're doing?"

The abrupt end of the fight sapped the last of King's strength and for a moment, he thought he might collapse. But as he panted to catch his breath, he saw the other faces in the room. Tremblay was grinning in unabashed admiration. Parker was doing a slightly better job of concealing the same emotion. Even the big Ranger, Somers, looked impressed. Zelda was leaning wearily against the ropes, but her face wore the same expression.

He had proven something to her...to all of them.

He took a deep breath, let it out, then another. He straightened to the best approximation of a position of attention that his exhausted limbs could muster.

"Well sir, you instructed me to put together a new unit—the best of the best. I was just conducting tryouts." And then, as if he needed to say nothing more in his own defense, he turned to Zelda. "She's hired."

Keasling continued to scowl at King, but the simple fact of his silence told King that he'd said the right thing. His new mission—the new unit, whatever it was—had already taken him out from under Keasling's direct authority. After a moment, the general shook his head. "Fine. She's all yours."

Zelda's eyes went wide in disbelief. "Now just a damn minute—"

"Deal with it." Keasling kept his gaze on King. "Your new handler wants to brief you, ASAP. Get cleaned up."

It didn't appear to be in Zelda's nature to "deal with it," but she refocused her ire on the man chiefly responsible for it. She stalked forward and put a gloved fist against King's chest. "You don't own me, and you sure as hell don't get to just claim me like some prize."

King gently pushed her hand away. "Zelda... Sergeant Baker, I think you're going to like the job I've got for you."

"I already have a job."

"Now you've got a better one." He smiled. "Welcome to Delta."

NINETEEN

THERE WAS JUST enough time for King to towel off the perspiration and get Parker to slap a butterfly suture on the cut under his right eye, before Keasling took him aside for the conference call with the new handler.

The general handled the introductions...sort of. "I have Jack Sigler—callsign: King—here with me."

King didn't know what to say, so he ventured a vague: "Hello?"

The voice that issued from the speaker sounded strange. It wasn't just the normal crackles of squelch or the vagaries of radio transmissions. The voice had been electronically distorted, making it impossible to even begin guessing at the person's identity. King couldn't say with certainty whether it was a male or female voice. "King?" The distant unseen person seemed to be savoring the word. "A rather fortuitous choice. You can call me Deep Blue."

"Deep Blue?" King could just imagine what Tremblay's response to that declaration would be—something off-color, no doubt—and the thought brought a smile to his face. King however, correctly recognized the origin of the name. "Like the chess computer?"

"Exactly. It's my job to know everything and be one step ahead of our enemies."

The auto-tuned and digitally modulated voice could have been the voice of a computer, for all King knew. It was not a very comforting thought. The obvious implication was that this mysterious Deep Blue was going to be playing chess on a grand scale, with King and his new unit as the pawns. He didn't like the idea of his fate being controlled by some mysterious entity, much less one that might not even be human.

"Or rather I should say," Deep Blue continued, "to keep you one step ahead of *your* enemies."

"I'm listening."

"Operational Detachment Delta was created to give the President the ability to act—or react—rapidly, without having to wade through the mire of politics and command structures. But like everything else in government, it has gradually become a victim of the bureaucracy it was supposed to circumvent. Now, as you have personally witnessed, it has been compromised. The worst part is that we have no idea where this attack came from, much less who can be trusted. It will be General Keasling's job to root out any bad actors still lurking in the shadows, but last night underscores the importance of having a quick response team—one with virtually unlimited resources—as a surgical option for the President to use as an alternative to the military."

"You don't need to sell me on this, sir." King wasn't sure if he was supposed to refer to his handler as 'sir,' but when in doubt... "What's the mission?"

"First, build your team. From what the General tells me, you've already started recruiting." The electronic distortion made it impossible to tell if Deep Blue was joking.

"Why me?"

"I think you already know the answer. Right now, you and your men are above suspicion. Additionally, the fact that you survived last night tells me that you are someone who can beat long odds."

"I had a lot of help."

"Don't sell yourself short, King. You were thrown into an impossible situation, and you held it together."

King wondered if the men who hadn't made it back would agree with that assessment.

Deep Blue quickly switched gears. "However, our most pressing need right now is to bring those rogue operators down. Need I add, with extreme prejudice?"

King thought about what Parker had said earlier, during the first meeting with Keasling. "I think maybe we should be more focused on the question of why this happened, and what it is the enemy wants."

"The CIA is working that angle, but gathering intelligence will be an essential part of the mission."

"So you don't have a clue?" It came out with more sarcasm than he intended, but Deep Blue let it slide.

"It would be dangerous to assume anything at this early stage. It appears that this action was completely unconnected to current military operations, but whoever is behind this was able to coordinate with the insurgents that attacked you last night. We can't dismiss the possibility that this is a bold new terror plot."

"The CIA contractor—Therion—was the target," King said. "They wanted her for something. She's a code-breaker; maybe they want her to hack into the Pentagon computers? Steal nuclear launch codes?"

"Now you understand why we have to act quickly and without full knowledge of our enemy's goal." Deep Blue must have sensed King's earlier concerns, and after a pause, he continued. "You probably think that I'm playing a game with your life, and the lives of your men. Perhaps in a way that's true, but it's a game we have to win. In chess, you can never know exactly what your opponent is thinking, but you can draw conclusions from the moves he's made. But you must never think that you are a pawn to be sacrificed for victory. As soon as I know something, you will know it, and when it comes to operational decisions, you have the final say."

In King's experience, assurances like that came cheaply and were worth even less. He wished he could look the other man in the eye, read the sincerity—or lack thereof—in that promise. "All right, let's talk about those resources. We know where Rainer is, but that's about all we know."

"I've already made contact with Shin Dae-jung—the man currently conducting reconnaissance on the target. With the GPS coordinates he gave me, I've tasked a KH-12 satellite to get some real-time satellite imagery. That should give you a better idea of what you're looking at."

For a moment, King thought he misheard. The nation's network of 'eyes in the sky' was controlled by the National Reconnaissance Office, an independent and specialized agency that kept a very tight rein on its product—detailed satellite imagery—and was positively miserly about the satellites themselves. Requests for pictures of a target had to go up one chain of command and down another, a process that could take days and could be very costly in terms of political capital. Actually changing the orbit of a satellite, a procedure that required the craft to use up some of its very limited and irreplaceable fuel supply, was something that almost never happened.

Deep Blue wasn't kidding about having unlimited resources.

Maybe this new team was going to work out after all.

TWENTY

THE EXCITEMENT SASHA had felt as she donned the level-four biohazard safety suit in preparation to enter the sealed room where the relic was being kept, climbed to a fever-pitch of elation as she got a chance to actually behold the object—real, tangible evidence that the Voynich code was not a unique occurrence. That was about all that it revealed.

She was able to touch and interact with the object—albeit with a barrier of latex rubber between her and it, but there was little to be gleaned from such physical contact. She laid her hands upon it, turned it this way and that and then poked experimentally at the strange protrusions that were marked with the distinctive letters of the Voynich alphabet. She could tell that the pegs extended into the larger body of the thing, and deduced that they were something like the keys on a typewriter. That would be consistent with the idea that the device had been a type of encryption machine, but somehow it didn't feel right. She saw no evidence of gears and wheels inside the thing—the kind of things that would be necessary for a rudimentary cipher machine to work. Rather, the hollow body, broken though it was, contained only the remains of a few hollow tubes. The tubes and the wooden body of the thing reminded her of something, but what exactly that was, eluded her.

What she did know for certain was that eight of the keys contained exact matches to the Voynich script, and that was somewhere to start. She went back to an adjacent office just outside the containment area, shedding her environment suit. Rainer was there and began looking over her shoulder, but he otherwise let her work undisturbed.

Her laptop contained a complete version of the Voynich manu-script in digital form, along with a program that allowed her to plug in values for the distinctive characters of the mysterious alphabet. She highlighted the eight that were marked on the device. Without any context, they offered absolutely no insight.

It can't be a code machine, she decided. If it was, other examples of the code would have shown up. So what did that leave?

What else has levers like that? Buttons? Keys...

"A piano has keys!"

Rainer threw an inquisitive glance her way.

"It's a musical instrument," she said, and she knew with absolute certainty that she was right. The wooden body was similar to a drum or a stringed instrument, hollow with thin curved panels to amplify the sounds. The tubes inside were like the pipes of an organ or a pan flute.

The Voynich manuscript was a book of music. The mysterious characters that had challenged code breakers for nearly a century were not enciphered letters, but musical notes; each symbol corresponded to a specific tone, a sound frequency.

Sasha didn't have a deep aesthetic appreciation for music, but she did recognize its perfection as a mathematical language. If the code was an expression, not of individual letters but of sounds, then there would be a pattern to it.

There wasn't enough of the device left to even approximate what specific notes each lever would have created, but the simple knowledge of the artifact's purpose was enough to get her started.

She turned to Rainer. "Do you have a broadband Internet connection here? I need access to the Cray at Langley."

He shook his head. "That's not going to happen."

She blinked at him in disbelief. "You want this cracked, don't you?"

Rainer shrugged indifferently. "I can allow you supervised Internet access, but there's no way in hell I'm letting you interface with the CIA."

For a moment, Sasha couldn't comprehend the reason for this, but then she remembered that she wasn't here by choice. The Cray would have allowed her to employ a brute force attack, trying every permutation of the code, a grueling task that would have taken a lifetime using conventional methods, but would require only a few hours or days at the most, for the supercomputer. Denial of access to the agency's resources meant that she would have to do this the old-fashioned way.

The idea was not without some appeal to her.

The subroutines weren't discriminatory; the computer would treat every permutation as having equal potential, whereas a human cryptanalyst knew how to winnow out the obvious false trails.

But there were still too many variables.

She glanced through the window at the artifact—the instrument. If it had been a piano or a flute—something familiar—she would know the expected range of possible sounds, but there was nothing familiar about this device. She knew only its country of origin...

She turned to Rainer again. "This was found in China? Yunnan Province?"

"That's what I was told."

That didn't make any sense. There was nothing in the manuscript that even hinted at a Far Eastern origin; everything—the artwork, the style and the distribution of the text, even the parchment on which it was written—pointed to Europe as the place where the manuscript had been created.

"I need to know more about where this was found."

Rainer stared at her thoughtfully for a moment, and then he produced a cell phone. He dialed it and after a moment, he spoke. "She has some questions about the find."

He nodded in response to an unheard reply, then set the phone on the desktop, pushing a button to activate speaker mode.

The voice of Rainer's employer—Sasha couldn't recall if she'd been told his name—sounded tinny as it issued from the mobile device. "What do you wish to know, Ms. Therion?"

"You said it was in a crypt? Whose crypt? Was there anything else there? Has it been dated?"

"We think it was the tomb of a Chinese prefect named Guo Kan. Several of the artifacts appear to be war trophies from his campaigns with the Mongol Empire."

"Mongol?" Sasha tried to recall what she knew of the Mongolian era. "That would have been...12th century?"

"A bit later than that. Historical records say that he died in 1277, during the reign of Kublai Khan."

Kublai Khan. History had never held much interest for her, but that was a name she knew well. Kublai Khan had ruled most of Asia during the late 13th and early 14th centuries, but he was perhaps best known for being the exotic ruler described in *The Travels of Marco Polo.*

Had the Voynich manuscript and the strange musical instrument, which evidently held the key to unlocking its secrets, traveled on the Silk Road from Europe to China? Had the manuscript traveled back again?

It was another variable, and one that didn't square with the carbon-dating of the Voynich manuscript to the 1400s, but it would place the device and the Voynich script nearly fifty years ahead of the outbreak of the Black Death.

"What else did you find? Was there anything that might explain where this artifact originated?"

There was a sound that might have been a sigh. "Just stick to deciphering the code, Ms. Therion. I've already investigated all the other angles."

"It's a musical instrument," she blurted. "Did you discover that in your investigations?"

A long silence followed. "A musical instrument, you say? Could it be an organ of some kind?"

"Yes. A primitive one."

"Some of Guo's writings refer to an *'urghan'*—something he took as spoil from the siege of Baghdad. It's a Persian word and possibly the root word from which we get the name 'organ.'"

Baghdad. Iraq again. The search was bringing her full circle.

"I need to see everything you have on this *urghan*. If I am going to crack this code, I need to rebuild the thing."

TWENTY-ONE

"**KING, THIS IS** Irish, over."

In the front seat of the rented Ford Galaxy minivan, King keyed his throat mic. "This is King. Send it."

"We're moving out now."

King consulted his mental map of the area in which his team would execute the raid—an image that had been burned into his brain during the hours spent planning the op—and visualized Parker's vehicle concealed a hundred meters or so off the main road, about five miles southeast of the objective. "Roger. Radio checks every half hour. King out."

In his mind's eye, he saw Parker and the two snipers—'Dark' Meyers and 'Race' Banion—moving like dots across the terrain map. Their job was to rendezvous with Shin Dae-jung and establish over-watch positions around the compound. King would be leading the main assault force up the single road that connected the compound with the main highway.

He'd felt a twinge of regret at assigning his friend to lead the recon team. He and Parker had been working together for a long time. They were like brothers, and it felt strange to be going into a potentially hairy situation without Parker at his side, especially on a mission like this, where they were practically flying by the seat of their pants. But recon and over-watch was just as important to success as the assault, and there wasn't anyone he'd rather have watching his back. Besides, it was a foregone conclusion that Parker would be his top NCO in the new team, and this was a chance for his friend to show his abilities as a leader. King had no doubt that Parker was up to the challenge.

He was less certain about his own ability to take the reins of command, especially with the motley group crammed into the Galaxy that now sped along the main highway out of Mandalay, traveling east into the deepening dusk. Zelda Baker—who thanks to their 'sparring match' now looked like a supermodel on her way to a domestic violence shelter—was at the wheel, a logical choice given her familiarity with the country and its roads. King sensed that she was secretly pleased by the invitation to join the new team, but it was just as obvious that she didn't yet trust him. She wasn't happy to have been handed over to him like a trophy of war.

Behind him, Tremblay chattered away easily, bemoaning the fact that he had been unable to find replacement ammunition for his recently acquired Desert Eagle pistols, and generally throwing out observations about the scenery and one-liners that weren't nearly as funny as he seemed to believe.

King liked the solid Delta shooter and his ability to shrug off the uncertain and ever-changing circumstances in which they all now found themselves—that kind of adaptability was essential to special ops, but he wondered if Tremblay was bottling up negative emotions deep inside, hiding the grief at having lost two of his teammates behind a façade of humor. He worried about what might happen if and when that bottle finally overflowed.

Still, he preferred Tremblay's near-constant monologue to the implacable silence of the other three men in the van. He'd served with Casey Bellows for over a year, so he was used to the man's reserved nature, but he couldn't say the same for the other two: Travis "Silent Bob" Roberts, Tremblay's teammate from Alpha team, and Erik Somers.

Somers, in particular, concerned King. Although King had personally witnessed Somers's extraordinary strength and unwavering dedication in the face of enemy fire, there was something unsettling about the big man. It wasn't just that he was quiet. Silent Bob was a regular chatterbox next to Somers. There was an intensity to Somers. There was some unspoken passion or rage, smoldering just below the surface, like hot coals under a crust of ash, waiting for a stiff breeze to fan them into a full-blown wildfire.

King had briefly considered assigning Somers the callsign of "Terminator," but he figured the big guy had probably had his fill of comparisons to 'Ahnold.' Instead, he pulled a different iconic name from the well of Hollywood inspiration; Somers was now 'Eastwood,' and given his personality, that seemed even more apropos.

It didn't surprise King at all that Somers hadn't been selected to a Delta unit. Operators tended to be extroverts by nature, able to kick back over a brew with their teammates after a mission, shedding the stress of combat as easily as dropping their gear. He couldn't imagine what 'kicking back' would look like to Erik Somers.

Parker had recommended Somers, and that counted for a lot, but whether or not the big man found a place on King's new team would depend on how tonight's mission went.

I suppose that's true for all of us, he thought morosely.

They passed through a small town, and King spied a billboard written in several languages, including English, indicating the National Botanical Gardens lay just ahead.

"Almost there," Zelda announced. "Shin says it's just a couple miles past Pyin Oo Lwin."

Tremblay's face appeared at her shoulder. "What a coincidence; that's the name of my favorite noodle dish at PF Chang's. Speaking of which, I'm famished. Is there a Mickey D's hereabouts?"

Zelda purposefully ignored him, as did King. "All right. Let's find a good place to park."

A few minutes later, she pulled the van off road and threaded it into the woods, where it wouldn't be readily visible from the highway. The trees shut out the last few rays of daylight, plunging them into a world of shadows. They would be making their final approach to the objective on the dirt road, but before they could begin that journey, they had to deal with the gate guard.

King, Bellows and Silent Bob left the van behind and hiked through the woods toward the guard shack. There was no sign of the old man Shin had reported meeting the previous day, but the windows of the small structure glowed with artificial light—probably from a television set. Bellows crept to one of the windows, cautiously peered inside and then used hand signals to relay what he had seen: one man, sitting near the wall, facing east.

Silent Bob nodded, and then, with the stealthy swiftness that had earned him his nickname, he swept through the door. King, half a step behind, glimpsed movement in the dark interior room—the guard reached for his rifle but Silent Bob's suppressed MP5 coughed twice, and all motion ceased.

King scanned the small room, noting the old television set and a radio transmitter station that looked like little more than an off-the-shelf citizen's band radio. He decided that was a good sign; the triad, or whoever was running this little operation, evidently didn't think it warranted more aggressive security measures. He keyed his mic. "Legend, this is King. We have the gate. Move up now."

Zelda, who had made her displeasure at the callsign he'd chose for her abundantly clear, answered with a terse: "Roger, out."

King backed through the door and turned to Bellows. "Casey. You're staying here. Set up an observation post and watch the door."

Surprise and dismay flickered across his teammate's face, but Bellows was too much of a professional to protest. Deep down, the man was probably relieved to be sitting on the bench for this raid. They had all used up a lifetime's worth of luck, but Casey Bellows had a pretty wife and a newborn baby waiting for him back home. Every Delta shooter knew the risks that came with the job, even those with families, but King believed there were already too many kids without fathers in the world, and he didn't want to be responsible for one more.

Bellows assented with a nod and melted into the woods behind the shack, while King and Silent Bob headed for road where Zelda and others were waiting.

TWENTY-TWO

THE COMPOUND GLOWED brightly over the hilltops, or at least appeared to when viewed through night-vision goggles. It had been visible even from the road where they had parked their rented vehicle, but Parker had nonetheless let his Garman GPS guide him rather than relying on the distant source of illumination. The most direct route to their goal—a straight line—would have required them to climb hills and traverse the valleys in between, where the forest cover was thickest and the uneven terrain in between could easily cause injuries that would jeopardize the mission. Instead, they had programmed a more circuitous route into the GPS, one that kept them mostly on the high ground, at the expense of adding a couple of miles to the cross-country trek. The compound was still about five hundred meters away, but according to the GPS, they had reached the last waypoint marker, the place where they were to rendezvous with the forward observer.

A strident hiss issued from the darkness. Parker and the others immediately brought their weapons up, scanning the area for the source of the noise, but even with their night-vision, there was nothing to see.

"Take it easy, Irish." The voice was pitched just above a whisper, but Parker couldn't fix its location. "We're all on the same side. Safe your weapons, and I'll come out."

Parker breathed a sigh of relief. It had to be their contact, but he remained alert. "What's the word?"

"Nighteyes."

It was the callsign that King had assigned to their advanced scout. Parker thumbed the safety on his MP5 and lowered the weapon, nodding for the other men to do the same. As soon as they did, something rose from the ground just a few steps from where he stood. The figure was man-shaped, but camouflaged with dirt and tree branches, so he was nearly indistinguishable from the surrounding terrain. The only indication that there was a real person standing before him was a broad smile that glowed like a Cheshire Cat grin in the display of Parker's night vision.

"Took you guys long enough," the man said, extending a hand. "I'm Nighteyes, but please, just call me Shin."

Parker accepted the handclasp, and after a quick round of introductions, unslung his field pack and passed it over. Shin opened the pack and began sorting through its contents—a radio, a bottle of water and a partially disassembled M21 sniper rifle.

"Now we're talking," Shin muttered as he fitted the parts of the weapon together. In the dark, he had work by feel alone, but his fingers knew exactly what to do, and in less than thirty seconds, he was performing a dry-fire functions check. When he was done, he slid a magazine into the well and advanced a round, after which, he turned back to Parker. "Okay, here's the good news. There's virtually no security. No patrols, no cameras or perimeter sensors... Hell, I don't even think they have a night watchman."

"And the bad news?"

Shin shrugged. "This place is remote, and the triads don't exactly follow military procedures...but there should be some kind of security here. The fact that there isn't any has me worried."

"You don't believe in luck?"

"I don't trust it."

"Words to live by."

Shin clipped the radio to his belt and fixed the headset in place. He turned his head away and whispered into the lip mic. "This is Nighteyes. Radio check, over."

Parker heard the man's voice as clear as day in his own earpiece, followed immediately by King's voice. "This is King. Good copy, Nighteyes. Irish, you there?"

"Right next to him," Parker answered. "We're about to move out. Should be romeo-tango-golf in five mikes."

"Waiting on you, Irish. King out."

Parker turned to the other men. "Dark, you're with me. Race, you and Nighteyes head to OP-Two. Call in when you're set. You heard the boss; the clock is ticking."

TWENTY-THREE

ZELDA FELT LIKE she'd been reborn.

King, in inviting her to join Delta—or rather, as it had been explained to her, a new elite team within Delta—had done something no man had ever done so quickly before: he had earned her respect. One of the reasons she had joined the Army in the first place, was to be part of something big, something important. She had been relentless in her pursuit of that goal. She had certainly earned this advancement, but it still felt good to finally, at long last, be appreciated for more than just her looks. Of course, she wasn't about to let the rest of the men in the van know how pleased she was to be 'one of the boys.'

That was only part of the reason for the elation she now felt. Mostly, what had her feeling so energized—so alive—was the fact that she was charging down an unfamiliar dirt road, bouncing over potholes and ruts at nearly forty miles an hour and barely slowing for the turns, all without headlights and in near total darkness. She was aided by night vision technology, but she was trusting more in her memory of the satellite photos the team's new handler had provided.

It was a pure adrenaline rush, made all the sweeter by the fact that, for the first time since meeting him, Stan Tremblay had finally shut up. He actually looked like he was about to throw up, but maybe that was just a trick of the night vision.

She didn't actually mind Tremblay. In truth, she had passed the point where his relentless sophomoric humor was irritating; it was, strangely, almost charming, and while he still seemed unable to look at her without cracking a shit-eating grin, she sensed that he, like King, was beginning to see her as a teammate and a fellow soldier, first. She got the same sense from the others, particularly Somers, the dark and brooding Ranger, who she was given to understand, was very much an outsider like herself.

"This is good," King announced from the passenger seat. "Stop here."

Zelda stamped the brake, stopping the minivan in the middle of the road.

King half-turned so he could see everyone. "All right, kids. The new boss is watching, so let's make this look easy."

The team had been outfitted with equipment and weapons from the cache at the safe-house: PVS-14s; sound-suppressed Heckler & Koch MP5s with M68 Aimpoint red-dot aiming sights and tactical body armor vests with load carrying pouches for spare magazines, grenades and their radio sets. They exited the vehicle in silence and made their way on foot up the final hill, with King in the lead and Somers bringing up the rear.

King called a halt at the top of the rise and radioed the sniper teams for a final visual report. Just as Shin had reported all afternoon, the compound was quiet.

King brought them all forward for a final brief. "We do this fast, quiet and by the numbers."

There were four buildings in the compound. Buildings Two and Four were two stories each. The helicopter, which had arrived at midday, was still parked on the roof of Building Two, but most of the activity Shin had observed occurred in and around Building Four. Based on his description, Zelda felt certain that Building Four was a holding area for the triad's captives—future slave laborers, child soldiers or organ donors. It was also where the team would probably face the stiffest opposition.

She couldn't begin to guess what business Chinese gangsters had with rogue Delta operators. 'By the numbers' meant Building Four would be the last one they entered.

"There is one presumed non-hostile—"

Zelda recalled her brief glimpse of Sasha Therion at the airport the previous day. She had no doubt that the CIA cryptanalyst was a hostage.

"—so positive ID before you pull the trigger. The good news is, she's the only one you need to worry about not killing." He looked at each of them in turn. "Any questions?"

There were none.

"Irish, this is King. Give me a weather report?"

Zelda heard the echo of his transmission a millisecond later in her radio earpiece, followed by Parker's voice. "Nothing moving on the south side. Nighteyes, how's the north look?"

"All clear. Watch yourselves. It's spooky quiet."

King took a breath and then spoke again. "Deep Blue, this is King. Give the word."

A weird electronic voice burbled in Zelda's ears. "The word is 'Go.' Give 'em hell, team!"

"Well, I guess it beats 'break a leg,'" Tremblay muttered.

King gave the signal to move out. They walked in a straight line, staying about twenty feet apart. Tremblay took point, followed in turn by Silent Bob and King. Zelda was next in the formation, and Somers brought up there rear.

They reached the gate, where it took Tremblay all of ten seconds to cut away a section of wire mesh big enough for even Somers to slip through, and then they were moving again, dashing across the open ground to the front of Building One. As soon as they were all lined up outside the door, King gave another hand signal and they swept inside.

The reception area, like the rest of the structure, was dark and deserted, but they methodically cleared each room just to be sure.

The same would not be true of Building Two.

Although there were no windows, a thin strip of light was visible beneath the front entrance of the two-story building. King gave the order for everyone to switch off their night vision, and then he threw the door open.

Tremblay rushed inside, sweeping the area to the left with his weapon. Silent Bob went right and did the same, but there was no one to shoot at. The brightly lit hallway beyond was as quiet as a cemetery, but Zelda saw closed doors on either side.

King waved them all forward. "Juggernaut, Bob—take the right. Legend, Eastwood—left side. Leapfrog."

Tremblay and Roberts hastened forward, and moved through the first door in the same dynamic way they'd come in through the front entrance. Zelda waited for the noise of battle, but heard only Tremblay's voice in her earpiece: "Clear."

Now it was her turn. She advanced to the next door and felt Somers tap her shoulder with the ready signal.

That was when it finally hit home for her. She had done this more times than she could count in training, but she had never been given the opportunity to test herself in combat. This was the real deal; this was what she'd been waiting for.

And she was ready.

She gave the go signal, and in a single smooth motion, she turned the doorknob, threw the door open and moved into the room.

This room was not empty.

She processed what she saw in large chunks of information. There were two people, right in front of her: a woman, sitting at a table staring at the screen of a laptop computer, and a man right behind her, mostly hidden from view. Zelda recognized them both; the woman was Sasha Therion and the man was Kevin Rainer.

Zelda adjusted her aim, putting the targeting dot on the narrow sliver of Rainer's torso that was visible behind Sasha, but in the instant it took her to do so, he moved, ducking out of view.

With no shot, Zelda took a step back, bumping into the solid mass of Erik Somers who was entering the room right behind her, still unaware of what she had found.

"Contact!" she shouted.

Before either of them could move another step, Rainer's arm extended past Sasha. There was something dark in his fist, and there was just enough time for Zelda's brain to recognize that it was a gun, before Rainer pulled the trigger.

TWENTY-FOUR

SASHA WAS ONLY vaguely aware of the intrusion, at least up until Rainer's pistol thundered right beside her.

The noise was so loud it hurt her ears, and she jerked involuntarily in her seat. The blonde woman standing in the doorway jerked as well, stumbling backward as Rainer's bullet punched into her chest. Rainer yanked Sasha to her feet and dragged her away from the table...away from her laptop.

Panic flashed through her, but it wasn't fear for her life that set her heart pounding. "No!" she shrieked. "Not now. Let me finish!"

She couldn't tell if she said it out loud; all she could hear was a ringing in her ears. Rainer gave no indication that he heard her. Holding her in front of him like a shield, he began advancing toward the doorway. The fingers of his left hand were curled around her biceps, but his right hand, which rested on her shoulder, no longer held a pistol. Instead, he clutched a round green object, about the size of a baseball—a hand grenade with the safety pin already removed.

No...let me finish.

This time there were no words. Sasha tried to look back, to reach out for the laptop, but her captor gave her a rough shake, asserting his dominance.

I was so close.

The variables swirled out of control in her head, screaming like white noise.

A large man dragged the blonde—Sasha couldn't tell if the woman was still alive—out of the doorway, retreating from before Rainer, who advanced relentlessly behind his human shield. Rainer thrust her out into the open, staying behind cover. Sasha saw the large man and the blonde woman, as well as three other men, one of whom she recognized from Iraq. The woman was struggling free of the big man's grip—evidently, she was not seriously injured, but the others had their guns aimed at the doorway...at her.

"Bravo, Jack," Rainer called out from behind her. "You made it. I'm impressed. And you got yourself some new Mouseketeers. I guess there were some openings on the team."

When no one answered his taunt, he continued, "I'm gonna go out on a limb here and say that you've got orders to keep this one alive, right? Otherwise, this place would already be a smoking crater. I'm right, aren't I? Let's test it and see."

Sasha was nudged forward again, out into the open.

One of the men spoke. He was the one Sasha recognized. "Kevin, I want to keep her alive only a little bit more than I want you dead, so I guess it's your lucky day. Let her go, and that will be the end of it."

Rainer laughed mirthlessly. "You know, I almost believe you, Jack. You've got this whole 'honor' thing going on; it's why I didn't even think about asking you to join me for this paycheck. No, I think I'll do this my way." He waggled the hand grenade. "You might want to stand back."

Sasha was abruptly yanked backward, down the hallway, deeper into the building's interior. She caught a last glimpse of the five commandos before Rainer pulled her through another doorway and into a stairwell leading up. His earlier deliberate stride now gave way to a haste that seemed to verge on panic. He darted up the stairs, two at a time, nearly dragging Sasha along, but she barely noticed. The only thing that mattered to her was the ever-increasing distance between herself and the answer she had been so close to uncovering.

"You have to let me go back," she managed to say. "My computer."

"I'll get you a new one." Rainer didn't slow. He reached the second-story landing and burst through the door into a hallway that was nearly identical to the one below. He pulled her to the second door on the right and threw it open. Sasha couldn't see past him, but she heard him say: "Richard! Company's here."

"Who?"

Sasha recognized the voice of Rainer's employer.

"Does it matter? We need to get out of here." Rainer dragged Sasha to another door and barked commands to his two co-conspirators, ordering them to join him. Then he hastened back into the stairwell, hauling her up the next flight, with the other men close behind.

"Where are we going?" Richard demanded.

Rainer answered without looking back. "The helicopter. They'll probably be covering it with snipers, but they won't do anything to jeopardize her." Then he added, "I hope."

Sasha's eyes found Richard's. "I have to go back," she pleaded. "My computer is down there."

The man just shook his head.

"You don't understand. The answers are on that computer. I've almost figured it out."

The man's face registered dismay, but only for a second. "Nothing we can do about that now. We can start over when we're safely away from here."

Rainer finally seemed to acknowledge her concerns. He paused at the top of the stairs. "There might be information on that computer that they can use against us."

Richard shrugged. "It won't matter. They're not getting out of here alive."

He took a phone from his pocket, and after dialing, he held it to his ear. "We're being attacked," he said, without preamble. "Turn them loose."

TWENTY-FIVE

KING WATCHED RAINER disappear through the doorway with a cold knot of rage in his gut, but his anger wasn't directed at the escaping traitor; he was mad at himself.

A litany of his failures ticked off in his head. *We moved too soon... Should have gotten more intel... Should've planned better.*

None of those measures would have really made a difference, and waiting would only have given Rainer a chance to slip away completely. No, this wasn't a failure of planning or leadership; it was just plain bad luck, but that didn't lessen the sting.

I should've just taken the shot, consequences be damned.

Glowering, he shouldered his weapon and started forward, moving toward the door through which his quarry had vanished.

"Jack?" an anxious voice called from behind him. It was Tremblay. "Talk to us, boss. What's the plan?"

King ignored him and kept moving. Rainer had to be stopped, no matter what.

"Jack? Sigler? King!"

That stopped him.

King.

He wasn't just Jack Sigler, pissed-off Delta shooter. He was King; he was their leader.

He pivoted on his heel. He saw, as if for the first time, Zelda leaning against the wall, struggling to breathe. "Legend, are you hit?"

Zelda winced, but there was fire in her eyes. "The vest stopped it. I've been hit harder than that." She managed a grin and added, "Not by you."

"Then on your feet, soldier. Eastwood, you and Legend head back and bring the van up. Juggernaut, Bob...you're with me. We're gonna get what we came for."

A flicker of disappointment crossed Zelda's pained visage—she probably thought he was benching her and blamed herself for not having taken out Rainer when she'd had the chance—but she grabbed Somers's shoulder and pulled herself erect.

Tremblay likewise seemed heartened by King's decisiveness. He and Silent Bob quickly caught up to their team leader and cautiously followed him through the doorway.

King swept the muzzle of his MP5 up the stairwell and checked for blind spots before heading up the steps. At the second floor landing, he waited for the other two operators to line up behind him before throwing the door open and moving through. His finger was tight against the trigger, ready to shoot, no matter who was on the receiving end or what the ultimate consequences were, but the hallway was vacant.

"Shit."

He knew Rainer was too smart to retreat to a dead end, but he also knew that the turncoat Delta officer had not come here alone; were his co-conspirators waiting behind one of the closed doors, waiting to ambush them?

Only one way to find out.

Before he could approach the first door, a voice sounded from his radio receiver. "This is Nighteyes. We've got activity at Building—"

The transmission broke off in mid sentence, and for a moment, King feared that somehow the sniper had been discovered, but then Shin's voice came back. "I don't even know how to describe this. You guys need to get out of there right now."

King heard the urgency in the man's voice, but turning back wasn't an option he was prepared to consider. The mission came first, and the mission was to take down Kevin Rainer and the other traitors; his own survival was a secondary priority.

He advanced to the first door, and as soon as Tremblay and Silent Bob were in place, he threw the door open and moved in. As before, he was poised to fire at the first target of opportunity, but nothing could have prepared him for what he saw in that room.

Unlike the ramshackle interiors they had encountered in every other corner of the compound, this space had been scrupulously maintained. The walls and ceiling, and even the floor, were a brilliant, almost sterile, white. The effect was intensified by the bright overhead lights that blazed down with sun-like intensity. The place looked clean enough to be a surgical operating room.

Which was exactly what it was.

There were four people in the room. Two wore blue surgical scrubs, complete with caps and face masks that hid all clues to their identity. The other two were laid out on gurneys. One of the latter was barely visible; just pale white arms and legs protruding from a tent of blue fabric, transfixed in the glare of the lights; he was the focus of the surgeons' attention.

The last person in the room was male, a dark-skinned Burmese man in his early twenties or perhaps younger. He lay naked on a stretcher, which had been pushed to one side of the room. He was unmoving, as if unconscious, but it was plainly evident that he wasn't simply sleeping. His upper torso had been opened like the petals of a rose. King caught only a momentary glimpse into the man's chest cavity, but it was enough to see that there was a dark bloody void where his heart and lungs ought to have been.

King had seen terrible things in his life—children blown apart by IEDs and American serviceman horribly burned in fuel explosions— but those raw savage experiences were nothing alongside the sanitized, precise and utterly inhuman evil he now beheld.

He brought his gaze back to the surgeon who stood above the patient—the recipient of the organs that had been taken from the body of the unwilling donor. The doctor's eyes were fixed on King's gun, but after a moment they flickered up to meet his gaze. He raised his hands in a supplicating gesture, his latex gloves painted with blood.

"I don't know what you want," the man said in a voice that was unnaturally calm. "But you have to leave, now."

"Or what?" The question came from Tremblay, but it had none of his customary humor. He was as shocked as King.

"Or my patient will die," was the haughty answer.

King took a menacing step forward, close enough to see inside the chest cavity of the patient; the stolen body parts lay flaccid and seemingly lifeless within. Only now was King aware of the complex web of tubes that sprouted from the supine form, connecting the man to IV drips and bypass machines—devices that were keeping the man's blood oxygenated and flowing while the surgeons methodically spliced in the hijacked organs.

The patient's face was hidden beneath a shroud of blue cloth, but King didn't need to make a positive identification to know what sort of person lay on the operating table: a true human predator, someone who bought the organs of another living human to sustain his own miserable life, as casually as someone might order a cheeseburger.

"And why the fuck should I care about him?" King asked.

Parker's voice abruptly sounded in King's ear. "Movement on the roof. They're going for the helo... It's Sasha! I have eyes on Sasha."

There seemed to be an unasked question there, but it took King a moment to disengage from the horror unfolding right in front of him. *Roof? Helo?* Then the picture came into focus; Rainer was about to slip through his fingers again.

For the briefest instant, he considered telling Parker to take out the helicopter. A burst of some 7.62 millimeter rounds into its turbine engines would probably disable it and leave their foe trapped on the roof.

Trapped... Backed into a corner... There was no telling what Rainer might do if that happened.

King keyed his mic. "Deep Blue, this is King. Will you be able to track that helicopter?"

There was a brief delay before the mystery figure answered, with no small measure of urgency: "Affirmative, King. You've done all you can there. Abort the mission and exfil immediately."

Done all you can... Abort... King felt his earlier self-directed rage rising again, but he fought it back. "Roger. Irish, hold your fire. Let them go."

On the other side of the operating table, the surgeon relaxed visibly, as if sensing that King's radio transmission signaled the end of the incursion. "What we're doing has nothing to do with whatever it is you want. Please, just go, so I can get back to saving this man."

King adjusted his aim ever so slightly, and squeezed off a single shot. The only noise from the suppressed MP5 was a faint metallic click as the internal mechanism ejected the spent brass casing and ratcheted another round into the firing chamber. The sound of the surgeon, screaming in pain and disbelief, as the nine-millimeter bullet punched through the palm of his right hand, was much more satisfying.

King threw a mock salute with the smoking muzzle of the weapon. "Good luck with that."

TWENTY-SIX

EVER SINCE LEAVING his Ranger unit behind to join with King's Delta team, Erik Somers had felt like the odd man out.

A change of assignment always brought with it a period of adjustment—it took a while to get used to new teammates and procedures—but the whirlwind of activity that had engulfed him in the last twenty-four hours was unsettling, especially for someone like himself, who kept a tight rein on his emotions. The private rage that defined him was always simmering just below the surface, but the rigors and routines of military life provided a purposeful way for him use that anger.

That was missing for him now. He had gone from being a Ranger with a clearly defined set of responsibilities and objectives, to being...what exactly? Even Zelda, a woman in a profession dominated by men, seemed to have staked out a niche for herself, but he was still waiting to see how he would fit in. From the moment he'd joined King's team on the plane to Myanmar, Somers had the feeling that he was just a warm body filling an empty seat, and that uncertainty about his place in the scheme of things was eating at his self-control. He felt an almost overpowering urge to destroy something...anything.

He swallowed the bubble of rage down and turned to Zelda. "Can you walk?"

"Been walking most of my life, big guy," she said, but the words came out in short bursts, as if she lacked the breath to utter a complete sentence.

He acknowledged with a nod and headed for the door, but she forestalled him. Moving stiffly at first, she hastened back into the room where they had confronted Rainer, and emerged a moment later, shoving the abandoned laptop computer into her backpack. "Might be something useful on this."

"Good thinking." It seemed like the right thing to say. Without further comment, he headed for the exit, only peripherally aware of Zelda a few steps behind.

He immediately sensed that something was different about the exterior of the compound. A low indistinct noise, like the hum of conversation in a crowded room, pervaded the still night. Before he could identify the source, he heard Nighteyes's anxious voice warning of activity in the compound, and he knew that his ears had not deceived him.

As he and Zelda moved from the building, he saw a torrent of human figures pouring out of Building Four, less than a hundred yards away. Most of them looked like refugees, slack-jawed and dull-eyed, wearing clothes that were little more than rags, but there were a few men who stood out from the crowd, partly because of their garish attire and partly because of the AK-47s they held at the ready. The gunmen seemed to be herding the others, but their eyes were sweeping the compound, as if searching for targets. One of the gunmen looked directly at Zelda and Somers, and with a shout to the others, raised his rifle.

Somers started to bring his MP5 around, but before he could put the red dot on his chosen target, the man's head snapped back in a spray of red. Someone was looking out for them.

Another of the armed men was downed by a quiet but deadly shot from the distant sniper. Yet even as the shepherds were felled, some of the herd revealed their true nature. Their eyes were no longer dull, but focused on the fleeing Delta operators like laser beams, and with a noise that sounded almost like the braying of coyotes, a dozen of them lurched forward.

Somers grabbed Zelda by the arm and propelled her ahead of him, even as he broke into a run. "Go!"

She seemed to grasp the urgency of the situation. After a few faltering steps, she sprinted ahead, racing for the gap in the gate and the perceived safety that lay beyond. She easily outpaced Somers, but it wasn't because she was lighter or more athletic; he was intentionally hanging back, just in case the pursuing horde caught up to them. Without even looking, he crooked his arm backward and triggered a long burst from the MP5 into the oncoming mass of bodies.

Zelda slipped through the fence and resumed her dash up the road. In the moment it took for Somers to thread himself into the gap, she vanished completely into the darkness. A spur of metal snagged his shoulder, raking his skin through the fabric of his shirt, but he wrestled free and ran after her.

Behind him, there was a metallic rattle of bodies hitting the fence, and he risked a look back. Some of the pursuers were squirming through the hole, but several more were scaling the fence, as nimble as squirrels on a tree trunk. Somers fired out the magazine, but the rounds from his silenced submachine gun seemed to produce about as much effect as a swarm of gnats.

There was no time to reload. He kept his grip on the weapon as he bolted up the hill, but the seconds he had spent getting through the fence had cost him his scant lead. Before he'd gone twenty steps, they were on him.

He felt it first as a weight crashing against him, and then something wrapped around his legs. The impact wasn't enough to knock him down—he was too big and too powerful to be taken down by a hit from just about anyone but an NFL linebacker, but the grip that tightened around his legs was fierce enough to break his stride. He swiped at the clutching arms, using the MP5 like a club, but even as his assailant fell away, another body crashed into him, and then another. Then he was buried under a deluge of human flesh.

They swarmed over him like warrior ants guided by a common mind, attempting to immobilize his limbs and render him defenseless. Against almost anyone else, this tactic would have achieved its intended purpose, but he was not just anyone else. The ferocity of the attack catalyzed him, burning through his practiced self-restraint, releasing his fury in a titanic eruption.

The next thing he knew, he was free of their grasping hands, kneeling in the center of a circle of broken bodies. His ability to think rationally returned by degrees...

I was supposed to be doing something... The van...

He stood, aware that some of the bodies that lay around him were moving, stirring from the stunning violence he had inflicted on them. Despite the darkness, he could distinctly make out that the attackers were small-bodied—some of them looked like very young teenagers—but their arms and legs were thick with muscle, almost grotesquely so. Clothes had been torn away in the struggle, revealing torsos that ballooned with the kind of unnatural tissue growth that was a side-effect of steroid abuse.

But that was the only the tip of the iceberg.

Enormous scars mapped their bodies, white and purple marks with crisscrossing patterns like the laces of a football. The coarse black hair that covered their scalps was patchy in places, revealing where incisions had been made. Some of the wounds were not completely healed, but oozed fluid; plastic tubes sprouted from some, external veins that ran around their bodies and disappeared again somewhere else. In some distant corner of his mind, he registered the fact that these weren't merely child soldiers. They were living science experiments, enhanced with chemicals and probably lobotomized, stitched together like something from Frankenstein's laboratory. Whatever had made them human once, was now gone completely.

Somers felt a different kind of fury welling up inside him.

What the hell is this place?

He wanted to turn back, storm the compound and tear it down to its foundations. He wanted to find the monsters responsible for such atrocities and rip them limb from limb...but that wasn't why he was here.

He was vaguely aware that he had lost his weapon in the battle. His radio set had also been torn away, leaving him deaf to the needs of the rest of the team. More of the... What should he even call them? 'Frankensteins' was the first thing that came to his mind... They were rushing up the road from the compound, but the majority of them were massing at the entrance to Building Two, where King and the others were pinned down.

He had to get to the van, join Zelda and then get the others out of the compound. The mission was his first priority, and right now his team needed him.

TWENTY-SEVEN

KING'S SATISFACTION AT disrupting the macabre surgery was short-lived. As he returned to the main hallway, he heard the low rumble of footsteps in the nearby stairwell, a sure sign that trouble was approaching. Then, even that sound was drowned out, as the roar of engines coming to life sent a tremor through the entire building.

Rainer was getting away, and there wasn't anything he could do about it.

Suddenly, the door to the stairwell burst open, and human shapes began rushing through. King had his MP5 up and ready to meet the attack, as did Tremblay and Silent Bob, but for a moment, all three were too stunned by what they beheld to pull a trigger.

Christ, they're just kids, King thought.

Except they weren't. They might once have been innocent children, but not anymore. In the hallway lighting, he could clearly see what Somers had only been able to glimpse—the sprouting tubes, the surgical scars and mismatched limbs and muscles bulging from artificial growth hormones. The children they had once been were as dead as the young man whose organs had been callously harvested, and in their place there were only these monsters.

In an instant, they swarmed over Silent Bob, who stood nearest to the stairwell. He scrambled back at the last second, swinging his submachine gun like a club, but then he was gone, buried under a wave of bodies. The unmistakable violence brought King out of his horror, and he squeezed the trigger, hurling lead soundlessly into the onrushing mass of human flesh. Some of the monsters flinched as the bullets tore into them, but driven by steroids and raw primal fury, they did not slow. Before he could even think about changing his tactics, the leading edge of the wave crashed into him.

Suddenly, King was yanked backward. He struggled for a moment before realizing that it was Tremblay who had seized hold of him, dragging him into one of the rooms that opened off the hallway. The Delta operator slammed the door shut and braced it with his back. A moment later, the entire wall shook as the attacking mob began hammering against the barrier.

Tremblay grimaced. "Any bright ideas, boss man?"

"Working on it." King gave the room a quick look. It contained a few desks and chairs, but nothing that seemed to offer a way of holding off the attackers, much less an escape route. The door shook again, and a long dark line appeared in the wood as it began splitting in two. The walls rattled with the relentless pounding, and then even floor began to shake.

Okay, we can't stay here and we can't get out... What does that leave?

The flimsy construction gave King an idea, and in a rush of inspiration, he tipped one of the desks over and slid it toward Tremblay, positioning it so the desktop was facing away from him.

"I don't think that will hold them for very long," Tremblay said.

"It's not supposed to." King dipped a hand into a pouch on his vest and brought out a green-gray spherical object identical to the one Rainer had used to effect his escape.

Tremblay's eyes went wide. "Oh, you're not."

King's only answer was to pull the safety pin on the grenade. "Better get down."

As Tremblay slid to the floor, seeking cover behind the desk, the top of the door split completely apart. King tossed the grenade underhanded, so it arced through the room to drop near the far wall, and then he threw himself down next to Tremblay, likewise bracing the door. Grasping arms slipped through the gap above their heads, trying to force the opening wider. It seemed inevitable that they would succeed.

And then the world exploded.

The detonation unleashed a storm of kinetic energy in all directions, compressing the air into a wall as hard as steel, which expanded outward in a millisecond. The overpressure wave superheated the air in the small room, and would have vaporized everyone inside if the walls had been made of stiffer stuff. Because the building was little more than plywood on a stick-built frame, the side of the structure was blasted open, relieving some of the pressure. The shockwave picked up loose furniture and hurled it away from the blast center. The walls bulged outward, as if the room was a balloon being inflated by a breath from a giant. The broken door was blasted off its hinges, which not only hurled the attacking mob back, but also caused King and Tremblay to fall backward. This proved fortuitous, because it helped protect them from a deadly spray of steel fragments that surfed the leading edge of the blast wave. The nearly molten metal shredded everything it touched, including several of the monstrosities massed in the hallway beyond. The desk caught some of the fragments that would have ripped into the Delta operators, but even as it did, the cheap wood was smashed apart by the blast, and the two men were pummeled by the broken pieces.

Although they had done everything they could to prepare for the blast, their survival was as much a matter of luck as it was forethought, and it took them a few seconds to recover their wits. King rolled over to find Tremblay also shaking off the effects. The blond soldier mumbled something—probably one of his trademark one-liners—but King couldn't hear anything except a loud and steady high-pitched tone inside his head. He gave Tremblay a thumbs-up, and when the other man returned it, he gestured toward the gaping hole where the wall had been. The two men crawled forward, skirting along the edge of a newly created opening in the floor, and lowered themselves into the compound.

For a few seconds, they had only the dead for company. Several bodies—many of them Asian men dressed like wannabe hip-hop performers with AK-47s clutched in their dead hands—lay scattered about the courtyard, felled by sniper fire. King realized that he and Tremblay were now probably in someone's scope, but with his ears still ringing, there was no way to make contact.

He chose the shortest path back to the gate and motioned for Tremblay to follow, but before they had gone fifty feet, a glimpse of

movement revealed one of the living atrocities prowling the compound. The thin figure—a patchwork that was equal parts teenage girl
and professional wrestler—just stared at them for a moment, and then
she tilted her head back and opened her mouth, as if she was trying to
catch a raindrop on her tongue. King didn't need his faculty of hearing
to know that she was sounding the alarm. The silent scream lasted
only a few seconds, after which the thing lurched toward them.

Suddenly, monstrosities were all around them. They did not
charge this time, perhaps having learned wariness, but they circled
like a pack of wolves. King slapped a fresh magazine into his MP5 and
started firing. A few went down, but the 9-millimeter rounds seemed
to be more of an irritant than anything else; the pack pulled back and
began to move faster, orbiting the Delta shooters like a cyclone.

Try as they might, King and Tremblay could not watch every
approach, and before long, the things attempted to attack from their
blind spot. King spied movement and whirled to find one of the things
dead on the ground just a few feet away; the snipers were still watching
out for them. Another of the monsters went down in a spray of red as a
high-velocity rifle round tore the top off its head, but for every one that
fell, two more crept out of the shadows to join the circle.

Then, without any warning and for no discernible reason, the
circle began to close. It was if some kind of critical mass had been
achieved. King fired out a magazine, and two of the monsters stumbled
forward and died at his feet, but the rest engulfed him. He swung the
MP5 wildly like a club, but a dozen grasping hands wrapped around his
arm, arresting any further movement. They grabbed his other arm, and
then his legs. Then they began to pull in opposite directions.

King howled, more in frustration than in pain, though there was
plenty of the latter. He felt his joints grinding in their sockets, his tendons
stretching like rubber-bands pulled to the breaking point... They were
going to pull him apart like a wishbone from a Thanksgiving turkey.

And then, just as quickly as they had seized him, the fury of the
attack began to wane. King twisted free of his assailants' hands, and
scrambled away, flailing his arms in an attempt to drive back any other
would-be attackers.

There weren't any. The only people still standing were himself, Tremblay and the hulking form of Erik Somers.

In the stillness that followed, he became aware of the van, idling about a hundred feet away, Zelda Baker behind the wheel. The front end of the vehicle showed scratches and dents, presumably from having plowed through the gate leading into the compound, but King also noted streaks of red on the fenders and bits of fabric caught in radiator grill.

Somers's face was uncharacteristically animated, and it took King a moment to realize that the big man was shouting at him.

If we make it out of this alive, everyone is learning sign language, King decided. *Executive decision, number one.*

He pointed to his ear and shook his head. Somers shouted even louder and began gesturing wildly toward the van. King could just make out a few words this time; it was faint, as if Somers was shouting into a pillow. "We need to get the hell out of here!"

Oh. Well, obviously.

TWENTY-EIGHT

CAN THIS NIGHT get any worse? Zelda Baker thought to herself as King, Tremblay and Somers climbed into the van. King shouted for her to drive, a bit louder than necessary, she thought, but she chalked it up to adrenaline. Things clearly had not gone well inside Building Two, and it did not escape her notice that they were short one man. She didn't ask. If Silent Bob wasn't with King, it meant he wasn't coming back. Period. Full stop. End of story.

Zelda stomped the accelerator and cranked the steering wheel around. The van's tires threw gravel as it carved out a wide U-turn and headed back toward the gates—or more precisely, the gateposts, since she'd flattened the actual moving parts of the perimeter defense a few moments earlier.

She spied movement in the rearview mirror. The things Somers had taken to calling 'frankensteins' were regrouping and giving chase, but even at a full run, they couldn't hope to keep up with the van. By the time the vehicle crested the hilltop, the frankensteins had vanished into the night.

She was just about to allow herself to breathe a little easier when the radio came alive. "King, this is Roadrunner."

'Roadrunner' was the callsign for Bellows, the man that had been left back at the gate. If he was calling in, it couldn't be good news.

King didn't reply, and after another half a minute, the voice repeated, but again the only answer was silence. Zelda glanced sidelong at the man in the passenger's seat. "You gonna take that call?"

He was staring straight ahead, but after a moment seemed to realize that she was addressing him. He turned and shook his head. "I can't hear you!"

His shout was loud enough to make her wince, and she could tell from his excessive volume that he wasn't kidding. She craned her head around and saw Tremblay and Somers both scanning the darkness, oblivious to the radio message or anything that had been said.

She keyed her transmitter. "Roadrunner, this is Legend. Send your traffic for King."

"Legend, be advised that two five-ton trucks just rolled past me, headed your way. If I had to guess, I'd say they're military."

Before Zelda could respond, the distorted voice of the mysterious Deep Blue broke in. "That's affirmative. I'm now monitoring their army radio net. Rainer must have tipped them off. They've dispatched a company of infantry soldiers to investigate."

Christ. It never rains... In her mind's eye, she saw the trucks with their big wheels rolling effortlessly over obstacles that had slowed the van to a near crawl. There were no other roads, no places to turn off and let them pass. If they stayed on the road, they would run headlong into the army trucks. She'd dealt with the Burmese military a few times in the course of her posting here, and she knew that if they were caught, the best they could hope for would be a swift death. The alternative was an indefinite stay in Myanmar's infamous Insein prison—the name said it all—where they would be subjected to brutal tortures, or worse, turned into propaganda puppets.

She turned to King. "More trouble! The Burmese army is headed our way!"

He shook his head and spread his hands helplessly.

Wonderful. For a moment, she wondered how she was going to make him understand the situation; should she try writing it down for him? Did she even have paper to write on?

"Oh, screw this." She stomped on the brake and threw the van into a three-point turn.

She heard the immediate protests from the others, but since there was no way to explain herself to them, she ignored their shouts. There were more important things to do.

"Nighteyes, this is Legend, do you read me?"

Shin's voice came back, sounding both concerned and relieved. "Loud and clear, Legend. Are you turning back?"

"You know it. There's no way out of here except on foot. If we ditch the van in the compound, the army might not even know we were here."

A new voice cut in. "Negative, Legend. The place is crawling with hostiles." It was Irish—the guy leading the sniper teams and King's acting First Sergeant.

Zelda felt the hairs on the back of her neck bristling. Was he actually trying to give her orders? She swallowed down her rising anger and with all the coolness she could muster, replied: "I guess it's a good thing you guys are looking out for us, because unless someone can find me an exit, we're doing this my way."

To her surprise, Deep Blue cut in. "Irish, Nighteyes... The road is closed. You need to provide cover for the rest of the team. Rendezvous in the woods and proceed to the second vehicle as Legend recommends."

The vindication was cold comfort. The truth of it was that they were now caught between a rock and a hard place. Somers had successfully beat the frankensteins off twice now, but this time there wouldn't be a moving vehicle to come to the team's rescue.

In seemingly no time at all, she found herself at the hilltop, staring down into the compound.

"Stop here," King said.

His comment surprised her, and when she looked over, she saw him nodding his head. "I caught some of what you said," he confessed. "My hearing's coming back a little bit. You made the right call. But I have an idea."

She glanced down into the compound where the massed frankensteins had noticed their return and were starting to move toward the gate. "I'm listening, but make it quick."

"Everybody out!" This time, King's shout was intentional. He leaned toward Zelda, and in a less strident tone, he added: "Leave it in neutral."

At last, Zelda understood. She straightened the wheel, shifted the gear selector to 'N' and then applied the parking brake before sliding out of the driver's seat. When everyone was out, she released the brake, whereupon Somers gave the van a hearty push and sent it careening down the hill.

Many of the monstrosities leapt out of the way, but nearly a dozen of them decided to meet the charge head-on—wild dogs facing down a charging elephant. Broken bodies went flying in every direction. The multiple impacts caused the vehicle to veer slightly to the right, and as it reached the compound, the front bumper crashed into one of the gateposts with a crunch that reached their ears a moment later.

"I guess we're not getting our deposit back," Tremblay said.

TWENTY-NINE

SHIN WATCHED THE van crash into the gateposts, and then he lowered his eye once more to the rifle's scope. Human forms flitted across his field of view, moving past the crosshairs, but they never lingered in one place long enough for him to take a shot.

The men with the Kalashnikovs—the 'gangstas'—had been the first priority targets. They were armed, and to all appearances, they had acted as the leadership element. They were the head of the serpent, as it were—for the larger body of unarmed slave soldiers. Taking the leaders out had been easy enough. Even when their comrades in arms had begun to fall, they had done what men in combat always do; they sought cover and started looking for a place to direct their answering fire.

Unfortunately, cutting the head off the snake had not killed the snake. Shin realized that he had misinterpreted the relationship between the triad officers and the slave force. They were not leaders or shepherds, marshaling a force of unwilling conscripts; they were the leash restraining a pack of wild animals, and now that they were gone, the beasts were running wild. Deprived of intelligent leadership, they simply reacted to anything that moved. Right now, their collective attention seemed to be focused on the small group escaping into the woods surrounding the compound.

There was nothing more for him to do. "Time to go," he announced.

'Race' Banion, acknowledged with a nod and stowed his spotter's scope in his backpack, as Shin broke down his rifle and prepared to move out.

True to his callsign, Banion sprinted ahead, and Shin, still nursing a sore ankle, had to push himself just to keep the man in sight. Worse, the Delta sniper wasn't following their original route, staying on the high ground where the terrain was more solid and there was less foliage, but he chose a direct route, bushwacking through the woods. Shin gave up trying to dog the man's footsteps, and kept to the longer but more familiar path he had used earlier.

The noise of the helicopter, which had been steadily powering up for several minutes, abruptly changed in timber and pitch as the aircraft lifted off the roof of Building Two, and for a moment, the deafening thump of its rotors beating the air overwhelmed all other sounds. Then, just as quickly, the sound began to diminish. Shin glanced skyward and saw the running lights of the helicopter moving away to the southwest.

Just before the din of the departing craft vanished altogether, Shin heard a rustling noise in the undergrowth, from the general direction Banion had gone. He stopped for a second, craning his head to locate the source of the noise, but the woods had already gone silent again.

"Race?" He spoke in a stage whisper. This far from the compound, there wasn't a need for absolute stealth. He didn't want to use the radio, preferring to keep the net open for communication with the rest of the team. "You out there?"

No reply.

He listened a few seconds longer, then he resumed his trek. In his night-vision display, he could see several glowing objects directly ahead, and he correctly guessed that they were infrared chem-lights Parker had deployed as a beacon to guide the disparate elements of the team to the rendezvous. A minute later, he saw Parker and 'Dark' Meyers, both in the prone firing position and facing in opposite directions.

Parker glanced up at him and then looked past him, searching the woods with his gaze. "Where's Race?"

"He took a shortcut. I expected him to be here already."

Parker frowned. "Damn it, doesn't anybody pay attention to what I say?" He keyed his mic. "Race, this is Irish. Do you copy?"

There was no response.

Shin's forehead creased in concern. It wasn't impossible that Banion had gotten turned around in the dense undergrowth and wandered off in the wrong direction, but if he wasn't responding to the radio, it portended something more dire. Shin thought about the injury he had suffered moving through the low areas in broad daylight; Banion could have similarly fallen and been knocked unconscious.

Parker repeated the message again, with no more success, then shook his head with a scowl. "King, this Irish. What's your ETA?"

Zelda's voice came over the radio. Her words were in short, clipped bursts, and Shin thought she might be running as she spoke. "This is Legend. King's comms are out. Estimate five mikes to the rally point."

"Roger, Legend. I have to go collect one of my wayward children. The rally point is marked with IR glowsticks, but we'll try to be back and waiting for you."

"Good copy, Irish. Legend out."

Parker rose to his feet and faced Shin. "Do you remember where you lost him?"

Shin felt a twinge of irritation at the implication that he was some-how responsible for what had happened, but he let the misdirected criticism pass without comment. Instead, he simply waved for Parker and Meyers to follow.

He had no difficulty retracing his steps, but as he returned to the spot where he had been standing when the helicopter had taken off, he realized that he couldn't recall exactly when he'd last seen Banion. He gestured down a gentle slope at the general area where he had heard the rustling noise.

Parker peered into the unlit shadows. "Race! You out there?" When there was no answer, he turned to the others. "Okay, spread out. We'll walk a police line. Maybe we'll trip over him."

Shin moved to Parker's left and placed himself about twenty feet away. Meyers moved to the other side. At a signal from Parker, they all started down the slope. After just a few steps, the tangle of vegetation broke up the orderliness of the effort, but Shin could still see Parker, and less distinctly, Meyers through the trees.

There was sudden thrashing in the foliage. Meyers let out a yelp and then simply vanished, as if a trapdoor in the forest floor had opened beneath him. A squeal of static and noise burst over the radio, followed by loud staccato cracks overhead—the sound, Shin realized suddenly, of bullets striking and breaking tree branches.

Parker, closer to the source, reacted first. He brought his MP5 around and moved toward the disturbance, shouting Meyer's name.

"Watch it!" Shin called out, moving quickly but in a low crouch, just a few steps behind Parker. "He's shooting wild!"

The random gunfire ceased. Shin reached Parker's side a moment later, and even though he knew that something bad had happened, nothing could have prepared him for what he saw.

Meyers appeared to have fallen into a waist deep hole, but that alone could not account for his look of raw terror. He thrashed wildly, directing frantic blows into the hole as if trying to beat out flames.

Parker thrust a hand out. "Take it."

Meyers looked up at him, his face twisted with both desperation and pain, but before he could reach out or do anything else, something moved beneath him, and he was gone, sucked completely into the dark void.

Meyers's screams rose up from the opening, but then were abruptly silenced, replaced by a very different sound—the sound of bones crunching.

Parker pulled back involuntarily, but then he started forward, as if intending to go into the hole after Meyers. Shin hastily threw his arms around the other man to prevent him, because he had caught a glimpse of something moving inside the hole. Something that wasn't Meyers...

Something that wasn't human.

Then he saw more movement, not in the pit that had swallowed the Delta sniper, but in the undergrowth all around them. Shapes were squirming out from beneath the trees all around them... serpentine... reptilian... enormous.

Shin recalled the words of the old gatekeeper. *"Buru... Nagas... Very dangerous."*

So this is what he was talking about.

THIRTY

AS THEY MOVED, King tried to assess the team's operational capability. The outlook was not good. Zelda had emerged unscathed—if bruised ribs could be considered unscathed—and she retained most of her gear, but she was the exception. In their respective scuffles with the frankensteins, he, Somers and Tremblay had either lost most of their equipment or it had been destroyed. They had a decent supply of ammunition in their vest pouches, but only two MP5s between them. Zelda had the only working radio and the only remaining night-vision device, which meant they all had to stay together or risk becoming hopelessly lost in the woods. To further complicate matters, the monstrosities were beating the bushes to pick up their trail.

The one piece of equipment King did still possess was his GPS unit, and he consulted it now to locate the rally point where Parker and the rest of the sniper team would be waiting. He focused on the dot in the backlit display that showed the direction of their destination. It was the only thing that mattered now.

The mission was a complete disaster; Rainer had slipped away, Sasha Therion was still a hostage, Silent Bob was almost certainly dead and it had all happened on his watch. Even worse, the night wasn't over yet; there was still a lot that could go wrong.

King's hearing had returned sufficiently that he could now hear the hooting of the frankensteins behind them and the snap of tree branches breaking from their passage. They were close, and even arrival at the rally point would not necessarily guarantee safety. Speed alone would save them, speed in reaching the rendezvous and speed in getting through the woods to the waiting vehicle.

They moved together in a tight knot, with Zelda leading the way and everyone else lined up behind her, close enough to maintain physical contact. In the darkness, it was the only way to keep from being separated.

He heard her voice and realized she was getting radio traffic. After a few seconds, she looked over her shoulder and relayed the message that Parker had just sent.

"Are they under attack?"

"I don't think so," Zelda breathed. "Sounds like someone got lost."

Damn, King thought. *More problems.* "Just get us there." He pointed in the direction indicated by the GPS. "That way, about five hundred meters."

"It's overgrown. Shin said he was able to move faster on the high ground."

A blistering retort rose to King's lips, but he bit it back. She was right, of course. Trying to blaze a trail, in the dark no less, was an exercise in futility. "You pick the route, and I'll keep us moving in the right general direction," he said. "But if we get lost, you have to promise not to blame the officer."

Zelda actually laughed. "Deal. This way."

She guided them up a hill where they could see the compound. The place looked completely deserted. A glow appeared in the distance, in the direction of the road, and then it abruptly rose like a tiny sun over the crest of the hill. It was the headlights of a Burmese army truck. A second pair of lights followed right behind it. As the truck charged down the hill, a few of the abominations stirred from their refuge in the shadows, and went out to meet the arriving forces. With a little luck, King thought, the Burmese would be so occupied with the frankensteins, they wouldn't even realize that his team had been there. He wanted to watch the chaos unfold, but a bestial hooting sound from behind them, answered by several more similar cries from all around, reminded him that most of the monstrosities were already in the woods and hunting him.

Another two hundred meters brought them to the place marked on his GPS as the rally point. Zelda picked up a plastic chem-light tube, which gave off light only in a spectrum visible through her night vision device, and confirmed that they had arrived.

"Those things are everywhere," Tremblay remarked without his customary humor. "We can't stay here."

King was about to agree when another cry tore through the night, only to be silenced as abruptly as the fall of a guillotine blade.

Zelda immediately keyed her mic. "Irish, come in." She listened for only a moment before raising her head to the other. "They're in trouble."

"Where?"

Zelda asked the question of Parker at the same moment King asked her, and when the reply came, she didn't bother to put it into words, but broke into a run, heading northwest.

Though Zelda had only been given a rough approximation of where Parker, Shin and the others were, the noise of a disturbance in the underbrush, growing louder as they moved, brought them to the spine of a low ridge. In the darkness, King could barely make out two human shapes struggling to climb the slope below. He started down to assist them, but Zelda snagged the back of his shirt.

"Wait!"

It wasn't her grasping hand or her admonition that stopped him, but rather her tone; she didn't sound frightened exactly—King didn't think anything could frighten Zelda Baker—but she was definitely rattled.

"There's something down there."

"What?"

"I—I can't tell."

The men on the slope were definitely fending off some kind of attack, alternately shooting into the darkness below their feet and trying to advance up the incline.

"You'll have to give me a better answer than that." King started to pulled free, but Somers was faster.

Moving with a speed and agility that seemed unnatural in some-one so big, he charged down to the other men and grasped one with each hand, heaving them bodily halfway up the hill. It was the boost the beleaguered Delta operators needed. Bounding to their feet, the two men—Parker and Shin—scrambled up to join the others.

Somers started to follow, but he had time only to turn around be-fore something snatched his feet from under him. The big man toppled like a tree, crashing heavily to the ground. He was whisked away into the underbrush.

THIRTY-ONE

SOMERS FELT AS though his left foot had been caught in a bear trap. Only the heavy leather uppers of his combat boots had prevented the vise-like jaws from snapping his ankle.

Jaws—yes, he'd been grabbed by something with jaws and teeth. It was an animal of some kind, impossible to identify, but low to the ground like a crocodile or alligator. The beast was dragging him back, into the thicket where, presumably it would do more than just nip his ankle.

Not today you won't.

Somers drove the heel of his free right foot into the ground and tried to wrench his trapped left foot loose. He was only partly success-ful. The creature didn't let go, but his mighty heave overcame the power of its retreat, and for a moment the beast was lofted into the air, still clinging to his foot. Somers caught just a glimpse of a thick, torpedo-shaped body with stubby legs paddling at the air and a long thrashing tail before his leg and the attached animal crashed back to the ground.

His earlier comparison to an alligator wasn't far off the mark. He judged it to be some kind of crocodilian reptile, easily twelve feet long from tip to tail.

The impact accomplished what Somers's initial display of strength could not. He felt the pressure around his ankle vanish; he was free. But he did not scramble back to the relative safety of the ridgetop. Instead, he twisted around and dove down the hill, probing with his hands until his fingers felt the rough, scaly skin of the thing that had attacked him. The creature wasn't moving, stunned perhaps, but Somers wasn't going to take any chances. He wrapped his arms around the thick body and wrestled it out into the open.

As soon as he lifted it off the ground, it began thrashing like a live wire, slamming its tail into the ground with such force that Somers nearly toppled over.

Nearly...but not quite.

When he had charged into the fray, he had released the cork on the bottle of his primal anger. There was no turning back. Driven by an inner fire that the ancients had once called *berserkergang*, Somers just squeezed even harder.

He felt his arms start to burn with the build-up of lactic acid. He was hugging the beast against his chest so tightly that he couldn't even draw breath. The creature's thrashing seemed to build to a feverish climax, and then, with a hideous cracking sound, its bones snapped and its torso deflated like an empty balloon. Somers held on through its death throes, but when he was certain of his victory, he heaved the carcass into the bushes from where it had originated.

The reptilian body landed with a crash amid a rustling of broken vegetation, but Somers's victory was short lived. A cold sliver of doubt insinuated itself into his battle-rage as he saw three more shapes dart out from the thicket to avenge their fallen brother.

Oh, he thought. *Shit.*

He backpedaled, but the things moved like dark lightning across the open ground. Then, seemingly without reason, the nearest of the things began to jerk spasmodically. Its tail swept out, knocking one of the remaining animals off course, sending it tumbling back down the slope. The third creature seized the advantage and hastened forward, only to suffer the same fate as the first.

Something had killed these two scaly behemoths.

He glanced up the hill and saw the silhouettes of the rest of the team—five in all—including a short man standing next to Zelda, aiming a large rifle into the thicket.

Somers felt the tide of his fury start to wane. "Good shooting," he said, his voice a low rumble that might not have even been audible from where the team now stood.

"Just returning the favor," replied the man with the gun. "It was the least—"

The rest of his words were lost as the din of automatic rifle fire erupted in the distance. The Burmese troops had engaged the frankensteins in the compound. Almost simultaneously, several dark shapes appeared on the ridge line and charged the team's position.

THIRTY-TWO

ZELDA WHEELED AND unleashed a burst from her MP5 that nearly tore the head off the frankenstein leading the charge. Parker also fired into the horde, but his shots were less precise, only wounding the attackers.

Unable to clearly see the abominations, King and Tremblay could do little more than step back and let the others carry the fight, but in an instant, two of the monstrosities broke through and closed with them.

King drew his only remaining weapon, a razor sharp KA-BAR combat knife, and thrust it forward. The frankenstein impaled itself on the blade, but its momentum knocked King back, and both tumbled down the hill. Somers bounded forward, arresting King's fall and hurling the frankenstein into the underbrush that concealed the reptilian creatures' nest.

Tremblay faced the remaining foe, but as it reached for him, he deftly stepped aside, grasping its ragged shirt as it passed, and redirected its momentum to send it crashing headlong into a tree trunk.

Just like that, the skirmish was over, but the threat was far from past. King recovered his footing and hastened back up the hill.

"We're out of here," he rasped. "Buddy up, everyone. Nighteyes, you know the way. Eastwood, stay with him. Juggernaut, you're with Legend. Danno, you lead me."

They moved out without further discussion, running—at least to the extent their various injuries made that possible—where the terrain would allow. For King, Tremblay and Somers, the journey was surreal; a game of blind man's bluff, requiring absolute trust in their guides, who not only had the ability to see in the near total darkness, but could also talk to each other and to the distant Deep Blue.

The long silence was too much for Tremblay. "What the hell were those things? They looked like alligators."

He had hoped the mostly rhetorical question would ease the tension with a little soldierly commiseration, and the only soldier within earshot was someone with whom he was particularly interested in commiserating.

"Shin says the locals call them *buru*."

Zelda's answer indicated that she had already asked the same question and received an answer. While informative, it wasn't quite the banter for which Tremblay had been hoping. "You mean he knew about them? Nice of him to share."

She didn't respond, and he decided to let it drop. Being attacked by some kind of weird mountain crocodile wasn't the craziest thing that had happened tonight. As he mentally ticked off the litany of horrors they had witnessed and the sacrifices that had been made, the fact of Silent Bob's death finally sank in. The realization led to another: he was now the last surviving member of Alpha team.

Damn.

After that, Tremblay wasn't much in the mood for bantering, even with the lovely Zelda Baker.

THIRTY-THREE

GENERAL KEASLING WAS waiting for them at the safe-house. He stood with his arms folded across his chest, saying nothing as the thoroughly dispirited Delta operators filed into the room and collapsed wearily onto the floor.

Ten had gone out. Only seven had come back.

They had reached the van after a harrowing hour-long cross-country trek. On three different occasions, they had encountered *buru*—the crocodilian species was evidently a nocturnal predator—waiting in ambush along their chosen route, but in each case, Shin spotted them in time to avoid a repeat of the earlier battle. The frankensteins had dogged their steps relentlessly for the first half-hour, but after that, the noise of pursuit had dwindled. When they finally reached the rented van, they climbed inside with barely a word exchanged among themselves. Zelda had handed her radio over to King, who promptly informed Deep Blue that they had reached the extraction point. He hadn't added that the mission was a complete failure; that was self-evident.

They picked up Casey Bellows on the return trip. Despite the fact that his role in the night's disastrous events had been peripheral, he shared their sense of defeat. Now, back in the relative safety of the Mandalay op center, there seemed little left to do but lick their wounds.

Keasling continued to survey the team with a stern look, then turned on his heel and scooted a large blue Igloo cooler into the center of the room. He threw back the lid to reveal several brown glass bottles sloshing about in a bath of ice cubes.

As if by unanimous accord, the members of the team stared at the offering like it was a crate full of spent nuclear fuel rods.

Tremblay finally edged forward and picked up one of the bottles. "Samuel Adams Boston Lager. General, I could..." He stopped in mid-quip, as if recognizing that this most definitely wasn't the time or the place, and instead he commenced distributing the beers. When he had completed that task, he raised his bottle. "To missing friends."

Everyone raised their drinks to the toast, but when they finally began to imbibe, it was perfunctory. King just stared at the bottle and shook his head. He raised his eyes to Keasling. "Sir, I'd like a word with you and Deep Blue...in private, please."

Keasling regarded him thoughtfully, as if divining King's intent. "Want to call it quits, son?"

"I blew it, sir. Three men are dead, and nothing to show for it."

"The fact that you made it out of there is a testament to your abilities." He gestured around the room. "That goes for all of you. So you got your asses handed to you; shit happens. The important thing is that you took the fight to the enemy, and he's the one that ran. You were ordered to run him down, and that's what you've got to do."

King remained unconvinced. "So, we're just going to watch and see where he lands next, and then go charging into another little shop of horrors? Do we just keep doing that until we finally run out of bodies to throw at him?"

"If that's what it takes."

Parker spoke up unexpectedly. "Jack, it's not just about beating him or getting payback. He's got Sasha. As long as she's alive, we have to keep trying."

King looked like he was about to throw up his hands, but instead he just rubbed the bridge of his nose as if trying to massage away a headache. "Kevin told me something back there; he talked about a paycheck. He's just the hired muscle. We need to know who's writing that check and why they need Sasha. Maybe if we can figure that out, we can get ahead of him. That's the only way we're going to win this."

There was a loud pop as Zelda smacked a hand against her thigh. She shrugged out of her backpack and rooted in it until she produced a laptop computer. "I completely forgot about this. I grabbed it from the room where we ran into Rainer. She was working on it when we walked in."

Parker reached out for it, and after a nod from King, Zelda surrendered it. Parker opened the computer and hit the power button, but a moment later he let out a frustrated sigh. "Password protected."

"If anyone can figure it out," King said, "it's you, Danno."

Parker however wasn't quite as enthusiastic. "Sasha Therion is a mathematical genius and a professional cryptographer. I think her password is going to be a little more complicated than the name of her pet goldfish."

"Is there another way to get around it?"

Parker stroked his chin thoughtfully. "Well, Lew taught me a few tricks... He's the guy you really want working on this."

"Done," declared Keasling. "It just so happens that Staff Sergeant Aleman has been assigned to the headquarters element of our new team. You should be able to link up with him using the equipment here."

"Crack that nut, Danno." King's expression was no longer that of a defeated commander ready to tender his resignation or fall on his sword. Whether it was Keasling's exhortation or Zelda's revelation, he had a little of his fighting spirit back. "Figure out what that bastard wants, and where he's going to go next, and just maybe, we'll be able to get her back."

THIRTY-FOUR

THE PASSWORD TURNED out to be child's play, relatively speaking anyway. Sasha's user settings were protected by factory-standard security software, which was not in itself unsophisticated. There was no way around the password lock without reformatting the hard drive and overwriting the disk's contents, and the password options were virtually unlimited, but it had one weakness that Lewis Aleman was able to exploit, and in short order, he opened Sasha's computer like it was Pandora's Box. That weakness was that there was no limit to the number of attempts that could be made to enter the correct password.

Ordinarily, that wouldn't have mattered. Even with unlimited guesses, it might take a lifetime to physically enter all the possible combinations.

A skilled hacker might be able to accomplish the same task in a matter of days instead of decades, but it would nevertheless be a daunting task even for the fastest commercially available computers.

Deep Blue had given Aleman access to something even better: the National Security Agency's XT3 Red Storm supercomputer.

The most time-consuming part of the process involved creating a virtual clone of Sasha's computer inside the NSA's system, a procedure that was limited by the download speed of the satellite Internet connection at the safe-house. The cloned version eliminated the laborious chore of manually entering all possible password permutations, or waiting for the laptop's comparatively ponderous Intel Core processor to run the security subroutine.

It took all of three minutes.

Trying to make sense of the contents of the computer took slightly longer; about half an hour altogether.

"It really is about trying to decode the Voynich manuscript," Parker announced after scanning the most recently created document files.

King, exhausted and sporting a veritably mummy's wrap of bandages over cuts and abrasions too numerous to count, didn't look particularly impressed. "Alright, Danno, you've been talking about this manuscript for a couple days now. What is it?"

Parker took a breath and affected his best professorial manner. "In 1912, a rare book dealer named Wilfrid Voynich came across a very unique book in a church in Italy. It was an antique, hand written on parchment and illustrated with full color paintings. That was pretty common for books from the Middle Ages, before the invention of the printing press, but what made this book really special was the fact that it was written in cipher text."

"Symbols instead of letters? Like the page we supposedly found in Ramadi?"

"Right. At a glance, you might think it's just another language or a different alphabet, but the symbols in the manuscript have never appeared anywhere else. Even so, there are ways to break a cipher, and usually the longer the message, the easier it is to crack. All you have to do is figure out which characters appear most frequently, and then compare them to the letters of the alphabet that are most often used, and you're on your way to breaking the cipher."

"Just like Wheel of Fortune; you start with RNLST and E. But what if it's not written in English?"

Parker shook his head. "That's not as important as it might seem. But in the case of the Voynich manuscript, professional and amateur code breakers from all over Europe have been trying to crack it for nearly a hundred years. The fact that no one has succeeded has led many to believe that it's a fake—a randomly generated message, created by a medieval con man."

King frowned. "Okay, for argument's sake, let's say that it's real. What difference does it make? What are we talking here: lost books of the Bible? Templar treasure maps, or something else? What makes this thing so damned important? What makes it worth killing for?"

Parker took a deep breath. "Remember how I said the manuscript was illustrated? It's full of detailed drawings, mostly of plants, but other things too, like star charts and animals. The popular theory is that it was a book of herbal or alchemical lore. That would explain why it was coded in the first place; it's a book of secret recipes, and who ever wrote it didn't want those recipes falling into the wrong hands."

King nodded slowly. "Secret recipes. Like the formula for some kind of nerve agent?"

"Or worse." Parker turned the computer around so that King could see the file he had been looking at. The screen displayed a picture of a badly damaged wooden box with several levers sticking out from the sides. "This was found in a crypt in China. It has markings that are identical to the cipher used in the manuscript. The crypt where they found this thing was hot with a strain of plague bacteria. In fact, the place where they found it might have been ground zero for the Black Death back in the fourteenth century."

"Okay, now you have my attention." King pointed at the image. "What is it?"

"It's a musical instrument, similar to an organ. The code isn't cipher text. It's musical notation. That's why no one has been able to crack it. The letters don't correspond to any alphabet; they're musical notes."

King just stared at him.

"Sasha figured it all out...well, almost. She couldn't verify any of her historic suppositions because they wouldn't let her have outside Internet access, but it all checks out."

Parker tapped the screen again. "This is what started it all. Some kind of primitive pipe organ, found in the crypt of a Chinese general who led the Mongol armies that destroyed Baghdad in 1258; it was a war trophy taken from the House of Wisdom."

"That was almost a hundred years before the Black Death," King pointed out. "How could they be connected?"

"Maybe they're not, but somebody obviously thinks they are. That's why they want Sasha to decode the manuscript."

King still didn't appear convinced. "Back up. You said it's musical notation. What did you mean by that?"

"Think of it as another layer of code. Each symbol corresponds to a specific musical note—we even use letters to symbolize those, A to G—so music is a form of language. The Voynich notation is obviously more complex, but that could be the difference between octaves or semitones—sharps and flats. I don't understand it all, but Sasha did. She was in the process of trying to create a virtual copy of the organ when you showed up tonight."

"Would that have worked?"

"The original was badly damaged. There wasn't enough of it left to even begin guessing how the symbols and notes corresponded. But Sasha was researching someone named Nasir al-Tusi, a Persian scientist and an advisor to the Mongol ruler. Al-Tusi was the Leonardo Da Vinci of the Islamic world. No, scratch that... He was more like Leonardo and Galileo and Isaac Newton all rolled into one. Based on what Sasha turned up, he's a good candidate for having been involved in the creation of the manuscript. He was also present at the destruction of Baghdad, and he even managed to save some of the documents from the House of Wisdom. Sasha wanted access to al-Tusi's writings, to see if the plans for the organ were there somewhere, but she never got a chance."

King considered this for a moment. "Those documents he saved; where did they go?"

"A place called Maragheh. It was an astronomical observatory, and after the destruction of Baghdad, the last bastion of science and learning in the Islamic world."

"I don't suppose it's still around today?"

"Yes and no. It's currently undergoing restoration." Parker clicked a few keys and the picture on the display changed to show an enormous white geodesic dome. "Everything in Sasha's notes indicates that she expected to find a copy of the plans for the organ in the archives of the Maragheh Observatory. There are thousands of documents there, but hardly any of them have been preserved digitally."

"So, the only way to get the specs for the organ is to physically visit this observatory." It was more a statement than a question, but King's next inquiry wasn't rhetorical. "The organ is the only way to decode the manuscript?"

Parker nodded.

King's lips curled into a smile that was both grim and satisfied. "Rainer will have to go to Maragheh. And we'll be waiting for him."

"Jack, there's a problem. Maragheh..."

"Yeah?"

"It's in Iran."

King blinked at him. "Oh. I guess that is a problem."

THIRTY-FIVE

WHEN HE FINALLY found a map that showed Maragheh, King's first thought was that it wasn't as bad as he'd first thought. The ruins of the ancient astronomical observatory were located in the remote northwestern part of Iran, only about a hundred miles from the borders with Iraq and Turkey, and at least four hundred miles from Tehran.

When he'd showed Keasling, the general had just rubbed his forehead as if the news had given him a migraine. "God damned Iran," he muttered. "Well, it's not my call. You'll have to take it up with your new boss."

Deep Blue received the news with no discernible reaction whatsoever; one of the advantages to being little more than a disembodied voice was that you could always just hit the 'mute' button if you didn't feel like letting the person at the other end of the line know just how pissed off you were. After a longer than expected pause, Deep Blue said simply: "What do you need?"

King explained his plan for the team to execute a High Altitude, High Opening (HAHO) jump. Unlike the High Altitude, Low Opening jump that Tremblay and Alpha team had used to get on the ground fast by free-falling most of the way and opening the parachutes at almost literally the last second, at HAHO jump required a paratrooper to deploy his chute at around 25,000 feet, and then glide the chute to a drop zone as far as thirty miles away.

"That will get you in unnoticed," Deep Blue replied, "but you'll still be a good fifty miles from the objective. Let me see if I can't come up with a better alternative."

The mysterious handler didn't give any details, but directed them to proceed immediately to the airport, where Keasling's plane would bear them to their next, as yet unrevealed destination. With that, Zelda and Shin packed up what few personal belongings they had accumulated during their time in Mandalay, and buttoned up the safe-house. Forty minutes later, they were in the air, and four hours thereafter, they were on the ground at Bagram Air Field in Afghanistan.

A five-ton military transport truck, driven by a pair of US Air Force enlisted personnel, rolled out to meet them on the tarmac. Bagram was a primary entry point for Afghanistan, and over the course of his military career, King had spent more than a few days cooling his heels in transitional housing there while waiting for a connecting flight or ground transport to some remote FOB. This time however, they didn't leave the flight line. Instead, the truck delivered them to one of several non-descript semi-cylindrical hangar buildings along the perimeter of the airstrip; the only noticeable difference about this particular structure was the fact that it was shrouded in darkness.

With only the beams of the airmen's flashlights to guide them, they were escorted into the Quonset-hut style hangar and up the boarding ramp of a large aircraft. King suspected it was some kind of stealth plane, but its interior looked more like a cargo transport. When they were all aboard, the ramp closed and the interior space became filled with an escalating whine as the aircraft's engines started powering up.

As if to answer the question King knew better than to ask, Keasling gestured airily about the hold. "I know I don't need to tell any of you that you were never aboard this plane. Officially, it doesn't exist."

"And unofficially?" asked Zelda, beating everyone else to the punch.

"Unofficially... Welcome aboard the CR-41 SR, stealth reconnaissance and transport aircraft, code named 'Senior Citizen.'"

Tremblay snorted disdainfully.

"Don't get too comfortable," the general said, without missing a beat. "Once we're aloft, we'll be flying at Mach 2—which should put you at the drop zone in a little less than two hours. That's how long you've got to get ready. Oh, and King...got some Christmas presents for you."

Keasling gestured to a stack of large plastic containers that were secured to the deck with heavy nylon straps. King immediately went about loosening the straps so he could remove the lids. Inside the containers, nestled in hollows cut from protective foam, was all the equipment they would need for their mission, but this wasn't just the replacement gear he'd asked Deep Blue to provide. The box held the newest, most cutting-edge—and most expensive—military hardware available.

One box held five sets of AN/PSQ-20 infrared/thermal night-vision devices, ASIP satellite radio sets with earbuds and lip mics and two ruggedized laptop computers. Another contained a bulky olive drab pack, labeled with stenciled letters that read: 'STARS.'

King was impressed with that. Deep Blue had actually signed off on his crazy plan.

A third was opened to reveal five XM8 carbines equipped with custom sound suppressors—one was also outfitted with an XM320 grenade launcher, and King passed it to Somers, who inspected the weapon almost reverently.

Beneath the top layer of foam lay dozens of plastic box magazines. These were already loaded with 5.56 rounds for the XM8s. There were also several ammunition cans containing grenades and other ordnance. King picked out a cardboard box that was not rendered in bland military olive green, like the others, and he handed it over to Tremblay.

For a moment, Tremblay stared at it uncomprehendingly, but then his eyes lit up as he deciphered the strange code printed on the label: *.50 AE.* "Oh, Santa," he crooned. "Stan was a very good boy."

As if transported to heaven, the blond Delta operator sank into one of the jump seats, took out his Desert Eagle pistols, and began pushing rounds into the empty magazines.

The normally quiet Shin watched him for a moment, and then with a grin said: "You'll shoot your eye out."

Tremblay threw him a one-fingered salute.

King indulged in the laughter that followed, but only for a few seconds. He wasn't looking forward to his next task. "Danno, Casey...a word in private."

He could see in their faces that they'd already done the math; seven Delta shooters, but only five sets of gear. Bellows's expression momentarily creased in disappointment, but then just as quickly transformed into a poorly disguised mixture of guilt and relief. Parker's eyes however, flashed dark with rage. Keasling seemed to sense that an eruption was building and stepped over to join the men, but he did not speak; this was King's show now.

No point in sugar coating it, King thought. *Just tear the band-aid off.* "You guys are staying in the rear on this one."

Parker, who was incapable of concealing his emotional state, trembled visibly with the effort of holding back an explosion of anger. In a tight voice, the words scraping past the knot in his throat, he said, "May I ask why, *sir?*" The last utterance was filled with palpable contempt.

King regarded his friend coolly for a moment, but then he turned to Bellows. "Casey..."

"No need to spell it out boss. There's always gonna be bad guys that need killin' but I'll only get this one chance to hug my kid."

He offered his hand, and King took it. "It was an honor serving with you, soldier. Now, make us all proud and do something really important: change some diapers, and shit like that."

The joke lightened the mood, but only until Bellows moved off to rejoin the others, who were now making a conspicuous effort to look busy by taking inventory of the new equipment. When he was gone, Parker wheeled on King. "What the fuck, Jack? You wouldn't even have this lead if not for me...and now you're leaving me behind?"

"Danno, that's exactly *why* I have to keep you back."

Parker blinked, uncomprehending.

"There's too much that we don't know, like what Rainer plans to do with the manuscript once he's decoded it. The only way to get a step ahead of him is to figure out a way to translate the manuscript first. That computer we recovered contains everything we know about the Voynich manuscript, how to read it and what it can be used for. And you're the only person who can make any sense of it."

"Sasha can." As soon as he said it, something seemed to click in Parker's head. "God...you're going to kill her, aren't you? That's why you won't take me."

"At ease, soldier," barked Keasling.

Parker stiffened, but his ire was approaching full boil.

King wasn't sure what tone to take with his friend; he'd never seen the man so spun up before. Parker continued to glower at him, breathing rapidly. "You don't need to leave me behind. In fact, you need me with you."

King shook his head. "No. If everything goes to hell—and lately, that seems to be happening a lot, I don't want that computer falling into the wrong hands. I need it, and you, to stay somewhere safe."

"Someone else can—"

"There *is* no one else. Just you." He gripped Parker's shoulder. "Dan, I'm going to do everything in my power to bring her back safe."

King could tell by the subtle shift in his friend's demeanor that he had chosen the right pressure point. There was more to Parker's outburst than his schoolboy crush on the stand-offish cryptanalyst, but it was certainly a factor. And that, perhaps more than anything else, was why King didn't want his friend in the field on this mission.

Because if it came down to it, and there was no other alternative, King absolutely would kill Sasha Therion.

He let the matter drop, sensing that further discussion would only rub salt in the wound. Instead, he moved back to the others. They had almost completely pilfered the contents of the containers, and now they were all settling into their jump seats in preparation for take-off. King braced himself against a bulkhead as the aircraft lurched into motion, beginning its short taxi to the runway.

"If I can get your attention please," he said to the others. "We're going to skip the standard pre-flight briefing—"

"Good," chortled Tremblay. "I think we all know that our seat cushions will do fuck-all in the event of a water landing."

King nodded, but kept talking. "I do have a couple of administrative announcements that might be of interest to you. As you know, in about ninety minutes, we'll be invading a sovereign nation—one that would very much like to tangle with us, if only to show the rest of the world that they've got the balls for it. If all goes as planned, we'll do what we need to do and beat feet out of there without anyone being the wiser. But you all know how quickly things can go FUBAR, so we need to be ready for anything.

"Each of you should now have an AN-M14 TH3 incendiary grenade. You have this for one reason only. If you are killed in action, one of your teammates will use it to cremate your remains and completely destroy all your equipment. There can be no evidence whatsoever connecting us and what we are about to do, with the government of the United States of America. Is that clear?"

There was a scattering of somber nods.

"If you are about to be overrun or captured, you will use your incendiary device to ensure that no evidence remains. Do I need to repeat that?"

He didn't.

"One last thing. We all kind of got thrown together without any preparation; it sucks, I know, but we're all professionals. The only constant is change, and you either roll with it or get rolled over. Here's the latest order." He made a purposeful decision not to look at Parker. "We have a new team designation, and each of you will have a new operational callsign. Tremblay, you will be called 'Rook.' Shin, you are now 'Knight.' Somers, henceforth, you will be 'Bishop.' Baker, you're 'Queen.' I will continue to use the callsign: 'King.' And just in case it's not already clear—Tremblay, pay attention, this is for you—those are all chess pieces.

"Kids, we are now the Chess Team."

INDIVISIBLE

THIRTY-SIX

Maragheh, Iran

THE CHESS TEAM dropped from the sky like avenging angels descending from the heavens, but no one took note of their arrival. They were silent wraiths, moving through the darkness, like their namesake pieces on a game board, maneuvering for maximum strategic effect, preparing and pre-positioning for the battles that would surely come.

Their LZ was just north of the bulbous white temporary structure that had been erected over the ruins of the Maragheh Observatory. Ironically, their ultimate destination also happened to be the best place to land their parachutes, well away from the orchards and vineyards that lined the outskirts of the city. While it was possible that they might have escaped notice in the agricultural fields, it was equally likely that they might spook a dog or do something else to wake up the occupants of the nearby farmhouses.

Working quickly, they established two concealed over-watch positions, each about a hundred yards from the white dome. Dawn was lightening the sky as they finished this task, and they hastily retreated into the camouflaged dugout blinds. King crowded into one with Knight and Bishop, while Queen and Rook took the other.

As the day passed, they studied the exterior of the observatory, following the movements of the archaeologists and researchers who came and went without ever suspecting that there were never less than two gun barrels trained on them at any given time. The observers took careful notes, assigning a number—and in some cases, a nickname—to each person they saw.

King's greatest fear was that Rainer would show up during the day, when the team didn't dare move from concealment, but that did not happen. Most of the people who visited the site exhibited a familiarity that could only indicate that they were employed there.

Dusk fell, and activity at the site dwindled to nothing, but the team remained where they were for two hours more. King would have preferred to wait until well after midnight, but time was a critical variable. He keyed his mic. "Queen, meet me at the door."

"Roger. Moving."

In the display of his night-vision device, he saw her, a bright human shape rising from the grass like some kind of spirit emerging from out of the ground, but in the near total darkness, she was virtually invisible to the unassisted eye. She stayed low to the ground, but hastened toward the dome.

King also rose from hiding. "Bishop, you're with me."

The big man didn't say a word, but unfolded himself from the cramped burrow, and fell into step right behind him. They crossed the open ground in less than a minute and joined Queen at the large doorframe set into the west side of the dome, which provided the only access to its interior.

Queen tried the door—locked—and then produced a set of lock-picking tools. King felt a momentary twinge at the sight; Parker had always been his go-to guy for opening doors, and watching someone else do the job was a reminder of the hard choice to leave his friend behind. He still believed it was the right decision, and he hoped Parker would eventually understand that.

The door knob yielded to Queen's efforts, and she eased it open a crack, watching and waiting for an alarm to sound. When that did not happen, she swung the door wide and moved inside.

The interior of the dome looked little different than the surrounding terrain. There were few structures inside; all that remained of the Maragheh Observatory were the cut stone foundations and a few crumbling walls. The trio of intruders fanned out, familiarizing themselves with the ruin under the dome, identifying several places where the archaeological team had begun the two-fold task of excavation and restoration, and more importantly, verifying that the site was not being actively monitored with remote surveillance devices. After about ten minutes of reconnaissance, they regrouped at the first dig site and descended a cut stone staircase into a sub-chamber.

A scattering of artifacts—strange devices and machines that had once been used to map the night sky—were arrayed on folding tables, but there was no indication that the room had once been a repository of documents. King photographed everything with a digital camera, then gestured for the others to follow him back out.

The second site, another subterranean chamber, had been only partially excavated, but the artifacts that had been recovered were strictly utilitarian—cooking utensils and pots, plates and cups. They moved on.

The next site was very different. The vast stone room had been completely excavated, revealing a maze of wooden shelves, the wood splintered and decaying, but nevertheless laden with ceramic tubes and leather chests. More interesting however, was a collection of tables with a dizzying array of modern laboratory equipment and hibernating computers.

King swept the room with the beam of his flashlight, which had been equipped with a dark filter that emitted only infrared light—invisible to the naked eye. He saw paper tags, inscribed with elegant modern Persian script, affixed to the shelves.

"Bishop. What do those tags say?"

The big man scanned a few of them. "Numbers and letters."

"Some kind of filing system?" ventured Queen.

King nodded and gestured to the tables at the center. "See if you can find the catalogue."

Bishop stared at him. "Me?"

"You're Iranian aren't you?"

"I grew up in Illinois."

Queen snorted in amusement.

Behind his night-vision goggles, King rolled his eyes. "I read your file. It says you speak Farsi."

"I took a couple of classes. I know how to order coffee and ask for the restroom." Bishop heaved a sigh. "I'll do my best."

As Bishop began flipping through notepads and ring-binders, perusing their contents with no evident confusion, King decided that his teammate was either selling himself short or he had picked up more in those classes than even he realized.

"I'm looking for anything written by al-Tusi, right?" the big man said after a few minutes. "There's a lot here. Is there any way to narrow it down?"

Before King could initiate a call to Parker, his earpiece crackled with an incoming transmission. It was Rook. "King, there's a vehicle approaching. You're about to have company."

THIRTY-SEVEN
Incirlik Air Base, Turkey

THE PASSAGE OF time did not cool Daniel Parker's ire. Instead, the longer he sat, alone with his thoughts, chewing the gristle of his bitterness, the more convinced he became that his old friend had forsaken him. Why exactly, he could not say. Maybe King was enamored with his new teammates...*maybe just having me around reminds him how badly he bungled the last mission...*

Yes, that had to be it.

Maybe he's trying to cover his ass, put the blame for the screw-up in Myanmar onto me, somehow.

Damn him.

He didn't buy for a second King's story about needing him to decode the Voynich manuscript. King didn't really believe there was anything worthwhile in the mysterious old book; its only value to him was the fact that Kevin Rainer seemed to care about it.

That thought gave Parker pause. Maybe King wasn't a believer, but Sasha definitely thought the book was important, and that was reason enough to take it seriously.

After the team exited the plane 30,000 feet above northwestern Iran, the stealth transport had headed for Incirlik Air Force Base in Turkey. The plane was refueled and refitted for the eventual extraction of the team. Parker found an unused office near the airstrip, and as he listened in on the team's radio transmissions, he went to work on the riddle of the Voynich manuscript.

He reviewed Sasha's notes more thoroughly, and he discovered that his initial perusal had only scratched the surface. Sasha Therion had been thinking about the Voynich problem for a long time, and she had recorded her musings in a personal journal. Parker scrolled through the entries, going back to the day that she had been contacted by Scott Klein and told of Cipher element's discovery in Ramadi:

There is a new lead on the Voynich manuscript. A page has been found among documents captured from an insurgent cell in Iraq, and preliminary findings indicate a connection between the manuscript and plague research. While it is a tenuous connection, it supports my hypothesis that VM contains information that might offer insight into the origin of life.

Parker couldn't recall Sasha mentioning any such hypothesis. He did a search of the journal, and found an entry from nearly two years earlier.

I am so weary of them all. Just when I think I have figured out the secret of what makes them tick, they do something completely unexpected. The human variable confounds me. I don't even want to leave home anymore.

I am going to take that government job. Now that I think about it, I don't even know why I hesitated. It's perfect. The Voynich manuscript. It's always fascinated me, but I never would have imagined that I could actually get paid to solve it.

He was surprised to learn that her CIA contract had been primarily for the purpose of cracking the Voynich code. He had always assumed that it was just one of many projects she consulted on. Based on that new information, he realized that deciphering the Voynich manuscript had become Sasha's entire reason for living. He skimmed through the subsequent entries until he found something more substantial.

The pictures must be the key to understanding VM. It cannot simply be, as many think, a book of herbal lore. The paintings show plants that do not exist, or rather, plants that we have never seen before. Those plants must have existed when the book was written; how else can the level of precision and detail be explained?

I am convinced that Bacon is the author of the book, though perhaps he did not work alone. I'm also convinced that the VM contains a record of his experiments. What kind of experiments? Did he conduct some kind of primitive genetic manipulations? That would account for the mysterious plants. Perhaps he created them in his laboratory.

"Bacon" had to be Roger Bacon, a 13th century Franciscan friar who was often credited as the father of scientific investigations. His published writings included detailed reports of his experiments with lenses, acoustics, botany and even a primitive form of gunpowder. One popular theory held that Bacon was the author of the Voynich manuscript, and indeed many of the illustrations in the manuscript were similar to known examples of his work.

Yet, I have to believe there is more to it than that. Methods of cross-pollinating and plant grafting were widely known in his day. He would not have felt the need to hide his research using such a complex cipher if that was all it was. No, I believe he must have uncovered something even more profound, something that could have made him liable for a charge of heresy.

What could that possibly be? I can think of only one thing. If the plants shown in the VM are not the result of genetic manipulation, and they do not exist in the natural world, I see only one logical conclusion: they were created. Bacon discovered the alchemists' secret, the Elixir, the Philosopher's Stone. Nothing short of the discovery of the secret of creating life from inorganic matter could account for his compulsion to conceal the knowledge in a code that seems, quite literally, unbreakable.

The Elixir of Life? Parker had missed that reference during his earlier reading. It was difficult to believe that the ever-pragmatic cryptanalyst's quest to decode the Voynich manuscript was anything but an academic exercise; this idea seemed so fanciful, and yet, he could not disagree with her simple logic. The complexity of the Voynich code demanded that its contents be of exceptional value.

Subsequent entries in Sasha's journal variously restated that hypothesis, but evidently her insights had not been sufficient to crack the code. He skipped forward to the most recent entry—made less than an hour before the disastrous raid and failed rescue attempt in Myanmar. Parker read it again, this time from this new perspective.

I cannot allow myself to think about what has happened. It is beyond my comprehension. The human variable confounds me yet again. If only I could find the solution that would allow me to subtract that unknown and balance the equation.

The answer lies in the VM. I am sure of it. If I can decipher the VM, maybe I can work backward and find a solution for the human variable.

I think I understand the connection between the urghan and the manuscript. Guo Kan led the Mongol armies that sacked Baghdad. He also traveled with Nasir al-Tusi. Now it all makes sense. It was not Bacon that wrote the VM, but al-Tusi, an Islamic scholar. I should have made that connection sooner. After all, 'elixir' is an Arabic word; it translates as 'the effective recipe.' Effective could be understood in the causative sense; not just a healing substance, but something that can bring life out of lifelessness.

Al-Tusi must have discovered the secret of the elixir and created the code to keep it safe. Perhaps, in his writings, I will find the key to deciphering the book. Perhaps he even kept a copy of the plans for the urghan with the documents he rescued from Baghdad and took back to Persia. It might be there at Maragheh.

I still do not understand the connection between the plague and the book, but I am no longer willing to dismiss it as a coincidence. Guo Kan had the urghan; did he use it to decode the book? Perhaps he tried to make the elixir, but accidently unleashed something else—an elixir of anti-life? Or maybe it was no accident.

When I have deciphered the book, I will know for sure.

Parker realized that he had been holding his breath.

Sasha's long effort to understand the Voynich manuscript was nothing less than a quest to divine the secret of life. It had become her sole purpose for living.

In a rush of understanding, Daniel Parker realized that his own purpose was to help her succeed.

"Damn you, Jack," he muttered under his breath. "You'd better bring her back in one piece."

As if in response to his utterance, a voice blared from the radio: "King, there's a vehicle approaching. You're about to have company."

THIRTY-EIGHT
Maragheh, Iran

SASHA FELT AS though her head was about to implode.

The variables had multiplied beyond her ability to enumerate them. They were coalescing in her consciousness, becoming a veritable black hole of chaos and uncertainty that consumed her thoughts. Her sleep had been erratic; there were huge gaps of time in her memory; dark periods where she must have slept deeply, but she felt exhausted and physically ill. Her techniques for tuning out the world—working through prime numbers, performing complex mathematical operations in her head—seemed beyond her ability now. She barely understood where she was; even the simplest of sensory inputs were scrambled in a fog of confusion.

She sat in the back of a large vehicle, an SUV of some kind. There were five other men there. Four of them had been on the plane; Chinese men, whose tailored suits did not quite conceal their true identity as thugs working for the triad. They had told her their names, but that information had already vanished beyond the event horizon. The fifth man had been picked up shortly after their arrival. He was different; he cowered fearfully in his seat, nursing superficial wounds that oozed blood. Sasha sensed that he was not there of his own volition.

A prisoner. Like me.

The realization slipped away, engulfed by the blackness of chaos.

Some time later—perhaps just a few minutes, perhaps days or weeks—she became aware of someone tugging at her arm. The SUV had stopped, and all of its passengers, save for her, had already disembarked. She allowed herself to be coaxed from her seat, but as soon as she was standing on the rough ground outside, she felt her legs go weak. She tried to lean against a fender, but the man holding her arm did not permit this; he drew her toward the front end of the vehicle.

She gradually came to understand that it was nighttime. The headlights of the SUV were illuminating a rather plain looking metal door set into a much larger white structure. The man—the prisoner—was propelled forward, and one of their captors barked a rough order. The prisoner fumbled with a ring of keys, and after a few moments, he succeeded in unlocking the door, after which they all filed in. Sasha and her minder brought up the rear.

Flashlights came out, but their beams revealed little about the interior of the white structure. Sasha wasn't paying any attention. This new experience only compounded her sense of dislocation; the dark tumor of uncertainty throbbed in her head, consuming even her desire to know what was happening.

The group descended a flight of carved stone steps, and they halted at last in a room that might have been the office at a construction site. One of the men barked something, and then repeated himself, but Sasha paid no heed until she felt someone shaking her arm violently. Through a monumental effort of will, she fixed her gaze on the man who had been speaking.

"Tell him what you want." The man spoke in a harsh, clipped manner, possibly a result of his relative unfamiliarity with English but more probably because he was a man of violence, used to getting his way with bellicose displays of aggression.

"What, I—?" Sasha shook her head. What was he talking about?

"We bring you here to Maragheh, like you ask. You say you need writings." He gestured forcefully at the prisoner. "Tell him which papers you need."

Maragheh. That was important, and she struggled to remember why. "Al-Tusi," she murmured. "In Nasir al-Tusi's writings, is there anything that describes how to construct an *urghan*?"

The prisoner, a middle-aged man with a full head of gray hair and a bushy beard, looked at her blankly for a moment, and he seemed on the verge of answering in the negative, but a menacing growl from one of the other Chinese men gave him pause.

"An *urghan*, you say?" He bent over a table and began flipping through a ring binder.

This simple act of compliance was a lifeline to Sasha in the midst of the whirlpool. *Maragheh. Al-Tusi. The* urghan.

These were not variables. They were the constants that anchored her to the world; they were known quantities and values that, while not yet completely understood, were fixed properties.

The manuscript.

Yes.

The Voynich manuscript was the ultimate constant. The knowledge locked within its mysterious cipher text would not change once she decoded it. It would be the same tomorrow as it was when al-Tusi had first written it down. But she would change.

The book was the irreducible prime factor that would enable her finally to balance the equation of her life...of the very nature of human existence. She believed this to be true with every fiber of her being.

I need to be here...right now...in this moment.

She willed herself back from the swelling tide of chaos and straightened, at long last taking in her surroundings. She knew that she was in the ruins of the Maragheh Observatory, which now rested inside a protective geodesic bubble that preserved its ancient stones and the scrolls and codices from the ravages of the elements. The man—the prisoner—was an Iranian, and probably one of the archaeologists or caretakers of the facility. Her Chinese captors had rightly deduced that they would not be able to simply walk into Maragheh and find what they needed lying out on a table. Sasha wondered if she would even recognize the document when it was finally procured.

"This must be it," the prisoner announced, tapping a page. "A treatise on the mathematical nature of harmonies. Al-Tusi's authorship is suspected, but not proven. It appears nowhere else, and it is not mentioned in any other writings of the time."

"Get it," ordered the leader.

The man moved into the maze of shelves, followed closely by one of the Chinese men, and then he returned a moment later with a copper tube. The lead captor snatched it from his hands and handed it to Sasha.

"You must wear gloves," admonished the Iranian, but before he could explain why, a savage blow to the gut put him on his knees, hunched over and moaning in pain.

Sasha witnessed the violence with detachment; her attention had already become focused on opening the case and teasing out the roll of parchment inside. The outermost curl, which had received the most exposure to the environment, felt stiff and cracked a little at the edges when she began to unfurl it, but above that, the vellum had, for the most part, remained supple. She carefully unrolled the document and spread it out on a tabletop.

It was immediately evident that she would not be able to read it; the careful and elegant script looked to her untrained eye like Arabic, but the accompanying illustrations filled her with hope. This was, unquestionably, a set of instructions for building the device that had been recovered from Guo's crypt. One illustration even showed the levers, marked with Voynich characters, and each one was connected by a line to the pipes of varying length contained in the body of the *urghan*. Though she could not grasp the specific musical tones that the pipes were intended to produce, Sasha could already see the mathematical progression that al-Tusi had employed. Given enough time, she might be able to work it out in her head, but she felt certain that, if afforded access to a computer and supplied with translation tools, she could build a virtual replica of the device, and with it, at long last, she could decode the Voynich manuscript.

"This is it," she breathed.

The lead captor did not appear to appreciate the gravity of her discovery, but he understood well enough that they had accomplished their objective. He dipped a hand into the folds of his jacket and produced a pistol, which he promptly trained on the other captive.

The Iranian's eyes grew wide, and he threw his hands up in a supplicating gesture. "No. Please. I did what you asked."

The Chinese man glanced at Sasha again. "You need him for anything else?"

Sasha blinked, not fully comprehending the question. The man might be able to help her translate the document, but there were other ways to accomplish that. What she really needed was a computer; her computer. "I don't think so."

That was answer enough for the Chinese man. He adjusted the barrel of the pistol so it was trained between the captive's eyes...

And then he abruptly pitched backward onto the ground. Before any of his cohorts could react, they too went down, pistols and flashlights clattering to the floor, the latter describing wild and random arcs of illumination before coming to rest.

Sasha stood motionless, unable to fathom what had just happened. She picked up the flashlight she had been using to inspect the document and swept it around the library. Her beam found a large figure, dressed in desert camouflage and heavily laden with military gear, emerging from behind one of the shelves. His face was partially obscured by a night vision device, and at the touch of her flashlight beam, he raised a hand to shade his eyes. Sasha saw that he held a gun in the other hand; wisps of smoke were issuing from its long barrel.

"Miss Therion!" The voice, a man's voice, came from another direction, and she turned to see two more similarly dressed figures moving toward her from a different part of the room. "It's Jack Sigler. Are you all right?"

Sigler?

She remembered him. One of the Delta commandos who had accompanied her in Iraq, and had tried to rescue her in Myanmar.

Her head started to pound with the effort of processing what had just happened. More variables. More chaos.

But this time, she was able to resist the pull of the vortex. She now had the key to unlocking the manuscript, and with it, the secret of the Elixir.

The solution was within her grasp. Soon, she would have the means to balance the equation, and at last, wipe away all the uncertainty.

THIRTY-NINE

KING HEARD A voice, a low whisper. It was the Iranian man, the hostage they had saved from a triad bullet, cowering on the floor, mumbling incoherently... No, not mumbling...talking into a cellular phone.

"Bishop!"

Bishop darted forward and smacked the phone from the man's hand, sending it flying across the room to shatter against a wall. He brandished the barrel of his carbine, thrusting it toward the man's face. "Who did you call?" he barked, and then he repeated the question in Farsi.

The fearful hostage muttered something in the same tongue and then continued pleading.

"What did he say, Bish?" asked Queen.

"He called the police. They're probably on their way."

"Damn." King continued forward until he was standing in front of Sasha. His gaze fell on the unrolled parchment. "It that it? Is that what you were looking for?"

She nodded.

King let his carbine hang from its sling and took out his digital camera. He snapped several photographs of the document before rolling it up and stuffing it into a pocket. "We need to get out of here, now." He keyed his mic. "Rook, Knight, sitrep."

Both men succinctly reported that everything was clear outside the dome.

"Deep Blue, this is King. It looks like we're going to be needing that extraction soon."

The electronic voice responded immediately as if anticipating the request. "Understood. The bird left the ground five minutes ago. ETA to the rendezvous point is twenty mikes."

"Roger, out." He turned to the Sasha again. "Where's Rainer?"

She gave him a blank stare, as if unaware that he was addressing her, but then she snapped out of it. "He didn't come. He thought the Iranians would be suspicious of a Westerner."

King felt only a flicker of disappointment. Taking down Rainer would have been the icing on the cake, but rescuing Sasha and recovering the information to decode the Voynich manuscript was nothing to sneeze at. He gestured to the bodies on the floor. "Who are they?"

"Triad foot soldiers," muttered Queen.

Sasha nodded. "Posing as a Chinese cultural delegation."

That made sense. Iran and China had a cozy relationship, with the latter buying most of the former's oil exports, keeping the regime flush with cash in spite of the sanctions imposed by Western nations. King hoped Queen's assessment was correct and that they hadn't just killed actual Chinese diplomats; one international incident was more than enough.

"Queen, stay with her. Bishop, check these guys for a set of keys. We're gonna borrow their ride."

Bishop jerked a thumb at the Iranian hostage. "What about him?"

King regarded the frightened man. "Let's hope that when the police get here, he remembers to tell them that we're the good guys."

They hastened out of the library chamber and back to the dome's entrance. Knight and Rook were waiting for them at the SUV—a Toyota Hilux Surf—and without any discussion, they piled inside. Bishop settled into the driver's seat and started the engine, while King, in the front passenger seat, busied himself with establishing a satellite data-link. The others crowded into the rear, with Knight and Rook taking the door seats.

By the time they reached the edge of the open area surrounding the ruins, King had started uploading of the images of the al-Tusi document to

Parker. Now, if they didn't make it out, the secret to decoding the Voynich manuscript would survive. Nevertheless, he was cautiously optimistic about their prospects. It would take a while for the police to arrive, and hopefully by then, they'd be long gone, en route to the remote pick-up location several miles west of Maragheh.

His good feeling lasted about a minute, the length of time it took for Bishop to navigate through the maze of exterior ruins and around old foundations to the paved road south of the dome. There, in the small parking lot, waited another vehicle identical to their own. Several men with Asian features stood vigilantly around its exterior, and as Bishop drove past them without slowing, they all began moving, shouting and gesturing animatedly at the departing SUV.

King felt a knot of dread in his stomach. "Miss Therion, how many men were in that cultural delegation?"

Sasha seemed blissfully unaware. "About a dozen. Why?"

King sighed and shook his head. "One of these days, everything is actually going to go according to plan; I truly believe that. Bishop...drive like hell."

FORTY
Incirlik Air Base, Turkey

PARKER FELT A wave of relief at the news of Sasha's rescue, but that did little to dull the sting of having been cut out of the operation. He couldn't begin to imagine the hell she'd gone through, and the fact that he wasn't there to comfort her only compounded his bitterness.

The computer chirped an alert, signaling that a download was in progress. He waited until the transfer was complete and then opened the file. There it was; Nasir al-Tusi's instructions on how to build the device that would decode the Voynich manuscript.

He scrolled over the text, cutting and pasting it into a translation matrix, and in a matter of only a few seconds, he was able to read the Persian scholar's words in English. He skimmed the introductory paragraphs and focused on the specifications for the *urghan*. Sasha had already constructed a virtual replica of the exterior body—the wooden sounding chamber that would amplify the musical tones—and the bellows system that supplied air to the pipes. All that was missing was the pipes themselves. Al-Tusi had fashioned them out of wood, and provided extensive information about the size, thickness, and shape of the pipes. The units of measurement were unfamiliar to Parker, but as he read on, he saw that even that detail was unimportant. The last section of the roll contained information on how to verify that the *urghan* was tuned correctly; each character of Voynich script corresponded to a specific note on the Persian harmonic scale.

Almost trembling with excitement, he began inputting the values into Sasha's program for the virtual *urghan*. With each addition, the program transferred the information into the deciphering subroutine, seeking out every instance where the Voynich character occurred, and replacing it with an alphanumeric character based on the musical scale, but Parker did not check it until the last value had been entered.

He had hoped that the manuscript's secrets would simply pour off the pages, but the book did not give up its treasure so readily. The output was an incomprehensible jumble of letters and numbers. He tried different variations on the musical scale, but each time the result was the same.

That wasn't a surprise really; all he had done was employ a common substitution cipher, and that approach had been tried innumerable times. There was an added layer to the Voynich code.

He returned to the al-Tusi document and read it again. Aside from the appearance of the unique script, there was nothing to explicitly link the *urghan* to the manuscript. The explanatory paragraphs focused mostly on the mathematical properties of music. Then he noticed the final paragraph.

"When once you have fashioned the organ, the music of the book may be understood with the indivisible numbers, each one in turn and one for each number, in the language of civilized men but according to the fashion of the infidel."

Parker gaped at the words on the screen. The 'book' could only be the Voynich manuscript, but what did the rest mean? The numbers part seemed straightforward enough; assign each musical note—as represented by the Voynich script—a number and then employ an alphabetic substitution.

Language of civilized men? To al-Tusi, the civilized world was the world of Islam, and the common language of Islam, even in Persia, was Arabic. That made sense, and offered one possible explanation for why the manuscript had resisted all previous decoding efforts. But something about that explanation nagged at him.

Of course!

Arabic, like many Middle Eastern languages, was written from right to left. The Voynich manuscript however was clearly written in the manner of the Western world, from left to right. That was what al-Tusi meant by "in the fashion of the infidel." The original text had been composed in Arabic, but then written backward, in the Western style, to confuse the uninitiated reader.

But the difference in language and composition style did not sufficiently explain the mystery. Read forward or backward, the text output from the manuscript remained without any sort of recognizable pattern.

He read the clue again. *Indivisible numbers.* The only whole numbers that could not be divided were the primes. Each one in turn. Could that be it?

A standard substitution cipher assigned a value for each letter of the alphabet: A=1, B=2 and so forth. With a cipher wheel, you could change the starting point: A=4, B=5 and on until you started the numbers over so that X=1, Y=2 and Z=3, but even this substitution could be easily defeated by looking at the frequency of certain oft-used letters. There were other ways to tweak the system, such as by using a keyword variation, but frequency analysis remained the Achilles heel of any substitution cipher. However, one way to render the cipher nearly unbreakable was to change the substitution pattern with every letter, rotating the cipher wheel a prescribed number of places with each letter. That way, letters and numbers would not correspond with any regularity.

Had al-Tusi done that, using prime numbers to adjust the cipher pattern with each new letter?

Parker plugged the new parameters into the decipherment sub-routine and let it run. He tried to keep his expectations in check, and braced himself for yet another disappointment. When the screen finally displayed the results, he was stunned to discover that he was able to do something that nobody had done in over seven hundred years.

He was reading the Voynich manuscript.

FORTY-ONE

Maragheh, Iran

BISHOP STOMPED THE accelerator but had to brake just as quickly, when a sharp hairpin turn loomed ahead.

"You do realize," he said in a low voice that was not altogether unlike the sound of rocks grinding together, "that just because I was *born* in Iran, it doesn't mean I know my way around."

Before King could respond, Deep Blue's voice came over the net. "Bishop, I'm tracking you on GPS. I'll guide you to the rendezvous point."

"Well that's handy," Rook said.

"The road continues straight for about a quarter-mile, then there's another sharp turn to the left."

The play of light on the embankment behind them betrayed the fact that the second SUV was moving; they weren't going to be able to just slip away. Bishop floored the gas pedal again, racing down the straight stretch, but before he got to the turn, a pair of headlights dawned in the rearview mirror.

King glanced back. "Knight, see if you can't shoot out their radiator."

Knight answered with a nod, and depressed the button to roll his window down as he twisted around in his seat. But as he started to lean out, something smacked into the rear window, shattering it. There were several more loud noises, the hammer-strike sound of bullets striking the rear of their stolen SUV. Knight pulled back without firing, and everyone ducked low, but Rook immediately popped back up, and aimed through the opening where the window had been. The sound-suppressed weapon made hardly any sound; the only indication that he was firing was the sudden storm of hot brass shell-casings that started pelting the other passengers.

The headlights started swerving back and forth as the other driver tried to evade the incoming fire, but then Bishop reached the turn, and for a moment, the pursuing vehicle was again lost from view.

King listened in as Deep Blue advised Bishop about the road ahead. There was another short straight stretch, followed by a hard right, but beyond that the road was straight for almost half-a-mile. King saw city lights ahead on the right; in less than a minute, they would be driving through an Iranian suburb.

"Let's take 'em on," suggested Rook. "We've got the firepower."

Queen chimed in as well. "I agree."

King felt like saying. *Great. When this is a democracy, I'll be sure to count your votes.* But instead, he just shook his head. "Negative. We can't risk getting pinned down here. Shoot back if you can, but we're not stopping."

The headlights reappeared behind them, just as they came along-side the residential area. If the police were not already on their way, they would be as soon as the people in those shops and houses heard the sound of shots from the triad soldiers' guns...or as soon as they started catching stray bullets.

"Bishop! Hard right now!" The electronic voice of Deep Blue crackled strangely, as if the software used to mask his identity wasn't sure how to interpret his urgency.

There was a broad paved boulevard running almost parallel to the narrow access road on which they now drove, but neither Bishop nor King saw any sign of the turn Deep Blue was telling them to take.

"Turn," Deep Blue repeated, even more stridently. "Right turn."

With unexpected suddenness, the road ended and merged onto the main thoroughfare...going the wrong way.

Bishop realized his mistake a moment too late. He stomped on the brake and hauled the wheel hard to the right, but it was an impossible angle, and the stolen SUV had too much momentum. The brakes locked, and there was a tortured scream of metal and rubber as the Toyota went into a spin.

The next few seconds were a blur of movement, but when King's disorientation passed, he became aware of honking horns and the head-lights of traffic on the main road swerving around the now stationary SUV. He also saw a pair of headlights coming from a different direction, and he realized they were the lights of the pursuing Hilux Surf, still on the access road, but about to reach the intersection. The vehicle carrying the team had spun around too many times to count, but had come to rest facing back the way they'd come.

"Bishop! Go!"

The big man, thankfully, didn't ask him to specify a direction, but cranked the wheel hard to the left and stomped on the accelerator.

Nothing happened.

The spin out had caused the engine to stall.

Bishop frantically threw the shift selector into neutral and jiggled the keys until the whining noise of the starter sounded, but the engine refused to turn over. He tried again, once more with no success.

"It's flooded!" Rook shouted from the back seat.

King didn't think it was possible to flood a modern fuel-injected engine, but Bishop didn't challenge the diagnosis. Instead, he pressed the accelerator to the floor and held it there as he tried the starter once more.

The engine roared to life with a plume of blue smoke, and the smell of burning petroleum wafted into the interior through the shattered rear window, momentarily overpowering the pervasive sulfur odor of gunpowder. Bishop threw the SUV into gear and they lurched into motion, joining the flow of traffic heading west, at almost the same instant that the vehicle carrying the Chinese thugs reached the intersection.

Their pursuers had to slow to make the turn, but the spin-out and stall had cost Chess Team several seconds of their lead. The pursuing headlights continued to get closer until Bishop was able to build up a head of steam.

King couldn't see the speedometer, but it felt like Bishop was doing close to seventy miles an hour. He swept around the other vehicles on the road like they were standing still, weaving in and out, and sometimes creating his own lane with a blaring horn. Unfortunately, the pursuing vehicle didn't have to contend with the same obstacles, because Bishop was clearing a trail for them, and so despite his best efforts, the gap continued to close. Two hundred meters...a hundred...fifty.

The triad thugs hadn't fired at them again, and King thought he knew why; they wanted Sasha back—alive and preferably unharmed. But if the pursuing vehicle got much closer, the gunmen inside would be able to shoot out their tires and bring the chase to an abrupt end.

"Rook. If they get any closer, use those cannons of yours to take them out."

Rook grinned as he drew his Desert Eagle pistols, and then leaned over the back of his seat and took aim. Before he could fire though, the SUV swerved left, out of his field of view, and made a move to overtake them.

Without prompting, Knight aimed his XM8 out the window and tried to hit the Surf's front tires. He squeezed off a few shots, but the moving target eluded him, and his rounds just sparked off the vehicle's chassis or burrowed harmlessly into the pavement.

Now the Surf was beside them, only a few yards away and nearly even with them. Knight gave up trying to hit the tires and instead aimed at the windshield, which he could now see was already fractured with a spider web pattern from earlier impacts.

Something was happening on the far side of the vehicle, but because his attention was fixed on the picture in his gun sight, Knight didn't see what the others did: a figure had crawled out of the rear driver's side window and was clambering onto the roof of the SUV. Queen saw it and so did Rook. The latter leaned over his fellow passengers and tried to aim his Desert Eagle up at the man on the roof, but before he could fire, two things happened almost simultaneously: Knight fired a burst from his carbine that shattered the front passenger window and filled the interior of the chasing vehicle with lead, and the figure on the roof coiled like a spring and then jumped.

The pursuing SUV abruptly veered right, evidently out of control, and ground against the side of the team's vehicle. Just as quickly, it rebounded and careened to the left, going off the pavement to smash into the exterior of a building. The members of Chess Team barely noticed the demise of their pursuers however; their attention was consumed by the crunch of something heavy landing on the roof of their vehicle.

"We've got a stowaway!" Rook shouted.

Bishop reacted immediately by tapping the brakes. Everyone inside was hurled forward by the sudden deceleration, and King expected to see their unwanted passenger thrown from his perch like a stone from a catapult, but that didn't happen. Instead, something crashed down on the windshield right in front of Bishop, but somehow, impossibly, it refused to be dislodged.

King stared at the outline of their attacker, splayed out on the other side of the glass, arms and legs stretched out, feet digging into the narrow seam between the hood and the windshield, and he understood how the man, seemingly in defiance of the laws of physics, had managed to hang on.

Man was perhaps the wrong word.

The thing clinging to the front of the SUV was human in the literal sense, but one look told King that this was no ordinary foot soldier of the Chinese mob. The head and unkempt hair were that of a Burmese youth, perhaps in his mid-twenties, but the arms and legs were grotesquely muscled, straining at the fabric of the man's clothes. The torso was malformed, as if he had been taken apart and reassembled by someone who had only the vaguest grasp of human anatomy.

This was one of the monstrosities they had fought in Myanmar—a frankenstein—but unlike those, this one seemed to be a new-and-improved model.

The thing dropped its head low and peered into the interior of the SUV, swiveling its gaze back and forth, searching for something.

It was looking for Sasha.

It found her.

The thing released one of its clutching hands, drew back, and punched through the windshield. The blow would have broken a

normal person's hand, but this creature was in no way normal. The
fist smashed out the upper corner of the glass, folding it over like a
dog-eared page in a book. Just as quickly, it grasped the exposed metal
of the Surf's roof in both hands and then braced its feet against the
hood as if getting ready to lift something.

That something was the SUV's roof. With a torturous shriek, the
metal skin of the Toyota began peeling back like the lid of a sardine
can.

King brought his XM8 up and let lead fly. The already compromised windshield fractured into a web of cracks, and beyond it, the
bullets tore into the monstrosity's chest. Blood, erupting from the exit
wounds and blown back by the wind, sprayed across the windshield,
but the thing barely flinched from the wounds. Driven by rage and
augmented by a stew of chemical enhancements, it shrugged off the
lethal wounds like they were mosquito bites, and commenced giving
the Surf a ragged sunroof.

Rook stabbed one of his Desert Eagles in the direction of the
thing's exposed head, but even as he pulled the trigger, unleashing a
thunderclap of noise in the semi-enclosed space, the creature moved.
It ducked out of the way, and then with a gymnast's agility, vaulted
from the hood, up and over the opening to land behind the gap,
impacting the roof with such force that the vehicle bounced on its
suspension.

For a moment, King thought the frankenstein had been thrown
clear, but a moment later the shredding of the car resumed. He twisted
around, trying to get a shot at the thing, but it stayed out of view, using the
curl of torn metal like a shield. King knew the 5.56-millimeter ammunition from the XM8 would pass through the thin sheet like it was tissue
paper, but so far the high-velocity rounds hadn't done much to slow the
monster down.

"Rook, blast that fucker!"

Rook didn't wait for a clear shot. He aimed the Desert Eagle at a
spot roughly in the center of the roof and fired into the headliner. The
entire chassis rang like a bell as the .50 caliber round punched an
enormous hole in the roof. Rook adjusted his aim to a point twelve

inches behind the hole and fired again. He didn't need to hit a vital organ; a bullet from the Desert Eagle could rip off limbs.

The tearing stopped.

Suddenly Knight's window was filled with the creature's head and shoulders. Blood streamed from dozens of wounds, but the thing was relentless. It had swung down from the roof and was now reaching into the Surf, stretching its fingers out to snare Sasha's arm.

Knight was pinned against his seat by the monster's bulk. Rook threw both arms around Sasha, trying to pull her back, but the prodigiously strong creature effortlessly dragged him along. Queen was the only thing between the frankenstein and its prey; she threw an uppercut that snapped the thing's head back. The monster gave a low growl and shook its head, shrugging the punch off as effortlessly as the bullets, but in that brief instant, Queen did something that no one expected. She reached under the shredded fabric of the monster's shirt, closed her fingers around the tubes that curled like external veins between its head and chest, and pulled. The tubes came free like clumps of hair, with scraps of bloody flesh clinging to the ends.

The frankenstein's limbs went rigid for a moment, like it was being electrocuted, but whatever Queen had done, it was still not enough to permanently stop the beast. With an agonized howl, it resumed pulling Sasha across the interior.

Queen kept raining blows into the thing's face, pummeling it unmercifully, but the monster did not relent. It drew its human prize closer, pinning Queen's arms down and crushing her against the already immobilized Knight.

King twisted around and tried to find something to shoot at, but in the tangle of bodies, there was no way to separate friend from foe. Instead, he reversed his hold on the carbine and slammed the butt of the weapon into the monster's head. There was a sickening crunch of bones breaking, but the creature refused to die.

Bishop stomped on the accelerator again, and as the Surf lurched forward, he swerved to the left. Locked in a mortal struggle, the other passengers were barely aware of the maneuver. None of them saw the delivery truck in the lane beside them.

The side panel of the truck was like a solid wall outside the windows of the SUV as the two vehicles scraped together with a hideous grinding noise, and then suddenly the Surf shot forward again, breaking free of the momentary effects of friction.

Rook and Sasha fell back as the creature's efforts abruptly ended. The frankenstein—or rather what was left of him, head and shoulders—toppled forward into the SUV and landed in Knight's lap. The monster's lower torso and legs had been crushed and sheared away by the collision with the delivery truck.

For a few seconds, everyone just stared in disbelief at the twitching remnants of the monster. Then Knight, with a shudder of revulsion, pushed the bodiless corpse away, inadvertently putting it right into Queen's arms.

"Oh, hell no!" She shoved it back at him.

King put an immediate stop to the gruesome game of hot potato by reaching back and heaving the remains out the open window, and for a moment thereafter, they all just slumped in their seats, too physically and mentally drained to say a word. Even Rook seemed unable to add his customary pithy insights.

It was Bishop that finally broke the silence. "Guys, we've got another problem."

That was when King heard the sound of sirens in the distance. Behind them, weaving through the traffic on the road and quickly gaining ground, was a long serpentine chain of flashing police lights.

FORTY-TWO

KING COUNTED SEVEN different sets of flashing lights, the nearest perhaps two hundred meters behind them. Then he became aware of something else; Deep Blue, was telling them that they'd missed a turn.

In the mayhem of the battle with the frankenstein, the task of navigating the unfamiliar roads hadn't seemed all that important. "Sorry, boss man," he broke in. "We're a little busy here."

"The road you are on will end in less than half a mile. You have to turn around."

Bishop glanced over at him. "Now he tells us."

King masked his concern with a sigh of mock-frustration. "I guess you should turn around."

"Yep," agreed Bishop and slammed on the brakes.

King was thrown forward against the dashboard, and he heard a collective howl from the back seat as everyone succumbed to the sudden deceleration. The Toyota skidded forward, enveloped in the tumult of noise and a noxious cloud of rubber smoke, and then it drifted across the road. It almost went into a spin, but Bishop kept making minor corrections with the front wheels to keep its nose forward until most of the momentum was gone. When the SUV was nearly at a complete stop, he let off the brakes and cranked the steering wheel hard to the left.

King felt his center of gravity shift and thought for a moment that the Surf was going to roll, but Bishop knew what he was doing. He stomped the gas pedal down, racing out of the turn, and headed back the way they'd come...and right down the throat of the advancing squadron of police cars.

For just a moment, King thought Bishop was going to challenge the Iranian National Police to a game of chicken. It was just the sort of thing Bishop might do, and—live or die—King felt certain that his teammate would never 'lose' in such a game. The police however, had no intention of playing along; as the Surf swung around to meet them, the lead chase vehicles broke formation and spread out to block both lanes. It was a hasty affair, and King felt sure that they could blast through with a minimum of damage. Unfortunately, the Toyota wasn't the only vehicle on the road, and now a traffic jam several cars deep was piling up in front of them. Bishop, undaunted, kept accelerating toward the impasse.

Rook leaned forward, staring into the sea of bright red brake lights. "Ummm..."

King resisted the urge to comment, waiting to see what fancy evasive maneuvers Bishop would employ to get them past the barricade. As they closed the gap however—eating up the distance in mere seconds—King started to question his assumptions about Bishop having a plan...or for that matter, being sane.

A millisecond or two after passing what King thought surely must be the point of no return, Bishop nudged the wheel to the left. The Surf missed the rear bumper of a stopped car by millimeters as it veered into the opposite lane, now cleared of traffic thanks to the roadblock.

The next few seconds were like an amusement park ride from Hell. King was thrown sideways by the sudden turn, and then pitched forward as the SUV slammed into the front end of a blockading police cruiser. The impact sent the smaller vehicle spinning, but barely slowed the Surf. Bishop cut back and forth, attempting—not always successfully—to thread his way through the maze of vehicles. The Toyota's bumper absorbed most of the damage, but each impact crumpled the fenders and the hood, and as Bishop slipped past the roadblock and into the now wide-open lane, King saw wisps of steam rising from the front end.

"There's a turn coming up on your left," Deep Blue intoned.

Bishop saw the side road, which angled away from the opposite lane, before anyone else. Without warning, he cranked the wheel over hard. To his credit, he managed to keep all four tires on the pavement, but everyone inside was subjected to more punishment. Over the screech of the controlled skid, the sound of gunshots was audible, but none of the rounds found their mark, and as Bishop straightened the wheels, the tumult momentarily diminished.

"Stay on this road," Deep Blue said. "It will get you to the pick-up zone."

"How far?" King said.

"Twenty klicks, give or take. Senior Citizen will meet you there."

King covered his microphone so that only Bishop would hear him. "Can we make it that far?"

Bishop glanced at the dashboard where the temperature gauge was starting to climb, and then shook his head.

Behind them, the police had regrouped and were now filing onto the side road to resume the pursuit. Even if they were able to reach the rendezvous, the police would overtake them as soon as they stopped.

They needed a new plan.

King glanced up, through the gaping hole the frankenstein had torn in the roof. Somewhere up there, a supersonic stealth transport plane was racing to a rendezvous that Chess Team would never make.

Suddenly, he realized the answer was staring him in the face.

He twisted around to the others. "Queen, get Sasha into a STARS harness. Rook, Knight... We need to turn this thing into a convertible."

Rook was the first to figure it out...or at least the first to say something. "Tell me you are not thinking what I think you're thinking."

"It's fundamentally the same thing we were planning to do anyway." King wasn't sure if he was trying to convince Rook or himself.

"I can think of one pretty fundamental difference," Rook grumbled.

Knight rolled his eyes and started digging in his pack.

"Don't be such as sissy," Queen chided. "It's probably not the craziest thing you've ever done."

She had already retrieved the large rucksack that contained the STARS gear, and after digging out a rig of nylon web belts identical to the ones they were all wearing, she rested a hand on Sasha's shoulder to get her attention. The cryptanalyst, who had been practically catatonic since the battle with the frankenstein, nearly jumped out of her skin.

"Hey, it's okay." Queen's manner was surprisingly soothing, a striking contrast to the tone she'd used with Rook. "It's all going to be over in few minutes."

She's right about that, thought King. *One way or another.*

While Rook and Knight set to work, affixing small shaped charges to the door posts and support beams that held the SUV's roof in place, King called Deep Blue and told him the new plan.

There was a long silence.

"Deep Blue, did you copy my last?"

"I copied, King. I'm just not sure it will work."

"Unless you've got a better option, we're going to make it work."

"I admire your 'can-do' attitude, but this is a question of physics. I'm not sure this can be done. Or that you will survive it."

King eyed the temperature gauge. The needle was creeping toward the red zone. "No time to discuss this," he said. "We're going ahead with it. Let Senior Citizen know. King, out."

"Jeez, it sounds like you're asking grandpa for a ride," Rook muttered. "We really need another name for that damn plane."

"Put it in the suggestion box," King replied. "Give me some detcord. I'll get the front."

Knight passed forward a spool of what looked like thick orange wire, but which was actually Primacord—plastic tubing filled with a thread-thin strand of the high-explosive compound pentaerythritol tetranitrate. King reeled off about two feet and carefully cut it with his KA-BAR.

"All set here," Queen announced, giving Sasha's harness a final cinch for good measure.

As King wrapped a length of detcord around the front doorpost on his side, Rook and Knight signaled that they were ready to go. There was a blast of warmth from the Surf's vents. Bishop had turned on the heater in an effort to bleed off some of the rising engine heat. It was a stopgap measure, and one that wouldn't keep up with the spiking temperature from the near constant acceleration. King tied the detcord off and then pressed a small blasting cap into one end of the tube. He repeated the procedure on the driver's side, awkwardly reaching past Bishop to do so, and then settled back into his seat.

"All set."

"Get down if you can." Knight's voice was eerily calm, but everyone took his admonition seriously. "Three... two... one... Fire in the hole."

The charges all detonated simultaneously with a noise as loud as a gunshot, but the smoke and heat of the small explosions was whisked away in the rush of air that swept through the now exposed interior of the SUV. The roof, cut loose from its supports, was gone, skittering along the road in their wake.

King now had an unobstructed view of the landscape in all directions. They had left Maragheh behind and were now traveling through the lightly wooded countryside. That was something in their favor at least. The open road meant almost no traffic to impede them, but it also meant there was nothing to slow down the pursuit. Behind them, the line of flashing colored lights swerved around the remains of the Surf's roof; the lead police car was perhaps only a quarter-mile behind them.

Queen passed King a pair of heavy-duty locking carabiners, both of which were connected at intervals to a long rope that sprouted from the rucksack. Everyone in the back seat was already clipped in. He hooked one to Bishop's harness and then secured the remaining one to his own.

Despite the noise of rushing air, King could now hear a rapid ticking sound, the noise of the engine block starting to expand as it heated up. In a few seconds, one of the pistons would probably seize and the motor would stall, leaving them at the mercy of their pursuers.

"Rook, send up the balloon."

Rook pulled a shapeless mass—it looked like an enormous deflated red football—from the rucksack and held it over his head. "Ladies and gentleman, in preparation for our flight, please make sure that your seat backs and tray tables are in the upright position, and I want to stress this, make sure that your seat belts are *not* fastened."

There was a whooshing sound as the object in Rook's hands suddenly expanded, filling up with pressurized helium. The wind whipped against the inflating bladder, but Rook held on until it was nearly bursting at the seams. When he let go, the rush of air seemed to yank it straight back, but as soon as it was clear of the Surf, it started rising, trailing a heavy line out behind it—the same rope to which they were all attached. There was a weird zipping sound, like two pieces of fabric rubbing together, as the cable spooled out from the rucksack. The balloon rose up and out of sight, and then with a *twang*, the line went taut.

Sasha gaped in disbelief, finally overcoming her shell-shocked paralysis. "That balloon isn't big enough to lift all of us."

"Nope," agreed Rook, sounding almost miserable. "But grandpa is."

"What?"

King heard a new voice over the radio. "Chess Team, this is Senior Citizen. We have visual contact. Hang on to your nuts."

Queen gave a derisive snort...and then she was gone.

FORTY-THREE

IN 1950, THE CIA and the Air Force decided to tackle the problem of how to quickly retrieve personnel who were deep in enemy territory, well beyond the range of the helicopters of the day and in areas that were too unsafe for a plane to land. The ultimate product of that endeavor was the Fulton surface-to-air-recovery-system—STARS—named for inventor Robert Fulton Jr. who had spent nearly a decade designing and refining the system. It was known more commonly by the nickname 'Skyhook.'

Subsequent advances in aircraft design and stealth technology, as well as improvements to air-tracking radar systems employed by unfriendly nations, had rendered the Skyhook system effectively obsolete; there were much better ways to rescue downed pilots and deep-cover agents, much safer and much more pleasant ways.

The principle behind Fulton's system was fairly simple. A transport aircraft would make a foray into enemy territory and airdrop a package containing all the necessary equipment: a harness, five hundred feet of high-tension rope, and a self-inflating balloon. The man on the ground would don the harness, connect himself to the balloon and then send it aloft. The whole process could be accomplished in just a few minutes. Once the balloon was in the sky, the plane would make one more pass, driving straight at the balloon. A special trap attached to the nose of the aircraft would snag the rope and yank the man into the sky.

That was where the really uncomfortable part began. The first thing the person in the harness would experience was sudden rapid acceleration—zero to two hundred miles an hour in the blink of an eye. The elasticity of the rope alleviated some of this effect, but the G-forces involved were enough to make some people black out. Next, came the high-altitude double whammy: freezing temperatures and low air pressure. While the plane beat a hasty retreat back to friendly skies, the unlucky CIA asset would experience the equivalent of climbing an Alpine mountain in the space of a few seconds. Last but not least, there was the spinning; an object trailed at high speed through the air had a tendency to spin like an out-of-control kite. This spin could induce dizziness, nausea or even unconsciousness. Fortunately, there was an easy way to stop the spin: the disoriented man dangling at the end of the rope needed only to extend his half-frozen arms and legs, spread-eagling like a body-surfer, until the air crew in the plane managed to reel in their catch.

Capture and torture by the enemy was almost a preferable alternative.

Officially, the Air Force ceased using the Skyhook in 1996. Unofficially, the equipment and the capability to employ the Skyhook was maintained by the Joint Special Operations Command as a 'just in case' measure.

No one had been especially thrilled by King's suggestion that they use the Skyhook to whisk them out of Iran, least of all King himself, but with time and resources in short supply for the team, and with secrecy a paramount concern, Deep Blue had signed off on it. There was the matter of retrofitting Senior Citizen to accommodate the thirty-foot long horns that would be used to snare the balloon—no simple task since the craft was designed for super-sonic travel. There was also the question of whether the pick-up line could hold the weight of six passengers; it was theoretically possible, but the system had never been used to pick up more than two men at a time.

What was most certainly not in the original plan was deploying the STARS from inside a moving vehicle while being chased down a rural highway by half the Iranian National Police force.

In a rare instance of serendipity, the forward momentum of the Toyota actually made things easier. Like with a kite pulled along by a running child, the line pulled taut, and the balloon—which was festooned with blinking infrared lights—cut through the sky in an almost perfectly straight line, providing an easy target for the pilot sitting at the controls of Senior Citizen.

Unseen by anyone on the ground, the stealth plane came from out of the west and streaked across the sky. Even without the constantly updated GPS coordinates supplied by the mysterious entity known only as Deep Blue, the pilot would have been able to find the target vehicle simply by following the string of flashing red and blue lights trailing behind it.

The pilot banked the aircraft to the right, carved a tight turn in the sky and with his computerized targeting system, locked onto the balloon. The plane advanced unerringly toward the blinking lights, and then, with textbook precision, it snared the balloon in the V-shaped trap.

One at a time, like an unraveling chain-stitch, the six passengers in the SUV were plucked from their seats. The empty vehicle cruised forward a few hundred yards before veering off the road and crashing into a stand of trees. By the time the police cars arrived, the plane, still trailing the Chess Team plus one, was already several miles away.

Because they were already traveling forward at about seventy miles per hour, the effect of the sudden acceleration was considerably reduced, though understandably, this was of little comfort to the six people dangling daisy-chained from the nose of the aircraft.

King had imagined that being jerked out of his seat would feel a little like what happened when his parachute opened during a jump— a sudden bone-jarring snap. He would later reflect that his erroneous assumption had been for the best; if he'd actually known what to expect, he never would have gone through with it.

For several long seconds, he struggled through a barrage of sensory inputs, all of them unpleasant. Biting cold ripped into him, blasting his face with such intensity that he couldn't breathe, much less open his eyes. Somewhere in the back of his mind, he knew that he was spinning uncontrollably, but the accompanying disorientation, coupled with the relentless assault from the wind, confounded his efforts to take any sort of action to arrest the spin. Mustering his last vestiges of will power, he unclenched his limbs from the protective fetal curl he had instinctively assumed, and extended his arms.

The sense of vertigo started to abate after a few moments, emboldening him to stretch his legs out as well. Now, instead of corkscrewing through the sky, he felt himself bouncing up and down, buffeted by invisible currents of air. He felt like he was trying to swim up Niagara Falls, but there wasn't a single thing he could do to end the ordeal.

Then, almost without being aware of the transition, the pervasive Arctic blast and the jarring turbulence stopped, and he felt something solid beneath him. His face felt like a frozen mask, but he managed to open his eyes enough to see two men in cold-weather flight suits dragging him up a metal ramp and into the relatively protected interior of the stealth transport's cargo hold.

There was a loud whine and a deep rumble as the ramp began moving, and then a metallic thump, completely cut off the howling of the wind.

At first, he didn't see anyone except the crewmen, and a wave of panic crashed over him. He tried to ask them for an update, but the words wouldn't come out. One of the men said something, a reassuring comment that barely registered through the lingering fog of the experience, and then King was wrapped in a heavy blanket. There were other blankets strewn about the floor of the hold, and after a few more seconds, he realized that nestled within each of the shapeless heaps was one of his companions.

He did a quick count. Five altogether.

They'd made it.

He huddled his arms around his torso, pulling the blanket tight, and savored the warm feeling of relief that came with that realization.

Eventually, they emerged from their cocoons, imbibed hot beverages supplied by the flight crew and displayed fits of outrage at the nightmare they had just gone through—some of it was directed at King, and not all of it was playful. King kept his distance, focusing his attention on Sasha, who seemed practically comatose; he wondered if she actually understood that she had been rescued.

When the plane touched down at Incirlik Air Base half an hour later, and the team members roused themselves and prepared to disembark. Rook loudly announced that the first thing he was going to do was kiss the tarmac. Sasha just sat in her seat, staring blankly ahead, as if she was waiting for further instructions. King gently grasped her arm and coaxed her to rise.

As they descended the ramp, a van rolled up and Daniel Parker jump out to greet them. King felt a moment of apprehension at the sight of his old friend. He had been so focused on the mission in Maragheh that he had completely forgotten about their earlier tense exchange.

But if Parker was nursing a grudge at having been cut out of the mission into Iran, he gave no indication. In fact, he barely seemed to notice King at all. He raced up the ramp and homed in on Sasha like a moth to a flame, his earnest face concealing none of his eagerness. He managed to stop himself before crashing into her...or hugging her.

"Sasha!" he said, unable to contain his excitement. "I did it... Well, you did. Your program and al-Tusi's writings."

She regarded him like he was crazy. "What are you saying?"

"The Voynich manuscript! You solved it!"

For the first time since meeting her several days earlier, King saw something like life in Sasha's eyes.

FORTY-FOUR
Incirlik Air Base, Turkey

KING HAD THE distinct impression of being a third wheel. On a unicycle.

Parker had always been an open book emotionally. He wanted to be alone with Sasha; King could read that in his friend's face as clearly as he could discern that Parker was mostly over any resentment at having been sidelined.

It had been the right decision, but King knew that one of the burdens of leadership was that you couldn't make everyone happy.

As far as Parker's crush on Sasha was concerned, King would have happily stepped aside to let his friend try out his best moves, though he didn't think Parker stood much of a chance with her. Where Sasha had earlier appeared indifferent to that kind of attention, she now seemed to occupy an entirely different plane of reality where Daniel Parker did not even exist. There was only one thing that mattered to her now: the Voynich manuscript.

King was also very interested in learning what the mysterious document had to say, though for a much different reason.

He considered the mission in Iran to have been only partly successful. Yes, they had rescued Sasha and retrieved the key to deciphering the manuscript, but one goal had eluded him, perhaps the most important objective, at least on a personal level. Kevin Rainer was still at large.

King didn't think his former CO cared much about the contents of the book. Rainer's motives were purely mercenary, but King felt sure that Rainer's big paycheck was connected to the matter of deciphering the Voynich manuscript. Understanding exactly why the man wanted it might give King the edge he needed to accomplish that one remaining mission objective.

While the rest of the team had gone off in search of food, beer, hot showers and a place to crash, King had accompanied Parker and Sasha to the office where a digital version of the book, with its secrets revealed at last, was displayed on the screen of her laptop computer.

Parker quickly recounted how he had used the information from al-Tusi's treatise along with Sasha's own deciphering software to crack the code. Sasha nodded, as if the explanation validated a cherished belief, but then dismissively turned her attention to the computer.

King glanced over her shoulder and read a few lines. Deciphered or not, the book was still incomprehensible to him.

"What's it say?" he asked Parker.

Without taking his eyes off Sasha, Parker said, "Let me give you some background first. The book was actually written by two men: al-Tusi and Roger Bacon."

"Bacon, I know that name from somewhere." King could almost hear Rook making a crack, probably in his best approximation of Homer Simpson, so he quickly added: "Some people think he was the guy who really wrote Shakespeare's plays, right?"

"No, that was Sir Francis Bacon. Although the two men had very similar interests, they lived about four centuries apart. Roger Bacon was a Franciscan friar who lived in the thirteenth century. It's long been thought that Bacon might have been the author of the Voynich manuscript; now we know it for certain.

"In 1247, Bacon was living in Paris, lecturing at the University, when he made an unusual discovery. He was conducting experiments with ground quartz lenses and realized that in addition to their other properties, the crystal could be made to vibrate at different frequencies—musical frequencies, like the way a soprano can make a wine glass vibrate and shatter. Even stranger, he discovered that when they were aligned with each other and facing in a specific direction, the effect was much stronger. He repeated his experiments in different places throughout Paris. When he compared the results, he realized that the crystals were pointing him toward something."

"What?"

Parker shook his head. "Bacon didn't know, but he decided to share his findings with another scientist; one of the most learned men in the world at that point in history."

"Nasir al-Tusi."

"Bingo. Of course, al-Tusi was a Muslim and theoretically an enemy, so they had to correspond in secret, using coded messages. Al-Tusi recreated Bacon's experiments from Mosul, where he was living at the time, and based on the results, they were able to triangulate a possible source for the effect, a place they called 'the Prime.'"

"Where was it?" King asked.

"They didn't record the exact location, but it was somewhere in southern France. The maps of the day weren't very precise, and they were relying on the crystal devices to guide them. Al-Tusi journeyed west, in disguise of course, and they met at the source to conduct further experiments." Parker took a deep breath, as if gathering his courage to broach the next topic. "That was when things got really weird. Bacon began to notice strange plants, like nothing he'd ever seen before, and he had quite literally written the book on botany. Eventually, he realized that there was a connection between the appearance of the plants and the timing of the experiments with the crystal devices. He tried different frequencies, and he was able to produce different varieties of plants, as well as lichens, mosses, fungi—all of them different than anything he or al-Tusi had ever seen before. There was only one explanation that made any sense; somehow, the plants were being spontaneously generated."

"Wait...what?"

"Life from lifelessness," Sasha said, not looking away. "They found the source; the Elixir of Life."

"I guess you could call it that," Parker said. "It wasn't a magical power like the Philosopher's Stone, but a combination of being in the right place and triggering the right frequency."

King shook his head in confusion. "Back up. Life from lifelessness? What does that mean?"

"One thing science has never been able to adequately explain, is where life came from. All life on Earth—every single living thing down to the tiniest microbe—comes from a living parent organism. If the theory of evolution is true, then all life probably traces back to one single organism—an amoeba or something—that got the process started, but no one can explain how that happened. Scientists have been able to create conditions where amino acids and protein molecules will naturally occur, but they've never been able to make the final leap—to bring them to life."

"You're saying that Bacon and al-Tusi found a way to do that? With...what? Crystals and music? Sounds pretty New Age to me."

Parker however nodded enthusiastically. "It's not so farfetched. There have been all kinds of studies to show that music can influence plant health. It happens at a molecular level. The crystals weren't even important. It was the music, or rather the specific harmonic frequencies that produced the effect. Al-Tusi built his pipe organ so that they could pin down exactly which musical notes did what."

"Is it possible that their experiments were just creating some kind of funky mutations in the plants that were already there?"

"Maybe. Even that would be a pretty significant discovery for the time, but they tried to control for all the variables, and they were convinced that they were actually giving life to inanimate matter."

"Okay, let's say I believe all that. What's Rainer's angle?" King turned his gaze to Sasha. "You were with him. Did you get a sense of what he wants from all of this?"

Sasha's eyes remained riveted on the screen, as if the information there was far more interesting than anything King had to say. She clicked to the next page, her eyes moving back and forth as she read.

"Black Death," she said finally. "The plague. Guo Kan, the Chinese general who fought with Mongols, got his hands on an al-Tusi's *urghan*. His experiments with it created the organism responsible for the Black Death outbreak in the fourteenth century."

"That's exactly why Bacon and al-Tusi encoded the manuscript," Parker added. "It's a how-to manual for creating new kinds of life. They were afraid of what might happen if it fell into the wrong hands."

"I thought that could happen only at that one special place, the prime location."

Parker shrugged. "The effect is most pronounced at the source. They weren't able to replicate their experiments when they left the area. But maybe there are other places on Earth with the same properties. Or maybe it just takes longer to see results; the Black Death didn't show up until several decades after Guo's death."

King pondered this possibility for a moment then switched gears. "Does the book say what's so special about this 'Prime' place?"

"Bacon speculated that it might be some kind of confluence of Earth energy. He had only a vague understanding of what that meant, but we know there are invisible rivers of geo-magnetic energy called Telluric currents that run through the whole planet. Crystals—like the ones he was using—align themselves magnetically. Maybe that provided the extra boost needed to start life."

Sasha shook her head. "The Prime is important because it is the original source. Every living thing on Earth is mathematically connected to it."

There was a hint of mania in her voice, and King knew he had to tread carefully. He had no idea what she was talking about, but Parker was nodding. *At least it makes sense to someone*, he thought. "So, bottom line, if the wrong person goes to this Prime place and plays the wrong song, all hell breaks loose, and that's a bad thing. Do Rainer and company know all this?"

Sasha appeared to consider for a moment. "I don't think so. That wasn't the direction they were going. But they understand that the *urghan* is the key to deciphering the manuscript."

King's hand moved to his pocket where he'd stashed al-Tusi's parchment. It was the only one of its kind, aside from the digital copy he'd sent to Parker.

The Voynich manuscript...the Prime location...the origin of life on Earth—none of that was really important. What mattered was that Rainer needed the information on that parchment, and King knew the rogue Delta operator would move Heaven and Earth to get it.

When he came for it, King and Chess Team would be waiting.

FORTY-FIVE

KING WAS WRONG in one respect. Parker had been glad to have him in the room, because it had given him someone to talk to. Sasha didn't seem the least bit interested in conversation. After King left, Parker watched her reading and tried in vain to come up with a way to break the awkward silence. He was surprised when she spoke up.

"You figured this out?"

He shook his head quickly. "No, you did all the work. I just plugged in the variables from what al-Tusi wrote."

"I'm not accusing you of anything." Something like a smile twitched across her face, and she nodded toward the door through which King had just passed. "Do you think he understood any of it?"

"Jack's a smart guy. But truthfully? It's a lot to swallow. The source of life? It seems a little farfetched."

"You're right." She looked at the screen thoughtfully. She was silent for a long time. "I want to go there," she said finally. "To the Prime. I want to see it for myself; to know if it's true."

Parker stifled an urge to laugh. She was serious. "I think Jack has a different set of priorities."

She crossed her arms, looking almost petulant. "Your team was supposed to be helping me, remember?"

"Sasha, we solved it. Isn't that enough?" He already knew the answer. The quest to understand the Voynich manuscript had come to define her life, and now, with the ultimate goal in sight, he was telling her to back off. He sighed. "You said that all life is mathematically connected to the Prime. What did you mean by that?"

"Why do you ask?"

"If I'm going to sell Jack on the idea of finding the Prime, I'm going to need a more persuasive reason than just to satisfy your curiosity."

It must have been the right thing to say, because when she looked at him, there wasn't a trace of irritation in her expression. "Life is a mathematical process. Each of us is the product of countless permutations that began with the Prime event.

"Think about your own life as a mathematical expression. You are the product of DNA from your two parents. And they are each the product of two. We are each the result of millions of such computations, and our DNA contains all those factors."

He nodded to indicate that he understood, but he still didn't see what she was driving at.

"But at some point, the process flips. The branches of the family tree start coming together and the number of factors reduces down to primes."

"Adam and Eve."

She inclined her head. "Figuratively speaking. Somewhere in history, all humans share a common ancestor, or, put another way, a prime factor. Of course, the prime factor for humans is just one point on a much larger continuum, but that too can be mathematically reduced to a prime factor—*the* Prime factor."

"Okay, I get that. Everything starts with something, chicken and egg. But that's not what you meant by a connection, is it?"

She pursed her lips. "Life is more than just the mathematical distribution of genetic material. There's something else involved that we still don't understand; some component or catalyst that got the whole thing started. It's in every living thing; it's what separates living cells from organic matter and a living human from a dead corpse. And the really remarkable thing is that this life-force—whatever you want to call it—is the same now as it was at the beginning."

"You mean it's the same kind of energy, right?"

She shook her head. "The same energy, undiluted and indivisible."

"How is that possible?"

"It's like using one candle to light another. The original candle might die out, but as long as you keep lighting candles, it's the same original flame you started with. It goes on forever." She turned her head. "Are you familiar with quantum entanglement?"

"Two particles interact, then separate but remain connected, no matter how far apart they are."

"Everything in the universe is entangled because all the matter in the universe originated with a single event, the Big Bang. But living things are quantum entangled in a very specific way, linked to the Prime event. Every living thing on Earth is connected, through time and space by quantum entanglement, to the Prime. It's like we're all plugged into it by an invisible extension cord. Do you see now why finding and protecting the Prime source is so important?"

Parker certainly did. "I'll take this to Jack. I'll make him understand."

"And if he doesn't?"

"If he doesn't, then I guess we'll have to go with Plan B."

FORTY-SIX
Langley, Virginia

THE PHONE ON Domenick Boucher's desk started ringing as soon as he stepped into his office, almost as if the caller somehow knew that he had arrived to start his workday.

That couldn't be a coincidence.

Like everyone else in the civilized world, Boucher had begun to think of his desk phone as a relic from another age. He hardly ever used it. He was so accustomed to using his encrypted digital phone that he preferred to make calls with it, even when in his office, and anyone who might want to contact him directly, would almost certainly know that and have used his cellular number.

With a frown, he picked it up and cautiously said: "Hello?"

"Good morning, Director Boucher," said an electronically distorted voice. "This is Deep Blue."

Boucher's forehead creased in concern. He was one of a select few who not only knew about Deep Blue—the one man the President trusted enough to run his new super-secret black ops team—but he also knew the man's true identity. Chess Team however, had no ties to the Agency, and Boucher couldn't think of a single reason why Deep Blue would contact him like this. There were other, much more direct routes of communication.

"I'm listening," he finally said.

"The team recovered your missing contractor last night."

"Sasha Therion?" Boucher's anxiety eased measurably. "Alive and well, I hope."

"That remains to be seen. There's been a new development."

Boucher listened without interruption, and when Deep Blue finished, he simply said: "I'll make it happen."

He then hung up and called for an emergency meeting with all senior department heads. Ten minutes later he addressed a conference room full of harried-looking staffers.

"As you all are no doubt aware, a few days ago one of our own, Field Officer Scott Klein, was murdered by a group of traitors. Sasha Therion, one of our contracted cryptanalysts was abducted in the same event.

"I'm pleased to say that last night, a Delta team rescued her. The team also recovered information relating to the development of an unspecified biogenic weapon."

He briefly glanced at the Director of Sci/Tech, the only man in the room who knew the full details of what Sasha Therion had been sent to find. The man's face creased in confusion at the seeming incongruity. No one else knew anything about the Voynich manuscript or what it purportedly contained, nor did they need to know.

A ripple of relief circled the room like a crowd wave at a sporting event. Boucher let them savor the news for a moment before dropping the other shoe. "At approximately 0900 Zulu time this morning—so about eight hours ago—our contractor and a Delta operator named Daniel Parker, went AWOL from Incirlik Air Force Base in Turkey. Their purpose is unknown, but it is believed that they might be on their way to the south of France, looking for a component necessary for the manufacture of the aforementioned biogenic weapon.

"It isn't known at this point if Therion or Parker were involved in the original incident. They could be acting as free agents, or they might even be working under the assumption that they have the best interests of the nation at heart. Regardless of their motives, it is imperative that they be found and taken into custody.

"The Delta team will be handling the operational aspects; our job is to provide them with actionable intelligence—review video camera feeds, cell phone calls, get our assets in airports and train stations... Hell, get out a damn Ouija board, if it will help track them down."

Boucher let that sink in for a moment before concluding. "Coordinate with my office for sectors of responsibility. Let's make this happen, people."

Boucher retreated back to his office and spent the rest of the morning assigning specific tasks to the different departments of his agency. He didn't expect immediate results; it would take several hours to collect enough data to get started, and perhaps days to sift through it all. Worst of all, there was no guarantee of success, especially considering for whom they were searching.

Parker had received the very best training in escape and evasion techniques; if he didn't want to be found, he wouldn't be.

FORTY-SEVEN

Shanghai, China

RAINER THUMBED THE button on his phone to end the call. He turned to face his employer with a satisfied grin. "We just caught a break that might make up for the disaster in Iran."

The other man, who had been lounging on a couch and idly watching television, looked up with a frown at the implicit insult. "I work with what I have. We both agreed that it was too risky for you to make that trip. Obviously, our gangster friends weren't up to the task of taking on the US Special Forces, but to be fair, we didn't know they would be there."

Rainer suppressed a chuckle. He had known; he had even said as much, but the billionaire had dismissed his concerns, claiming that Sigler and the others were almost certainly dead in Myanmar. Rainer hadn't believed that for a second, if for no other reason than that he and Jack Sigler had unfinished business.

Still, going to Iran had been a risk he wasn't eager to take, so he'd bowed to the other man's wishes. While the triad soldiers, in the guise of a Chinese cultural delegation, were getting their asses handed to them, Rainer and his men had been indulging in a veritable smorgasbord of pleasures afforded to guests of the five-star Renaissance Shanghai Pudong Hotel, where they had been holed up since their escape from the facility in Myanmar.

He waved off the excuse. "My agency contact reports that Sasha has gone off the reservation, and she's got help from Danny Parker."

"Should that name mean something to me?"

"Parker was in my unit. He's a good soldier and a smart guy, but I think he has a soft spot for Sasha. You know, she says 'jump'...well, it sounds like he jumped."

The billionaire still didn't get it. "Why has she left?"

"The official word is that it has something to do with—get this— 'biogenic weapons.' Does that sound familiar?"

The man's eyes flitted back and forth as he pondered the news.

Rainer went on. "I think our girl solved the problem, and learned something important from the book. The Company is looking for her and Parker in the south of France."

"France? What on Earth could be there?"

"I guess I'll find out when I run her down," Rainer answered confidently.

"Your decision to implant the RFID tracking chip in her when she was unconscious was fortuitous. That bit of foresight is going to pay off a huge dividend."

"Yeah, well that's me. Mr. Prepared. Speaking of which, I don't want to get caught flatfooted like those jokers in Iran."

His employer just smiled. "I think I can help you with that."

FORTY-EIGHT
Vallon-Pont-d'Arc, France

DANIEL PARKER BREATHED in the cool air and turned slowly to take in the panoramic vista laid out before him. Thousands of years ago, the Ardèche River had cut through the soft limestone landscape, leaving a deep gorge, and although the river's course had changed long ago, the place still remembered. He felt that it remembered something else too, something much more ancient.

Sasha got out of their rented Renault, but she didn't seem the least bit aware of the magnificent scenery. Her attention was completely fixed on the strange device she placed on the hood of the car—really nothing more than a board on which several irregular looking quartz crystals hung suspended by fine copper wires. Roger Bacon had once possessed such a device, and he had probably stood with it on this very spot.

They had built Sasha's version of the crystal array shortly after arriving in Paris, though hers was an upgraded model. The bare copper wires were spliced to a length of speaker wire that trailed from the microphone jack of her laptop computer. All she needed to do was push a button, and the computer would play a harmonic frequency that would vibrate in the crystals. The computer would then translate those vibrations into a graphic display, allowing for a much greater degree of precision than Bacon could ever have hoped for.

Sasha studied the display as she adjusted the position of the crystal device, just as she had done in Paris, from the roof of the hostel where they had spent their first night, and several times thereafter, to verify that they were on the correct path, following in Bacon's footsteps.

They kept to the back roads and avoided human contact. Parker knew they were being hunted.

He gazed once more at the wooded slopes that ran up to the sheer walls of the gorge, wondering if they were being watched right now, and if so, by whom.

Sasha made a disapproving sound as she fiddled with the device. He watched her for a moment, marveling at her single-mindedness, then finally he asked, "What's wrong?"

She pointed at the looming cliff wall to the north. "The signal is strongest in that direction, but it's not strong enough."

He circled around the car and looked over her shoulder. Based on her earlier calculations, they should have been practically on top of the Prime source, but sure enough, the crystals weren't vibrating with the feverish intensity he expected. He turned the crystal array back and forth, but the action only had the effect of further diminishing the vibrations. He returned them to their original position and stared in the direction in which they were pointing.

Had Roger Bacon and Nasir al-Tusi been confronted with such a puzzle?

"Right at the cliffs," he muttered. He tilted the array up, toward the place where the rock face met the sky, but once more the signal strength faltered.

No, not up, he realized with a growing sense of excitement.

He tipped the array so that it was angled down.

The pattern of oscillations on the screen practically exploded with intensity.

"You did it," Sasha said, almost breathlessly.

He savored the rare praise. Despite all that he had done for her,

Sasha still seemed unable to think of him in anything but the most utilitarian terms. He was a tool to help her accomplish her purpose, just as the CIA, the Delta team and even Rainer and his triad allies had been, each in their own way and without even suspecting it. This wasn't a cynical calculation on her part; it was just how she was.

Driven.

His initial physical attraction to her had cooled somewhat over the course of their days together, but his fascination with both her intellect and her personality had grown stronger. She was an enigma, a puzzle even more intricate than the Voynich manuscript, and just as he had solved it, he would also solve her. He would give her what she wanted, and when she had it, he would unlock that part of her that was capable of compassion, friendship...and love?

Well, he could hope anyway.

Her elation faltered. "But I don't understand. We have to go down? How is that possible?"

He scooped the array up and tucked it under one arm, then picked up the computer. "Let's go find out."

They left the road, skirted a small field of grape vines, and pushed into the pine forest. Parker thought he could feel the crystals vibrating against his skin. It was probably his imagination, fueled by the anticipation of success, but with each step forward, he could sense the energy of the Prime rising out of the ground, invigorating him and filling him with possibilities.

The woods ended abruptly at the foot of the cliff. Parker checked the array again; if the crystals were to be believed, the Prime lay somewhere within the limestone wall, perhaps fifty feet below them.

"Do you suppose this is as close as they got?"

Sasha's brow furrowed, as if she had never considered this possibility.

"We could test it here," he continued. "Try one of the formulae from the book. If it works, we'll have our answer."

She shook her head. "No. They found it. The book said they found it. You read it, too."

He knew she was right. While the Voynich manuscript had been short on details about what and where the Prime was, nothing in the account suggested that Bacon and al-Tusi had been stopped short of their ultimate goal. They had found it; somehow, they had found a way into the Earth's interior.

They skirted along the wall, scanning the rough limestone face for some shadowy niche, crevice or crack that might conceal a cave entrance. What they found instead, barely a hundred yards from where they started, was a door.

It was so incongruous that, for a few minutes, Parker could only stare in disbelief. There was a gray metal door with a U-shaped handle above a metal box with numbered buttons, pasted into a gap in the cliff face with dark concrete. It looked like the entrance to a utility corridor at a mall or an amusement park. Then he remembered where they were, and he realized what lay on the other side of the door.

He turned to Sasha, unable to contain his excitement at this revelation. "This is Chauvet Cave."

She blinked at him, the name evidently ringing no bells.

Parker laid an almost reverent hand on the door.

Discovered in 1994, Chauvet-Pont-d'Arc Cave was the site of what was arguably the most impressive example of paleolithic art on Earth. Carbon dating of charred timbers—wood used for fires to illuminate the cave for the artists—dated back more than thirty thousand years, making the paintings in Chauvet Cave the oldest known examples of human artwork. The walls of the cave were adorned with extraordinary detailed images of horses, bears, panthers—more than a dozen different species of animals, many extinct. Some of the paintings seemed to represent mythical creatures, chimera combinations of beasts that had never actually lived on the planet, or perhaps, like the plants painted in the Voynich manuscript, had existed only here and only for a brief time.

He had read about this place in National Geographic. What was truly remarkable about the cave was how well it had been preserved. Similar discoveries across Europe, such as at the one at Lascaux, had been severely degraded by thousands of visiting tourists, but almost immediately after its discovery, Chauvet Cave had been locked up tight. Even the scientists authorized to conduct research on the site had to observe stringent procedures to minimize their impact.

Parker felt his excitement roll back like the tide. "'Hitherto shalt thou come, but no further,'" he muttered.

"What's that? Something from the manuscript?"

He shook his head. "No. It's from the Bible...the Book of Job. Bacon and al-Tusi might have been able to get closer, but this is the end of the line for us."

"It can't be. We haven't come this far to be turned back now. Can't we break in?" She looked around, belatedly checking to see if they were being observed.

Parker balked momentarily at the cavalier suggestion; it wasn't just the illegality of the action—he did illegal things on a routine basis in the interest of a greater good—but rather the immorality of it. This was a sacred place; a treasure to be preserved, not desecrated.

Yet, what if the very reason it had been venerated by those ancient artists was because it contained the thing they now sought? What if those primitive cave painters had, perhaps even without really knowing it, intuitively recognized that this place was a source of life?

The source of life.

Sasha was right. They had come too far to turn back now.

He stared at the door a moment longer, trying to think of the best way to get past it. He hadn't been able to bring along explosives for a breaching charge; he didn't even have a Swiss Army knife.

"Something's not right here." He turned to Sasha. "The original entrance to this cave was sealed up by a landslide about twenty thousand years ago. That's why it's so well preserved."

"So?"

"So, this entrance wasn't discovered until just a few years ago. And I would be willing to bet money that Bacon and al-Tusi didn't come this way."

"Then there's another entrance?"

"Maybe. But I think there's another answer; an answer worthy of the men who wrote the Voynich manuscript." He offered her an outstretched hand. "Do you trust me?"

He saw immediately that she did not, not unreservedly. His heart sank like a stone. After everything he had done for her, all the risks and sacrifice... She still couldn't find it in her heart to give him the benefit of the doubt. She stared at his hand warily, but finally took it, clasping his fingers as if to indicate that she would comply, but only on her own terms. Parker struggled back from the event horizon of his emotions, and he gave her hand an awkward squeeze. Then, he led her back the way they'd come.

Parker set down the computer. In response to an unspoken question, he said: "What do we know about the Prime? It's a place where harmonic frequencies can be used to radically alter the composition of matter, right?"

"You don't mean...?"

"It's what the alchemists were always looking for. They understood the connection, but they didn't have the technological know-how. We already know that wave energy can have an effect on the states of matter; what do you think a microwave oven does? It causes water molecules to vibrate, which releases heat."

Her eyes began darting back and forth, processing his suggestions, calculating. Then her expression changed.

Not just her expression.

He felt her hand shift in his, sliding up so that their palms were facing.

Then the moment passed. She let go and knelt at the computer, once more consumed by calculations that had nothing at all to do with him.

He heard the sound of her fingers tapping on the keyboard, but then he heard something else that drew his attention away. It wasn't a distinctive sound, more of a change in atmosphere than anything else, but it chilled him nevertheless. He scanned the tree line and saw movement.

Then he saw people, and before he could utter even a word of warning, he recognized one of the men striding toward them.

Kevin Rainer.

FORTY-NINE

FOR JUST A few moments, Sasha felt the sublime satisfaction of a balanced equation. Order had come into her world at last. The Voynich manuscript had given up its secrets, and in so doing, had shown her the underlying arithmetic of the entire universe. She deftly entered information into the virtual *urghan*, instructing it to play a combination of notes—a specific low frequency sound—and then hit the key that would turn data into music.

The next sound she heard however was not a deep resonant bass tone, but a human voice; the voice of her former captor. "Hello again."

Even before she could look up, a lighting bolt of pure chaos ripped through her. *No. Not now. Not again.*

Rainer and four other men stood in a semi-circle around her and Parker. She recognized two of the men—the two rogue Night Stalker crewmen—but the other two were not really men at all; short but massively muscled, they were the hideous science projects that the Chess Team had dubbed 'frankensteins.' The renegade soldiers were armed with compact machine pistols but the frankensteins needed no weapons.

Parker had gone rigid beside her, as if straining to hold back an eruption of fear or rage—probably rage—but when he spoke, his voice was flat, emotionless. "Kevin. How did you find us?"

"I took the liberty of tagging your little girlfriend when she was my guest."

"GPS trackers have a very limited range. You couldn't have known we'd be coming here."

Rainer smiled. "You hear all kinds of funny rumors these days. For example, I heard that you might be thinking of changing careers. I just might have a place in my organization for you, especially if..." He nodded toward Sasha. "...you can help me babysit our girl genius."

Sasha squeezed her eyes shut.

Go away!

The words were a silent scream in her head.

Go away. Leave me alone. Let me finish.

"Here's how I see it," Rainer continued. "You're on your own right now. Jack is looking for you; he knows you're here in France. How long do you think you can stay ahead of him? Come with me and you get to spend as much time with her as you want. You'd like that, right?"

"Just like that?" said Parker. "I'm supposed to believe that you would trust me?"

"Danny, you've always had a lousy poker face. I can see the wheels turning in your head. You know this is the best option."

Sasha barely heard the words being exchanged between the men, the striking of a bargain in which she was merely an object. Parker was no different than any other human variable; unpredictable, inconsistent and driven by animal passions and irrational emotions. He wasn't interested in helping her resolve the equation, but only in possessing her.

Chaos swirled around in a haze of white noise.

No, not white noise...a real sound, vibrating through her bones.

Her eyes flew open.

The others hadn't noticed it yet; they were too consumed with their mundane game of life and death.

The ground beneath her was rippling faintly, like the surface of a pond disturbed by a cast stone. She turned her head slowly and saw that the effect was spreading to the limestone face of the cliff. The dull white rock seemed to be shimmering, as if made of fog.

It's working!

The door to the Prime was opening, just as Parker had said it would. *So close.*

The thing she had sought for so long—the solution that would balance the equation of existence—was about to be taken away from her by another damnable human variable.

Rainer drew in a deep breath and then let it out with a dramatic sigh. "Maybe I was wrong about you, Danny. Here's the thing. We're leaving with your girlfriend. You can come along, or I can put a bullet between your eyes. Seems like a simple choice to me, but..." He shrugged.

"Don't make me go," Sasha whispered, barely able to get the

words out. She reached up and found Parker's hand. She squeezed it tight. "Please."

He looked down at her, his earnest face hiding none of his fear and concern...his affection. Then he turned his eyes back to Rainer and muttered. "Could use a little help here, Jack."

Confusion flickered across Rainer's face, but before it could give way to comprehension, there was a loud *smack*, and the head of one of the frankensteins blew apart in a fine red mist.

FIFTY

IN THE INSTANT that the bullet from Knight's Barrett M82 sniper rifle erased the frankenstein's head, King and the rest of the team broke from cover and swept toward the rock wall. They bounded forward in pairs. King and Bishop stopped and fired off a few rounds, aiming high so as not to hit Parker and Sasha, while Rook and Queen raced forward a few feet, and then they would switch roles.

Knight managed to get a second shot off before Rainer and the others could fully process what was happening, but this time his bullet only grazed the target.

They had debated how to best use that first decisive shot; eliminate Rainer, cutting the head off the snake as it were, or take out the frankensteins. The latter won out. Based on their experiences with the monstrosities in Burma and Iran, the frankensteins were the bigger threat. Deprived of leadership, they could still wreak unimaginable harm.

As he hit the ground, rolling left and coming back up into a prone firing position, King saw that the decision to target the frankenstein had yielded the expected results: Rainer and his men were retreating, Parker had thrown himself over Sasha and they were huddled near the rock face, and the sole remaining frankenstein, bleeding copiously from its left shoulder, was charging headlong toward Rook and Queen. King turned the barrel of his XM8 toward the creature, but before he could get a shot off, Rook came up with one of his enormous

Desert Eagle pistols.

His first shot caught the frankenstein full in the chest, the .50 caliber round staggering the creature back like a battering ram. For most living things, it would have been a lethal shot—it probably was for the chemical-crazed frankenstein as well, but Rook didn't take chances. He fought the massive pistol's recoil with a two-handed grip, brought it level and fired again. This time, there was no uncertainty about the outcome; the bullet tore off the top of the abomination's skull.

King swung his barrel back toward Rainer, but the rogue Delta commander and his men were zigzagging back into the tree line, returning fire blindly to cover their escape. King got off a few shots before the running men disappeared into the boughs.

"Rook, Queen, go after them."

King wanted to give chase as well—hunt the rabid Rainer down and personally put him out of everyone's misery once and for all—but first he had to make sure that Parker and Sasha were okay. He had used them, dangled them in front of Rainer like bait, played them like pawns in his own private chess game, and even though everything seemed to have gone according to plan, if anything happened to them, it would be on his head.

He keyed his microphone. "Irish, this is King. I'm coming to you."

Parker had known the risks. When he'd come to King in Turkey and asked for permission to take Sasha on some kind of treasure hunt, King had seized on it as an opportunity not only to lure Rainer into the open but also perhaps to smoke out any security leaks at CIA and JSOC. Nevertheless, he had been forthright with respect to the dangers he and Sasha would be facing.

"It will have to look absolutely real," he had told Parker. "You'll be unarmed, no support, the CIA will be hunting for you. We'll try to stay one step ahead of you, but if Rainer makes his move and we're not ready..."

Parker had obviously been concerned about putting Sasha at risk, but he understood what was at stake. "Make sure that doesn't happen."

It had been a close thing, but the plan had worked. Thanks to

Parker's stealthy radio calls, the team had finally gotten ahead of Rainer and been waiting to spring the trap. Now King just had to make sure that Parker and Sasha were okay.

"Danno!"

Parker raised his head just a little, mindful of the fact that bullets were still flying not far away. "Cut it pretty close, Jack."

King breathed a sigh of relief. Sasha looked a little freaked out—when didn't she?—but both were unhurt.

"Come on. Let's get you guys out of here."

Sasha's head came up. Her gaze flitted between the men for a moment, then her eyes locked on Parker. "This was a setup?"

Parker gave a heavy sigh. "Sasha, I'm so sorry. We had to flush Rainer out. It was the only way."

She kept staring at him with such intensity that King feared his friend might melt, figuratively at least, from the rage she was putting out. He wondered if this was a risk Parker had considered when he'd agreed to the plan.

Sasha abruptly dropped her gaze and looked around furtively. Then, moving quicker than King had ever seen her move, she grabbed her computer and hurled herself toward the looming rock wall...

And vanished.

King's mind refused to accept what he had just seen.

Parker however reacted instantly. "Sasha!"

He too bolted right at the wall, and this time, King knew that his eyes had not deceived him. Parker had not ducked behind a bush or slipped into an unseen crevice in the cliff face. He reached the wall and kept right on going, as if it were no more substantial than smoke.

Disbelief hit King like a physical blow, leaving him numb all over.

You saw what you saw, he told himself. *It's a trick—smoke and mirrors—nothing more.*

But if it was a trick, it was a damned good one.

"Okay, Danno," he said. "How'd you do that?"

He took a step toward the place where the others had disappeared. He extended a hand. Where he expected to feel solid rock beneath his fingertips, he felt only the barest of resistance, like the push of air from an electric fan.

"Smoke and mirrors, my ass," he muttered, and with a deep breath to fortify his courage, King took another step forward.

FIFTY-ONE

ROOK SAW MOVEMENT in the trees and followed it with the business end of his XM8. The Desert Eagles were great for putting down those inhuman freakshows but not very accurate past about thirty meters.

The right tool for the right job, as Grandpa Tremblay always used to say.

A head appeared from behind a trunk—one of the rogue Night Stalkers—and Rook squeezed the trigger.

"That was for Houston, motherfucker," he muttered as the distant figure slumped to the ground. He searched for another target but saw nothing.

"Let's go!" Queen urged.

Rook gave a terse nod. There were still two more debts to collect on the balance sheet for Alpha team. Rainer owed a lot of other men for the pain he'd caused, but unfortunately, they would be able to kill him only once.

They crept into the woods, moving quickly but cautiously, and emerged at the edge of a small vineyard. Rook glimpsed movement in the rows of vines, but the running figure stayed low, depriving him of a target.

Rook stared at the perfectly straight parallel rows of vines, seeing them for the trap they were. "We go in there, and we'll be easy pickings."

Queen groaned at the pun. "Really? That's the best you've got?"

Rook shrugged then gestured to the perimeter of the vineyard. "Do we go the long way around?"

"You're asking me?"

"You're the Queen."

"Now that's funny," she returned, deadpan.

He chuckled to hide an unexpected feeling of embarrassment; he hadn't meant it as a joke. Keeping his carbine trained on the vine tops, he struck out along the edge of the field.

He had gone only about twenty feet when something hissed through the air right in front of him, accompanied by the simultaneous report of a pistol. As he threw himself flat, he realized that the shot had come from the woods, behind him.

Damn it! They suckered me.

As he scrambled on all fours for the concealment of the vines, the ground all around him started exploding, bullets striking like lightning bolts to the accompanying thunder of gunshots. Dirt sprayed into his face, stinging like the bite of wasps, forcing him to close his eyes, but he nevertheless brought his carbine up and returned fire.

Someone grabbed his shoulder.

He gave a yelp and twisted around to meet this new threat, swinging the gun like a club, but through the ringing in his ears and the pounding of his heart, a female voice reached out to him. "Slow down, hero. I got him."

Rook slowly unclenched, breathing heavily to damp down the deluge of adrenaline. He opened his eyes and saw Queen kneeling over him. "Which one?" he finally managed to say.

"Not Rainer." There was a trace of disappointment in her voice.

"You saved the big fish for me? How thoughtful of you."

"Fuck that. The asshole shot me, remember? He's mine."

Rook got to his feet and then flashed a grin. "Not if I see him first."

With that, he wheeled around and sprinted headlong into the vineyard. It was a stupid, cocky thing to do, but so far, luck had played a more decisive role than caution in keeping him alive. Besides, Rainer was alone now.

In his peripheral vision, he glimpsed a flash of gold—Queen's blonde locks, trailing behind her as she matched his pace in the next row over. He threw her a wink, and then reached down into his deepest reserves and put on an all-out burst of speed.

He spied movement ahead; Rainer had broken from the cover of the vines and was racing for the parking area where Parker's rented Renault had been joined by two Volkswagen Eurovans.

Rook tried to get the fleeing man in his sights, but he couldn't hold a bead while he was running, and if he stopped for a better shot, it might give Rainer the extra few seconds of lead time he needed to reach his van...

Rook saw that his quarry was going to make it to the vehicles anyway. He loosed a burst in the direction of he nearest van. It rocked a little under the impact of the 5.56-millimeter rounds and then lowered a few inches, as the air rushed from two of its tires.

Rainer threw up a hand in a reflexive, if futile, attempt to protect his head from bullets and flying debris, but he did not falter. He darted between the parked vans and disappeared from view.

Rook let his go of his XM8, allowing it to hang by the sling, and drew one of his pistols. Even if Rainer somehow got the other van rolling, one .50 caliber Action Express round would shut it down, and one more would shut *him* down. That was the great thing about the Desert Eagle—like with horseshoes and hand grenades, you didn't have to score a direct hit to get the job done. The recoil was a son-of-a-bitch—he really needed to see about getting some kind of wrist brace—but it wasn't nearly as bad as being on the other end when the trigger was pulled.

He expected to hear the van's engine turn over at any second, but all was silent. He reached the parking lot, Queen still matching his full sprint, and charged toward the vehicles, the Desert Eagle thrust out ahead of him like a battering ram.

Something moved out from behind the furthest vehicle and Rook fired. The pistol bucked in his hands, and the round tore into flesh in a spray of red, but Rook kept his gaze steady on the target, waiting for Rainer's dead body to hit the ground.

The shape did not fall.

It wasn't Rainer.

With a howl of primal rage, the wounded creature stepped into full view. It was a frankenstein.

Rook skidded to a stop, not twenty feet away. His bullet had nearly taken the thing's arm off; it would die eventually from shock and blood loss, but its rage would sustain it long enough for it to do some real damage.

Rook steadied the pistol in both hands, and fired again...and again. Beside him, Queen had likewise stopped, and she was emptying her carbine into the thing's chest. The frankenstein pitched backward.

Then another one appeared to take its place...

And another...

And another...

FIFTY-TWO

BISHOP WASN'T NORMALLY given to making loud, emotionally charged utterances. Most soldiers believed it was a good thing to vent some of their pent up rage with outbursts of colorful language, but Bishop knew that even a small crack could weaken a dam, and if the dam holding back his anger ever failed... Well, he didn't like to think about what might happen. The safer course was to meet every surprise, every disappointment, every reversal of fortune, the same way: with silence.

Once in a while, though, he would make an exception.

"What the—"

He had been looking away, watching the tree line for enemy activity, and so he had missed Sasha and Parker disappearing into the rock wall. He almost missed King's exit as well; he turned just in time to see King plunge into the stone face as if it were merely a curtain stretched over an opening in the wall. For a few seconds, he told himself that was exactly what he had seen, but when he approached the cliff and extended his hand, his fingers immediately encountered solid rock.

No, that wasn't quite right. It didn't feel solid exactly; more like stiff clay. He pressed harder and his fingers went in up to the first knuckle, but then stopped abruptly as if he'd hit something harder.

The substance was warm to the touch, almost uncomfortably so, and when he pulled his fingers free, he discovered that even that little bit of plasticity was gone from the rock; it had hardened once more into brittle chalky limestone.

"—fuck?"

He keyed his mic. "King, this is Bishop. Do you copy?"

Nothing.

He glimpsed movement from behind and whirled to find Knight jogging toward him, the enormous Barrett cradled in his arms. Knight's normally serene visage was twisted with concern; he had overheard Bishop's transmission, and the distinctive silence that had followed. "What's wrong?"

Bishop just gaped at the cliff face, silent mode re-engaged, but only because he didn't have the words to explain what he had just seen.

"Where's King?"

Bishop pointed at the wall. "He just...walked through it."

"Walked through it?"

The big man nodded. "Like a ghost or something."

"A ghost." Knight's forehead creased. "Bishop, you sound like my grandmother."

Bishop had no reply, but continued to probe the wall with his hands.

"You're serious, aren't you?" Knight came over to stand beside him. "So, is there a secret passage or something?"

The noise of gunfire—distant, but still close enough to warrant keeping their heads down—curtailed further discussion. Rook and Queen had engaged Rainer and his men. Knight opened the bipod legs for his Barrett and got down behind the weapon, ready to meet any threat that came their way, but Bishop went back to studying the rock. He felt a growing anxiety that had nothing to do with bringing down the rogue Delta operators.

King was inside the rock. There had to be a cave or a hidden tunnel entrance, but damned if he could find it. Had King gone in willingly? Was he in danger right now?

"Shit!"

Knight's rare expletive brought Bishop back to the moment. He wheeled around and saw the reason for his teammate's oath. Two figures—Queen and Rook—had broken from the cover of the pines and were bolting across the clearing toward them.

His concern deepened. It wasn't like those two to run from anything.

A frankenstein appeared behind them.

Why hadn't Rook dropped it with a couple of shots from his hand cannons?

Two more of the monstrosities emerged on the heels of the first, and the situation became clearer to Bishop.

There were two more behind those, and then more. Suddenly, the clearing was filled with the lumbering once-human things, moving so fast that Bishop couldn't accurately count them—at least ten, maybe a dozen, maybe more than that.

Knight's Barrett boomed, the muzzle brake throwing up a huge cloud of dirt as it vented the hot sulfurous gases that propelled a .50 BMG round with lethal accuracy into one of the monsters.

The sniper rifle thundered again, but without the same effect; the frankensteins were moving too fast for him to sight them in.

Queen and Rook were only a few seconds from reaching them, and their pursuers were just a few more.

"Knight! Let's go!" Bishop shouted.

"Where?" Knight must have intended it to be a rhetorical question, because he didn't look up from his grim but futile task.

A good question. King had gone into the rock, but they couldn't follow...

There was another way. He remembered the door they had passed when moving up on Rainer and his men; a door that led straight into the cliff, and to some old cave beyond. If they could get inside, that door would become a kill zone where they could repel almost any attack, even from the prodigiously strong frankensteins.

There was no time to explain all of this to Knight, so he simply reached down and plucked the smaller man up and threw him over one shoulder. The abrupt action startled Knight, but instead of struggling, he clutched at the rifle.

"This way!" Bishop shouted as he started running along the base of the cliff. He didn't look back to see if Queen and Rook were following.

The door seemed further away than he remembered—probably a trick of his battle-heightened perceptions.

Knight had stopped struggling against him almost immediately, but he didn't speak until Bishop reached his goal. "Put me down," he said calmly. "I'll hold them off while you get the door open."

Bishop complied without comment, letting his teammate slip to the ground. Queen and Rook reached them at almost the same moment. Four of the frankensteins were about a hundred feet behind them.

"Keep moving!" Queen was breathing so hard, she could barely get the words out.

Bishop shook his head. "We can make our stand here...inside."

"You got the key big guy?" panted Rook.

Bishop raised one foot and slammed it against the door, just below the U-shaped handle. The door buckled, practically folding in half around his boot, as it swung inward, revealing the darkness beyond.

"I guess you could knock," Rook said.

A piercing shriek filled the air as the cave's intruder alarm activated.

"Or ring the bell."

Bishop swept them all through the opening with one mighty arm; with his other hand, he fired his carbine into the approaching enemy. He didn't wait to see if his shots had any effect. He whirled and plunged headlong into the cave behind his teammates.

A narrow passage lay just beyond the door, and Bishop was forced to squirm through the tight throat of stone. Then, without warning, he was birthed into a great black void.

The oppressive darkness lasted only a few seconds. One by one, the tactical flashlights mounted to their carbines flared to life. Rays of tightly focused brilliance stabbed through the still air without really illuminating anything, but Bishop got the sense of being in an enormous enclosure, as big as an aircraft hanger. The floor alternated between loose chips of rock and a smooth surface that looked almost polished, but riding above both was a narrow bridge of steel plate—part of the conservation effort designed to minimize impact on the cave. The sweep of the lights revealed other discrete details: pillars of limestone and other minerals that stretched from floor to ceiling; stalagmites that seemed to be erupting from the floor like milky white mushroom clouds. One of the lights revealed something else, something that at first glance appeared to be moving, but was in reality an image painted on one wall—a buffalo or bison that appeared almost to be running. The illusion was gone even before Bishop could register it; the lights were sweeping back the way they'd come, shining on the narrow slit leading to the doorway.

Something was moving there.

Rook fired his pistol. The entire cavern rang with the noise of the discharge, and the acrid smell of burnt gunpowder obliterated the earthy odor of ancient stone. The shape in the entry twitched grotesquely with the impact, but then the figure began moving forward once more.

Rook fired again, and this time the damage was unmistakable; the bullet cratered the frankenstein's forehead.

Impossibly, it kept advancing.

Rook fired out the last of his magazine, but the monstrosity just seemed to absorb each hit as if it was impervious.

There was an ear-splitting report as Knight fired the Barrett straight into the thing's chest, nearly tearing it in half. This time it went down permanently, as did the frankenstein right behind it. But even before the bodies hit the steel decking, a third creature rushed forward and lifted the fallen body, holding it between itself and the Chess Team like a shield.

Bishop realized now why the first frankenstein had seemed invincible; it had been dead all along, and its body had sheltered the advance of its brothers through the chokepoint of the cave entrance.

Rook and Knight hastened to reload, while Bishop and Queen kept up a withering barrage of fire from their carbines, but the invading force just shrugged off the damage as they poured unhindered through the gap.

FIFTY-THREE

THE DARKNESS SURROUNDING King was becoming substantial. At first, he attributed this to some lingering vestige of claustrophobia, but as the air became viscous, like syrup clinging to his limbs, he realized that it was the literal truth. The strange effect that had opened this passageway into the Earth—science or magic, or maybe a little of both—was receding; the stone was returning to its solid state.

The realization triggered a surge of panic, and he started clawing his way forward, swimming as much as running. Abruptly, the resistance vanished. He stumbled forward, sprawling face down on hard stone.

What just happened?

He knew the answer. The rational part of his brain stodgily refused to embrace the reality of the experience, but what other explanation could there be?

Understanding the Voynich manuscript and securing the Prime had never been his highest priority, but he had been paying attention when Parker and Sasha had told their tale of medieval scientists discovering the secret source of life and using music to change the very nature of the physical world. If even a little bit of what they had told him was true...

I just walked through a solid rock wall!

There was a faint glow directly ahead, and King heard raised voices, conversing heatedly just a few yards in front of him.

"You have to let me do this," Sasha urged.

"And you can," Parker said. "Once Jack has secured the area."

"And what if he can't? What if Rainer kills him? Kills them all?"

Frowning, King got to his feet, and with his hands extended ahead, probing the darkness, he moved toward them. He could see their silhouettes now, lit by the glow of Sasha's computer.

He brought his carbine around and switched on the attached light.

The high-intensity LED bulb revealed a tunnel, cut and smoothed by the passage of some ancient subterranean river long since diverted, sloping gently downward, and standing partway down the slope were two human shapes.

Parker threw up a hand to shade his eyes, but Sasha seized on the moment to break free of his restraining hand. She charged ahead, deeper into the passage.

"Stop her, Danno!"

Parker was already moving. He caught her by the shoulder and spun her around. King could see the desperation in her eyes. She struggled in his grasp, her efforts becoming more frantic as King drew near.

"It's right there," she pleaded. "The Prime. I can fix everything, if you just let me go."

"Sasha..."

King reached them. "Miss Therion, I'm sorry, but you have to come back with us."

Sasha looked at him for a second, and then turned the full force of her gaze on Parker. She pointed ahead into the darkness. "The Prime is right there. It's why we came here."

King sensed that his friend's resolve was starting to slip.

"Danny, please let me. My whole life has been leading up to this. Don't let him stop me." She reached out and placed her hand over his heart. "You promised to help me."

Parker's restraining hand fell away. With a sigh of resignation, he nodded down the tunnel. "Go."

"Damn it, Danno." King reached out to restrain her, but Sasha was already forging ahead, deeper into the darkness. He started after her, but then felt a hand pull him back.

"Let her go, Jack." Parker's voice sounded weary, defeated. King tried to pull free, but what had at first been only Parker's token effort to forestall him abruptly became something more resolute. As he tried to wrench himself free, Parker yanked him back hard enough to spin him into the wall.

The impact stunned him, but not as much as the evident betrayal.

Parker, too, seemed surprised by what he'd done; he took a step back and raised his hands. He knew he had crossed a line, and now he had to decide whether to retreat and do some damage control, or commit with both feet.

"I don't have time for this shit, Danno."

King started forward, but Parker moved to block his way. "Jack, just let her do this. It's important to her."

"The last time someone screwed around with this stuff, it killed half the world's population, remember? You told me that. The Black Death? The Prime is dangerous."

The flame of Parker's resolve flickered, but then he shook his head. "That was different. Sasha knows what she's doing. I have to let her try."

"Well I don't."

King advanced again.

Parker, with arms akimbo, tried to block the passage, but King stepped to one side and lowered his head like a charging linebacker. He plowed into Parker, staggering him back, but even as he fell, Parker closed his arms around King, taking him to the ground in a bear hug.

Parker grunted from the impact, but instead of letting go, he wrapped his legs around King's, hobbling him, and then he started grappling for a better position. King quickly recognized what was happening, but before he could do anything about it, Parker had rolled him over and slipped an arm around his neck.

King knew how to break free of such a hold, and Parker knew how to prevent him from doing so. For several seconds, they struggled without appearing to move more than a few inches at a time. They had fought each other often in training, and sometimes just for the hell of it; they knew each other's best moves and Achilles' Heels. Neither man could hold an advantage against the other long enough to achieve a decisive victory. Experience told King that exhaustion would be the decider, and that was something he couldn't wait for.

He slammed his head back, driving the back of his skull into Parker's face. There was a white flash of pain, accompanied by a ringing in his ears, but he also heard the crunch of bones smacking together.

Parker let go and scrambled back. "Shit, Jack."

In the diffuse glow from King's light, he saw Parker holding a hand to his mouth, and bright drops of blood seeping through his fingers. "Shit," he repeated, the words distorted by the injury.

"You just can't let go, can you?" Parker continued, the accusation pouring out in an accompanying fountain of blood. "No wonder you didn't want me on your team."

King shook his head, and winced as another wave of pain spiked through his head. "Danno, we can talk about this later, but right now, you need to get her back. The Prime is dangerous. Don't let her mess around with it."

"Damn it, Jack. Would you just fucking back off for once? You don't have to be in control every God damned minute. It's not like the world is going to end."

A deep rumble shuddered through the cavern, throwing both men to the hard floor, and showering them with dust. The tremor lasted a few seconds, and when it stopped, King could hear the sound of the cavern walls groaning with the strain of holding up the earth.

The air was thick with falling dust, giving the beam of King's light the illusion of solidity but reducing its effectiveness. He could just make out Parker, struggling to rise a few yards away.

Between them, stretching from one wall of the passage to the other, was a shadowy line that swallowed the light whole, and as he peered into it, King saw that it was getting wider. The tremor had opened a fissure in the cavern.

The earth rumbled again, and King's side of the passage dropped six inches, with an accompanying shower of dust. Over the crushing of rock, other noises were audible, muffled but no less distinctive—the sound of gunfire.

"You were saying, Danno?"

FIFTY-FOUR

TWENTY-FIVE METERS FURTHER down the tunnel, Sasha Therion had reached her destination. While King and Parker fought, she had pressed forward, using the laptop screen to light her way. She arrived at a small, unremarkable looking cavern.

She saw a few stalagmites, looking like deformed white mushrooms growing out of the floor, but the feature that immediately drew her attention was man-made. In the center of the chamber, someone had laid down a circle of stones, each about the size a man's head. It looked like it might have served as a campfire ring, but instead of charcoal remnants, the entire circle—about six feet in diameter—was filled with soil, and poking up from the crumbly surface were the desiccated fibrous stalks of plants that had once grown here, in defiance of all the laws of nature.

This, she knew intuitively, was where Bacon and al-Tusi had conducted their experiments. This was the Prime—the place where life had begun—or as near to it as any human had ever come.

Not in this cave of course. When the spark of life had first caught, some three and a half billion years ago, the surface of the Earth had been a very different place. The land mass that would eventually become the continent of Europe would not be thrust up from the Earth's mantle until hundreds of millions of years later. The calcium carbonate that comprised the limestone walls of the cave network itself was an accretion of organic material—the skeletons of aquatic life forms settling to the ocean floor and compressing into sedimentary rock—and so the cave itself could not have existed prior to the genesis of life on Earth. Life had not begun in this cave, nor had it necessarily begun in the physical space the cave now occupied, but there was nevertheless something important about this place, something that was not bound to the fickle whims of geology.

There were many places like it, places long known and revered by humans even before the rise of civilization—power spots, rivers of invisible Earth energy, ley lines, vortices. They were places where the laws of nature could sometimes be bent, if not broken altogether. On a day lost to time, so long ago that the span of years was incomprehensible to the human brain, those laws had been distorted in a very special way, at this particular place, and the tinder of life had become a wildfire.

Sasha stood above the ring of stones, one hand extended as if she might be able to feel the unique energy of the Prime.

Oddly enough, she could feel something...a tingling in her skin, like the vibration of a tuning fork. She closed her eyes and savored the moment.

She had, at long last, arrived at a solution, discovered the common factor that would enable her to simplify the impossibly complex variables of the human equation. She had found the Prime.

She sat cross-legged in front of the stone circle and set her laptop in front of her. As she opened the hinged screen, she realized that the strange vibration wasn't coming from the Prime, at least not directly. It was coming from her computer, which was still streaming out the tonal frequency that had—in conjunction with the proximity of the Prime—made it possible for her to pass through solid matter. Now, the ground upon which she sat was starting to resonate to the same frequency, growing warm as the molecular bonds holding the stone in a solid state began to loosen.

She quickly closed the sound file, but at that very moment, an explosion ripped through the softened rock.

FIFTY METERS AWAY and about ten meters above the Prime location, the Chess Team had forced their way into Chauvet Cave and were now fighting for their lives. As the frankensteins poured through the entry, Bishop fired a 40-millimeter high explosive grenade from the XM320 launcher attached to his carbine. It had been an act of pure desperation; Bishop had known that the grenade might trigger a cave-in, collapsing the entrance and sealing them inside, but he had judged that a preferable fate to being overrun by the frankensteins.

What he could not have known was that the floor beneath him had been undergoing a subtle transformation; the stone was softening, and in some places, it had turned completely into a molecular slurry. When the small grenade detonated, its explosive energy ripped into the weakened stone and shattered it.

A SECTION OF the ceiling right above Sasha was pulverized, raining a fine powdery grit down onto her. Beyond that impenetrable dust cloud, long black fissures were appearing in the limestone as the cavern started tearing itself apart.

Sasha's sense of triumph was also on the verge of self-destruction. She huddled over the computer, taking shallow breaths to avoid inhaling too much of the choking dust, and fought back the rising tide of panic.

The solution, literally within her grasp, was about to be stolen away again, this time forever.

No. I won't let that happen.

She opened her eyes. The air still felt thick, but she could see the computer screen, and that was all she needed. Putting her face close so she could see the keyboard, she began inputting the solution.

She had worked it all out during the days that she and Parker had been on the run. The Voynich manuscript had provided her with all the information she needed about the musical notes that had the greatest effect on the Prime, so it had been a simple thing to isolate the relevant frequencies.

"Sasha!"

Parker's voice reached out through the gloom, but she ignored it. She didn't need his help anymore, and she certainly didn't need an unpredictable variable showing up now, not when she was so close to the solution.

"Sasha, are you there? Can you hear me?"

Go away.

She didn't say it aloud at first, but when his inquiries became more urgent, she realized that her refusal to acknowledge him was making him more persistent, and might embolden him to interfere with what she was trying to do. "I'm fine, Danny."

"Thank God." The walls groaned again, releasing another small shower of dust. "Where are you? Keep talking so I can find you."

"No. Don't come any closer."

"Why not? What's wrong?"

"I found the Prime. I can fix everything, but you need to just leave me alone for a little while, okay?"

There was a long pause, and Sasha was just starting to believe that maybe he had complied with her request when he spoke again. "Sasha, what are you talking about?"

She sighed. His questions were making it hard for her to concentrate, hampering her efforts to enter the new frequencies. Why couldn't he just go away?

"Sasha, what is it you are trying to fix?"

Exasperated, she smacked her palms against her thighs. "Everything! I'm trying to fix everything, okay? Does that answer your question?"

"And how are you going to do that?" He was speaking softly, but at the same time his voice was getting louder as he moved closer, trying to pinpoint her location in the near-total darkness. Maybe he couldn't see the glow of the computer screen in all the dust. She decided not to answer any more of his questions.

"How is the Prime going to help you do that?" he continued. "Are you trying to come up with your own Elixir of Life? Something to heal everyone?"

"Ha!" It was out of her mouth before she could think to suppress it. She clamped a hand over her mouth to stifle any further outbursts, then she went back to typing. *Almost done...*

Parker must have heard her. "Something else then? Not a cure for disease, but maybe a new disease? A new Black Death? Is that what you want Sasha? You can tell me. I can understand why you might feel like you need to do that."

His declaration surprised her. "Really?"

"Sure. I get it. Life sucks sometimes."

"It's the chaos I can't stand. It was all just a big mistake."

"What do you mean by 'a mistake?'"

She realized that he was toying with her, trying to keep her talking so he could find her. She shook her head, trying to shut him out. She went back to work.

"Sasha, tell me more about the chaos? I need to know more if I'm going to help you fix it."

"You wouldn't understand," she said, speaking slowly so as not to enter the wrong data.

"I might. You like things orderly, right? Precise? That's why you're a mathematician. You like solving equations. You like things that make sense."

Maybe he does understand.

"And people... Well, people are unpredictable. And with everything you've been through, I think it's perfectly understandable that you want to...you know, bring some order to the world. Let me help."

"I don't need your help," she declared. She could hear his footsteps crunching through the grit on the floor.

"Of course you don't. But I want to help. I want to be a part of it." Sasha felt his presence beside her. He knelt next to her and peered at the screen. "What are you working on there? Are you going to use the Prime to create a new plague? Is that how you're going to fix things?"

She looked over at him. His face was a mess of dust and blood, and he looked positively ghoulish in the diffuse glow of the computer screen, but there wasn't even a hint of accusation or condemnation in his eyes.

"No," she said finally. "The plague isn't a solution. It's just another variable; unpredictable like all living systems."

"Go on."

"Life was an accident, Danny. It was a mistake. A statistical impossibility that somehow happened anyway."

"Some people would call that a miracle."

She shook her head. "Not a miracle. Just something that happened; a random spark that caught fire and is destined to burn itself out."

"I know it might seem bad sometimes, but it doesn't have to be that way."

"It doesn't matter." She felt no emotion now. No fear at what would happen, and strangely, no satisfaction. "Three and a half billion years, that's how long the fire has been burning. We think we're so important—the center of the universe, but the universe doesn't even know we exist. Life is a plague, an infection that threatens the perfection of the universe. And it all started right here, with the Prime. But I know how to solve the equation."

"How?"

She looked into his eyes. "Simple math. You subtract known values from the equation until nothing is left."

His mouth formed the word: *subtract*.

"The Prime isn't just this place, Danny. It's the constant that makes all the variables possible. It's fixed in all dimensions, time and space."

"Then how are you going to...to solve it?"

"The Prime is only one factor. There is another; the frequency that made life possible. We'll never know what caused it...the wind maybe? Cosmic rays? Who knows, but it was the catalyst. The frequency and the Prime combined to equal life. I can't subtract the Prime from the equation, but I can nullify the frequency, and that will change one factor to zero."

"Nullify?" He nodded slowly. "You're going to create a phased wave to dampen the original one. And if, as you say, we are all linked through time and space to the Prime, eliminating one factor will pull the plug for us all. For all life on Earth."

She gazed up at him, impressed by how quickly he had figured it out. "You're very intelligent. I wish I'd met you sooner."

He smiled and patted her on the shoulder. "I want to hear all about this, but first we need to get out of here, okay?"

"No need," she said. She could feel it now, a tingling in her skin...an itch like pins and needles. "It's already started."

Parker jerked back as if he'd been stung. "Sasha, you've got to stop it. Turn it off now."

She gazed back at him. "Turn it off? Why would I—"

Her voice caught in her throat as the itching sensation blossomed into a spike of pain—a baptism in liquid fire.

The agony was transcendent, but it lasted for only an instant. Then the calculation was complete, and Sasha Therion was no more.

FIFTY-FIVE

BISHOP HAD CALLED out, warning them of what he was about to do. It was madness to fire a grenade inside the cavern, even as vast as it was, but what choice was there? The frankensteins had taken the entrance and were massing for an assault that Chess Team would never be able to repel. No one answered, and evidently taking the silence as assent, he had leveled the launcher and fired.

Queen heard the hollow pop as the spherical package of high explosive shot down the tube. She curled into a defensive ball in anticipation of the chaos that would follow.

The grenade exploded right in front of one of the monstrosities. There was a dull thump and a cloud of acrid smoke, and then the shockwave hit.

Queen was well outside the grenade's kill zone, but the energy of the blast slapped her to the ground and reverberated in her gut. She thought that was the worst of it, but then the ground beneath her fell.

She scrambled away from the crumbling floor, flinging her arms out in a desperate attempt to find a handhold, but everything she touched was moving, falling into the abyss that had opened beneath her.

Yet she was not falling.

She felt a strain in her right arm, the burden of her body weight suspended by that single appendage, and she realized that she must have snared something solid...but no, her fingers were curled into a fist around empty air.

"I've got you, babe!"

She couldn't see the face of her savior, but there was no mistaking the voice. Rook had somehow managed to snare her wrist, and now he held her, dangling over the brink of the newly formed fissure.

With a mighty heave, he pulled her up. She felt the rough stone edge of the abyss scraping against her body, and then she was on solid ground again, collapsing on top of her rescuer.

She pushed him away. "If you ever call me 'babe' again," she rasped. "I'll cut your balls off."

"Hey, slow down *chica*," he replied smoothly. "We should get to know each other better before you try getting in my pants."

With a growl, she snared his goatee in the darkness. She pulled him close, stopping just an inch from his face, causing him to suck in and hold a quick breath. If he puckered, their lips would touch.

"Keep dreaming, big guy."

She let go of his beard, and he smiled broadly. "If I dream about you, I'm going to have more nocturnal—"

The rest of his quip was lost as a peal of thunder boomed through the cave, and both of them scrambled back from the edge of the fissure. Then the noise sounded again, and Queen realized that it was the report of Knight's Barrett.

Squinting through the dust and smoke, she could make out pinpricks of light, marking the locations of Bishop and Knight respectively. Both men were firing across the cavern, over the yawning void of the fissure where at least five of the frankensteins were shaking off the effects of the grenade and preparing to move.

Queen breathed a curse, and raised her carbine. Bishop's grenade had improved the odds a little, but it hadn't been the equalizer they needed.

She played her light toward the fissure that had nearly claimed her. It was a good fifteen feet across, a ragged split in the limestone, sloping down almost vertically, with few handholds. An ordinary man would not have dared attempt to leap across the gap. Even an Olympic long jumper would have been daunted, but the frankensteins, fueled by steroids, and fearless, would be able to skip across it like girls playing hopscotch on a playground.

The expected charge however, did not come. Instead, the creatures moved out along the perimeter of the cavern, keeping to the shadows and staying low behind stalagmites for cover, heading for the narrow end of the crevasse.

"They're trying to flank us," she shouted, and the implications of that realization hit her like a slap. When the frankensteins crossed to their side of the cavern, the team would be trapped.

"They're smart," Rook remarked in a low voice. "Too smart. Like they've got some kind of hive mind."

She had been thinking the same thing.

"Well, your highness, any bright ideas?"

"All for one," she said, nodding toward Knight and Bishop. "We fall back as far as we can and form a defensive line. If they want us, they're going to have to get through a wall of lead."

FIFTY-SIX

A WAIL OF disbelief escaped Parker's lips as Sasha collapsed in front of the stone circle. He didn't need to touch her or check for a pulse to know that her life force had been completely extinguished.

He wanted to reach out to her, to hug her empty shell to his chest and demand that the heavens give her back, but he knew that to do so would be to join her.

She had found her answer, a solution to the incomprehensible equation of life with all its unpredictable chaos. Even if his rational mind balked at the idea, he could not argue with what he now beheld—Sasha, dead in an instant.

As if to affirm the testimony of his eyes, he felt a strange tingling in his skin.

He took a step back in alarm. The sensation faded but only a little and only for a moment. Whatever Sasha had done, it was still happening...and it was spreading.

He saw her computer, discarded and all but forgotten beside her body, but still functional. A thing of metal and silicon, it was immune to the anti-life power she had unleashed, and it would sit there casting its ambient glow until the battery died, a process that might take an hour or two...long after everything else on the planet had ceased to exist.

He had to get to the computer, turn off that sound and undo what Sasha had done.

But if he failed, if he died trying, there would be no second chances for humanity.

He spoke into the microphone taped to his shirt collar. "Jack, are you there?"

There was a momentary pause, and then King's voice, breathless, sounded in his ear. "I'm here, Danno."

"I'm sorry, Jack. I should have trusted you."

"Save it for later, buddy. I heard everything. You gave it your best try."

"She did something to the Prime, Jack. Turned it against itself. I have to get to her computer to turn it off. You heard what she said. If I can't stop this, everyone dies. Everywhere."

"Then stop it. Do what needs to be done, Danno."

"Listen to me, Jack. If this thing kills me before I can get clear, someone else is going to have to finish it. Do you understand?"

King was silent for few seconds then simply said: "Roger."

"I'll keep talking so you know what to do." Parker took a deep breath. The tingling sensation was getting stronger even though he had yet to take a step. "If I stop talking, you'll know what it means."

He lurched forward and instantly the itch became a fire burning on his skin, deepening into his muscles. One step forward, two... Despite his promise to keep communicating, the words were stolen away.

Another step...

He stood over Sasha's corpse, reached past her... The pain was deep inside him now, but his extremities felt numb and cold. He stretched out his hand, closed his fingers over the hard plastic of the laptop. He couldn't tell for sure if he was gripping it; his fingers had no sensation whatsoever, but through the haze, he could see the screen moving between his outstretched arms.

With what felt like the last of his strength, he staggered back down the passage, away from the Prime. Each step brought a measure of relief from the pain, but the coldness remained in his extremities.

"Jack, I have the computer."

He thought he heard his friend say something, "Thank God," perhaps, but he couldn't be sure. Something was happening to his hearing, to all his senses.

He peered through the fog now clouding his vision and stared at the computer screen. A sound file was playing from the virtual *urghan*, playing a single note in an endless loop. Below the graphical representation of the wave, he saw numbers: 7.83.

That's it, he realized. *The frequency of life—7.83 Hz.*

"It's the Schumann Resonance!"

He couldn't tell if King responded, so he kept talking.

"It's a constant waveform produced by the friction of the Earth's surface rotating beneath the ionosphere. You can't hear it—it's below the audible range for human hearing, but it's everywhere, all the time, and has been for billions of years. Some scientists called it the 'Earth's heartbeat.'"

Like a beating heart, Sasha had stopped it with something akin to defibrillation. It was a simple matter of wave dynamics; when two oppositely phased waves of the same frequency met, they cancelled each other out completely. It was the same principle used in sound-dampening headphones.

That was what Sasha had done; she had dampened the frequency of life, and plunged the Prime into deathly silence.

He tapped a few keys and shut down the waveform, trying to explain what he was doing to King, and wondering if it would make the difference.

The sudden flare of pain in his muscles told him it hadn't.

"It's not working," he rasped, and then he realized why. Sasha had stopped the beating heart of the Earth. It wasn't enough to stop the phased wave; he needed to start the heartbeat again.

His fingers fumbled uncertainly on the keyboard, making the adjustments that would play the Schumann Resonance again. A sine wave began oscillating across the screen, but that was the only change.

"It's not working. I think it needs to be closer to the Prime." He wasn't sure if the words were even coming out or if he was just imagining them. "There's a ring of stones... I think that's the marker. I'm going to try to put it there. You'll know if it works because we'll all still be here."

Gritting his teeth, he lurched forward, straight into the eye of the storm.

FIFTY-SEVEN

KING HEARD EVERY word.

When the fissure had first opened, separating him from Parker, he had lingered there, wondering if he should try jumping across. Before he could make the attempt, he heard Parker's voice in his headset, and he knew that whatever else had happened between them, his friend was still trying to do the right thing.

Confident that Parker was doing everything possible to coax Sasha away from the brink of madness, King turned his attention to what seemed like a much more immediate concern. The report of gunfire drifting down into the crevasse painted an incomplete picture, but it was enough for him to realize that the effort to capture or kill Rainer had taken an unexpected, and evidently dire, turn. Somewhere up above him, his teammates were fighting for their lives.

He played his light on the walls of the crevasse. It was almost vertical, but the break was irregular, with nubs of stone sticking out everywhere. What he could not see was the top; there was no telling how high he would have to climb.

He was just getting started on the ascent when he heard a crackle of squelch in his ear, followed by Parker's voice.

"A new Black Death? Is that what you want Sasha? You can tell me. I can understand why you might feel that's necessary."

What the hell?

Parker had opened the channel intentionally so that King would know what was happening. King didn't understand half of what was said, but he could quickly discern two things: Sasha Therion was bat-shit crazy, and Parker was doing his damnedest to rein her in.

King listened intently but kept his focus on the task at hand, moving slowly, methodically, patiently up the wall. The noise of fighting grew louder, and King realized that the crevasse did not lead outside, but rather connected with another cave where the battle was taking place. The good news was that the climb would be over soon.

The bad news was that he had no idea what he was about to step in.

When he reached the top, he kept his head down for a moment, wary of not getting caught in a crossfire. Off to his left, on the far side of the fissure, the team had just opened fire on a horde of the malformed creatures that were swarming toward them. Over the cacophony, King heard something else; a voice...a familiar voice...

Rainer's voice.

"Hold your position. Stay behind cover. Let them burn through their ammo."

Who's he talking to?

At that moment, Parker's voice sounded in his ear. "Jack, are you there?"

He didn't respond right away. If he was close enough to hear Rainer speaking, then he was close enough to be overheard. He lowered himself down below the edge of the crevasse and whispered. "I'm here, Danno."

"I'm sorry, Jack. I should have trusted you."

King's mind sifted through what he had overheard. He recalled Sasha saying something about chaos and how life was a mistake, and the realization had chilled him. What had she done? "Save it for later, buddy. I heard everything. You gave it your best try."

"She did something to the Prime, Jack. Turned it against itself. I have to get to her computer to turn it off."

King heard Rainer's voice again, almost simultaneous with Parker's. "Now, advance. Stay in a single file line. Continue to use the dead for cover."

Rainer was talking to the frankensteins through a radio headset just like the one Chess Team used. Not merely talking to them, but directing their movements, guiding them strategically, the way a chess player might maneuver pawns on the game board.

"You heard what she said," Parker continued. "If I can't stop this, everyone dies. Everywhere."

King heard, and on some level he understood what his friend was telling him, but there was nothing he could do to help. "Then stop it," he said. "Do what needs to be done, Danno."

"Listen to me, Jack. If this thing kills me before I can get clear, someone else is going to have to finish it. Do you understand?"

Parker's appeal stopped him cold. *What was happening down there?*

He shook his head. There was nobody better suited to dealing with whatever it was that was happening at the Prime than Daniel Parker. "Roger."

He pulled himself up again, peeking over the edge quickly to locate Rainer. He found his former CO, illuminated by indirect light from some kind of electronic device—a GPS unit or a PDA. Rainer's eyes were fixed on the scene playing out beyond the fissure, where his remaining force of four frankensteins were preparing to overrun Chess Team.

As stealthily as possible, King levered himself up onto the floor of the cave, never taking his eyes off Rainer. He brought his carbine up, but in the darkness, he couldn't get a good shot. He abandoned the effort, and in a smooth motion, he sprang to his feet and charged.

Rainer must have heard the ground crunching underfoot or sensed movement in the air, for at the last instant he swung around to face King. There was confusion in his eyes, as if he still didn't comprehend what was happening, but as King slammed into him, he threw up a defensive arm that somehow struck King in jaw. Then, in a tangle of limbs, both men went down.

The PDA flew out of Rainer's hand, shattering against the floor, its light instantly extinguished, but neither man noticed. King tried to get his hands around Rainer's throat, but a fierce punch rocked him back and sent stars shooting across his vision. As he tried to shrug off the blow, Rainer squirmed from beneath him, and launched a flurry of blows—fists and elbows—most of which missed completely or glanced off King's gear. A few however found their mark, and King's head rang with the impacts.

He lowered his head to his chest, trying to make himself less of a target and clutched at Rainer. His fingers tangled in the other man's shirt, then managed to snare one of the flailing arms. He tried to twist it around, but Rainer was not so easily subdued. The rogue Delta officer did not try to wrestle free of the hold, but spun around in the direction King was trying to turn him, and drove his body back into

King's chest, slamming him into the cave wall.

The breath was driven from King's lungs, and his arms flopped uselessly to his sides, his nerves buzzing. Rainer whirled and drove a fist into his gut. King doubled over, partly from the piston-like force of the blow, and partly in a desperate attempt to trap his foe's arm, but Rainer had already pulled free. With a savage growl, he gripped King's shoulders and heaved him to the floor, descending on top of him with another crushing impact.

King felt a stab of pain in both biceps as Rainer straddled his chest and drove his knees down onto King's arms, pinning him. Then, Rainer's hands closed around his throat, and a darkness that had nothing to do with the absence of light began to close over King.

Rainer leaned forward, close enough that King could feel the man's breath on his face. "Jack. I'll be damned. You threw me a party. Used that little bitch as bait to draw me out. I'm impressed."

King would have spit a curse in the man's face, but the breath to do so had been driven from him and the choking hands kept him from drawing another. He struggled to free himself, to get even a moment's respite, but Rainer's position was unassailable. King felt his limbs start to tingle from oxygen starvation, growing cold and numb.

Then, as if in answer to a prayer he had not even thought to utter, Rainer's grip went slack. He moved his hands away from King's throat and held them up, flexing them before his face.

"What the hell?"

The rush of oxygen brought King back from the brink of despair. His arms were still tingling...no, not just his arms... Every square inch of his body was pins and needles, and the sensation was deepening, becoming a painful itch.

Through the fog in his head, he heard Parker speaking, and realized that what he was now experiencing had nothing at all to do with the beating he'd received. Rainer was feeling it too.

Whatever Sasha had done to the Prime was spreading, growing in intensity.

"There's a ring of stones... I think that's the marker." Parker was saying. "I'm going to try to put it there. You'll know if it works because we'll all still be here."

A low wail of pain came over the radio, grunts of exertion and agony, and then an abrupt silence.

Danno!

King heaved against Rainer. Distracted by the strange pain that was creeping over his extremities, the other man was slow to react, while King's grief and rage opened a vein of untapped strength. He got one of his arms free and wrapped it around Rainer's waist, and in the same motion drove his feet against the cave floor.

Locked together, they rolled once, twice...and then suddenly there was no ground beneath them, and they plunged into the void.

FIFTY-EIGHT

KING HAD ACCOMPLISHED one of his objectives in the first moments of his struggle with Rainer. The destruction of the PDA had not only severed the link between the frankensteins and their leader, but it had also deprived them of their collective intelligence. Now, instead of four creatures working with a single mind, they were four wild beasts.

In every other way, they remained just as dangerous as before.

With a howl, they broke from cover and charged.

Knight felled one with a cannon-loud blast from the Barrett.

The other three continued, undaunted.

Rook leveled his Desert Eagle at the nearest target and squeezed the trigger again and again. The Action Express rounds hit with such energy that the frankenstein seemed to come apart before his very eyes.

The remaining two kept advancing.

With a bestial roar of his own, Bishop leapt forward and met the charge head on. He towered a full head taller than the monstrosity he faced, but the frankenstein did not show the slightest awareness of the fact. Its eyes locked onto Bishop, and it stretched its arms out to him, looking in that moment exactly like the iconic Hollywood character that had inspired its nickname.

As the two men met—one driven by steroids and inhuman surgical alteration, the other fueled by an almost incomprehensible primal rage—the frankenstein tried to seize hold of Bishop's arms, perhaps intending to rip them from their sockets, but Bishop was too quick. Instead of drawing back to avoid the reaching arms, he stepped in close and hugged the thing's face to his chest.

There was a sickening crunch and a wet tearing noise, as Bishop twisted its head completely around.

Only a few seconds had passed since the frankensteins began their final attack, and for those few seconds, Queen had felt completely useless. While she had stood by waiting for something to do, her teammates had seized the day and destroyed the enemy.

Not completely destroyed, though. One frankenstein remained. It had dodged Rook's bullets and slipped past Bishop, even as the big man had torn its brother's head off.

Knight brought the Barrett up, bracing it against his hip and firing point blank. The round punched a fist-sized hole clear through the creature's abdomen. The frankenstein staggered back a step, but before Knight could fire again, it started forward, seizing the barrel of the rifle. There was an audible hiss as the thing's skin blistered against the hot metal, but the frankenstein ignored the pain and pulled the gun, along with an unbalanced Knight, forward into its reach. The wounded beast seized Knight's arms, stretching them out like a child preparing to rip the wings off a captured fly.

Queen ran at the creature, pummeling it with the butt of her carbine, but she was disdainfully swatted away. She sprang up, desperate to do something...anything...that might keep Knight alive long enough for one of the others to come to the rescue, but she'd lost her carbine in the fall. She groped for the knife sheathed to her combat vest, but her hand found something else instead, a hard cylindrical object.

Yes!

Knight's cry of pain galvanized her. She leaped onto the frankenstein's back, wrapping her right arm around its head as Bishop had done, and clawed the fingers of her free hand into its eyes.

Though virtually immune to pain, the frankenstein reacted instinctively to the threat to its eyesight. It let go of Knight and reached up to defend against this new attack. Queen dug deeper, driving a finger between the orb and the eye socket, eliciting a howl of rage.

That howl was just what she had been hoping for.

"Cover up!" she shouted.

She dropped her left hand, using it to hold herself in place, and then jammed the object she'd been holding with her right hand into the thing's open mouth.

With a sharp hiss, the M14 incendiary grenade ignited and transformed the frankenstein's head into a miniature sun.

She threw herself back, scrambling to put some distance between herself and the bloom of white hot fire. Shading her eyes, she circled around to check on Knight.

He had heeded her advice and gotten well clear of the creature before the grenade had ignited, but even though he was several meters away from the blazing pyre of flesh, he was rubbing at his skin.

"You okay?"

"Yeah." He managed a wan smile as he looked up at her. "Weird thing though; I've got pins and needles all over."

That was when Queen realized that she did too.

FIFTY-NINE

TWO THINGS SAVED King's life.

The first was the shape of the fissure. The rift narrowed with depth, coming together at a seam so tight that a piece of paper could not have slipped into it. As he and Rainer fell, still locked together in combat, the shrinking gap between the walls caught them like friction brakes, slowing and ultimately halting their downward plunge.

The second factor that had made the difference between life and death was Kevin Rainer. Positioned as he was beneath King, Rainer's body cushioned the eventual impact just enough to spare King from serious harm. King was bruised, battered and bloody, but none of his injuries were life-threatening.

The same could not be said for Rainer; King's body drove into him like a hammer, forcing him deeper into the fissure than seemed possible, leaving him sandwiched between slabs of limestone about three inches apart. The pressure crushed the man's ribcage, driving nails of bone through his lungs and into his vital organs.

King felt the walls pressing in on either side of him as well, and he started to panic. He was afraid to move, fearful that doing so might cause him to slide deeper into the crevasse, to a place where it would be impossible for him to get free. Then he felt the tingling in his skin, and he knew that being trapped in stone was the least of his worries.

His awareness of what was at stake did not make his task any easier, but Rainer's body was a stable platform from which to begin clawing his way out of the abyss. With each inch he climbed, the press of stone against his chest diminished.

There was light now, bright but indirect, pouring down from high above to reveal his destination: the dark passage that led to the Prime.

Parker's words came back to him.

If I can't stop this, everyone dies.

Parker hadn't been able to stop it, though.

King's skin was burning, and the tingling was sinking deeper into his limbs. He wondered how much worse it would get before the end.

Pulling himself up into the tunnel was like sticking his head in a furnace, only in this case, the fire was inside him. He gritted his teeth against the pain and forced himself to move forward.

His brief respite from the darkness ended when he started down the passage, but there was a faint glow ahead, and he fought through the blossoming agony toward the beacon.

It was a computer—Sasha's laptop. He saw that much from a distance, but it was only when he got closer that he saw Parker's body crumpled in front of it.

There's a ring of stones, Parker had said. *I think that's the marker. I'm going to try to put it there.*

Further down the tunnel, King saw another body—Sasha's—lying prone in front of the stone circle. It was tantalizingly close; Parker had fallen just a few steps from the Prime.

If this thing kills me before I can get clear, someone else is going to have to finish it. Do you understand?

He understood.

King reached for the computer, but even as his fingers closed on the hard plastic, his legs simply gave out.

No, damn it!

He planted his elbows on the hard stone and pulled himself forward, one ahead of the other, over and over again, until he reached Sasha's lifeless form. The stone circle was just beyond her, but he could go no further.

With what he thought was surely the last of his strength, he flung the laptop toward the stone ring that marked the location of the Prime, and then collapsed in pain. His body curled up, feeling ready to implode, but then, as though he was suddenly touched by the divine, his pain faded. Still wary, he sat up.

The cave was silent.

His body felt untouched by the destructive force that took Sasha's and Parker's lives.

The world—he noted with a hint of surprise—had not come to an end.

EPILOGUE: LIMBO

Pope Air Force Base, North Carolina

"SO WHAT DO you think is going to happen?"

It wasn't the first time Rook had asked the question, but as before, the only answer he got was silence.

The truth of it was, King had no idea what was going to happen.

There had been a few moments, as he lay unmoving on the floor of the Prime cavern, where he felt something approaching satisfaction. But then, like the painful sting that accompanied the return of sensation to his nerves, the bitter reality of the situation hit home.

Parker was dead. That by itself was almost more than he could bear, but the way it had happened...

He thrust the thought from his mind. Yes, his friend had died. Parker had made a rash decision to help Sasha and it had cost him his life, and therein lay the problem.

King couldn't tell the truth, and not just because of how crazy it sounded; he was much more worried about the possibility that someone would actually believe him.

He had dragged Parker's body into the stone circle that marked the location of the Prime, laid him next to Sasha, and then ignited an incendiary grenade to erase all evidence that either of them had ever existed. He'd fed Sasha's computer and al-Tusi's treatise to the flames as well; maybe someday, someone would figure out how to read the Voynich manuscript and would discover the Prime and what it signified, but with a little luck, that day wouldn't come until the world was a much better place.

The official story would be the same one he had told the rest of the team: Sasha had been spooked by Rainer's arrival and fled into the cave. Parker had followed and both of them had fallen into a crevasse and died. King had used Sasha to bait the trap, and even though they had succeeded in running down Rainer and the other rogue operators, a CIA contractor and a Delta shooter had paid for the victory with their blood.

King knew that the others had questions about what had happened in the cave; he could see it in their eyes, but none of them had pressed him for details. He was grateful for that. He alone would take responsibility for what had happened, and if it meant the end of his career—or even criminal prosecution—then he alone would bear the burden.

No one could ever know how the world had almost ended.

The team had escaped Chauvet Cave to the eerie melody of sirens bouncing between the limestone cliffs of the Ardèche River valley. Chess Team was long gone by the time the gendarmes arrived. Less than an hour later, they were back aboard Senior Citizen and on their way back home.

Almost home, he amended.

As soon as Senior Citizen arrived at 'The Pope,' the team was moved to Decon, an isolated quarantine area where teams were debriefed after returning from particularly sensitive missions. Decon— short for 'decontamination'—was a place for operators to 'come down' from the adrenaline high of combat before going home to their families. It was also the last chance for the teams to get their stories straight before making an official report.

They had been in Decon for two full days, sleeping on cots, eating MREs, watching TV and playing X-Box games and generally going stir-crazy waiting for the hammer to fall. Rook had joked that they were "stuck in Limbo," and King thought that was pretty close to the truth.

Then, on the afternoon of their second day, the door was thrown open. General Keasling strode into the room. He made a low growling sound when Rook, sprawled on a couch with a game controller in hand, threw him a casual wave, but his expression was otherwise unreadable. He strode to the corner of the table where King was sitting with the others, and calmly put his hands behind his back.

Keasling wasn't alone.

A second figure entered right behind him. King had to do a double-take to recognize the man who had traded in his combat fatigues for blue jeans and Star Wars T-shirt; it was Lewis Aleman.

"Lew!"

Just seeing the Delta sniper filled King with a stew of emotions. Parker and Aleman had been friends, and the latter's presence was a harsh reminder of just how much King had lost along the way. Still, it was good to see a friendly and familiar face.

Aleman's right hand looked like the end of a Q-tip, swathed in bandages, but he looked otherwise none the worse for wear. He had a laptop computer tucked under his arm, and he promptly stepped in front of Rook and plugged a cable from the computer into the X-Box.

"Hey!" Rook protested as his virtual re-enactment of D-Day was replaced by a blank screen, but Aleman just threw him a mischievous grin and started tapping on his keyboard.

"Game over," Keasling said in flat voice. "Deep Blue wants to talk to you."

Here it comes, King thought.

"Got it," Aleman announced.

A spherical object—King recognized it immediately as a web cam—now rested atop the television, but it was the image on the screen that commanded the attention of everyone in the room.

The silhouetted figure, a fit-looking man with short hair—either a military buzz cut or a receding hairline, King couldn't tell for sure—was framed in the display. The man regarded them for a moment before speaking.

"It's good to finally see you all," he said, in the same electronically distorted voice they knew well from previous radio communications.

King realized that the others were all waiting for him to respond. "Likewise," he began, and then added. "Sort of."

"Forgive the theatrics," Deep Blue said. "At present, it is necessary to keep my identity a secret, but I sincerely hope that one day I will be able to meet you face-to-face. And let me apologize for keeping you here so long; I had my hands full trying to cover your tracks in France. That said, I think congratulations are in order."

King was by nature suspicious of praise from his superiors, but usually he knew better than to question it aloud. This time however, his caution kicked in a moment too late. "Sir?"

"You all showed exceptional valor. If you were in a traditional unit, I would see to it that you all received the highest commendation. Alas, all I can offer you is more work."

King glanced at the others.

Queen's eyes were alight with anticipation. This was what she had dreamed of when joining the Army; a chance to prove herself, to test her limits in the most extreme ways possible. There was no better reward for someone like her than to be thrown back into the fire.

Bishop was not so easy to read. Although he kept a tight rein on his emotions, he always looked like he was just a few seconds from critical mass...except right now, he looked almost serene, or at least as close to it as he would ever get.

Knight shrugged, feigning indifference to the news, but King knew it was an act. The Korean Casanova was an adrenaline junkie, eager for his next fix, and whether it was at a nightclub full of supermodels or in the thick of battle, he lived for the thrill of beating the odds.

Even Rook seemed to greet Deep Blue's statement with his own brand of enthusiasm. "More work? In this economy, what could be better than that?"

King returned his attention to Deep Blue. "Am I missing something here?"

Although he could not see the man's eyes, King got the impression that he was being scrutinized from across the electronic ether. After a moment, the silhouette shifted slightly and the auto-tuned voice said, "General Keasling, would you give us the room for a moment?"

An irritated scowl flickered across Keasling's face, but he smartly executed an about-face and strode through the door. Deep Blue waited a full ten seconds after his departure before speaking again. "Is there a problem, King?"

King took a deep breath. "I...don't think I'm the right man for this job."

There was a low roar of protest from the others, though Queen's voice was distinct above the others. "Bullshit."

"You're wondering how I can call this a win," Deep Blue said, as if reading King's mind. "You feel responsible for their deaths; for Daniel Parker and Sasha Therion."

"I am responsible."

"No, you aren't." There was a sadness in Deep Blue's reply that the artificial voice modulator could not disguise. "The ultimate responsibility lies with me. But if I had it all to do over again, I would make the same decision."

When King didn't respond, Deep Blue continued. "One of the burdens of command is that you feel personally responsible for every soldier lost on your watch. In my book, that doesn't make you unfit to lead; it makes you human.

"There's something else you should consider also. Lewis hasn't been able to figure out why, but instead of blocking radio signals, the limestone in that cave amplified the outgoing transmissions. You couldn't receive, but I was able to monitor your comms." His electronic tone lowered almost to a whisper. "I heard everything that happened in that cave."

The revelation hit King like a cold slap. He looked around at the others, expecting to see unasked questions on their faces, but none of them would meet his gaze.

They know, he realized. *They all know.*

Deep Blue went on as if the former matter was permanently concluded. "You were given an impossible task, and you accomplished it. You went up against an enemy with resources that—speaking frankly—still boggle my mind, and you beat him. So, by any standard, that's a win in my book. So pull it together, and get back on the horse. I can't think of anyone else I'd rather have leading this team."

Rook stood up raising his hands like an old-time preacher. "Amen, brother."

The others just nodded in silent agreement.

King was speechless for a moment, but when no one else—not even Rook—filled the silence, he gathered his wits. "So, what's next?"

"For the moment: recovery. Mandatory R&R. Stay loose, but stay sharp. Chess Team is going to be on alert status 24/7."

"Chess Team," Rook said. "I still think it sounds like an after-school club for nerds."

Aleman threw him a withering glance. "I *never* played chess."

King ignored them. "We're going to need an HQ."

"You're sitting in it," Deep Blue replied. "It's temporary until we can come up with something better, but feel free to redecorate as you see fit; just submit your requisitions to General Keasling."

Rook rolled his eyes at that news, but then his face seemed to brighten. "Dudes. We've got to have a horseshoe pit!"

Bishop's face creased in annoyance. "Horseshoes? Really?"

"Just promise me this," King said, cutting Rook off before he could launch into an impassioned defense of his favorite hobby. "Next time, can we just go up against some normal bad guys; you know, tangos with loose suitcase nukes and nerve gas? No more freaky science experiments, killer mountain crocodiles, historical voodoo...no more weird shit."

Deep Blue laughed. "I won't make promises I can't keep, but it's hard to imagine that you'll ever have to deal with anything quite so extreme in the future."

King had a sudden urge to knock on wood, but before he could rap his knuckles against the tabletop, he realized that it was molded plastic.

Ah, hell, he thought. *Deep Blue's right. Nothing could be as weird as what we just went through.*

Shanghai, China

THREE DAYS WAS long enough—too long, really.

Rainer wasn't coming back. The rogue Delta operator had failed, and given the resources he'd taken into the field, that was a frightening prospect indeed.

The telephone trilled once, twice...

Damn it! They know they need to pick up on the first ring.

"Reinhart."

"What took you so long?" He didn't wait for an answer. "Never mind. You've just been promoted; congratulations."

"What?"

God, the man is thick. "Rainer's not coming back. He's either dead or—God forbid—captured. Either way, you're running the show now. First order of business is damage control."

"Got it; no loose ends. I'll make sure there's nothing that ties us to him."

To his credit, Reinhart seemed to grasp what was being asked of him, but was tidying up after Rainer going to be good enough?

The whole situation had been a farce from the beginning. He had no interest in plague research; that had been Katherine's passion, and the only reason he'd even started down that road was to honor her memory; he'd thought that perhaps if he could salvage something useful from her work, her death wouldn't feel like such a waste.

Sentimentality is for suckers. It's time to write this whole fiasco off.

"Good. And while you're at it, I think it's time to dissolve our partnership with the Chinese."

"When you say 'dissolve?'" Reinhart let the question hang.

"Complete liquidation of our assets."

"Clear as crystal."

Reinhart hung up first, which would have been a further irritant to his employer under any other circumstances, but the breach of protocol barely registered. Things were finally looking up.

He had never been comfortable with the idea of dealing with the triad. Criminals were so unsavory, and while the partnership had been useful for procuring test subjects and generating untraceable revenue, the risk of exposure was just too great.

Besides, that line of research was a dead end—literally. Richard Ridley had no use for dead ends. He was going to live forever.

ABOUT THE AUTHORS

JEREMY ROBINSON is the bestselling author of thirty novels and novellas including ISLAND 731, SECONDWORLD, and the Jack Sigler series including PULSE, INSTINCT, THRESHOLD and RAGNAROK. Robinson is also known as the #1 Amazon.com horror writer, Jeremy Bishop, author of THE SENTINEL and the controversial novel, TORMENT. His novels have been translated into eleven languages. He lives in New Hampshire with his wife and three children.

Visit him online at: www.jeremyrobinsononline.com

SEAN ELLIS is the author of several thriller and adventure novels. He is a veteran of Operation Enduring Freedom, and has a Bachelor of Science degree in Natural Resources Policy from Oregon State University. Sean is also a member of the International Thriller Writers organization. He currently resides in Arizona, where he divides his time between writing, adventure sports and trying to figure out how to save the world.

Visit him online at: seanellisthrillers.webs.com

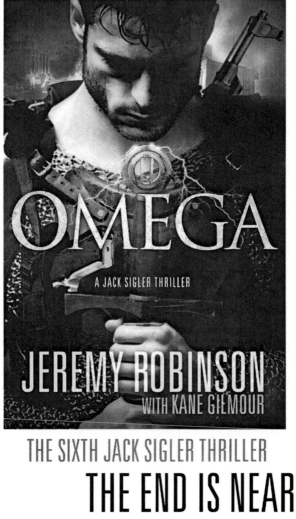

M

CPSIA information can be obtained at www.ICGtesting.com
Printed in the USA
LVOW07s2257310814

401793LV00002B/202/P